Dedication:

To the memory of Vonda McIntyre.

MERCEDES LACKEY

EYE SPY

FAMILY SPIES BOOK II

TITAN BOOKS

Family Spies Book II: Eye Spy
Print edition ISBN: 9781785653469
E-book edition ISBN: 9781785653476

Published by Titan Books
A division of Titan Publishing Group Ltd.
144 Southwark Street, London, SE1 0UP
www.titanbooks.com

First Titan edition July 2019
10 9 8 7 6 5 4 3 2 1

A CIP catalogue record for this title is available from the British Library.

Printed and bound By CPI Group (UK) Ltd, Croydon CR0 4YY

I

"**R**emind me again why we came out in this weather," Abi grumbled, as the cold rain found the seam in the hood of her waterproof gray cloak and dripped onto her neck. A dismal gray sky poured down water that was just short of being ice. It was not raining hard enough that Abi had even a prayer of persuading Kat to turn back, but it was raining hard enough to give Abi, at least, a miserable ride. She so envied the people in the expensive mansions they were riding past right now . . . not because of the expensive mansions, but because of the simple fact that they were *in there* and not out here.

"Because Mama is pregnant and feeling horrid, she has a craving for Ma Sendle's tart apple jelly, and the old lady won't give the Palace cook the recipe," Kat said agreeably. "And we're both going so we can buy the old girl out and won't have to go down into Haven again for it until after the baby's born."

"Hopefully," Abi groaned.

"Hopefully," Kat agreed.

Abi glanced over at her best friend, riding easily on her Companion, Dylia, and grimaced. "I am *never* getting pregnant." Personally, she was not a big fan of marriage right now either, but it didn't do to ever say that out loud. As one of her father's agents in and around the Court, she reckoned that for every one happy marriage there were a dozen that ranged from "distantly friendly" to "armed truce." While the King and Queen and Mama and Papa were definitely in happy marriages, with few exceptions, the rest of the courtiers were not exactly an advertisement for matrimony.

Princess Katiana, known as "Kat," or now, "Herald Trainee Kat," answered her with a wry smile. Kat didn't seem at all bothered by the rain. Then again, Kat didn't seem at all bothered by much anymore, now that she'd been Chosen. Of all of the Royal siblings, she was the most even-tempered, and she didn't look like either of her parents. In fact, Abi would have said, if she'd been asked, that if the Palace portraits were accurate, she looked like an exact copy of her great-grandmother: medium brown hair the color of autumn leaves, dark eyes, oval face. Kat's expression was generally cheerful though, and the old Queen's had been sad and sober, at least in the painting.

One advantage of being a Princess rather than just a regular Trainee was that Kat's uniforms had been custom-made for her, so maybe her cloak was a bit more waterproof than the one Abi had purloined from the storage room. Actually, now that Abi thought about it, Kat's cloak not only was probably quite waterproof, but she knew for a fact it had a woolen lining, something Abi's lacked.

No wonder Kat looked unfazed by the rain.

So unfair . . .

Abi wasn't a Herald Trainee, but Rolan, her mama's Companion, had offered to carry her on this errand because the weather was so bad, and she wasn't going to turn that down. So she'd dressed in gray and swiped a Trainee cloak from the spares, figuring in weather like this no one was going to look too hard and realize one of the Trainees—wasn't. *That might have been a bad miscalculation. I probably should have asked to borrow Trey's cloak instead. He certainly isn't going anywhere outside today.* The last she'd seen of Trey, he'd been firmly ensconced in front of the fire in the Royal Suite, deep in a history lesson, and not about to be shaken out of it by anything less important than dinner.

My own fault for trying to pose as a Trainee without thinking things through.

That's not to say that Abi wasn't training in something. She was training, at least in the sense that she was learning a lot of things, all the time. Her papa, Herald Mags, was the King's Spy, and all three of his children had been learning the craft from the time they were able to understand what that was. Partly, that had been to keep them out of mischief. But that had also been because they played with and fundamentally lived with the royal children, and Papa and Mama counted on them to help keep the royals safe—and to notice what went on and was said around them. And finally, it was to impress on them how important it was that no one else should know that "good old solid Mags," whose glory days of being a Kirball champion were long past, and who mostly did boring work in the law courts, was in fact the King's Spy and thanks to the rigors of the job could probably run every current Kirball champion into the ground and dance on them afterward.

Actually, the training now had gone far past that. Once they were old enough to understand exactly why they were getting this sort of training, Papa had asked them if they actually wanted to *help* him.

Her older brother Peregrine had said "yes," and after a fantastic adventure in the Pelagirs that had turned out to be *way* more exciting than anyone had guessed it would be, had settled right in as one of Papa's regular agents. *She* had said "yes" but had yet to do anything to come close to Perry's adventure; mostly she was just collecting Court gossip. Tory was still too young to be asked, but she was pretty sure he would say "yes" too.

To be absolutely honest, right now there really wasn't anything else she did want to do with her life, though how long she was going to be useful as Kat's best friend was debatable, and how else she could serve as a spy was unknown. Unless, perhaps, she could take over Aunty Minda's brood of orphaned and abandoned street younglings and oversee that part of her father's "business."

But almost anyone could do that. She just wished she could think of something that would suit her uniquely.

She was only sure of one thing. She absolutely, positively, did not want to have babies. The poor Queen looked absolutely miserable, as if someone had grafted a melon to the front of her. And as if that wasn't bad enough, her feet and back hurt all the time, the first part of her pregnancy had involved a lot of throwing up, there were still foods she could not stand to have around, and Abi wouldn't have been in her shoes for all the crowns of all the Kingdoms she could name—and she could name quite a lot.

So she did little things for Papa, and she spent the rest of the time learning things. She took classes at all three of the Collegia. She trained in weapons-work with the Collegia Weaponsmaster and with Master Leandro, who had trained her father. Her father trained her in spycraft, her mother in statecraft—in the latter case, mostly by allowing her to observe what went on in Council meetings and other business of the King. She did that by serving as a page—a heavily armed page. In effect, as the sort of guard that an attacker would probably overlook, should anyone be stupid enough to try anything in a Council meeting. And she had about as much leisure time as any of the Trainees, which was to say, quite a bit more than most girls her age, who were already hard at work every waking hour either as servants or working on a farm. And she made a point of enjoying every minute of that leisure, because she had the feeling that when she figured out what it was she wanted to do with the rest of her life, most of that leisure time would vanish like snow in a fire.

Today, however, she was *not* enjoying her "leisure." Then again, this wasn't so much leisure as it was a chore.

At the moment, they were riding on a cobblestoned street that ran past all the fine mansions of the merely rich (as opposed to the rich *and* highborn). The road was practically deserted; there wasn't a soul in sight who didn't have to be out in this weather. But from the windows of these varied manses came warm, golden light that looked very inviting right now, and Abi wished she were inside, toasting her toes in front of a nice fire, preferably with a book.

She didn't envy the people her age who were in those houses though; the ones who weren't already apprentices in the businesses that had made their families wealthy were involved in a complicated and sometimes cutthroat social dance to acquire the perfect spouse, and that brought her right back to marriage and babies and . . . *ugh*.

She really envied Perry right now. He was snug in the pawn shop, and if he wanted anything, he could send one of the littles from Aunty Minda's next door out after it; they were either runners or runners-in-training (also in Papa's employ) and completely expected to be asked to do things like that. He probably wouldn't do that, though. He'd go fetch it himself rather than make a child trudge around Haven in miserable weather.

Which, really, was why she and Kat were out here. The Queen wouldn't make a page go out in this muck, no matter how urgent her cravings were. But Kat knew how badly she wanted that fruit jelly—Kat had Mindspeech and a touch of Empathy—so Kat had volunteered, and the Queen wasn't about to let Kat go down there alone, even on her Companion. So it had to be at least one bodyguard from the Royal Guard or Abi, and Abi would be a lot less conspicuous. Having a Trainee accompanied by a Guard pretty much shouted *Oh, look, the Princess!* Having Abi along looked as if two Trainees had been sent on an errand down into Haven.

Kat was armed, and perfectly capable of using those arms . . . but Abi was *armed to the teeth*, and before Kat, for all her training, noticed that something was not quite right, Abi would already have decided what weapon to use, whether to be lethal or nonlethal, and dealt with the problem.

Another trickle of cold water made it inside her hood, sending a shudder down her body. *I should have let the Guard come after all. Or borrowed Trey's cloak.*

"Maybe we should turn back," Kat said, giving Abi a sidelong glance. Abi gritted her teeth, and shook her head.

"No, we promised your mother her jelly, and by the gods she'll get her jelly," she replied stoutly. "It's just a leak in my hood, it's not going to kill me."

"Yes, but I'd rather it didn't make you sick," Kat protested. Kat's Companion Dylia nodded her head in emphatic agreement.

"If Rolan thought I was going to be sick from this, he'd have already said something." As the Companion to the King's Own, Rolan was able to make anyone hear him, even those, like Abi, without Mindspeech. And he hadn't said a peep. "He hasn't said anything to you, has he?"

Rolan cocked his head back at her a little and snorted. Kat smothered a laugh.

"What?"

"Rolan says you are nowhere near sweet enough to melt in the rain," Kat choked.

Abi stared at the Companion's one blue eye looking at her. Was he smirking? *He's smirking*, she decided. "No pocket pies for you, horse," she told him. He snorted again, knowing very well that he could cozen all the pocket pies he wanted out of virtually anyone in the stable. After all, he was the King's Own's Companion, and what he wanted, he usually got.

He made a noise that sounded exactly like a smirky laugh. Kat laughed too. Abi decided not to ask what Rolan had said.

The mansions and stately homes of the highborn behind them had each been set in their own expanse of gardens and lawns behind their fences and walls. In this part of the road, the slightly less impressive homes of the very wealthy were closer together and had a lot less in the way of greenspace. A few lengths more and they had passed another unspoken but very visible divide. These two- and three-story houses were owned by the "merely" wealthy, and were separated by just enough space for a wall between them, and room between the wall and the houses on either side for a human to walk. And ahead of them, where the houses of the well-off rather than wealthy were, the homes were packed so closely together that neighbors could pass things from the window of one to the window of another without straining. And ahead of that—

Was her least favorite bridge in all of Haven.

If you asked anyone else, they'd probably tell you that it was a very fine bridge indeed, a good, stout stone bridge big enough and strong enough that two lanes of large drays could use it, bringing up oversized goods to the wealthier parts of Haven and even the Palace itself. The parapets at either side were barely knee high, and she never liked crossing it even in the best of weather. This was the only bridge like it in the entire city and the only place where the river could be crossed by such oversized vehicles. The river was on a downhill slope at this point in town, one of the places where the water ran really fast when it was high, and looking at the foaming water from the roadbed of stone always made her feel as if she were likely to topple into it. Given the choice, she'd go halfway across town to avoid crossing it.

Partly that was because this was where her grandfather, Herald Nikolas, had died. He'd come back to life again, thanks to her father, but he *had* died for a few moments. Papa's good friend Bear had taught Mags what to do with a drowning victim, or he would have stayed dead.

That was when Rolan had Chosen his daughter, Kat's mother; then a new Companion had Chosen Grandpapa, and for the first time ever, the former King's Own and the new King's Own had been alive at the same time. And that near-death was what people told her was the reason for her unease. But she knew the truth; all that really had very little to do with how she felt about the bridge. If anything, she would have felt pretty good about the whole thing; after all it was a story with a very happy ending.

No, she hated this bridge for a different reason altogether.

Even in the best of weather, when the river flowed smoothly under it, the bridge had always felt wrong to Abi. As if it were sick. It made her a little nauseated to cross it, as if it were moving under her when of course it wasn't. And in weather like this, when the river raged beneath it? It felt to her as if it were shaking itself to bits, even when other people would just remark it was vibrating a bit.

And yet, anyone she talked to about her feelings assured her that the bridge had been constructed perfectly, there was nothing wrong with it, it had stood for two hundred years and would stand for another two hundred. And if it vibrated a little when the water roared around its supports? Well, that was to be expected.

This was of no help whatsoever. And if she had had any choice at all, she wouldn't go within a mile of this cursed thing.

But Ma Sendle's little fruit shop, where she sold mostly preserves, jams, and jellies along with her small store of the finest of offerings from the orchards around Haven, was just on the other side of that bridge. And it would be stupid, especially in this weather, to go halfway across Haven to get to it.

So she was going to grit her teeth, and cross the bridge with Kat, and endure the sensation that the thing was about to fall to pieces at any moment.

They turned a corner, and there it was, in the middle distance. At this time of the day—and in this awful weather—there weren't too many people crossing it. No heavy drays, thank goodness—those usually waited until most of the traffic had cleared out of Haven anyway, making their deliveries at night or in the very early morning. But there were some carts, a few horses, and several people carefully making their way on foot alongside the parapet.

The thundering of the river was audible even from here. She shivered. Kat cast her a sympathetic glance. Kat's touch of Empathy meant that Kat knew quite well how she felt.

But this time was vastly different from every other time she had neared this bridge. With every step Rolan took nearer the bridge, the worse she felt. And then, as he actually set his forehoof on the bridge, it struck her, like a blow to the stomach—

—this time was no false alarm. The bridge had stopped merely warning. Now it was about to crumble.

She didn't need to say anything to Kat; Kat picked it up from her. "We have to get people off the bridge!" Kat shouted as those nearest them turned and stared at her. "Go to the middle and split, I'll go south, you go north!"

She couldn't answer for a moment around the swelling nausea, the actual *pain* she felt. But Rolan followed Dylia out onto the bridge as they cantered to the center of it, turned and faced the opposite ways. She shook off her pain and nausea, knowing deep inside her that *this* moment was critical, that *this* time it wasn't just a bad feeling, that *this* time, unless they did something, people were going to die.

The next few moments were a blur. She knew she was shouting but not *what* she was shouting, but at least people reacted the way she wanted them to and fled in the direction of safety. Rolan backed up her orders with stamping hooves and, when needed, snaps of his jaws. Everything was a confusion of screams, people running for the river bank, nausea, the feeling that her bones were about to snap, her voice growing hoarse.

And then it all suddenly cleared. There was only one person left on her side of the bridge, an old man on a cart, who was stubbornly trying to force his way past her, shouting at her. The bridge shuddered in warning, and she didn't even think; she reached over and grabbed the front of his tunic and with superhuman strength dragged him over the front of her saddle.

And behind Rolan, a roar of stone and water. She felt the bridge giving way behind them and cried out, clutching the old man and the saddle. She sensed the rocks falling away under Rolan's hind hooves, felt the impossible strength of his legs as he scrabbled for purchase on the disintegrating stone, the slip and the catch, and, finally, the muscle-straining leap that took them to safety as the cart and screaming horse plunged into the river behind them.

The nausea and pain vanished as if they had never been there at all. She shook her head clear and passed the old man down into the hands of those on the bank. And then remembered who else had been on that bridge.

KAT!

She whirled in Rolan's saddle, peering frantically through the mist thrown up by the collapse of the bridge, and with a sob of relief, spotted Kat on the other side, waving vigorously to her.

"Rolan," she said aloud. "We need Guards and Heralds on the other side, and we need them *now.*" Because now Kat was all by herself over there. . . .

Wearily, Rolan nodded his head, and she realized that he must be hurt—muscles torn and tendons strained from that death-defying leap carrying her and the stranger to the bank. Hastily she dismounted and turned again, just in time to see four of the City Watch shoving their way through the crowd up to Kat's side. And shortly after that, a pair of Guardsmen and a Herald. From here, she couldn't tell who the Herald was, but it was clear the Princess was in good hands.

"Let's get you back up the hill before your injuries stiffen," she said to Rolan, just as another of the Watch turned up on her side of the river. She let the bystanders babble out whatever explanations they wanted to; Kat would give an accurate report, and right now, the most important thing she could do would be to get Rolan back to the stable and into the hands of the Healers.

———

There was an entire group waiting for her at the front gate of the Palace/Collegium complex. She'd expected a Healer or two and a crew from the stable—after all, Rolan was in need of tender care. She hadn't expected to be descended on by Heralds herself. Before she could object, or even say anything at all, they'd bustled her into an empty classroom at Heralds' Collegium and began a methodical interrogation.

It was definitely an interrogation; she'd been a witness to a few of those conducted by her father.

They did make sure she wasn't hurt, of course, got her hot tea and a blanket to wrap around her, even got a cushion for the hard bench seat. But it was very clear once they knew that she was fine that they weren't letting her go anywhere until they got some answers.

The classroom was oddly quiet. It wasn't on a side of the building where the rain was hitting the windows, so weather sounds were all muted. It smelled of chalk dust and ink. She'd never noticed that before, probably because when she was actually in a classroom she was too busy taking notes or listening to pay any attention to how it smelled. The three Heralds who had brought her here sat in a semicircle in front of her. She answered each question, carefully, in detail, and just as methodically as they asked them. Being Mags' daughter certainly helped in a case like this.

When they'd ascertained exactly what had happened *today*, they paused for a moment, which gave her a chance to get more of that hot tea into herself. She didn't recognize any of the three Heralds, which meant they probably taught the use of Gifts. She'd have had no reason to be in contact with them or in any of their classes, since up until now, no one had ever thought she'd had a Gift. Two, both males, were brown-haired. One was short and slender, the other had gray in his hair. The third, a woman, looked as if she had been a weaver at one time; she had that kind of upper-body strength and large, strong hands. She had hair of a color between red and brown.

"Have you ever felt that way about a place before?" the woman asked.

"Well, I always felt that way about that bridge, just not as strongly as I did today," Abi replied. "I've always hated it, always hated crossing it. It always felt . . ." she thought about her feelings for a long time, trying to pick the best words. ". . . like there was something wrong about it. That it was *sick* in some way. Or like an instrument that was out-of-tune, except that the consequences of being out-of-tune were going to be much worse than a horrible rendition of a song."

"You mean you heard things?" the graying man asked. She shook her head.

"No, it was definitely a feeling, inside. I never heard anything but the same things other people heard. This was something I *felt*, except I always knew it wasn't me feeling it, it was the bridge. The bridge was *wrong.* I don't know if it was built wrong, or grew wrong over the years, but by the time I was old enough to cross it, it had gotten to that point."

The three of them locked eyes, and she was pretty sure they were Mindspeaking. *Good, I'd rather they did that than talked in front of me as if I wasn't there.* The tea was very good; something with a lot of rose hips in it, and a little mint, and a generous dollop of honey. Now that she was warm, she didn't mind being here. Mind? It was far better than being out in that miserable rain. From the sound of the drops outside the window, in fact, it was getting worse. If they'd gotten to the shop, even Kat would have been drenched by the time they got back. *Did she make the Herald go with her to the shop? I bet she did. So she's drenched. Poor Kat.*

No one had died, that was the important thing. She actually felt very good about how things had worked out. No one had died, Kat was safe, and she'd personally been responsible for all of that! Not that she wanted a medal or anything, but it did feel really good to know she'd saved peoples' lives. *This is probably how Papa feels when he does the same thing.* If so, she wouldn't mind doing it again. Only maybe without bridges collapsing.

The Heralds interrupted her thoughts. "Are there any other places where you've felt like you felt about the bridge?" the woman asked.

"Not nearly that strongly," she replied. "There are a couple of places in some highborn houses I've been in where I felt that faintly, but not to the point where I'd avoid going to a party there. One is the minstrel's gallery at Lord Corveau's house, and the other is the balcony over the back terrace at Lord Spenaker's. And I feel that way all the time down in Haven, in the impoverished districts where the houses are just about ready to fall apart."

The woman nodded with satisfaction. "So it's always buildings?" asked the graying man.

"I don't know. I've never been outside Haven to find out," she pointed out. "I'm pretty sure after what just happened that what I've been sensing is stress or strain, but the city is built on pretty stable land, so I wouldn't know if I can sense the same thing in natural locations—like maybe a spot that was likely to have an avalanche. I know for a fact Rolan probably strained tendons and muscles, maybe tore them, and I didn't feel anything from him, I just knew like anyone would know that he must have been hurt."

The woman seemed extremely pleased with her answer. "I agree with you, Abi—can I call you Abi?" At Abi's nod, she continued. "I think you've made the right deduction. We weren't sure if what you have is Foresight or something else, but it seems very clear that you're right. You sense the physical strain in things that are not living. And we Heralds are the wrong people to try to teach you, since that's what it appears to be. If you want to learn how to use this thing, that is."

She snorted. "Of course I do. A fat lot of good it's going to do me or anyone else if all I can do is sense vaguely that something's under stress. Right? I mean, think of the potential if I can tell something's in need of repair before it's obvious! Or better still, if I can tell *how* and *where* to fix it!"

The woman grinned. "Quite so. I'm fairly certain the closest Gifts we have to yours are going to be among the Healers, but I'll ask around to be sure. When I know, you and I will make arrangements for lessons. I'm Herald Stela, by the way." She held out her hand, and Abi shook it, very much liking the firm handshake she got. "But there's something else I'd like to ask you to do, and that's to join the Artificers, the Unaffiliated students who are learning things like building, construction, and the making of things."

"I can do that?" she exclaimed. "I thought places in the Artificers were only open to people who got recommendations because they were good at math and things like that!"

"You're getting a recommendation from me, and that's all it takes," Stela replied. "They'll open up a place for you. You can become good at math with practice, but it isn't every day when someone comes along who can intuit that a bridge is about to collapse. As you yourself pointed out, it would be good to have someone out there who can tell us the points of weakness *before* something collapses and it would be even better to have someone who knows how to fix those points of weakness before the weaknesses become an issue." She stood up, and the other two followed her example. "I'll come talk to you and your parents in the next couple of days, as soon as

I can make the arrangements. I'll see you then. Meanwhile you can go join your family and be the hero of the hour."

Abi stood up, holding the blanket around her, and clutching her mug of tea. The gray-haired Herald held open the door for all of them, and she made her way back into the Palace and the suite of rooms her family lived in feeling both excited and bemused.

But the moment she got into the corridor leading to their suite, her brother Perry charged down it and enveloped her in a hug. "Holy fire, Abi!" he exclaimed into her hair. "You're a hero!"

She *oofed*, the wind knocked out of her for a second. "Is Kat back?" she asked, more concerned about her friend than anything else.

"Yes, and she made Herald Seth go with her to get the apple jelly, so the Queen has every speck of it that there was in the shop." He hugged her again. "She got soaked, and so did he, but it was worth it, she says. Everyone's in our great room, so come on." He grabbed her wrist and pulled her along behind him, too impatient to put up with her sedate walk.

The suite of rooms that Mags and Amily's family lived in was a bit peculiar, even for the Palace. It was several small rooms surrounding one big one, and the big one was where everyone gathered most of the time. The whole family and all the Royal offspring were there now, most of them clustered around Kat, who by her gestures, was describing the bridge collapse. Her mother, Amily, intercepted her before her siblings could co-opt her; she was still in the semiformal Herald's Whites that she wore when she was serving at King Stefan's side. *She must have come straight here from the Throne Room.*

"How wet are you?" Amily demanded.

"Damp," Abi admitted. "They gave me this blanket, though, and the classroom where they took me was pretty warm."

"Then not another word out of you until you get changed into something dry and comfortable," her mother ordered. Abi was not at all reluctant to do so; damp clothing was somehow even less appealing than fully wet clothing.

She emerged from her room in her favorite old, worn, long-sleeved canvas tunic and trews, both soft enough with hard wear to feel like lambswool. Gray again; this was part of the camouflage she and her brothers took on to protect the Royals. They *all* wore gray or brown, so anyone charging into this room wouldn't know which of the children were the King's—until one of the three who were *not*, eliminated him, one way or another. *I have a very strange family,* she thought, not for the first time.

By this time, her mother was pouring out hot, spiced cider for everyone, and she was very happy to get her share. She sat down with the rest of them on the old rug between the hearth and the huge table on one side of the room, a table they all used for eating and everything else. She did wonder a little why her mother was here, and not attending the King . . . but maybe the King figured that she needed to be a mother right now, not the King's Own. Besides, he had Mags with him, and everyone in the King's inner circle knew that what Amily knew, Mags knew, and vice versa; if anything important was happening in the Throne Room, Amily was getting a full description.

"We got Kat's version, and Mama told us Rolan's version, so we don't need to hear about the bridge," Perry proclaimed, before anyone could pelt her with questions. "So what did the *Heralds* say?"

"First I want to know if Rolan is all right," she interjected, looking over their heads to her mother.

"He strained his back legs and hips and sprained his back, but you did the right thing by keeping him moving at a slow pace and getting off of him immediately," her mother told her. "He'll be just fine in a couple of days at most."

Well, that's a relief. Mama entrusts me with him . . . and I go and get him hurt. Although I don't know how we could have avoided that situation except by not being out there at all. And if they hadn't been there, people certainly would have died. At least Rolan's injuries were minor.

"Well, I guess I've got a Gift, but it isn't one they've ever seen before," she said. "They said the closest thing to it is how a Healer can sense when you've got a muscle or bone that's under stress and damaged, except my version works with things that aren't alive. Built things, as far as I know, but I've never been out of Haven, so I don't know if I could tell if there was a hillside that might have an avalanche or something."

Her little brother Tory's mouth made a little "o" shape, though he didn't say anything. Perry asked the important question.

"You're going to train in it, right?" He grinned. His Gift was unusual, but not unheard of: an exceptionally strong version of Animal Mindspeech. That might have been what allowed him to bond to his partner, the giant *kyree* currently acting as a back-brace for him. The *kyree* nodded sagely.

"Rood rain," he mouthed, meaning "should train," of course. All of them understood Larral the *kyree* as easily as they understood each other.

"They seem to think the Healers can come up with something," she said, and accepted a slice of bread and cheese from her mother. Then, once it was in her hands, she realized she was starving, and she ate it so fast it was gone before Amily had gotten done passing out the snack to the rest of the group. "They also want to put me in the Artificers," she continued, feeling suddenly gleeful as Perry whistled.

"You mean they're going to *make* a slot for you?" he asked. "I've never heard of them doing that before!"

"I have, but it isn't done often," Mama replied. "You have to have something quite special to bypass the queue to get in, but I suppose a Gift that allows you to tell when a bridge is dangerous would certainly qualify."

"That's a lot of math," Trey said doubtfully. Kat hit his shoulder.

"You trying to say you think she can't do it?" Kat demanded, as her oldest brother rubbed his shoulder.

"Not so hard!" he protested. "I'm just saying *I* couldn't do it, is all!"

"I'm not bad at math," Abi said slowly. "I just didn't see much use for it before. It's not as if anyone was going to invite me into the Artificers."

"Well, now they have," Niko pointed out. "Do you think you can do it?"

She pondered that a while. "They said math is a matter of practice. So if you idiots can manage to practice hard enough in six months to hit the bull's-eye nine out of ten, I expect I can practice enough to do math well."

Niko smirked; the fact that he and Trey had brought their archery skills up from abysmal to top of their group in half a year was a point of pride for both of them. They hadn't cared enough to bother about it, pointing out that it wasn't as if the Heir and the Spare were *ever* going to be allowed out of Haven where they'd need archery, until Kat had shamed them both by being good enough to be made an instructor.

"But is it what you *want* to do?" asked Tory, simply.

She thought about the question a moment, then shrugged. "Don't know yet, because I haven't tried it. I guess I'm going to find out!"

Her mother nodded. "Meanwhile, being in classes is going to keep people from wanting to trot you around the kingdom like a living flaw-detector," she pointed out. "And that includes Heralds, because every one of them in the field is going to want your help. Perry had enough adventure at a young age for the entire family, and I'd much rather you didn't emulate him, at least until you are much older."

She nodded, although she had mixed feelings about that statement. On the one hand—Perry'd had an *amazing* time, and he'd seen and experienced things that likely no one else would, ever. Including real magic. On the other hand, he'd almost died. She was not sure even the most amazing adventure was worth that kind of risk. Today she had come much too close to death to ever want to feel that terror again.

Her mother was watching her closely, as if she could read Abi's mind—which she couldn't, since her Gift, like Perry's, was Animal Mindspeech. But she was awfully good at reading faces, and what she saw in Abi's made her lips relax and curve up again.

"Well, on that note, who's going to volunteer to run down and get the pocket pies from the Heralds' Collegium kitchen?" she asked, and looked at the four Royals. "Your mother's given permission for you to have supper with us."

"She can't even *look* at anything but fruit and vegetables and bread and jelly," Kat said wisely. "Father will have dinner with the Court, and he's not mean enough to make us do that with him on pocket pie night. I'll go. Trey, Niko, Perry, you can go with me."

"You can use Larral as a backrest," Perry said generously to Abi, as the *kyree* got to his feet, padded around to Abi, and flopped down behind her. She relaxed into the curve of his body. He was lovely and warm and didn't smell at all "doggy," more like a bed of pine needles and ferns. "We'll be back as fast as lightning!"

All things considered, Abi thought contentedly, *life is awfully good.*

2

Herald Trainees wore gray. Healer Trainees wore a light green. Bardic Trainees wore a sort of dark reddish orange. But there were people who attended classes here at the three Collegia who weren't Trainees at all. And this particular classroom was full of them, so there wasn't a trace of any of those colors to be seen here. Abi had taken a desk at the back of the room, the only place that was open, and what she saw was a lot of blue-clad backs that matched her own brand new blue tunic and trews.

Abi was used to the Collegia classrooms; they all looked pretty much alike, whether they were in the Heralds', Healers' or Bardic Collegium buildings. Each room held about twenty bench seats and simple slanted wooden desks for the students, a larger desk and actual chair for the instructor, with a slateboard at the front of the room, another at the back, and one on the side facing the wall. The remaining side was all windows. There was a door at the front of the room with a transom over it, so on hot days there was a breeze coming through the open windows and the transoms. The floor was polished wood, the ceiling whitewashed plaster. The room smelled of wood polish, chalk dust, and ink. Abi had been taking lessons in rooms like these since she'd been about six, just like her older and younger brothers and Kat and her siblings.

Most of the young people taking classes here who weren't Trainees were the offspring of those highborn or wealthy families that didn't want to bother with personal tutors for them. That was a smaller number than people might think, as Abi well knew. If you were highborn, and especially if you were wealthy, you didn't want people to think you couldn't *afford* private tutors for your sons. So generally the only highborn or wealthy boys taking classes at the Collegium were those whose abilities had outstripped most tutors . . . or, of course, whose parents actually *couldn't* afford private tutors. There were very few girls among the highborn coterie of the Unaffiliated students; the vast majority of highborn girls were here at their parents' manors or living at the Palace itself solely for the Serious Business of getting husbands, and they were expected to invest all of their time in activities that would bring them to the attention of eligible males or the mothers of eligible males. Taking academic classes was not on the approved list of such activities, unless it was dancing lessons, or etiquette, or a little rudimentary lute or harp playing.

Abi had heard that there were a *couple* of highborn girls studying seriously here, but she hadn't met them yet. She might never, if they weren't associated with the classes that the Artificers took.

All the Unaffiliated students were supposed to wear uniforms in a blue that was about two shades lighter than Guard blue and tailored to match the Trainee uniforms. That was something more often seen in the breech than the observance with the highborns or moneyed. Yes, their expensive outfits were blue . . . and they might on occasion be in the correct shade. But mostly, they weren't, and they definitely did not match the simple tunics and trews of the three sets of Trainees. And there were always a few who wore whatever they wanted to.

That accounted for a small number of the so-called "Blues."

But the Unaffiliated students were much more than a place to put an academically inclined younger son because you didn't want him to sit idle and get into mischief. Almost all of the girls, and a great many of the boys, were not from highborn or moneyed families at all. They were here on their own merit, and since most of them couldn't afford uniforms, the appropriate uniforms in the right color were supplied to them by the Crown.

They came from all over the Kingdom and had generally been sponsored by some temple or other in their home towns and villages, since most formal schooling was supplied by temples large and small. And the majority of the boys were in the Artificers—the students who would, at the conclusion of their studies, go out and do *things* with their knowledge. Build. Invent. Improve. Granted, you didn't have to graduate from the Artificers to learn how to do the same things— there were apprenticeships available in all the Trades that did that sort of work, such as the Building Trades. But apprenticeships were expensive, and even when the student's parents could afford such a thing, apprenticeships were limited by the scope and interest of the master and did not encourage innovation. Everyone knew that if you were going to go out and do *new* things, you had to come to the Collegia to learn the tools to let you do that.

There were more Unaffiliated students with interests outside the Artificers and the highborn, who were also in the blue uniforms and also sponsored here by various temples. But they were fewer than the Artificers, and were pure scholars, studying history, literature, the arts. It wasn't likely that Abi would ever run into any of them.

Right now she was sitting in her first Artificers class, at the back of a classroom full of boys mostly in those standard blue uniforms. In this class at least, there were no girls. Some of the boys were ignoring her. Some, surreptitiously watching her. Some watched with curiosity, some with resentment. She completely understood the resentment. There was a waiting list to get in here, and a special place had been made for her, jumping her ahead of others who had been waiting, sometimes for years. Probably most of these boys assumed she'd gotten that place because her mother was King's Own and both her parents were Heralds. The story of the collapsing bridge that had swept through Haven and Hill like wildfire had featured Kat as the heroine, not her.

People like things simple, and Kat is a Princess as well as a Herald Trainee, she thought, as she and the others waited for their instructor to arrive. *They don't like stories with two heroes or that involve a Gift no one has ever heard of.*

And it wasn't as if Kat hadn't actually been a hero. She could have been killed out there; she'd done half of the saving and done it well. And it wasn't as if Abi begrudged her the attention—it was attention that she hadn't wanted for herself, and the story was doing good things for the popularity of the Royal children.

But it would have been useful if these boys had known why she'd gotten this special place before she turned up here.

That's all right. Dealing with a lot of resentful lads is a whole lot easier than infiltrating a magic city taken over by a crazy cannibalistic magician. I'd rather be doing this than dealing with that.

The instructor, Master Morell, entered and immediately commanded the attention of the room. He was a short, balding man with a prominent nose and piercing green eyes. He had with him, curiously enough, a box that seemed to contain pieces of wood. "I assume that all of you are aware of the new student, Abidela. I also assume that all of you are making the assumption that she is here because her mother is the King's Own."

He waited for a moment, and some quiet murmurs made it clear that his assumption was correct.

"Rather than simply *tell* you why you are all wrong, I'm going to have Abidela demonstrate," he said, as he began taking the pieces of wood out of the box and assembled them into what was apparently a bridge model. "You all already know the answer to this particular problem, but she does not. Abidela, come show me the weak spot on this model."

She got up from her desk and moved to the front of the class. This wasn't as easy as it looked—the model was small, all the pieces were painted the same dun color to hide what they were made of, and the strain in it wasn't anywhere near as obvious as it had been every other time her Gift had been at work. In fact, she had to slowly move her hand over and around the model before she sensed it, as a very faint unease, so faint she wouldn't have noticed it if she hadn't been concentrating. "Here," she said, pointing to one of the under-supports. "That can't take more than the weight it's already carrying."

Murmurs arose again, this time of surprise, as she went to sit down at her desk again.

The instructor swept all the pieces back into their box. "You all know about the bridge collapse, of course. What isn't common knowledge is that Abidela was not only there, she is the one that sensed the bridge was about to collapse and helped Herald Trainee Princess Katiana get people off the bridge before it fell. And *that* is why a place was made for her here, among us."

Now every one of those boys turned in their seats to stare at her. She licked her lips nervously. She'd never faced this much scrutiny before.

The instructor wasn't helping; in fact, he stood there with his arms crossed as if he was waiting for her to say something. She swallowed and gave it her best.

"I've . . . got some kind of weird Gift nobody ever heard of before. The Princess was running an errand for the Queen, and we're friends, so I came with her to help." *That sounds a whole lot less pretentious than 'I came along to guard her,' which they won't believe.* "My mother's Companion let me ride him so we wouldn't stand out as anything other than a couple of Trainees. So when I felt the bridge start to go, he picked that up from me, and told Ka—the Princess and her Companion, and we chased everybody off the bridge before it fell. That's all." She shrugged. "Really, it was the Companions that did everything. We just stuck to the saddles like a couple of annoying burrs."

That got a couple of reluctant smiles.

"Anyway, they want me to train as an Artificer while they figure out how to make this Gift reliable, and I guess when I know how to do repairs and reinforcement they'll send me out on bridge and building inspections." That was pure speculation on her part, but it did make sense, and the instructor nodded approvingly. *It also doesn't sound like someone who wants to make a big reputation for herself. You don't make a reputation doing bridge inspections, you make one designing famous temples and expensive manor houses.* If she was going to help her father, a reputation was the very last thing she needed or wanted anyway. Except, maybe, a reputation for keeping her mouth shut and getting the job done.

"But that's not fair!" whined someone at the front of the room where Abi couldn't see him. "She'll know how to tell where models are bad without having to work at it!"

"She'll be required to show her work just as the rest of you are," the instructor snapped, in a tone of voice that told Abi very clearly that he didn't care for this particular student.

Among the many, many useful things she'd learned from both her father and her mother so far, one of them was what they called "reading a room"—seeing where the power dynamics were. You didn't need Gifts to do that; all you needed was a pair of eyes, a mind, and careful observation. The moment that whining complaint emerged from the complainer's mouth, the room sorted itself in front of her eyes.

It was quite clear that the complainer was someone who expected not only to be listened to but to have any implicit orders obeyed. She could see right off that three of the boys in this room were his personal sycophants, as their own little nods of agreement or sullen expressions showed. The rest of the boys were not at all impressed, and in fact, the complaint had thrown them over to her side.

Interestingly the instructor was no more impressed by the complainer than she herself was, and she got the distinct feeling that if he could be rid of this student, he would happily throw him out. But that arrogance, that assumption of power, said the boy was either highborn or very wealthy.

Now, it was vanishingly unlikely that any of the highborn would have a son in *this* set of classes. Builders were Tradesmen, and while you might allow your second or third daughter to marry one who was sufficiently wealthy, you certainly would not let your son become one. That meant that this boy's parents were not highborn. But the fact that he expected to be heard and obeyed meant that they were very wealthy. These were all interesting things to know and take note of.

"Now we've wasted enough time satisfying your curiosity about Abidela. It's time to return to the reason we are here. Abidela, I expect you to keep up, and if you have questions, ask them. Now—"

Abi hadn't expected a class as specific as this one, which was entirely about the structural strength and flexibility of various materials in minute detail—what they were most useful for, and how to calculate the load-bearing potential for each one. She'd probably missed a few that the class had already covered, but she had a good idea that she could catch up on those if one of the boys would lend her his notes. Which meant she had to make friends.

Well, Master Whiner had already given her a head start on that.

She still hadn't gotten a good look at the whiner by the time the lesson was over, just a sense that he was taller than most of the rest, and a look at the top of his head, which sported blond hair. But luck, of a sort, was with her. She kept one eye on that particular head and saw from his body language that he intended to intercept her as they all filed out of this classroom and headed for the next.

Lovely. So he's a bully as well as a whiner.

He was not what she expected, though she had already known he was tall. She'd expected someone large, bulky—bullies usually were—but he wasn't especially muscled, and he did look very soft, quite in keeping with her assumption that he was wealthy. It didn't look as if he ever needed to lift a hand to do anything for himself. He had a perfectly square face, a shock of blond hair, small eyes, a pouty mouth, and oddly small hands. He smirked as he made brief eye contact with her, and she sighed. This was either going to be a verbal confrontation or—a physical one.

The boy does not know what he is shoving his face into.

There was some jostling as two of his sycophants pinned her between them for a moment, blocking Master Morell from seeing her and what was happening to her, and he grabbed for her breast under cover of the crowd. There was a sudden rush of anticipatory energy as she recognized what he was doing and a surge of indignation. She, however, was a lot faster than he was, and she had been learning dirty tricks since she was old enough to train with Master Leandro. She knew exactly what to do because she'd practiced doing it so often she could make the move without even thinking about it.

Before he or his toadies had any idea she already knew what he was up to, she intercepted his hand, got a firm grasp on the little finger, and twisted her hand quickly to the side and down.

Feeling the bone snap, she released his finger before anyone else had any idea that he'd reached for her, much less that she had retaliated against his assault—released it before even his nerves has registered pain. In fact, she wasn't even sure his toadies understood she'd made a move at all before her part in the little dance was over.

But his high-pitched scream of pain a moment later alerted everyone to the fact that something had just happened.

He staggered backward into the wall, holding his injured hand by the wrist, uttering girlish, inarticulate shrieks at the top of his lungs. Abi saw with a feeling of deep satisfaction that the little finger of his right hand was now bent backward at a right-angle to the rest of his hand. While some of the others paused to gape, she just made her way out of the door and down the hall to the next class as if nothing had happened. By this time, of course, the screaming attracted attention from the hall as well, and more people crowded around the door behind her. By virtue of all the attention her would-be tormentor had attracted, the room she ducked into was virtually empty, and she found a good seat at the front and to the farthest right.

The instructor for this class was already there, and he raised an interrogative eyebrow at her. "I assume you're Abidela. Aren't you curious what all the caterwauling is about?" he asked.

"Not really," she replied with studied indifference, as she willed her heart to slow and her emotions to cool down. "I believe some fool was engaged in horseplay, doing something stupid, and got himself hurt. I'm not a Healer, so it's none of my business."

The other eyebrow joined the first as the instructor pondered what she had just said—and the very careful wording. She had not lied. Some fool *had* done something very stupid, and the result was he'd gotten himself hurt.

Outside in the hall, the screaming faded to a whimper, then to nothing; the other students filed into the classroom. Abi noted that as far as she could tell, the makeup of this class was the same as the last, and as the last of them took his seat, the instructor got down to the business of teaching them geometry.

The third class of the morning added a couple of Herald Trainees to the mix; Abi vaguely knew them, and they gave her quick nods of recognition as they took their seats. Then it was time for lunch. She thought about approaching one or more of her classmates— but no. Not just yet, anyway. *Let them get used to me, to the idea of me being one of them. Maybe let some of them come to me first.*

Besides, she was starving. She spotted Kat and Trey immediately when she entered the dining hall; they spotted her at the same time, and waved at her. She wove her way through the crowd, and found herself sandwiched between them, being plied with food and what was evidently a burning question.

"Did you *really* break Dudley Remp's finger?" Kat asked, half laughing as she passed Abi the bowl of cooked cabbage and bacon.

"If he's a particularly repugnant blond bully who likes to put his hands where they shouldn't be, yes," she said tightly, willing herself *not* to give in to the anger she really wanted to feel. "Good luck him proving it, though. No one saw me. Or him, for that matter. He took advantage of the crowd at the door to make a grab for my chest. I did the same to apply Master Leandro's little-finger hold—and then I went all the way with it." She gave both of them a warning look. "If anyone but a teacher or a Herald asks, though, you don't know anything. And if anyone but a Herald asks *me*, I'm going to say there was a lot of jostling, I thought I felt someone pawing my chest, and I swatted the hand away and didn't think anything more about it. Accidents happen in crowds." She helped herself to pickled beets. "And he's lucky he didn't try to grab for anything lower. I'd have broken his whole gods-bedamned hand for him, and the wrist with it."

Kat stuffed her hand into her mouth to keep from laughing. Trey, however, looked serious. "Master Remp is very wealthy," he said, with a warning tone in his voice. "And what he wants, he generally gets. He owns a *lot* of property in Haven, and he rents it out, then lends the money he gets to powerful people. That's where he gets his fortune."

But Kat snorted. "He's a skinflinted landlord is what he is," she said. "He may own a lot of property, but most of it is in the poorest parts of Haven, where he'll neglect his buildings, knowing that if he doesn't make repairs, eventually the tenants will do it for him for free."

"Hmm," Abi replied, wondering why on earth such a man would have enrolled his son in the Artificer building classes. "Well, that doesn't give him any power here on the Hill. At least, not against someone like me."

"Don't count on that, and don't count on him not making trouble for you," Trey warned again. "He can try to get you expelled."

But while Trey had been talking, Abi had already come up with a plan.

The only question in her mind was, would she have to use it?

Abidela was not startled by the tap on her shoulder from behind as she left her last class. She'd been perfectly aware of the Guard's approach through the hall, even though he'd done his best to remain unobtrusive. "Abidela?" he said, sounding apologetic. "I'm afraid you will have to come with me. Someone has lodged a serious charge against you that requires answering."

It was a young man she vaguely knew from the rotations of Guards on the Royal Suite. Which made sense, whoever wanted her would have sent someone who knew her on sight.

She shrugged. "All right," she said agreeably, but she said nothing more. When the Guard didn't get any further response from her, he motioned to her to follow and took her from Heralds' Collegium, where the classes had been, into the administrative area of the Palace, to a hall full of offices. As she had expected, waiting for her were a red-faced, hand-bandaged Dudley Remp, an older, hard-visaged man who was probably his father, and behind a big desk, someone she didn't recognize, probably whoever was in charge of the Artificers. It was a larger office, which suggested this man was important enough to be the equivalent of the Dean of Heralds or Healers. There was more than enough room for the three people currently in it and a chair waiting for one more— her, she supposed.

"That's her!" Dudley blurted, jumping to his feet and pointing, as soon as she came in. "That's the bitch that broke my finger! I want her beaten! I want her beaten and thrown out, Master Ketnar! Right now!"

Anger brought with it energy, but she schooled herself not to show it. It looked as if she was going to have to implement her plan after all.

"I demand Truth Spell," she snapped, instantly, before anyone could say anything else. "As the accused, I am entitled to demand Truth Spell. *On both of us.* We're here at the Collegium, there are literally dozens of Heralds and Trainees that can do it at a moment's notice. I demand it now."

And with that, to demonstrate that she had no intention of saying anything until a Herald turned up, she picked up the empty chair, moved it as far from Dudley and his father as possible, and sat down in it with her arms crossed over her chest.

Dudley went from red to pale in an instant, though his father apparently was not bright enough to figure out that someone who demanded a Truth Spell was probably innocent. "This is nonsense. My son has been injured. *I* demand—"

But the Artificer cut him off. "She's within her rights," he agreed and motioned to the Guard. "Go find me a Herald that can—"

"Actually, sir, there is at least one, and possibly two of them on the way now," the Guard said apologetically. "You sent Greer after them. They're her parents." And within moments after he finished that sentence, Mags turned up at the door.

"I'm Herald Mags. Abidela is my daughter," he said, wearing that expression that Abi knew so well, the one that made him look amiable, but stupid. "What's all this about her being in trouble?"

At first, Remp the Elder protested that having the accused's father implementing the Truth Spell was—

Well, he wasn't allowed to continue. Master Ketnar frostily asked him if he was actually questioning the impartiality of a Herald. At that point Remp finally realized how dangerous the ground he was treading on was and shut up. Explanations were given which Abi didn't pay any attention to and didn't contribute to. What she was concentrating on were Dudley and his father.

Dudley's hair had started to clump as he sweated nervously. Clearly he hadn't thought this through at all.

Neither had his father, who had expected that money would buy him what he wanted, since it always had before. The difference between them, however, was that the father was concentrating on punishing Abi for hurting his son, regardless of his son's innocence or guilt. Whereas Dudley already knew he was guilty, and realized he was about to be caught red-handed.

Mags nodded when the Artificer had finished. "Well, then," he said. "Best that we get all the truth out at once, eh? Coercive Truth Spell it is. And just to be fair, I'll put it on Abi first."

Dudley, strangely, looked relieved at that. For a moment, Abi was puzzled as to why—but then she realized that he thought that what her father would do was ask "Did you break Dudley's finger?" and of course she'd be forced to admit she had, and Dudley would get what he wanted. She came very near to laughing at that moment, as she felt the Truth Spell settle about her. She faced her father, fearless and relaxed.

Because, of course, her father was a master at asking exactly the right questions. The very ones Dudley didn't want asked.

And that was precisely what he did.

"What happened this morning as you left Master Morell's class?" he asked calmly. Out of the corner of her eye she saw Dudley start as if someone had stuck him with a pin and start to sweat again.

"Two of the big fellows that had been up at the front of the class with Dudley got me pinned me between them in the scuffle to get out the door," she said, feeling absolutely nothing, because, of course, she had no reason to try to fight the Truth Spell. "Besides pinning me between them, they were trying to hide me from Master Morell. Dudley tried to assault me with intent to hurt. I grabbed his hand in that *handa* hold that Master Leandro taught us and broke his finger."

"There!" shouted Remp. "She admits it! She—"

"Shut up, Remp!" Master Ketnar shouted. "She just accused your son of trying to *assault* her! Are you stupid as well as deaf?" As Remp stood there, mouth agape, Master Ketnar turned to her. "What do you mean by 'assault,' Abidela?" he asked, his tone crisp.

"He tried to grab my breast," she said, matter-of-factly. "I guess he thought no one would believe me if I said anything. I reckon he must get away with that a lot."

Anyone who didn't know Mags would think that Abi's words had meant nothing to him, but she saw the slow burn of anger in his eyes, though his mouth continued to smile and his tone never changed. "What made you think he was trying to grab you there?" he asked.

"Well, the fact that he shoved right in front of his friend and lunged his hand at me, mostly," she replied. "But just to be sure, I let him get within a finger-width of his goal before I grabbed his pinky, and to tell the truth, an awful lot of what made his finger *break* was his own lunging. Honestly if I hadn't been pinned in by his friends, I'd have just stepped aside, stuck my foot out to trip him, and let him fall on his face, he's that clumsy. I thought about letting him grab and then cracking him in the chin with the heel of my hand instead of breaking his finger, or crunching him in the family treasures with my knee, but from the way he came in, he intended to hurt me, and I didn't want any bruises."

"Will that be enough, Master Ketnar?" Mags asked politely. Ketnar nodded.

Abi didn't feel any differently as her father turned away from her than she had when he'd put the Truth Spell on her, but that was the point. You weren't supposed to feel anything as long as you'd made no effort to hide anything.

"Now," Mags said, and whether or not Dudley and his father heard the steel in the Herald's voice, Abi did. "It's time for Dudley."

Mags didn't give them a chance to object, either. In less time than it took to snap her fingers, Abi saw Dudley surrounded by the bright blue glow of the Truth Spell—a glow that was invisible to those inside it but clearly visible to everyone else. Dudley's carefully groomed hair lay plastered to his scalp with sweat, and drops of perspiration ran down his forehead.

"Now, Dudley," Mags said, voice soft and emotionless. "What did you tell your friends to do with Abi?"

"I told them to get her pinned between them at the door, where Master couldn't see her, like we did with Brice a couple of moons ago, so I could teach him a lesson too." The words came freely, though from the contorted expression on Dudley's face, he was trying with all his might to keep them from coming out of his mouth.

"And what were you going to do to her?" Mags continued.

"Grab her booby, give it a twist, and show her it's best not to cross me," said Dudley. "I knew nobody'd believe her. I do grab boobies all the time, to show girls who's in charge of them, and nobody believes the girls. When you're rich, you can do anything, and they just let you."

Well, this was a lot more than Abi had expected to come pouring out without a more careful examination by her father. She glanced at Master Ketnar, who was listening, slack-jawed with astonishment. She glanced at Dudley's father—and quickly looked away. The man was in a white-hot rage. And she sensed it was not because of what his son had said but because his son had said it out loud.

"I think that's sufficient, Herald Mags," Ketnar said, before Mags could think of another question—as if another question was actually going to be needed at this point. "Master Remp, I have no option but to expel your son. Not only did he attempt to assault a fellow student and lie about it, he confessed to assaulting another. Such behavior has no place here. Please take him and leave. You do, of course, have the option of hiring whatever Master Artificers you choose to tutor him, but he is no longer welcome here on the Hill, and I will instruct the Guard to escort him off if he attempts to pass the Gates in the unlikely event you are tendered an invitation that includes him."

Remp grabbed Dudley by the upper arm and hauled him bodily out of the room. They had barely cleared the door when the *crack* of flesh on flesh rang through the hall, there was the sound of a heavy body hitting the wall, and angry whispers. Abi winced. But neither of the adults said or did anything as the sound of two sets of feet, one stumbling, retreated down the hall and, presumably, out of the building.

Now Mags turned to face Master Ketnar, his true feelings showing in his expression. "What kind uv a school are you runnin' here, Ketnar, when a pig like *thet* c'n run roughshod over weaker students an' get away with 't?" he stormed, his cultured manner completely gone as he reverted to the dialect of his childhood in his anger. "I've more'n half a mind t' take all this t' th' King his own self and git you and yer Masters thrown outa here! We c'n find other tutors fer th' classes they was teachin' here at th' Collegia!"

But Master Ketnar stood firm in the face of her father's controlled anger, and he answered it with calm and regret. "You have no reason to believe me, Herald Mags, but I swear to you, there has never been a problem here like this before. But I'll tell you this much—I am going to think twice and three times before I let someone with more money than ethics talk me into accepting his child in the Artificers college again! Those two *friends* that Dudley mentioned? They're going to be expelled as well as soon as I can find out from Morell who they are and summon them here."

Now he turned to Abi, to her surprise. "Abidela, I apologize for all of this, and I'd like to know what *you* want. After all, you are the injured party in this entire matter."

Abi thought about it for a long while. Truth to tell, she didn't have a hot temper, and her anger had cooled the moment her father had turned up. "I'd like to stay in the classes," she said, at last. "It's not as if something like this has happened before that they knew of, so I'd like things to stay the same for the Artificers up here."

"I'm perfectly willing for you to invoke the Truth Spell on me or any of my instructors, Herald," Master Ketnar said with immense dignity. Mags nodded.

Abi continued. "I'd like it if you expel those other two bullies, Master Ketnar, and I think you're going to make sure that no one like them gets in again. And right now, I'd like to go home and start my studying for tomorrow."

Master Ketnar looked at her father. Mags shrugged. "If that's what ye want—"

She nodded. "That's what I want," she assured him, then gave him a tight smile. "If I let one stupid lout run me off of something I want to do, I'm not my father's daughter."

Mags barked a tiny, surprised laugh. She took that as a good sign and left the office.

Let them work out whatever they were going to work out. She had studying to do.

3

"Well, what are we going to do with you?" Healer Sanje asked rhetorically. At least Abi assumed the question was rhetorical, since she had no idea how to answer it.

They were in a green-tiled examination and treatment room in the part of Healers' Collegium devoted to the sick and injured. Abi could not imagine how the Healers managed it, but somehow the atmosphere in here was welcoming and comforting, not cold and sterile, or ominous.

The Healer took Abi's chin in her hand and tilted Abi's face up to catch the light, looking deeply—and somewhat creepily—into Abi's eyes. No one had ever looked so intently at Abi before, not even her parents, and she found herself repressing the urge to squirm and look away.

Healer Sanje was an extremely tall woman, as tall as most men and certainly much taller than her father. She was also quite thin, with an oddly angular face, and slow, graceful movements, as if she thought out each movement carefully and choreographed it before executing it. Sanje's eyes were an unsettling silver, her hair, jet-black. In her green Healer's robes she was an unforgettable character.

"Walk with me," Sanje ordered, letting go of Abi's chin, and making a tiny gesture to indicate Abi should walk alongside her. They left the examination room, moved down the hallway of the treatment and recovery wing of Healers', and out into the herb garden. Sanje didn't say a word the entire time, just glided along with her head tilted down slightly, as if she were meditating.

The many scents of the herb garden tickled and teased Abi's nose. Some people found it dull because most of the plants did not have big, showy flowers. She never had and actually preferred it to the formal gardens. They paced slowly between the beds of herbs, tending in the direction of Companion's Field but taking little detours as Sanje paused to examine this plant or that.

"Do you know what synesthesia is?" she asked, finally, when Abi was already a bit unnerved by the silence.

"No," Abi replied.

"It's a rare condition. I personally would not consider it a defect, but rather an enhancement of the senses. Some people experience two senses at once with a single stimulus, such as hearing a particular note and at the same time, seeing a particular color." She hummed a note, and Abi was completely unsurprised to discover Sanje had a very good voice. "A person with synesthesia would hear that note, and see, say, the color blue at the same time. Another note, and instead of blue he would see yellow. More often, a person will see or experience particular letters or numbers as distinct colors. If you asked them how they saw the letter 'A' they might tell you it was red."

"Huh," Abi said, thinking about it. "That must make listening to or reading anything a bit distracting until you get used to it."

"Which is why I am known for treating it," Sanje said. "For some, especially those who are born with the condition, this is perfectly normal and enjoyable, and removing the ability would lessen their lives. For those who are older, for whom the condition has come on because of a head injury or illness, especially adults, it can be confusing and distressing to suddenly be able to taste shapes when you eat your food. I have had some success in removing the secondary sensations in people like that." She glanced sideways at Abi and waited.

Well, they want me to get this Gift under complete control, not get rid of it. So . . . "So they think you can *give* me synesthesia?" she hazarded. "So I can *see* stress in objects instead of just feeling it?"

Sanje smiled broadly, a very catlike smile. "They told me you were clever. Good. I like clever people. Dull ones irritate me, especially those who expect to be told what to do, and if they are not told, do nothing, even when something that needs doing is right in front of them. Yes, that is what they would like me to do. I think it's quite possible. I'd like to go farther than that, actually. I'm sure you realize that there is stress in anything that is not lying completely flat on the ground."

"Actually, there's stress even in something like that, but it's so weak it doesn't matter," Abi corrected.

Sanje nodded. "I'd like to train you to the point where you can sense and see how and where that stress flows in everything rather than seeing only the intolerable stress that makes things break. But how do you feel about that?"

She didn't answer right away. If she was actually going to become a full Artificer, and not just a mystical-damage-detector . . . such a Gift would be very useful. She would not just be able to correct and direct the repairs of things that were breaking down, she'd be able to help build them right in the first place. The more she thought about that, the better she liked that idea. These past few days of study and classes had been opening up new vistas in her mind. Until enrolling in Artificers, she'd had no interest in her entire life in building or designing things, but now . . . she'd changed her mind completely. Now whenever she looked at a building, she found herself imagining it if had been built differently. More pleasing. Stronger.

And becoming one of those Artificers who were known for designing beautiful structures would help her help her father too. Of course, when she'd first enrolled in the Artificers, she'd not wanted such a reputation, since everything she had done for her father until now had involved remaining fundamentally unseen. But this would be a different sort of disguise—like the times her father pretended to be highborn and gave himself a flamboyant personality. If others concentrated on what her persona of Master Builder could do, they might not pay much attention to what *she* was doing. Artificers with a reputation had extraordinary access to all manner of important *and* common people, from the ones who had the wealth to commission important buildings to the very secretive building tradesmen that constructed them. These were people Mags would ordinarily not be able to put an agent among. By honing her Gift to the point Sanje described, she'd be killing not just two birds with one stone, but an entire flock of them.

"If you can do it without driving me insane," she said, once she'd thought it all through, "I think that would be an excellent idea."

Sanje had a quite musical laugh. "Well said," she agreed. "I think I can promise that. So, if you have time to start, is there some place on the Hill where you know that a structure is under stress?"

"It'd be easier to build something," Abi pointed out. "A board up on two bricks or stones, then pile bricks or stones in the middle until it's ready to break."

Sanje laughed again. "Oh my, how very practical! You will make a fine Artificer, I think. Yes, let's do that, so that I can 'read' how you experience it."

There were always repairs going on the Hill; they followed the sound of hammering to the stable, where they found the Palace carpenter at work replacing the top of a stall that a horse had chewed on. He was perfectly willing to give them the damaged board, and the gardeners always had spare bricks. Then Sanje looked for a place they would not likely be disturbed and quickly spotted one. In less than half a candlemark, they were sitting together on a bench at the fence around Companion's Field, Sanje with one hand on Abi's shoulder, Abi slowly putting half-bricks onto the weakened board, and three Companions watching the proceedings with great interest.

"Hmm," Sanje said, at exactly the moment when Abi sensed that *wrong* feeling in the board. "Hm-hmm. Yes, I can work with this. Take the bricks off, and start again, would you?"

Anyone watching us is going to think we're daft, Abi thought, and glanced up at the three Companions with their heads over the fence, all in a row. *Including them.* But it was a lovely early-summer day, not too hot, not too cool. The bench wasn't particularly uncomfortable, and she'd been explicitly told that Sanje was to have her entire afternoon. And this wasn't any sillier looking than other Gift training she had seen. So with a mental shrug, she took the bricks off and began piling them back on again.

Now, when she'd taken them off, she'd counted them and laid them all to the left so she'd know when to quit even if this Gift of hers wasn't being reliable. But the moment she laid the second-to-the-last brick on the board, she felt the strain under her hand and stopped.

"Good," said Sanje. "Again."

Wondering if that had been a fluke, she took off the bricks and started again. But this time she felt the strain with three bricks to go. And Sanje took her hand off Abi's shoulder.

"Again," Sanje ordered. "This time without my help."

She sensed the strain as that uneasy, almost queasy feeling with three bricks to go, and Sanje dusted off her hands wearing a smile of satisfaction. "Keep working without me," the Healer told her. "If you start to get a headache, stop. I'll see you in a sennight at the same time in my examination room." And with that, the woman got up and left, leaving Abi sitting on the bench, gazing after her with curiously mixed feelings.

"Did she just—" she asked, looking at the three Companions. Two of them cocked their heads to the side, as if they didn't know either, but the third nodded vigorously. "Huh," she said, and unbuilt the bricks to build them back up again, over and over, still with the same result of sensing the strain with three bricks to go, until she started to get a sort of headache that actually felt more like "muscles" in her skull were tired. Figuring that was what

Healer Sanje had been talking about, she gathered up her pile of
bricks and her board and went in search of a place to keep them
for practicing later.

Since all her classes were in the morning and it wasn't time for
supper yet, she went back to the family apartment. Normally it
would have been empty—her mother and father at their duties, her
brother Perry minding the pawn shop down in Haven if he wasn't
doing something else for Mags, and her youngest brother Tory at
lessons of his own with the King's youngest, Kee. But it looked as
if lessons were over for the day, because Kee and Tory were in the
center room of the suite with their backs to the door, sitting on
the floor using Kee's great mastiff, Gryphon, as a backrest. The
other mastiff belonging to the Royals, Drake, was without a doubt
standing watch over the Queen, as he had from the moment she
first knew she was pregnant. But Gryphon was Kee's and Kee's
alone, from the time Perry had given the mastiff to the child. From
where she stood in the doorway, she could tell the two boys were
engrossed in something but not what that something was.

"Why were you stacking and unstacking bricks all afternoon?"
Tory asked, before she could announce her presence.

She blinked and walked farther into the room. "Did you Farsee
me?" she asked in return, as they both turned to look at her over
Gryphon's back.

Tory shook his head, then nodded, then shook it again. "Not
me," he said, sounding doubtful. "It was both of us together. We
can't see anyone but family, though. We've tried. You're weird."

"No, *you're* weird," she corrected, as Kee laughed.

"No, *you* are!"

They went back and forth with this a few more times, before Tory returned to his first question. "So, if you're not weird, which you are, why were you stacking and unstacking bricks all afternoon?"

She plopped down on the floor beside them, and when the great mastiff shoved his huge head under her hand for a scratch, obliged absentmindedly. "You know how I could tell the bridge was going to fall?"

Tory's pupils dilated. "Don't do that again!" he said with alarm.

"No, I have to do that again," she corrected gently. "I just have to make sure I do it a long time before the bridge is going to fall, so I can tell people to fix it so it doesn't fall down. That's what I was doing all afternoon. Learning to how tell a whole lot earlier. So I can get the bridges fixed and nobody gets hurt."

Tory relaxed. "Oh, all right," he agreed. "Who was that funny Healer?"

"Her name is Sanje, and I guess she has ways of making Gifts like mine stronger and easier to use." Just because she'd never heard of anyone who could do that, it didn't mean that ability didn't exist, right? And at least one of the Companions seemed to agree. She remembered how Sanje had specifically said "I can work with this" when she'd demonstrated her Gift, so probably Sanje couldn't work with everything. Maybe she was a kind of Mindhealer. That would make sense. That would make a lot of sense. If you could Heal something, you could probably make it stronger too.

Or maybe it wasn't a matter of making it *stronger,* maybe she was just making it easier to use? And it was Abi herself who was going to make it stronger by practicing with it?

And maybe I should stop speculating and just follow her instructions. As long as my Gift gets stronger, more reliable, and easier to use, that's all that matters. How it gets that way makes no difference.

"Can she do that with us? Make it so we can Farsee other people besides our families?" Tory wanted to know, interrupting her thoughts.

"And just who do you want to spy on, hmm?" she asked. "Little busybody—"

"Anyone Papa wants us to," came the unexpected answer, as Kee nodded vigorously.

"Well, you'll have to ask Sanje that yourself," Abi replied, "Because I don't know."

"Can't you ask?" Kee popped up with. "Then we could listen."

"No, I won't," she replied. "Ask her yourself. If she can, and she wants you to know she can, then she'll tell you."

"That's not fair! She's helping you and *you* didn't ask her to!" Tory protested. Kee looked doubtful.

"No, but that's because I didn't have to ask her. Someone else did, someone important, way more important than me. I was ordered to work with her, probably by the same person. And don't pout," she added, as Tory looked stormy. "Perry got to go off with Papa and got Larral when he was old enough. Now I'm getting my Gift trained up because I'm old enough. If you two want something done to make *your* Gifts stronger, you need to talk to Mama and Papa and see what they say."

"Don't want to," Kee said, but in a thoughtful way, not a rebellious one. "Don't want people to know yet."

"Well, all right, then. In that case, you'll just have to accept that the only people you can Farsee are family members." There. She'd just tied them all up in their own logic and put a neat little bow on top.

Tory made a face. So did Kee, but it wasn't the same face. It was more like one of surprise. "Abi, c'n I stay here overnight with Tory?"

"Uh—" Kee had done so before plenty of times but—"I guess so, but why?"

"Cause Mama's about to have the baby and people are going to start running around and everybody's going to forget I want to eat supper," he said, matter-of-factly, just as a commotion started in the area of the Royal Suite and there was a lot of running in both directions out in the hall.

———

"Well," her father said, when she had finished telling him *all* of the surprising things that had happened this afternoon. There was still activity going on in the Royal Suite, but things seemed to be moving along at the expected pace, and everyone except the Queen was happy with how the birth was going. And nothing was going to make the Queen happy except getting that baby out of her as quickly as possible. Abi was just glad not to be in the Queen's shoes—or, rather, lack of them. If being pregnant was bad, obviously giving birth was worse.

Kee talked a servant into bringing some snacks, then he and Tory settled into Tory's room for a game that involved picking straws out of a pile without making any of them move.

That had given Abi the chance to get her father to herself and tell him about her progress—and the boys.

Mags considered everything she had told him for quite some time. "Well," he said again. "I din't know Gifts c'ld be strengthened either. I knew yer use of 'em could improve over time an' with practice, but I din't know you could make 'em stronger."

"It may not be that," she pointed out. "It may just be this Healer can open things up a bit in my head."

"Still, somethin' t' file away. I am innerested that she c'n give you a way t' *see* things instead 'f just feelin' 'em." He sucked on his lower lip a moment. "Does th't mean yer gonna get t' be more precise once she does thet?"

"I think so. I'm pretty sure. Right now it's kind of hard to measure and compare levels of *I'm feeling sick*. I think it will be easier when I can see the stress and how it flows." The more she considered that, the surer she became, in fact. "And I'd *really* rather using this Gift meant I can use my eyes, and not feel like I'm going to throw up. If she can turn this 'sense,' whatever it is, into sight, that would be lovely."

"Well, I'll leave thet up to you an' her. Now 'bout the boys—"

Abi did her best not to roll her eyes. "Tory's probably going to pout when he finds out I told you."

"He didn' pledge you to secrecy did he?" Mags seemed very amused.

"No, he didn't say anything and Kee just said he didn't want anyone to find out," Abi told him.

"If they didn' want anyone t' find out, they shouldn't hev been doin' it in th' middle 'f th' great room in th' middle 'f th' day," Mags pointed out, and looked over to one side. "An' Kee an' Tory, if yer watchin' now, an' I am sure ye are, we're gonna to hev a talk in the mornin'."

He smiled suddenly.

"They *were* watching, weren't they?" demanded Abi, a little annoyed that her *private* talk with her father had been eavesdropped on.

"A' course they were, from the moment you walked inter my workshop. I jest don' want them to know yet I c'n tell when they are." Now he laughed, and grinned at her.

"So you've known they can Farsee all along?"

"I suspicioned it. But I didn' know their limitations, so thank you for findin' thet out, Abi." She felt mollified, and pleased. "Tomorrow they are gonna get the big Heraldic lecture on privacy an' what happens if'n they violate it."

Well, that made her feel a good bit better about telling her father. Tory could just get over his sulks at being told on.

"I gotta say that I've never heard of two childern only havin' a Gift when the two of 'em worked together, though," Mags continued. "I'll hev t' report this t' th' experts an' see what they can make of it." He sighed theatrically. "Why is it that none of you younglings c'n neither be completely normal, nor hev regular Heraldic Gifts?"

"Because you're our father," Abi teased.

He laughed, and sent her to her room to study.

But in the interval while she had been talking with her father, the entire set of four Royal children had invaded the main room of the suite again. Because of course they had; no one who didn't have to be there wanted to be with the Queen right now. "I am *so* glad there are thick walls between here and home," were the first words Kat greeted her with. "I might actually get some sleep tonight." She plopped down onto the floor in the main room and grabbed one of the cushions the youngest boys had been using.

Abi dropped down beside her friend and jabbed her in the ribs with an elbow. "Anyone would think you didn't care about your mother," she chided.

"Of course I care! But everything is going *fine*, there are four Healers there, and it isn't as if she hadn't done this four times already. But the *yelling!*" Kat shook her head. "Meanwhile the four children she has now need sleep if they're going to be able to pay any attention to their classes tomorrow."

"And food," Trey pointed out helpfully. "We also need food. Kee talked someone into bringing him and Tory snacks, but the rest of us haven't eaten since lunch."

Neither have I, she realized, and the thought awoke a ravening beast in her stomach. "Feel like coming with me to the kitchen?" she asked Kat, knowing that having one of the Royals with her was going to make scrounging food much, much easier. "Because I'll bet Mama is with the Queen, and that is going to leave all of us and Papa to starve unless we do something about it."

Kat's stomach chose to growl at that moment, and she laughed. "Obviously yes. Trey, you're coming too. Niko, you make sure Tory and Kee don't get up to mischief. No one is going to refuse the Heir. Particularly if you look wan and pathetic."

"Like this?" Trey asked, and put on a mournful face.

"That's too much. You'll start rumors that Mama is dying." Kat shook her head at him. "Just think about how hungry you are."

"That's not hard." Trey got up and joined them, and the three of them slipped down the servants' stair to the ground floor, which was where everything that kept the Palace going actually got done. Two corridors later, and they presented themselves at the side door of the Palace kitchen, well out of the way of the servers who were taking food up to the Great Hall where all the courtiers were dining. The King would probably be there as well, actually; it would start rumors that there was something wrong if he didn't go about his normal business. In the minds of the members of the Court, the only interest that a man should have in a birth was in the begetting of it.

As usual during a meal, the kitchen was a bedlam. Dirty dishes going to the sinks, scullery maids and boys scrubbing them, pots getting put down next to the sinks to soak, cooks shouting orders, servers rushing in with stacks of used dishes and plates of leftovers and more servers streaming out with laden plates of the next course. They waited politely to be noticed, and the moment finally came when the final dessert course went out and the cooks' jobs were over.

"Lady have mercy!" exclaimed the head cook loudly, startling everyone. "How long have you lot been standing there?"

"Not long," Trey said, and licked his lips with a longing expression on his face as he stared at half a ham. "Everyone's busy with the Queen and we kind of got—"

"How *is* the Queen?" asked a dozen voices at once.

"Yelling like she's on a battlefield," Kat said crisply. "And half of Healers' is taking care of her. But nobody's taking care of *us.*" She gazed meaningfully at a partly dismembered chicken sitting with the other leftovers on the worktables.

That was all it took. In very little time, the three of them were going back up the stairs, laden with big platters of leftovers. By this point it was all cold, of course, but they'd made sure to pick out things that were just fine eaten cold.

There was more than enough for all of them and Mags too. Rather than bother with setting the table, Mags declared a picnic, and they all ate with their hands, sitting together on the rug. And when the now empty platters were sitting outside the door to be collected by the servants, Kat and Abi went to her room. Abi had intended to study, but Kat had other plans.

"Tell me about the Healer!" she exclaimed, flopping down on Abi's bed, when Abi had taken out the firebird feather her brother Perry had given her, and stuck it in its holder to light up her little room.

"There's not much to tell," she protested, but she told it all anyway. Kat listened without interrupting until she was finished.

"I guess your Gift really *is* something no one knows what to do with," she said. "Trey and Niko and I all have very set lessons and exercises, and they even have Kee doing Shielding practice so he keeps his Shields up. A good thing too, or he'd probably be going crazy right now, what with Mama in labor."

Kee had demonstrated he had Empathy—usually a Healer's Gift—remarkably early. Fortunately, thanks to Perry among others, people had noticed before the Gift had developed enough to become a trouble for him.

"I really wish it was a normal Gift, or none at all," Abi replied, restlessly running the hem of her tunic through her fingers. "I like things to be . . . orderly."

"Which is why you're going to make a great Artificer," Kat teased. "All math and tidy numbers, where everything always works the same way every time."

"It's not like that," Abi protested, except she knew it actually was like that, and that this was the reason why she was beginning to enjoy the classes she had been a bit dubious about not that long ago. If you knew the way a problem worked, then working the problem always gave you the same answer. Math was reliable.

"You can't fool me, I'm your best friend and I've known you forever," Kat reminded her.

"I wouldn't want to fool you, except if it was a joke," she replied.

"You might order my head chopped off."

"They won't let me do that," Kat giggled. "Or I swear, I'd have had Trey's head off a long time ago. Here, read something besides musty math books," she added, shoving something with a cover Abi didn't recognize at her. "This just came into the Royal library, and I swiped it before anyone else could."

But Abi pushed it back toward her, much to her surprise. "Believe it or not, I'd rather read those musty math books."

Abi turned up at the refectory in Heralds' Collegium in the middle of the lunch mob all alone. She looked around, but she didn't see anyone obvious to eat with. Trey and Kat must have had an earlier lunch. Niko was in the middle of a huddle of his friends at a single table, and Abi didn't want to intrude on what was clearly a Very Male discussion.

About girls, she guessed with amusement, catching their covert glances at some of the more attractive girls among the Trainees. All the eyes moved to a particular target at once and then quickly away, and none of those targets were boys, so she was pretty sure she had read the group correctly.

Her presence would certainly end that discussion, considering that she tended to make fun of Niko's butterfly memory when it came to a girl he crushed on. It was a good thing that so far he'd never let the object of his desires know he was crushing on her, since he would have left a long string of broken hearts—or at least really annoyed girls—in his wake.

So she settled in a corner favored by Blues where her uniform wouldn't be conspicuous, helped herself to the bowls of food as they were passed around and proceeded to methodically work her way through her lunch. As always, she kept her ear open for bits of gossip that might be useful to her father, but today, there wasn't really anything of interest.

That wasn't such a bad thing, since it meant she could eat her lunch in peace; but she'd barely begun when she caught sight of three of the boys from her class moving through the crowd and working their way in her direction. There was no mistaking it after a few moments; they couldn't have any goal but her, because they passed several good seating opportunities. So the question was, was this a group of Dudley Remp's allies, or of his former victims?

She put down her fork and watched them with as neutral an expression as possible, making sure that they knew that she knew that they were making for her.

Their expressions as they neared were anxious, a little like a group of puppies who wanted to please but weren't sure of their reception. She relaxed and smiled. Unless they were the best actors in Haven, this was what she had been waiting for. Finally some of her fellow Artificer Trainees were ready to make friends.

When they finally got to her table, they stood there for a moment, shuffling their feet, uncertain of how to begin, and it occurred to her that they were acting—socially—much younger than their real ages. They seemed to have no idea about how to open a conversation with a stranger, especially a girl. So she made the first move.

"There's plenty of room, sit down," she said, in her friendliest tones. "I always like company over meals." All three of them looked a little startled, then enormously pleased, and took seats around her, two on her left and one on her right.

"I'm Emmit, he's Rudi, and this is Brice," said the boy on her right. "Uh, hello!"

"Brice—you're the boy Remp punched in the stomach!" she said to the third, who had probably incurred Dudley's wrath because he was a good deal handsomer than the bully, if a lot smaller. Brice started.

"How—"

"Dudley confessed under Truth Spell," she said, trying not to sound smug although "smug" was certainly how she felt. "It's one of the reasons he got expelled."

This, of course, was an immediate icebreaker, and she cheerfully detailed the entire experience. After all, no one had sworn her to secrecy. Unfortunately for their curiosity, once they got over gloating over Dudley's downfall, she couldn't actually answer a lot of their questions, which were about "how the Truth Spell works." She could describe the mechanics—the blue glow that hung about the person being questioned, the Coercive and non-Coercive spells, and why some Heralds could set one and not the other, and she could describe what it felt like to try and lie under the Coercive version, but that was all. They wanted to know what *made* it work, and why, and all she could do was say, "My Gift doesn't work like that, so I don't know."

"Pity," Brice sighed at last. "If you could just construct a mechanical apparatus to set it, you could have one in every village and not need to wait for a Herald."

"But even innocent people don't care for having it set on them," Abi pointed out. "Coercive makes you blurt out all kinds of things that are related to what you're guilty of, but maybe not directly.

That can be awkward. I mean, look how Dudley blabbed about Brice, and about how he likes to grab girls and get away with it."

"And people like my village headman would use it just because he *could,*" said Emmit. "At least in the Heralds' hands we know people aren't going to abuse it."

"Not on purpose anyway," Abi pointed out. "But embarrassing things do slip out without anyone intending them to."

"Which is why the threat is as effective as the Spell itself, I guess," Rudi pointed out. "But that's not what we came here for." He poked Brice in the ribs with an elbow.

"Oh! Aye," said Brice. "We brought you copies of the notes from the lectures in the materials class that you missed. We each took a section, so it wasn't a lot of work, really." All three of them reached inside their tunics and pulled out a folded packet of reused parchment. When she opened Rudi's, the scraped page was covered in carefully written notes in a very precise hand in ink. Brice's section was a lot smaller than the other two, and a bit oddly spelled. The other two were identical except for the handwriting and the fact that they were correctly spelled and much longer. She beamed at them, and they turned suddenly bashful. "This is exactly what I need!" she exclaimed. "I was going to ask to borrow someone's notes so *I* could copy them—thank you so much for doing the copying for me!"

"Oh, well," Brice said, blushing. "It's the least we can do for you getting rid of Dudley for us."

"What I don't understand was why he was in the Blues in the first place," Rudi said, as she tucked all three sets of notes into the front of her own tunic. "He didn't want to be there. He cheated all the time. And his father's rich, so it's not as if he isn't going to inherit a fortune."

"From what I saw, it was his father who wanted him there," Abi observed. "Really, really wanted him there."

"Too skinflint to hire tutors I guess," said Brice, dismissively, and the conversation moved on to other things.

But as the conversation flowed around her, she kept coming back to that question. Why had the elder Remp wanted his son in the Artificers so very badly?

4

With the Royals, her sibs, and her three new Artificer friends, Abi felt perfectly contented. None of her other fellow students had warmed up to Abi, but it wasn't as if she needed to feel that she was the most popular person in the class. Emmit, Brice, and Rudi were not unlike her: serious, not inclined to pranking or gossip, and genuinely interested in what they were all doing. "Dull," Perry called them, teasing her, but she didn't find them dull at all.

They generally worked together on the extra problems their teachers set to be done when lessons were over in an empty classroom or the dining hall. Today it was the dining hall.

"Well," Rudi said ruefully, as they checked the solutions they had gotten to a geometry problem, and they saw they had each gotten a different answer, "we'll never be brilliant."

"I don't want to be brilliant, I want to be reliable," Brice retorted, rubbing the back of his neck. "Well, Abi's the most likely of us to be right, so—"

Abi laughed. "I think the answer lies in the notes we all took. I think Master Ketnar spent a little too much time at the tavern last night--he sounded like he had a hangover. Let's compare those first."

Sure enough, they'd all misrecorded *something* in Master Ketnar's lecture; by comparing all four sets and applying some logic, they figured out where they'd each gone wrong, and finally all arrived at the same answer when they applied the corrected notes to the problem.

"All right, we've done this forward, now let's do it backward," Rudi said, in that tone that told Abi that he was going to do the problem that way even if they didn't. Of the four of them, he was the most thorough. She sighed inwardly; Rudi had a way of making you feel guilty if you sat there slacking while he worked. So they all put their heads down and joined him.

The refectory, or dining hall, was always a good place to get together to work between meals, and it wasn't that bad during them as long as you picked a table well out of the way. Abi would have liked to suggest that they all work outside, but it wasn't practical. Too many sheets of notes to blow away, too much scribbling on slates, and sitting crosslegged on the hard ground, with your head bent over your slate wasn't nearly as comfortable as sitting at a table. Of course, they could have brought pillows and rugs, but pillows and rugs suggested lounging, and if they did that they'd never get the assigned problems done.

Brice was the last to finish, laying his chalk aside with a sigh—no need to compare answers this time, they were all working toward the information they'd been given, and they already had that written down. "And that's the last," he said. "*Now* can we go sit in the warm grass while Abi reads history to us?"

"Meet you by our tree," Abi said, gathering up her notes, her sheet of written answers, and her slate and chalk to take them up to her room for safekeeping. None of them ever left anything behind to be picked up later. No one did. Although the "Collegium Prankster" incident had happened years ago, before Abi was born, even, no one ever left so much as a scrap or a book behind where it could be stolen or defaced. The details had faded in most peoples' minds by now, but not some of the lessons learned from the incident.

In fact, Abi was pretty sure that of all of the students at the Collegia, she was the only one who knew the truth about the tale, since her father and mother had been neck-deep in it.

Unfortunately, some people didn't learn the most important lesson, Abi reflected, as she came back down the stairs, now laden only with her history book and a small rug to sit on. *Women and girls are not the property of men and boys, to do with as they please.* Dudley's behavior was evidence of that much.

She'd taken to reading the history lesson aloud at Brice's request. He was not a good reader and labored through words she leaped over, and now she understood why his copy of the set of notes the friends had given her was smaller than the other two. He'd worked twice as hard to achieve half as much. He understood words when spoken; he just had trouble reading and writing them.

Well, the Artificers weren't here to learn how to read, she reasoned. So she had volunteered. History was the only nonmath class her group was required to take this quarter anyway. It wasn't as if she was doing all their work for them.

Rudi and Brice had also brought small rugs. Emmit, however, turned up a few moments after the rest laden down with so many cushions it was a wonder he didn't lose any.

"What did I say about lounging?" Abi demanded, eyeing the pile.

"I *knew* you were going to say that!" Emmit protested. "I just brought cushions for all of us, because I *knew* you were going to say that!" He dropped his pile and tossed pillows to Brice, Rudi and Abi, who caught them. "Look, we're none of us going to be Heralds. We're none of us going to have to get used to roughing it, because all of us are going to be working in nice, civilized places where it's not hard to find a pillow for your bum. And besides, the last time I gave in to your ridiculous demand that we martyr ourselves by sitting on the hard ground, I got ants."

"Your pockets were full of cake crumbs," Abi pointed out. "You want ants? That's how you get ants."

"You ate the cake too!" he protested, but he turned out his pockets and shook them vigorously before he sat down, using two cushions, one to sit on, and one leaned up against the tree trunk as a backrest. "When I produce my Master Work and I'm a full Artificer, I am never going to sit on the ground again. I'm going to have a servant just to carry around a folding chair for me."

Abi just laughed, sat down herself, and read out the lesson. Rudi and Emmit took notes; Brice listened intently with a line of concentration between his brows. He really had the most extraordinary ability to remember what he'd heard, almost amounting to a Gift. Abi often thought that if he somehow did not manage to become an Artificer, this ability alone would make him invaluable to her father.

Or maybe even if he does become an Artificer. It would depend on how he felt about it. She resolved to keep that in mind, for some time later, when the right moment came to ask him.

When she had finished, it was just too nice outside to even think about going in. Especially since more cold rain was expected, at least, according to what Abi had heard. It had been a very unsettled spring. "I don't want to go back inside," Rudi grumbled, echoing her thoughts. He somehow made his eyes look big and pleading and turned them toward Abi. "The kitchen gives you anything you want. Could you go get us some food so we can eat out here?"

She was tempted to throw a cushion at him, but instead, got to her feet and grabbed him by the elbow, hauling him to his. "Not if I have to carry it all. You're the one who asked for it, so you get to be my beast of burden."

Emmit and Brice snickered, and she turned to them. "And don't you get started, or you're coming too."

"The problem is, you don't know how to ask properly," she told Rudi, as he followed meekly beside her. "You barge into the kitchen while everyone is busy serving and get in the way. Follow and learn."

She led him to the Collegium kitchen, rather than the Palace kitchen, which at this hour would be frantic with activity. They went in—or rather slipped in—through the entrance to the kitchen garden and waited, just out of the way of everyone. Finally an undercook noticed them. He nodded and waved at the platters of food being prepared to go up to the tables. Abi looked around, found a handy basket that had held bread, and grabbed it. She lined it with a napkin, darted in and made selections from half-filled platters, and darted out again. "And *that* is how you do it," she said, covering the food with another napkin, and handing the basket to him. "Wait here while I get more."

She repeated the performance, and the two of them left without ever having made a nuisance of themselves.

Emmit looked a little disappointed at the selection, but didn't say anything—which was wise of him, as Abi would have reminded him that beggars could not be choosers. Besides, dinner tonight had featured big bowls of stew, which would have been very difficult to transport outside. The lads were going to have to be contented with buttered bread and cheese and crunchy raw vegetables. And she had gotten them honeycakes, after all!

———

"So when do I get to meet your new friends?" asked Kat.

The threatened rain had begun to fall just at sunset. As usual, Tory and Kee were playing in front of the fire, using Gryphon as a backrest. Perry was doing something for Papa, so that left Kat, Trey and Niko playing a game with cards with Abi. Not a card game as such, but a game where they built towers of cards, adding one at a time until the tower fell. They'd found that it wasn't much fun for Abi to play actual card games with them, since try as they might, the three royal siblings couldn't help occasional "leaks" to each other of which cards they held. On balance, Abi felt this was only fair. It wasn't much fun for them to play any sort of game involving a ball and a paddle with her because her accuracy was uncanny. The ball always went where she wanted it to, without benefit of any Gift, just an unerring eye and deadly ability to aim.

Abi was saved from having to answer that rather loaded question by the arrival of her father—whose entrance into the main room of the suite also created a draft that knocked down the half-built tower. "When I'm certain-sure they're safe fer you," Mags said, in that voice that told them all he was not going to accept any argument.

"But—" Kat began anyway.

Mags coughed and gave her a look that told Abi he was using Mindspeech with the Princess.

"Yes, sir," she sighed, and picked up the cards to begin the tower all over again.

Abi knew exactly what her father meant; the lads were perfectly safe for her to be around, but when it came to the Royals, Mags was going to make sure there wasn't anything lurking in their backgrounds that could cause a problem later. And he would be done only when he was completely satisfied that he had left nothing to chance.

Or rather, he and Perry would be done, since Abi was pretty certain that this was what Perry was doing tonight. The lads were all housed in the same place, a kind of annex to the "palace" of the Archpriest of Kernos, not a stone's throw from the Palace gates. It was an imposing edifice that would have been even more imposing if it weren't the home to a swarm of lesser priests as well as the Archpriest, who conducted all of the business of the Order across the entire Kingdom of Valdemar and well into Hardorn from there. All of the male Artificer students recommended by the various Temples of Kernos were housed there until the student either failed in some way or created his Master Work and became self-supporting. Other religions had similar arrangements, except for a very few Blue Trainees who actually boarded at the Palace. Of that minority, the girls were two to four to a room in rooms next to the Queen's Handmaidens—Mags' little network of lady spies who actually acted as ladies-in-waiting to those female courtiers who lived in the Palace. The boys were lodged with the Palace squires.

So it was almost guaranteed that Perry either had gotten actual permission to go over whatever records the Archpriest had on the boys or (far more likely) was getting at them covertly. And then he'd get his hands on the Archpriest's household livery, pose as a servant, and observe them himself. And meanwhile, one of her father's traveling agents would be checking back at the lads' home towns or villages to find out whatever he (or she) could find out there.

Because you just never knew. And what Mags didn't know, he made it his business to find out, when it came to the Royals. Just as Grandpapa had done, and Lord Jorthun. And just as some other Chosen would one day be singled out by Mags to be trained to follow him. Maybe someday there would be a Monarch of Valdemar who—for whatever reason—did not have a Herald-Spy, but Abi sincerely hoped that she would never see that day. That was trusting to luck a lot more than she felt comfortable with.

"Well, since I can't meet your friends yet, what do you four *do* all day?" Kat asked.

Abi laughed. "We'd bore you to bits," she said. "Mostly we study and do a great deal of assigned work outside of class. The Artificer students aren't like the highborn Blues. They're in a hurry to get to the point where they can do their Master Work and start making money, because if they haven't managed to do that by the time they reach twenty-one, they lose the support of their patrons and have to find a job any old where."

"Like where?" Kat asked.

"Well, they c'n become private tutors," Mags pointed out. "Not bein' up t' creatin' a Master Work don't make 'em dunces. But private tutors're jest servants, and not even th' kind'a servants who'll have a job guaranteed with the family they serve ferever. If the master or mistress takes a dislike to 'em, or the children they're hired t' teach learn enough t' satisfy the parents, it's out the door an' go find a new position, an' good luck to ye."

"Kind of a sad comedown if you were thought good enough to get patronage to come here in the first place," Niko observed, carefully placing a card.

"Is that likely to happen to your friends?" Kat asked.

Abi shook her head. "Not even Brice. He has trouble reading and writing, but there's nothing wrong with his ability at math. Even Master Ketnar says he's going to do well enough he can hire someone to read and write *for* him, and Master Ketnar finds fault with everyone. But they're all anxious to learn everything as fast as they possibly can, because the younger you are when you make your Master Work, the more attention that gets you. I'm the only one that doesn't have to worry about getting attention, because my Gift is going to do that for me."

"What's a Master Work, anyway?" Trey asked, completing the third level of the tower.

Abi looked at her father, who gave her a little nod. "Well, it can be an invention, something no one has ever seen before," she said. "It can be something as small as a new windlass, or as big as a new water mill. Like the boiler system that we get hot water for the bathing rooms from—that was someone's Master Work. But for us, who are going to be Builder-Artificers, there are always buildings and bridges and that sort of thing that need to be constructed for the Kingdom. So when our teachers reckon that we're ready to do that, we're assigned something of that sort, required to plan and design it without help, to oversee the actual construction. When it's done, and the other Master Builders are happy with it, we get to call ourselves Master."

"Well, whoever signed off on that bridge that collapsed under us should be demoted," Kat grumbled, adding her card to the fourth tier of the tower.

"It ain't gonna to be rebuilt," Mags informed them. "At leastwise not at thet spot. One of th' other bridges is gonna to be widened t' make it big 'nuff for large drays."

"Probably just as well," said Trey. "Though Father's not going to hear the last of it until it gets done."

Abi nodded; that was the problem with subjecting the rich and the highborn to inconvenience; they had daily access to the King and would clog up the business of the realm with complaints that they couldn't get their new gazebo built in a "timely manner."

"Amily or yer father'll think of somethin', I'm sure," Mags chuckled. "Prolly appoint someone t' be in charge of complaints 'bout it."

"And it probably wasn't anyone's fault that the bridge collapsed," Abi felt moved to point out. "There may be something going on with the flow of the river water and the former foundations there that we just don't know about. It's an old bridge, and it's possible that a newer one was built upstream that changed how the water flowed, and that undermined the foundations. You can't blame the original builders for that."

Niko, Trey, and Kat all stared at her. Finally Kat said, "You really *are* learning a lot!"

She flushed pleasurably. So often she'd hear about something the other three had done, especially things having to do with their Gifts or other specialized training, and she'd had nothing to show for herself—or at least things she was allowed to talk about. It was nice to have them throwing her looks of admiration for a change.

"Don't make a fool of yourself," Emmit said to Brice for at least the fifth time. "Don't start yammering on about nothing. Don't *highness* them every other word. Don't ask them personal questions. Don't—"

"Emmit, leave him alone," Abi said, trying to make the rebuke sound as mild as possible. "As far as you know, they're just Herald Trainees. Just treat them that way, all of you."

"Yes, but, *Herald Trainees!*" Brice burst out.

"You see Herald Trainees everyday," she pointed out.

"But we never, you know, have anything to do with them!" he countered. "I wouldn't dare go up and talk to one!"

"You know, you're an idiot," Rudi said in a kindly tone to take the sting out of it. "Herald Trainees are just people. But Princes and a Princess?" He swallowed nervously.

"But *Companions!*"

"Shut up, they're here," said Emmit.

The three Artificer students stood up nervously as Trey, Niko, and Kat approached them where they waited at a table in the library that took up the top floor of Heralds' Collegium. At this hour and as nice as it was outside, no one else was here, which was what Abi was counting on to minimize awkwardness.

Well, it had been a good plan, anyway. "Well," she said, "Here they are. Fellows, this is Trey, this is Niko, and this is Kat."

"I'm the handsome one," Trey said helpfully.

"I'm the smart one," smirked Niko.

"And I'm the one that's better looking than Trey and smarter than Niko," retorted Kat, elbowing both of her brothers at once.

"Hey!" said Trey and "Ow!" exclaimed Niko, both of them rubbing their sides, and the ice was broken all at once—which was probably exactly what the royal siblings had intended all along.

Abi's friends introduced themselves, although Brice still had stars in his eyes and a look about him that suggested he was smitten with Kat. "Well, here's the thing," Niko said, looking plaintive. "We've got an ulterior motive. We asked Abi to introduce us so we could ask you for help."

"Us?" squeaked Brice. "Help you?"

"Math," all three of them said at once, then Trey and Niko looked at Kat.

"We're in three different math classes, and there's only one Abi," Kat explained. "She can't help all of us at once."

"We left our books and things at Abi's rooms," Trey said helpfully.

Well, at that point there was nothing for it but for all seven of them to traipse down to the suite and take up slate and chalk. Fortunately no one else was there—and the siblings had, indeed, left books and supplies there. Abi had been more than halfway convinced this was a ruse, but a quarter candlemark later and she was convinced otherwise. Kat didn't need that much help—and after all, Abi had been working with her ever since she had been enrolled in the Artificers—but Trey was definitely in need of some assistance, and Niko needed both Brice and Emmit's help.

"I thought you said you were the smart one," Brice said, when Niko had finally gotten his head wrapped around the concept of calculating square acreage—and then conversions. Converting furlongs to lengths to arms'-lengths to thumb's-lengths and back again. Clearly Brice was now comfortable enough with his new friends to tease.

"I am, just not in math," Niko replied, rubbing his head. "You're my hero. I might be able to do the same problem and get the same answer twice in a row now."

Brice must have suddenly remembered who he was talking to, because he blushed a furious crimson, tongue-tied.

"Want to come with us and help us groom our Companions?" Trey asked. "It's about that time."

Brice was on his feet so fast he scattered the pages of their schoolwork and they had to pick them up and sort them out before they could go down.

Normally, Abi would have helped Kat with Dylia, but she waited to see if Kat would invite Brice to help before she offered. Which was exactly what Kat did, before Trey or Niko could say anything.

As always the "spy-wheels" in Abi's head began turning. She concluded that there were two possibilities here. Either Kat was as interested in Brice as Brice was in her, or she was not interested in Brice and was going to use Dylia as a distraction while she felt her way through a conversation intended to (somewhat) disenchant him. She was satisfied with either of those answers and busied herself with collecting the mane and tail hairs from the special combs and brushes used only for that purpose.

It was the habit of Heralds—and Trainees, for that matter— to braid little gifts for friends and loved ones out of the hair of their Companions' manes and tails. One might think, given the huge numbers of Companions that had passed through the gates of the Palace, that the Kingdom would have been flooded by such trinkets by this time, but as with all things mortal, even Companion hair turned brittle and fell to dust after a time, and so the demand for them was still high. There were plenty of unscrupulous people who sold plain white horsehair braids as the genuine article, but one look at the real thing showed the counterfeits to be what they were. The hair from a Companion was faintly translucent, with a silvery sheen, and the same pure white as new snow. The hair from white (more properly, "gray") horses—was not.

So Abi gathered up the hairs, made them into a tidy little skein, put a loose knot in the middle of the skein, and tucked the bunch into a little bag hanging from each stall meant for exactly that. It didn't take long, but when she had finished, an unpartnered Companion wandered into the stable from Companion's Field, walked over to her, and gave her a nudge with his nose.

Since this sort of thing had been happening to her since she was tall enough to come here on her own, she knew exactly what he wanted. She followed him into his own box-stall, took up the brush and comb there and went to work.

Even if he wasn't *her* Companion, the job was a pleasant one. The stranger radiated pleasurable content even she could feel, thoroughly relaxing her. *I should do this more often,* she reflected. The Companion turned his head slightly and nodded at her.

"You know," she said aloud, raising her voice so everyone could hear her. "You can come in here and groom unpartnered Companions any time you like."

"We can?" gasped Brice.

Kat laughed aloud. "Of course you can. Anyone up here on the Hill can, if you have the time to spare."

As if to underscore that, another unpartnered Companion appeared at the door to the Field and snorted happily when one of the King's Squires came in through the door to the stable yard. "All right, keep your tail on," the squire laughed. "Let me get your brushes."

Abi had completed her friend's grooming to his satisfaction, and he nuzzled his thanks, backed out of the loose box, and went back to his friends in the Field. She picked out the mane and tail hairs and put them in his bag—Heralds and Trainees who didn't have quite enough hair to finish a job generally helped themselves to whatever was in these bags. After all, it was still Companion hair.

"We should have just enough time to wash up before dinner," said Trey just as she finished. "You want to sit at our table?"

Abi peeked into Dylia's stall, Brice looked as if his cup of happiness was about to overflow.

The conversation at their table was dominated by Kirball, since the table itself was dominated tonight by Niko's friends. Niko had just been made a guard on the Red team and was possibly one of the most enthusiastic players in the Collegia. Trey was utterly indifferent to the sport, but not to giving his sibling a hard time over it. Kat, however, considered herself a connoisseur of the horses and ponies that the non-Heralds on the teams rode, and would happily debate the merits of any beast on any of the four teams currently playing.

Emmit and Brice fit right into this group, which left Rudi and Abi off to the side. "You were right," he said to her after a moment. "They're just people."

"Well . . . just people wealthy and important enough that rank and wealth don't matter to them," she temporized, but she couldn't deny that his words made her feel very warm and happy. "There is that. You can't get around that fact."

Rudi thought about that for a while. "That's true. I'm a blacksmith's son. My father is the most important man in our village. So he can choose to treat everyone else the same as himself. But with anyone else in the village there's a hierarchy and people know they had better respect it, pull their caps and say 'sir.' That never occurred to me until you said that just now."

"And don't forget that can change in a heartbeat." Abi warned him. "Not that it's going to happen with my friends, but when important people treat you as an equal and you actually aren't, never forget they can change their minds about that in the time it takes you to say or do one wrong thing."

Rudi smiled wryly. "Something they don't include in our rather brief lesson on manners and conducting yourself."

She nodded. "The younger they are, the more likely that is to happen, too."

"Then hopefully I'll only get commissions from the Crown or extremely old men. Who hopefully won't die before I finish their building."

At that point the conversation finally veered away from Kirball into Collegium legends and scooped them up again, along with a half dozen other people at the table. Most of the "legends" were ghost stories, which Abi didn't have an opinion on one way or another. But when it came to the Poltergeist . . .

"Oi," she objected. "That's not what happened at all."

"How do you know?" Brice demanded.

"Because her parents were there and probably involved at the time, idiot," chided Emmit.

"They were," she admitted, and gave them a very edited version. "There was a religious group called the Order of Sethor the Patriarch that moved into Haven and took over a temple in a very underhanded way. This Order was very much against women doing anything but staying at home and minding children. So they started a campaign of harassing and bullying women who weren't doing that. They smashed up shops down in Haven, and desecrated the Temples of Goddesses that didn't fit that role, and snuck people onto the hill to persecute female Trainees and female Blues. That's where the Poltergeist came from."

"What happened?" asked a very young Bardic Trainee.

Abi shrugged. "They got caught. Their leader attempted a murder. King Kyril threw them out of the Kingdom because of all the horrid things they had done. He threw the leader along with anyone who'd actually had a hand in the crimes in gaol, and confiscated their Temple and gave it to the Sisters of Betane of the Ax. That's why there's two Temples of the Sisters down there. Among other things, they'd harassed a Blue Trainee into almost killing herself, and the almost-suicide is what got tangled up with the Poltergeist which is why you've got the story of the girl who killed herself going after the work of Blues who are doing well and ruining it."

"In fact, the girl in question is one of the Sisters of Betane now," said Kat. "Not all of them are fighters; she's an historian, chronicler, and scribe for the Order."

"That doesn't make nearly as much fun of a story," Brice muttered.

If only you knew the whole truth, Abi thought. *Your hair would stand on end.*

When they all dispersed to go back to their rooms for the evening, Kat linked up arms with Abi. "I like our new friends," she said, as they went up the stairs together. "And not just because they're willing to help Niko and Trey with their math."

Abi grinned, once again feeling warm and happy. *Our new friends, hmm? Excellent. You always hope your friends will like each other, but that's never a certain thing.* "They seem to be the best of the lot that I'm in with," she agreed.

Completely not to her surprise, her father was waiting in his little workroom when she got back to the suite. "I reckon everythin' went all right?" he said with a half smile as she paused in his doorway.

"So far," she replied. "Kat likes them. They got over being dazzled pretty quickly. I did give Rudi the 'be careful around highborns, they can turn on you' advice, though."

"Prolly wise. They seem t' be good lads," was all he said—which told her his investigations hadn't uncovered anything to worry about. "You c'n bring 'em up here t' study whenever you like," he added, which told her he trusted them, which meant rather more.

"I was thinking," she said carefully. "They might be worth cultivating as informants later."

"Then start feeling them out 'bout it now," he advised. "Nothin' specific, 'f course, an' as vague as ye like, but yer right, they could be useful."

And that told her exactly what she needed to know. Mags was prepared to welcome them into his network. She smiled; that was almost better than that the Royals liked them.

She listened with one ear to the conversation over the dinner table. Her mother was relaxed and so was her father, and when they spoke of "intrigues," it was all petty nonsense. The King was a popular man, and thanks to the birth of a fourth son, the Queen had never been held in higher esteem. No, what was going on in the Court now was all maneuvering among the three current "factions," if you could call them that.

The first faction was composed of people who had made their money, rather than inheriting it—or who had inherited money and a lucrative trade. Because the Queen herself came from among those of that sort, rather than from the highborn, they alternated between a proprietary pride in her and the feeling that she somehow owed them favors. When she had been younger, Abi had never been able to understand the latter; now she knew it was just human nature. People who were not already divided into factions would *make* factions given the chance, and they would always want the most important people to belong to their faction, whether the person in question agreed with that or not.

The second faction was those whose titles stretched generations back, sometimes into the mists of time and the founding of Valdemar. Some of the fortunes of those people had increased with time, some had dwindled until they had little more than a name, a rank, and pride. And the third faction was, of course, the "newly" ennobled—which, so far as the old highborn were concerned, meant people whose titles went back "only" five generations.

It was the third faction that was the most diverse. Those who were "merely" wealthy tended to concentrate on the making and keeping of more wealth and were interested in the crown only insofar as the crown could facilitate both of those things. The second faction, while there were feuds among them, kept those feuds to polite venom and never brought out the fangs and knives. Abi knew why, of course. Before she was born, there had been a feud that did end in deaths, and the fact that there weren't more was due only to her father and mother intervening in the nick of time. That had quelled many of the other existing rivalries down to a bare simmer, and nothing had risen above that level to this day.

It was the third faction where rivalry was intense enough to threaten to boil over now and again. Every house kept a jealous eye on the preferments of every other house and was prepared to challenge anything that was added that they did not also receive. Alliances and antagonists could change in the blink of an eye. And every new addition to the peerage was met with smiles of welcome and hidden daggers, especially if the title (and possibly lands) had been awarded to a member of the first faction. Even the landed Knights were not an exception to this; it didn't matter that they had won their titles and property in martial service to the Crown, once they joined the new peers, they found themselves embroiled in a new and altogether silent war.

"Lord Sentean has taken his family back to their estate and put the manor up for rent," reported Mama, "And I'd like a little more bread please."

"So, there'll be peace for a while, leastwise, 'til everyone sorts thesselves out on sides again," Mags observed, passing her the bread. "Wonder who'll take th' manor?"

"Whoever does, it would be a good time to get one of Auntie's older boys into the household," said Perry. "It's likely it'll be someone with a smaller staff, so they'll need to hire. Kip or Neddy would be good."

"I'll leave that in yer hands," her father replied. "Pick one or both, and start 'em up at Lord Jorthun's. He can have 'em trained as household staff in no time."

The rest of the conversation consisted of her father and Perry discussing which boy might be best for what sort of service, so Abi went back to her own thoughts—which now that her friends were *all* friends together, were concerned with only one thing.

Would tomorrow's session with Healer Sanje be more of the same—or would Sanje finally decide it was time for Abi to go to the next stage of using her Gift?

5

It only took half a brick for Abi to sense the stress in their makeshift apparatus. She'd been practicing diligently, and not just with the boards and bricks, every single day for some time now. "Good," said Sanje, thoughtfully. "I think it is time."

Abi did her best to contain her excitement. Sanje had explained several times already that what she was going to attempt might not work the first time. In fact, it might not work at all. In the worst case scenario, Sanje might make a mistake and change how Abi sensed strain into some other sense—scent, which would be useless, or sound, which would be horrid. But Abi had confidence in the Healer, and Sanje herself did not seem too worried.

"Well, I'm more than ready," Abi told her, steeling herself. "What do I do?"

Sanje smiled. "You do nothing except close your eyes for a moment."

Abi obeyed her and heard Sanje getting to her feet, then felt the faint touch of fingers on either temple. After that, nothing, for a very long time.

Then she thought she saw a red glow, although that was likely nothing more than the sun through her closed eyelids. Was it? Wasn't it?

The glow got stronger . . . and more defined. It wasn't a vague glow anymore, but more akin to . . . to a spot that had been infected. In the center, it was brightest, then the glow dimmed along a clearly defined area on either side of the central spot. Clearly defined— like the board!

Her eyes flew open and in the direction her head had been pointing was the board with the half-brick still on it. Sanje *tsk*ed.

"So impatient," she chided. "Now, do you still feel the strain as well as seeing it?"

That ever-present sense of more-or-less unease was gone! "No!" she exclaimed, "But—now with my eyes open, I don't see it either—"

"Close your eyes again. You must walk before you can run," Sanje corrected. Abi closed her eyes. Once again, she "saw" the red "light," fading out to either side. She groped around until her hands fell on another brick, and placed it beside the first. The area lit up, roughly three times the original size and brighter.

"Healers must often close their eyes to 'see' illness and disease when they are first learning to use their powers," Sanje said. "And I think we will leave yours at this stage. You would not want to see the stresses in buildings all around you all the time. It would be most annoying."

"But could I learn how to . . . make it come and go when I

wanted?" she asked. "I mean, Healers don't go around looking at peoples' insides all the time."

"Still wanting to run, are you?" Sanje chuckled. "We will see. In the meantime, it is sufficient that we have steered your Gift into using another sense. Now you must sharpen it further. As you yourself pointed out, everything man builds contains stresses. It will serve you well if you can see them, whether they are balanced or not. This will be very useful to you."

Abi opened her eyes again, and looked up at Sanje, feeling a bit chagrined at her own bad manners. *Stupid, Abi, and rude, to demand something from someone who has done so much and asked nothing of you.* "I'm sorry. You've spent all this time with me, learning about my Gift and turning it into something a lot more useful than it was, and I haven't even said thank you."

"And now you have." Sanje nodded. "Now go and practice. When you can see the stresses in every thing, then send word to me, and we will *see* if it is possible for you to learn to make it come and go at will, and then to use it at the same time as ordinary vision."

She didn't wait for Abi to thank her again, she merely turned gracefully and glided away, back to Healers' and the House of Healing, her long black hair waving gently as she moved.

Abi would have liked to have spent the rest of the day testing this new aspect of her Gift, but Master Leandro was waiting to give her and Perry a workout, and he was not a patient instructor. So she carried off her bricks and board and left them in the waste area and ran off at top speed to Lord Jorthun's mansion, which stood in the area of the most impressive such buildings, just outside the gates of the Palace.

Perry and Larral were already there, Master Leandro was not. "How'd the session go?" Perry asked, lying on the grass in Master Leandro's practice yard in the garden, as usual, using Larral as a backrest. Abi dropped down on the soft grass beside him, reveling in the green scent and the feel of the warm sun on her back.

"Healer Sanje did something so that instead of just feeling where stress is, I can see it with my eyes closed," she said excitedly.

"How can you see it if your eyes are closed?" Perry asked, then shook his head. "Never mind, it's probably how I can see what animals are seeing. Well, that should make it easier to tell how much stress there is on a thing. Right?"

"A lot," she agreed, and that was when Master Leandro stalked into the yard and they both leaped to their feet. He regarded them thoughtfully.

He was a lean man with a prominent nose and large, intelligent eyes. He was not the first of Lord Jorthun's Weaponsmasters—that would have made him as old as Lord Jorthun, if not older—but he had studied at the feet of the man who had been from the time he was barely old enough to hold a stick and pretend it was a sword. Since he was older than their parents, that had been a great many years ago indeed. He was not only an expert in many kinds of weapons and none at all, he was also an expert in how to conceal weapons. In that, he had the aid of a very fine craftsman down in Haven, a man whose hands were as clever as his wits were feeble. All Master Leandro had to do was to imagine what he wanted and give detailed instructions as to what it should be like, and the fellow—whose identity their father kept secret even from them—could produce it.

But it appeared that they were not getting a lesson in one of those today. "It's been a very long time since I worked you two at stickwork," he said thoughtfully, as a puff of breeze stirred Abi's hair. "Abi, what is the likeliest such object that is going to come into your hands on a job?"

"Probably the stick we keep our chalk-string on," she said, after a moment. "We use it for measuring and laying out straight lines. It's about so long," she added, helpfully holding her hands a little farther apart than her hands were long.

"Yes, that will do. Go and get two each of the right size from the armory and come back here."

"We're going to get bruised knuckles," Perry said, grimacing, as they both headed for the armory.

She winced, but she nodded; there was going to be no way around that. They wouldn't put full force into their blows, of course, but they were still going to get bruises.

Oh, well.

She liked working out with Perry; they were nearly the same height and weight, and she could count on him neither to try to bowl her over nor go too easy on her. That wasn't the case with the others in the weapons-classes up at the Collegia. And the Weaponsmaster for the Collegia didn't always catch it when a partner was going easy on Abi because she was a girl. Or worse, because she was a girl and he was hoping she might be interested in him. The Blues that took weapons classes were not Artificers; most of them were highborn. The Artificers and the pure scholars were not expected to ever need to defend themselves; and indeed, why should they, any more than anyone studying outside the Collegia who was a scholar or a master of a skilled trade? So the weapons classes at the Collegia mostly held Herald Trainees, some Bardic Trainees, and the highborn Blues. Once in a while, about as often as a rare Artificer Blue with a penchant for exercise, a Healer turned up ready to learn how to fight, but it wasn't often. The only weapons class that everyone took was archery because no matter who you were—Bard, Healer, or highborn on a journey, Artificer on a job, or scholar being sent to a temple—there was always the chance, once you were outside of Haven, that mischance would overtake you on your journey, and the only thing that would keep you from starving was a bow and your skill with it. Mags' two older children didn't even bother with archery classes anymore, just practice. And pretty soon even Tory would no longer need a teacher as well.

Having chosen a pair of rounded sticks about the size Abi recommended, they returned to Master Leandro and presented themselves to him. When they had been younger, they would have done this exercise wearing padded tunics and even padded trews; now he trusted them to be able to land blows precisely enough to be felt, but not injure. Well, mostly. As Perry had said, Abi suspected there was no way they'd get off without bruised knuckles.

"Half speed," Leandro said, face thoughtful. "These are much shorter than batons; you're going to have to hold them in the middle."

Abi felt a great deal of relief at hearing they weren't going to go all out. "Begin," said the master.

"So are any of your friends in love with you?" Perry teased as he feinted for her shoulder and came in at her ribcage.

She let the point of his stick slide by easily. "No, but one of them is smitten with Kat."

"Which one?" He ducked under a strike to his temple.

"You're the clever spy who's two years older than me, you figure it out." The strike to her elbow would have made her drop her right-hand stick from suddenly numb fingers if she hadn't evaded it.

"You're no fun. Oof!" he exclaimed as she connected, not with a stick but with an elbow to the gut.

"Well done," said Master Leandro. "You're only half speed, she shouldn't have caught you. You're getting sloppy, Perry."

Before the session was over, Leandro had moved them up to full speed, but the worst Abi had suffered had been the loss of a little knuckle skin. Perry had done better, but he was two years older than she was with that much more practice.

"Maybe next time we should practice with bricks, Master," Perry said, as their mentor judged himself satisfied with their performance. "Abi should find a lot of bricks on the sites where she'll be working."

"Hmph," Leandro replied, his eyes gleaming. "Don't tempt me."

They were both dripping with sweat of course, and badly needed a bath, but Perry elected to head back at a run, and she knew he would beat her back home. Since there was only one bathing room in their part of the Palace, shared with the Royals, Abi got a clean uniform and went back down to Herald's Collegium and the girls' bathing room.

"Who let a Blue in here?" came a laughing voice out of the steam as she opened the door.

"It's not a Blue, it's Abi," she replied, and peered through the fog.

"Oh, well, then, we'll let you in, but you have to leave by the back door," came the retort. "We have to keep our standards you know."

Abi made a rude sound, and found the nearest unoccupied tub.

She wasn't the sort to dawdle over anything, much less a bath, so she was finished before the speaker emerged from her own tub.

By the time she was done, she was starving and raced back to the suite.

"Full Court dinner," her mother greeted Abi from her bedroom as Abi burst in through the door. "Lydia's first since the baby. Gather both tribes and either get something from the kitchen or—"

"I know, I know." She glanced in Tory's room, saw it was empty, and figured he was with Kee. The two were inseparable. Perry wasn't in his room either, so she ran her fingers through her hair to put it more-or-less in order, went back out into the hall, and turned toward the Royal Suite. The guards at the door grinned when they saw her.

"Going to mind the baby for Her Highness?" asked one.

She made a face. "I'd rather shovel manure," she replied as they waved her in.

"I hear nappies are worse," the guard said as she passed them.

The Royal Suite had the much more conventional layout of a public room where the King, Queen, or both could entertain special guests, the Queen's solar where previous Queens (who were not also Heralds) had probably spent entire days just embroidering and conversing with their ladies, a room common to the family that was not usually seen by anyone other than the family, with the bedrooms and nursery off that. The sibs were all in the family room, where Lydia's nurse was displaying baby Rafiel to them, with the mastiff Drake sitting watchfully at her side and Kee's Gryphon looking uninterested. Dutifully, Abi came over to look at him. At least now he looked like a baby and not a disagreeable old red-faced man. "Isn't he the most handsome little man?" cooed the nurse. Abi kept her mouth shut and nodded, standing just far enough away that the nurse was unlikely to thrust Rafi at her.

Instead she turned to the others. "The Queen's attending Court supper. Raid the Palace kitchen or eat with the Trainees?" she asked, as the nurse, trailed by Drake, went back into the nursery.

"Kitchen," said Tory and Kee. Tory glanced at Kee. "They won' let Gryphon in the dining hall," Kee explained.

"They won't let Larral in either," Perry said thoughtfully.

"That's because Larral inhales everything anyone is not actively guarding," Trey said with a laugh.

"Roo rot!" Larral barked indignantly.

"Do too," replied Niko.

Abi interrupted what was about to become an argument between a prince and a "dog." "Look, Perry, you raid the kitchen for you, Kee and Tory. The rest of us can eat with the Trainees. Everyone's happy."

"Mama didn't say we could do that," objected Tory.

"Mama didn't say that we *couldn't*, either." Perry often wasn't home at suppertime, but when he was, he wanted to be with Larral, and Kee didn't want to be parted from Gryphon under any circumstances. It seemed to her that leaving Perry in charge of the two younger boys solved all of their problems.

He made a face but nodded. "Come on you two," he said. "Kee, leave Gryphon here. Larral, make sure Gryphon stays here. I'm going to need both of you if we're going to get enough food to feed them too."

Of course, they didn't actually need to feed either the *kyree* or the mastiff. Both of them got proper meals twice a day. But without a meaty bone or some tidbitting, all three of the humans were going get big sad eyes and possibly whimpers all through supper.

And Kee, at least, would end up putting half of his own meal into his dog.

Kee nodded and ordered Gryphon to stay. With a mournful sigh, the mastiff sat down. Larral planted himself in front of the mastiff to ensure it, and the three boys headed out the door, followed by Abi and the remaining three Royals. They parted ways at the stairs, with Perry and the littles making for the kitchen and the rest for Heralds' Collegium.

Once at the dining hall, Trey and Niko made a beeline for their friends. Kat glanced over at Abi after surveying the tables full of chattering Trainees, mostly Heralds, but a leavening of Bardic and Healers among the gray. "Well, which conversation shall we join? Romance gossip, lesson whinging, artistic panic, or who's buying what at the Midsummer Fair?" she asked.

"Midsummer Fair shopping," Abi replied without a moment of hesitation. "Is it that close? I've lost all track of time." And she had; one day was pretty much like another for her now, she was so busy. Her family didn't attend services at any particular temple— Amily went with the King and his family, but Mags didn't go at all, and the siblings figured that their religions class taught at all three Collegia was enough holiness for anyone. So without regular services to mark the day and break up the time, and every day marked by classes or study, time had gotten away from her.

"A fortnight. But of course, people are already jabbering about it." Kat could be cavalier about the Fair; any time she cared to she could just join the Court for the evening's informal entertainment.

There was always music, generally performed by the best of the Bardic Trainees, and often acrobats or players, hoping for Royal accolades. But Trainees didn't get to attend the Court gatherings, informal or not, and most, if not all of them, wouldn't have had the time to if they could. But all Trainees got a day off during the Fair in rotation, so it was the high point of the summer.

There was, of course, another important day of the summer term—the annual day just before harvesting began, when those parents who could make the journey were invited to turn up to see what their offspring had been up to. There was a Kirball game, individual Bardic Trainees would perform throughout the day, there were booths where Healer Trainees could demonstrate remedies and techniques anyone could use, and demonstrations of martial arts and Companion riding for the Heraldic Trainees, culminating in a concert by the Bardic Trainees. But that tended to be a day devoted more to anxiety on the part of the Trainees than anticipation.

They picked up plates and place settings and joined a mixed table of all four types of Trainees. "I've got a half-finished Festival dress that—oh, heyla, Kat! Did you know Abi's taken to invading our bathing room?" teased one of the female Trainees, who, now that she wasn't obscured by steam, Abi recognized as Sofia, a year older than she was.

"It isn't 'your' bathing room, and Abi's been using it since before you were a Trainee, Fi," Kat said with a laugh. "And if you weren't usually the last one in there, you'd know that. What color's the dress?"

"Non-Healer green. Sort of a really dark blue-green, like longpine needles. I'm planning to try to find trim for it at the Fair." Sofia was a huge tease, but she didn't mind being teased back. "It's a hard color to match. And I don't want to use red because I'd look like a Midwinter garland."

"And blue and white would just be too, too Heraldy," Kat agreed. "Green on green is probably your best bet."

"Last year I heard there was a vendor that had lovely perfumes," sighed a Bardic Trainee. "Dione has some. There was a jessamine . . ." She didn't say anything else, so Abi assumed that she didn't have any pocket money to buy anything. Heraldic Trainees, because they were basically pledged in service to the Crown for the rest of their lives, got a regular small stipend, and most of them saved it up for the three annual Fairs. Healer Trainees could, and often did, make money concocting creams, lotions, scents, and other beauty products in their spare time from the herbs and flowers they were allowed to grow in the gardens. They had a brisk trade in such things with the ladies of the Court and got practice in making tinctures, salves, distillations, and other techniques without wasting precious medicinal herbs. Bardic Trainees could make money doing performances in the taverns and inns in Haven—but apparently this girl either hadn't learned that or hadn't managed to find anywhere that didn't already have a resident musician.

"Jessamine?" The sole Healer Trainee at the table snorted. "Pish, you don't need to buy that. I just finished a batch and it's not all spoken for. Come by my room and bring a bottle, and I'll decant some from the jug. I'll bet mine's as good or better than any trumpery Fair vendor." She thought a minute. "In fact, his might *be* mine."

The girl brightened and thanked her friend effusively. The Healer just grinned. "Oh, you'll owe me a favor, and I *will* collect. You can do my next three turns at kitchen duty."

"What are you going to buy, Abi?" asked Fi.

"Knives," she said shortly. "I decided my Midwinter presents to everyone are going to be knives. You can't go wrong by giving someone a knife."

Fi blinked. "Even Kee? Even Tory?"

Abi kept her smile to herself, because Tory had been training with Master Leandro since he was six and probably had no less than two knives on his person at all times. "Kee's more than old enough to have something besides an eating knife, and a good all-purpose blade will come in handy for him. Tory can teach him to carve." *How to carve up what's left of intruders that Gryphon takes down, that is.*

"Don't you want anything for yourself?" asked the Bardic Trainee. "Scents? Something for a new gown?"

Abi had to laugh at that. The only use she'd have for a scent would be to use one to reinforce a disguise. On the whole, she didn't have a lot of use or need for fancy gowns, and the one she'd gotten two Midwinters ago still fit just fine. "Actually . . . surveying and measuring instruments of my own would be awfully nice, but I don't think there are likely to be any vendors of those," she said, finally—because the sorts of things she actually could use were not the sorts of things she was supposed to be discussing with people who didn't know what her father did.

"Abi, you are exasperatingly practical," sighed Kat. "Don't you like nice things?"

"Certainly." Abi laughed. "But my definition of *nice things* and yours are very different. Besides, I need to buy my Midwinter presents *first*. Only if there's money left will I think about something for myself."

"And you're getting me a knife." Kat sighed.

"I never said what *kind* of knife, now, did I?" Abi smirked. "I've got something in mind you won't turn your nose up at."

In fact, this was something she wouldn't need to go down to the Fair to get. When her mother and father had gotten married, they'd had very special wedding outfits made—ones with several weapons sewn or built in. That had given Abi an idea. She'd gone to Master Leandro, and Leandro had had that mysterious craftsman in Haven make Kat's present, an identical present for the Queen, and one for Amily. These were pairs of slender stilettos disguised as hairsticks with beautifully inlaid hilts and bits of silver chain ending in mother-of-pearl beads attached to the pommels. Flick a catch and the blunt sheath remained in your hair and you were left with a wickedly sharp blade as long as your hand.

But like these ornaments, the other knives Abi intended to give as Midwinter gifts were not going to be bought at the Fair. She would have very little time for shopping. She and Perry and some of Auntie Minda's oldest younglings would be doing Mags' work down along the aisles between the booths and the tents.

She couldn't tell that to her fellow students, though. Not even Kat.

"Well, I don't know how you'd manage to resist temptation, with money in your hand and so many pretty things at the Fair," sighed Fi.

It was a rhetorical statement, obviously, since Fi and the others kept right on with their discussions of what they were looking for.

Abi leaned over the table to the Bardic Trainee. "I'm Abi," she said. "Is this your first year at the Collegium?"

The girl nodded. "I'm Harlee. You can call me Lee. I got here just this spring as soon as the roads were fit to travel on."

"So you didn't know that Bardic Trainees have leave to set up with a hat and play at the Fair?"

"Set up . . . with a hat?" the girl replied, bewildered.

So Abi explained how all the Bardic Trainees had permission to come down to the Fair during the day that they were given off from class, and after classes were finished for the day, set themselves up with a collection basket—or hat—and play for whatever money people would throw into it. "You have to wear your uniform, of course, and don't set up near anyone who has a performance tent or booth. Or near one of the big food tents; they generally already have musicians engaged for inside. My advice is to set up near a food booth in one of the quieter areas. Ask the booth owner first, but generally you'll both benefit."

"Oh, thank you, Abi!" the girl replied, gratefully.

"Oh, you'd have found out when they gathered you all together to tell you about which day off from classes you'd get, and give you the basic rules. All I've done was give you advance notice. Most people don't bother with a hat, because they have regular nights at a tavern or a regular job playing for gatherings up here on the Hill," Abi continued. "Though that's usually in duos or larger groups."

"I haven't been asked to one of those yet," Lee said, as the chatter moved on to speculation about what entertainers might be here this year. "I don't sing, actually, so that might be why."

Abi was a little surprised by that. Most Bardic students sang as well as playing instruments—usually several. "You don't sing?"

"I play the flute, the penny whistle, and the pipes," Lee replied, and blushed. "I know, very *country*. But I am from sheep country.

Maybe that's why I haven't been asked, everything I know is unsophisticated and old-fashioned."

"Well, when the Fair is over find someone who plays the hand drum who isn't already in a group, and try the taverns around the cattle market. That's exactly what the patrons of the inns there like. But for the Fair, find a good spot with a lot of room around it, start with the pipes and play dance tunes. The pipes will always get attention, and you'll want room in case people decide to start dancing."

"You're a Blue, not in Bardic, how do you know all these things?" Lee exclaimed.

Abi smiled. "You don't know; I've lived here all my life. Literally *here*. My mother and father are both Heralds."

Of course all my training in observation hasn't hurt either.

A little more conversation with Lee drew out the fact that her family were in hire to a small farmer, that she'd been self-taught on the penny whistle and shepherd's pipes and played in the local "tavern," which was really just the yard and main room of the house of the local brewer, and that was where an actual Bard heard her and her compositions and arranged for her to come to Bardic Collegium. Her family had not one copper to spare, and in fact, she'd gotten here by the arduous process of catching rides on farm carts from one village to the next—and walking when there were no rides to be had.

"I'd play in taverns every night for the night's meal, a place on the hearth to sleep, and food to get me to my next village," Lee continued. "My sponsor told me it didn't matter when I got here, as long as I made it in one piece."

It sounded cruel and callous, but Abi knew that the journey itself had been a test for the girl. If the roads hadn't been safe for a girl alone, the Bard would have escorted her himself, or found a safer way for her to get here—but since they were, finding her own way here was test of how badly she wanted the life of a Bard. It was a test she had obviously passed.

One by one the girls at their table excused themselves and went off to studies or a little leisure before bedtime, and Kat and Abi made their way back up to the Palace.

"You seemed deep in conversation," Kat said. "What was so interesting?"

"That Bardic Trainee. I was just giving her some advice so she can make some pocket money; her people don't have any to spare." Abi considered Lee a bit more. "She's smart and tough. All she needed was some information."

"She might make a good recruit for your father, then," Kat observed.

Abi chuckled. "You'd make a good recruiter."

Kat raised an eyebrow. "What makes you think I'm not already?"

"If you were, I'd know." Abi laughed as Kat stuck her tongue out at her. "I would, and you know it!"

"Well, it's not for lack of looking, I just haven't found anyone outside of the Heraldic Trainees I'd trust enough," Kat admitted. "And your father doesn't need agents among the Trainees, he needs a couple among the houses on the Hill."

"'Struth," she replied as they got to her door. "Coming in?"

"Not tonight. I have an exam in the morning. I'm a Princess, you'd think they'd just pass me without the work, but no!"

Abi laughed. "All right then, good night. Don't make your head explode with studying!"

"Small chance of that," Kat grinned back and went on down the hall to the door to the Royal Suite at the end of it.

Now, let's see how much farther ahead I can get than the rest of my class, so I can get as much time off during the Fair as possible. I have the feeling I might need it.

6

By dint of a *lot* of candle-burning and serious study, Abi managed to get a whole week ahead of the rest of the Blues in her class—and made sure her father knew about this. So when the first day of the Fair dawned, he had managed to wrangle a week's worth of time off for her, citing "family matters."

She and Perry went down together; their initial project was to memorize the layout of the Fair, which differed slightly every year, due to the placement of the large entertainment and food tents. They spent the entire first day just walking the Fair over and over, so that both of them knew the entire Fair as well as they knew the layout of the Palace, the Collegia, and the Great Houses on the Hill.

Having done that, they split up for the second day. This time, instead of concentrating on the Fair itself, they concentrated on the fairgoers. Both of them were dressed so as to be as inconspicuous and unmemorable as possible. They both wore simple outfits of a linen shirt, canvas trews that were well-worn but not shabby, and a canvas tunic that didn't match the trews. This outfit was not so good that it would attract the attention of a thief, but also did not signal poverty and thus might attract the attention of the Watch and suspicion from vendors. Insofar as the Watch was concerned, they wanted to avoid being trailed by a large, armed uniform fellow wearing a warning frown, because that would just draw unwanted scrutiny.

Abi kept her pace to the flow of traffic, waiting patiently when a bottleneck occurred, casually appearing to examine everything in the booths and tents on her side of the path, but all the while actually watching both the merchants and the people around her. This was oddly relaxing, and she found she had a tiny, satisfied smile on her face after a candlemark or so. *I guess this is fun. More fun than standing around in a page's tabard during a closed Council meeting, anyway.*

She really didn't expect anything to leap out at her immediately, although she did catch a couple of instances of merchants shortchanging their customers and suspected that many of the goods on offer were not what they were being touted as being. But those problems weren't her business. That was the business of the Fair-Wards, who policed the merchants and entertainers. And as for the thieves and cutpurses—those were the job of the Watch. Each of the Watch Houses was supposed to send at least two of their number down to the Fair every day to handle ordinary crime.

No, on this pass, what she was looking for was far more subtle. A merchant selling his goods at too *low* a price, for instance, which indicated he wasn't here to make money and didn't have a good idea of what his offerings should cost. Or a merchant who displayed things no one actually wanted, yet was showing no distress at all at his lack of customers. Either of those could mean the "merchant" was actually a foreign spy or a contact for spies already in place in Haven.

Or a contact for some other criminal activity that was far beyond the scope of the Watch.

"Remember who and what you are and live every moment as that person. You're fourteen," said her grandfather in her mind as he helped her establish a persona for this sort of work. *"You're a chandler's apprentice as you have been for two years. What little money you have is not in your pocket nor in a belt pouch, because you are from lower-class Haven and wise to the ways of cutpurses. It's in a bag around your neck tucked into your bodice. You will look and look and look again at everything, not just because you will ponder any potential purchase against the possibility that your mistress could dismiss you and that money will be all that stands between you and starvation until you get another place, but also because your mistress will quiz you when you return to the shop about things she might like to have."*

In her head, her father agreed. *"Nobody'll look at ye twice. Yer th' last person any'un's gonna think suspicious thoughts 'bout. You an' yer brother be my eyes an' ears down there."*

It certainly was no great chore, being set loose to roam the Fair all day, stopping now and again when someone was selling a treat actually worth the money, listening to musicians and watching the snippets of free entertainment.

The Fair kept going until midnight at night too—but there would be no chandler's apprentices here after dark, and she *would* be conspicuous—and worse. After sunset, an unaccompanied female of any age could be presumed to be available for whatever a man wanted from her. Boys too. She knew this because Mags believed in telling his children about things they were old enough to be affected by so that they weren't blindsided by them. Not that the Fair at night was dangerous, if you kept your wits about you. It could be quite fun, in fact, with shows taking advantage of the darkness to use lighting effects and one of the large entertainment tents hosting a nightly masked ball. But it was no place for anyone like Abi unless she was openly accompanied by Perry. Night was the time Mags or his adult agents would move through the pathways of the Fair.

Most likely it will be Papa's agents. He's got no need to be down here unless they find something interesting, and the fellows from the pawn shop would probably enjoy doing what I'm doing now as much as I am.

So far she had turned up absolutely nothing out of the ordinary, but it was a lot of fun looking. The people who placed booths had done a very cunning thing; they'd mixed everything up. So if, say, you were looking for glass beads, you would have to wander the entire grounds to find all of the vendors. Rather than being able to compare stocks and prices easily, this made it much more difficult. And that encouraged people to buy as soon as they found something *like* what they were looking for, even if the ideal item was at another booth. Because you never knew, and when you got back to the other vendor, what you wanted might be gone.

It was good for the food vendors too. Having food vendors mixed throughout the Fair meant that if a food had a tasty aroma, that smell wouldn't get trampled on by another food-vendor's wares. And encountering a good scent out of nowhere made people hungry, and inclined to buy.

It even had that effect on Abi, and she *knew* she was being manipulated!

You just ate, she reminded herself, as she was struck by the scent of fried dough and honey. *And that's just bread. You can get that for free in the kitchen.* A lot of Fair food was "just bread" and no surprise there. Bread was the cheapest thing you could make. Most bread down at the Fair was fried, though, since baking took a long time and needed an oven and a lot of fuel, but frying took mere moments. Now, it was true that the bread tended to be enhanced with herbs or spices, dotted with dried fruit or nuts, stuffed with a bite of cheese or sausage, glazed with salt or honey. So it wasn't "just" bread to most people, it was a seldom encountered treat.

Still, it's just bread.

It was at a spot where two of the paths through the Fair intersected, and she smelled pancakes *(just bread!)* that she heard the sound of shepherd's pipes playing a jig. Following her ears and nose, both led her to a booth beside which she found Lee, the Bardic Trainee she had advised a few days ago, vigorously playing her pipes to the delight of both the pancake-maker and his customers. By the nice layer of coppers in the straw hat she had put out, Lee had found a very receptive audience.

Abi smiled to herself, and faded back out of sight. Then, since her stomach protested that it was almost lunchtime, she went looking for a fruit vendor. Fruit would be food *and* drink and she wouldn't have to trust to the cleanliness of someone else's cups. If she was still hungry after that . . . well, maybe some bread after all.

By midafternoon she hadn't consciously noticed anything she needed to bring to her father's attention, and she'd encountered Perry twice. By that point she had the entire maze of the Fair memorized, she was hot and tired, and ready to make the trip back up the Hill. By the time she got there, it would be supper time, and she wouldn't have wasted her money on bread.

It was a long trudge, but once she was clear of the Fair, she made sure she was taking the route that the wagons taking Trainees to and from the Collegia also took. When she caught up with one on its way back, she flagged it down, showed the driver the little brass "pass" that all the Blues had to allow them in and out of the gates, and took her seat in the half-filled wagon. She didn't know any of the Trainees in it—they were mostly Healers—so she merely gave a friendly nod that included all of them and settled into the straw filling the wagon to rest.

After a quick wash at the pump outside the Companions' Stable, she headed for the dining hall and literally bumped into Trainee Lee.

"Abi!" the young woman exclaimed with pleasure, her eyes sparkling, despite the fact that she looked tired and there was definitely dust in her hair. "I was hoping I would be able to thank you!"

"For what?" Abi replied, heading for an empty table, and bringing Lee along by the elbow. It was light fare tonight, soup (and bread), since the kitchen staff assumed correctly that many of the Trainees would have stuffed themselves at the Fair and not be in the mood for anything substantial. Abi helped herself from the big bowl and platter in the middle of the table and waited for Lee to do the same.

"I wanted to thank you for your advice about the Fair, of course," Lee replied, when they had both provisioned themselves. "It worked wonderfully! And the booth owner asked me to come back any time."

"Take that with a caution," Abi replied. "Don't go back after dark without a boy. Girls alone are assumed to be available."

"Available for what?" Lee asked naively and blushed when Abi told her—bluntly. "Oh. Dear. I owe you thanks all over again!"

Abi drank off her entire mug of cold tea at a gulp and refilled it from the common pitcher. "You'll be fine by day. Just be back before the sun goes down, or have a nice strong boy along." Then she smiled. "I take it you had a profitable day."

"More money than I've ever had before at one time!" Lee said with glee, and with Abi listening attentively, she chattered for some time (between bites) about her success and some of the people who had enjoyed her playing. "Oh! And the best part!" she ended. "I met someone in the advanced classes whose partner just became a full Bard and is leaving! They had a similar duo, they already had a tavern spot once a week; she liked my playing and wants to partner with me!"

Abi smiled. "It sounds as if you have sorted everything out you need to do to earn your money. At least, until you make full Bard. Then you probably won't have to worry ever again."

"Yes, and if it hadn't been for you, I wouldn't have known how!" She sighed happily. "I owe you a very big favor now."

And I just might collect it by asking you to be one of Papa's agents, she thought with amusement. Lee's next question surprised her, though.

"You're in the Artificers, so you know all about buildings and things right?" she asked.

"Not everything," Abi corrected. "But quite a bit."

"Well, I have a silly question, but it's not about the Fair. It's something that's been bothering me since I got here." Now Lee looked very embarrassed.

"Say on."

"So . . . you know about the indoor latrines?" The last word was whispered.

Well, this has taken an interesting turn . . . "What about them?"

"Where does . . . it . . . go? I mean, at home, we have cesspits under our latrines, but you don't exactly seem to have that here—" Since she seemed perfectly earnest, Abi gave her the exact answer.

"They're all connected up to brick-lined sewer tunnels," Abi replied with authority. "The mansions and big homes on the Hill are connected to the same system. We send rainwater down it too, to keep it flushed out. From there it goes to a collection pond where it gets turned into fertilizer—I don't know how that's done, I just know that it is."

"What about down in Haven?" she asked.

"That depends entirely on where you live. There's another sewer system but not everyone is on it. Some people depend on cesspits, some on chamber pots and closed-stools. In either case there are collectors for it that come around every morning. It's valuable, especially if you're poor. Tanners need urine, and the rest can go as fertilizer. Or people who have their own small gardens keep the dung—and anything they can get off the street from passing animals—and compost it for their gardens." Abi realized that she was actually enjoying this, showing off what she knew.

"Why not just send it all into the river?" Lee asked innocently.

Abi raised an eyebrow at her. "People drink from the river," she pointed out. "And Haven has a lot of people in it. That's a lot of sewage you don't want going into your source of drinking water."

". . . oh."

"Anyway, it's quite an impressive feat of work, the sewer system,"

Abi concluded. "Or so I'm told. I'm not sure I could be persuaded to go down there, ever, but I am told that the tunnels are more than tall enough for a man to stand in them and that there is a crew in charge of making sure they stay in working order."

Lee shuddered.

"I would not mind at all being asked to design and build a system like that," Abi continued to muse aloud. "Think of all the good it does!"

Lee just shook her head, and as they were joined by other Trainees, the conversation turned to other things—most especially, what entertainers were at the Fair this year. Abi wasn't really listening to this, until one phrase caught her attention.

". . . all those children running loose. What are their parents thinking? Are they just giving them a penny and sending them to the Fair alone?" That was a Healer Trainee, and Abi blinked, suddenly realizing that he was right—there *had* been a lot more—a *magnitude* more—of children that were just running wild through the crowds. She hadn't paid any attention to them because they weren't what she'd been watching for. And that had been a mistake.

Why do we use Auntie Minda's littles? Why does Papa use us? Because no one notices children.

Now that she was combing through her recent memories . . . not only had there been far too many children moving swiftly through the crowd, they had all been dressed more or less alike. All of them in drab clothing slightly too big for them, with trews and loose tunics belted at the waist, with long, loose sleeves gathered at the wrist. All of them barefoot. Barefoot—for sure-footed running? Or because they were too poor for shoes?

The only reason she had noted them at all, and the only reason she remembered them now, was their behavior. Children, even poor children, didn't go running through the Fair. They stopped and stared. They sniffed hungrily at the treats. Poor ones, when the Watch or Fair-Wards weren't about, would try to beg. The only reason a child would be running would be if someone in charge of him had told him to run.

Now, this was a common practice for cutpurses and pickpockets—to have a distraction, such as a child running past the victim—to distract the victim while the thief made off with the goods. But so many children matching that pattern meant this was something out of the ordinary. This was an organized effort. And that was far past the authority of the Watch. Although this had nothing to do with enemy agents, this *was* something that came under her father's purview. The Watch would just arrest one or two thieves, knowing nothing about the rest. Her father would round up the whole gang.

She shook herself out of her thoughts in time to answer whatever Lee had just said satisfactorily. *I need to talk to Perry.*

A new influx of happy, tired Trainees came in at that moment, including some of Lee's fellows in Bardic. They carried her off to another table, leaving Abi free to make her way upstairs to see if her brother was there.

She caught him just leaving, in the hallway outside the suite. "Are you going back down to the Fair?" she asked.

"Papa's got me working with his group tonight," he replied with pride.

"Well, I need your ear a second." Quickly, she described what she had noticed and what she thought it implied. He pursed his lips and nodded.

"Seems sound," he agreed. "Let's go back in and relay to Papa."

By that he meant, of course, they would tell their mother, she in turn would tell Rolan, who would contact Mags. They could go through Larral, but this was surer and faster. So he and Larral turned around and they went back in together. Amily looked surprised to see her son again, but quickly understood why when she heard what Abi had to say.

Then it was just a matter of whiling away the time until Mags turned up.

It was dusk when he did, and he listened carefully to Abi's observations. "It do sound like a organized effort," he agreed. "What d'you think ye wanta do next?"

"I was thinking I could play bait," Abi replied, having given the situation a lot of thought while they were waiting for their father. "If I dress really well, I'll make a good target. I'll have a belt-pouch I've soaked with some sort of scent; Larral can pick that up and track it. If there is an organized theft ring operating, they're probably bringing their prizes to their leaders. Once we know where that is, you can tell the Watch."

"That's a good plan," Mags said with approval. "Perry, I'm taking you off duty tonight so you and Abi can work this plan tomorrow."

Perry looked a bit disappointed but nodded. Abi thought that Larral looked more relieved than disappointed. "Come help me pick something out to wear," Abi said to her brother. "You have a better eye for disguise than I do."

"I have a better idea," he suggested. "Let's get Kat."

Kat was only too happy to participate when they pulled her away from her studies. The moment Perry had suggested enlisting her aid, Abi had known he was right. Queen Lydia's family came of a long line of fabric merchants, and Lydia's uncanny eye for fabric and fashion had rubbed off on her daughter.

"Who are you?" Kat wanted to know immediately. Abi looked to her brother for that answer.

"We want someone rich enough to be a fat target, someone who'll go boo-hooing to her Papa and get another purse full of spending money—but not someone so rich that there will be Watch or a private guard keeping an eye on her," Perry said decisively. "Any poorer than that, though, and she'd be likely to fight for her pouch or run after the thief herself instead of running to Papa for more money."

One of the several rooms around the central living area was a storeroom. Mags had his own costume stash down in Haven, and Perry kept some of his own disguises down there as well, but now that Abi was helping, they'd added a wardrobe for her up here. Kat surveyed what was on offer.

"This chemise, this dress, and this set of sleeves," she said, picking them out. "This girdle, you can hang this pouch from it and you'll be a walking target."

The chemise was very fine linen, the dress was a plain twilled linen in a dull blue, laced up the bodice in front. The sleeves, however, were absolutely the *latest* in fashion, in two tight parts, an upper and a lower arm, both meant to allow the chemise to make attractive puffs at the shoulder, elbow and wrist. The girdle was heavily embroidered and had "hangers," loops of twill tape that allowed the wearer to suspend things from it. In this case, that would be a purse, a drawstring pouch, whose cords would make a mighty temptation for a cutpurse. Except for the girdle, the outfit looked quite plain—

But then again, Abi was more used to the clothing worn by the highborn and wealthy up here on the Hill, or the disguises she wore that would make her forgettable. She didn't have much experience with anything in-between.

"I could do this," Kat said wistfully. "It doesn't take any skill at all to play bait."

"Except you're the Princess," Perry reminded her. "I'm sorry, but—" Then he paused, then shook his head. "No, that won't work either. I need Abi free to help me and Larral, and if you play bait while she bodyguards you, she won't be free to do that. Sorry, Kat."

"Princesses don't get to have any fun," Kat grumbled.

"I doubt this is going to be fun," Abi replied, collecting the pieces of her disguise and draping them over her arm. "If these thieves are as good as we think they are, you wouldn't even notice the purse was missing until both the one playing thief and the one playing distraction were long gone."

"And once Larral tracks the purse to its destination, you absolutely would not be allowed anywhere near the next part of the job, which will be waiting and watching to make sure the criminals don't get away before we can bring the Watch down on them. Thanks a lot for your help, though!" Perry added, "Want to stay and play a game?"

But Kat shook her head. "I have a lot of reading to do for tomorrow. But I want to hear *everything* once you've caught the thieves!"

"I absolutely promise," Abi swore. "Everything!"

Abi even got the loan of a pony from the Royal Stables for this ruse, so she could ride down into Haven on an appropriate mount. Once she reached the Fair, there were tent stables for people who'd come from farther away than Haven—or were the sort that would not even consider walking—and she left the pony there, taking a chit in exchange for her fee and tucking it into the little bag around her neck that nestled in her cleavage where she was keeping money and anything else she actually needed to hold safely. Perry would be around this tent somewhere, waiting for her arrival, but she didn't bother looking for him. He and Larral both were extremely good at keeping themselves from being seen. An ordinary person would laugh at the notion that an animal bigger than a wolfhound could hide himself in a place like the Faire—or at least, he would laugh until he tried to spot the *kyree*, and failed. It was amazing how good Larral was—every bit as good as Perry or Papa.

So now Abi played the part of a rich, spoiled merchant's daughter. She spent a ridiculous amount of time looking over merchandise she had no interest in—jewelry and embroidered or brocaded purses, sets of sleeves like the ones she was wearing, hair ornaments, and utterly useless trinkets. She even bought a thing or two—making sure as she bargained to do the very opposite of what she normally would have done, which was to be inconspicuous. She wanted these merchants to remember her, and remember what she'd bought, because when the thieves were caught, that would form part of the evidence against them. If a merchant could say "Yes, I sold such-and-such to a girl in a blue gown," and the item turned up in the thieves' loot, it would cement the case.

So she bought an odd little hair ornament of a carved bone frog, stained green, clinging to the end of a hairstick, making quite a delighted fuss over it. And she bought a tiny doll also carved of bone, half the length of her little finger, perfectly made and cleverly jointed, with real human hair glued to its head, dressed in a gown of a blue that matched hers. She bought a *very* odd purple glass scent vial, with a stopper shaped like a coiled snake. It looked as if it must have been in the merchant's inventory for a decade and he'd despaired of ever getting rid of it, because it was half the price of any of the other vials on his table. Each time she made a purchase, she also took her time about lifting up the belt pouch attached to her girdle, getting out more money than was needed, putting back the excess, and then adding the change and her purchase to the pouch before letting it fall to her side again.

It was right after she'd bought herself a very nice pear and was eating it that she caught sight of one of those children, speeding toward her, dodging through the crowd to her right. As she'd expected, the child careened into her—enough to make her stumble, not enough to make her fall—and darted off again. And at the same time as the collision, she felt the weight of the belt pouch leave her side.

That belt pouch had been soaked last night in a solution of alcohol and oakmoss oil, then left to dry. Although it was used extensively in scentmaking, oakmoss was almost never used as a scent alone, and none of the scent vendors here sold it in its pure form, only as part of a formulated perfume. Larral should be able to track it easily.

Just to keep the guise up, Abi finished her pear, then made a show of looking for her pouch, dismay at finding it gone, and distress. She hurried to the Watch Tent through the crowd, a not unreasonable response to having found herself robbed.

Mags had warned the Watch this morning what was going on and that she'd be coming. She darted in through the open flaps of the tent and found herself facing a grizzled veteran of the Watch sitting at a "table" made of a board atop a pair of sawhorses.

He looked up at her. "Magpie," she said, before he could ask anything.

Without a word, he waved her to the back of the tent, where there was a canvas divider. The other half of the tent served as a place for Watchmen off duty to get a bit of a drink and a place to lounge. There was no one there at the moment, and she stripped off sleeves, gown and chemise to reveal the light shirt and breeches she'd worn under it all. She left her disguise neatly folded atop a barrel that seemed to be serving no other purpose at the moment. Her father would collect the gown and its accessories later.

She came back out again. The grizzled man had already gotten a sheet of paper and had a quill pen in his hand, an open bottle of ink next to him. "Blue embroidered linen drawstring purse," she said succinctly as he took her words down, laboriously writing them out. "Embroidered with a wreath of forget-me-nots around the initials JCS. Contains 10 bits, 5 copper pieces, eleven silver, a small bone doll from Eiron Edleson about this long—" she measured it for him on the paper "—dressed in a blue gown, with yellow hair. Also a purple glass scent vial with a coiled serpent stopper from Passal's Glasswork, and a hairstick with a green-stained bone frog on the top from Saveena's Fancies."

The Watchman finished writing it down and looked up at her

with a wry smile. "Snake vial? Frog ornament? Little poppet for sticking pins in? Sounds like the girl who bought all that is a budding witch."

She rolled her eyes. "Don't read too much into that," she replied. "I was trying to pick things the merchants would remember, and remember me."

"Then ye won't mind if I warn me girls not to go a-flirtin' with yer lad," the Watchman teased.

Why does everyone think I need to have a 'lad'? "Not at all," she replied, just to get it over with. Then before the man could blink, she whipped out one of her small concealed throwing knives and flipped it up and in the air so that it landed right beside his quill hand. "Though she'd have a lot more to fear from my knife skills than any witchery."

The Watchman's eyes bulged. "Wish I had more with yer skills on the Watch," he managed, finally, as she retrieved her blade and put it back where it belonged.

He didn't get a chance to say anything else; Larral shoved his huge head inside the flap and snorted at her. "Re's ro," he said. Her heart leaped. Larral had the target!

The Watchman's jaw dropped. "Did . . . thet dog just talk?"

"Yes," she said, and hurried to catch up with the *kyree*.

Larral ducked down a space between a couple of booths, and she followed him, discovering that he had brought her into a kind of back-passage that led behind the booths. The going was much faster here, and they needed to thread their way across and through the crowds only when they passed from one back-passage to another and had to cross one of the lanes. It was a lot less dusty; the grass on the field where the Fair was built had been pounded into earth by all the feet passing along those lanes. Her nose told her that they were nearing the stockyards, her eyes that the structures here weren't booths now, but simple tents for camping rather than dual-purpose living and selling spaces. Smart, to have your "headquarters" here. People were coming and going at all hours in the stockyard, and children were common.

Suddenly Larral dropped to the ground and began crawling on his belly; she did the same, very glad that there was grass here and not bare ground. Her heart sped up with excitement; this was the first time she'd actually been involved in a capture! Every other time she'd helped her father, she'd been left at home when the climax came and only told about it when everything was over.

She and Larral edged from one bit of cover to the next—here a pile of crates, there a corner of a tent, until they ended up next to Perry, who was flat on his stomach behind a water barrel, watching the side of a particularly big tent up ahead of them.

"Larral says that's where the purse went," he whispered. "Got any ideas how we can get closer?"

She spotted a couple of boxes not far from their target. *What we need is an excuse to wander up to those openly and sit down on them and loiter.* "We're right near the stockyards," she whispered back. "Let's get over there and see if we can find some halters that need mending."

They crawled out backward until they were out of sight of the tent, then followed their noses and ears to the stockyard itself, picking the section for oxen, horses, donkeys, and mules.

It didn't take much persuasion to get a couple of people to part with halters in dire need of fixing for a couple of coppers. And that wasn't an odd request. Younglings like the two of them often bought bits of harness in need of fixing, mended them, and resold them again at a small profit. It was one of the few ways by which someone whose only skills were as an animal tender could make a little extra money to spend at the Fair.

They returned to the back passage between the tents openly this time, casting about as if looking for a place to sit. "There!" she said aloud, pointing. "We can work there, and in the shade, too."

Larral was nowhere in sight, but that just meant he'd found a good place to hide. Unless someone decided to attack them, he'd remain in hiding. Perry could talk to him via Animal Mindspeech, and Larral in turn was talking to their father, keeping him apprised of what was going on.

No sooner had they plunked themselves down on the crates and begun to take the halters apart than there was a slight commotion in the tent at their backs. They kept their heads down as if they were concentrating on the work in their hands, just in case someone was somehow watching, but it didn't take much effort to make out the sounds of whimpering children.

"Shurrup an' mind yer manners!" someone growled. "Marster'll be 'ere soon!" The hair rose on the back of Abi's neck. She glanced over at her brother; he caught her eyes and nodded slightly. So, Mags knew. She hoped that he had gathered the Watch and was surrounding this tent! This might be their only chance to catch the actual head of this operation!

There was the sound of flesh smacking flesh, and the whimpering stopped. There was a little more commotion, then the sound of the flap at the front of the tent opening—

"I trust you have my money, Shackle," said a voice . . . one she knew!

It was Dudley Remp's father!

"Always, Marster." There came the chink of coins. "There be some goods too, as usual."

"And as usual I give you leave to dispose of them." Of course, Remp would have no idea how or where to dispose of stolen goods, and the few coins to be made out of them were not worth his time or effort.

"The rats been givin' me some trouble, Marster," Shackle continued. "Reckon ye c'n spare a word to 'em?"

A heavy sigh. "If I must." Remp cleared his throat ostentatiously. "Listen, you miserable little brats. You know who I am. Allow me to remind you why you are here. You are here to work off the debt your parents have to me. That means they owe me money, and I could have many bad things happen to them because of it if you don't obey. Now, you can do what Shackle tells you to, and at the end of the Fair, you can go back to your parents, and your parents will not be wandering the streets without a home. Or you can be ungrateful little wretches, disobey, and your families will find themselves sleeping in alleys with nothing more than what they have on their backs. And that's if they're lucky and I am feeling generous. If they're not, and I'm angry at your disobedience, they'll find themselves in gaol for debt, or in one of my workhouses, and once in one of those, they will never leave, you will all be separated, and you will never see each other again. Do you understand me?"

Silence, which seemed to be what he wanted.

"Very well then," Remp said, sounding bored. "Is there anything else I need to know?"

"Nothin' Marster," Shackle began. But he never got farther than that.

"Stand where you are! This is the Watch!"

The call came from somewhere near the front of the tent—and of course obeying that order was the very last thing that Remp was going to do. But Mags was no fool, as his children knew very well. They were already on their feet and scrambling out of the way as three Watchmen rushed for the back of the tent, and as Remp ran out a back flap, he ran straight into their arms.

———

"An' we got all th' littles back t'their families," Mags concluded, as Amily and Perry gathered up the supper dishes and left them outside the door to be collected. "Thet's what I call a good day's work. Abi, iff'n ye hadn't spotted thet all them littles was dressed alike an' runnin' a cantin' crew on th' same bung nipper, nobody'd have known it was organized. Well done. Perry, you an' Abi run a fine bait-an'-trap. An' Larral, good trackin'."

"Ran roo," Larral said politely from beneath the table, then went back to gnawing on his bone.

"What's going to happen to Remp now?" Abi wanted to know.

"That will depend on the King, I think," said her mother. "Someone as wealthy as Remp shouldn't be handled by the City Courts. Sedric will probably convene a High Court to try him, so he can't claim he's not being judged by a jury of his peers."

"Is that a good idea, though?" Abi persisted. "Brice said that Remp lends out money to important people so they owe him favors."

"Then I'll make sure that every juror has to undergo Truth Spell to ensure that they aren't among that group," Amily replied firmly. "The judges too."

"What about the families of all those littles?" Perry asked. "Are they going to be all right? After all, Remp's wife and Dudley aren't being charged, and they own those properties. What if they throw the families out on the street? Or worse, so the younglings can't testify?"

"I made certain sure t'bring thet up, no worries, Perry," Mags replied. "They'll be put somewhere safe."

"I wouldn't put it past Dudley to hire thugs to silence them," Abi said darkly. "He's worse than his father."

Mags looked at her oddly for a moment, then nodded. "Yer Mama'll make sure th' King knows thet."

"Well, what *I* want to know," Perry interjected. "Is what *else* you have for us to do at the Fair!"

7

Amily came in to the family dinner late and looking resigned. "Well," she said as she sat down, "it seems we are not finished with Fenris Remp quite yet."

Mags put his fork down. "What happen'd?"

"It appears that more people than I would have suspected owe him money, and he has been putting pressure on all of them to somehow get the charges against him dismissed," she replied. "It won't happen, of course. He was running a criminal enterprise. But this is making things very complicated."

"Am I going to have to testify?" Abi asked.

"No," her mother and father both answered at once. Mags nodded to his wife, who took up the tale. "No, because we have the reported goods that were stolen in the report of the Watch, and the goods were found in the possession of his underling. He was found in the tent, and, providentially, *your* purse is the one his underling chose to give him his ill-gotten gains in, and that was on his person when he was arrested. He's not going to be able to squirm out of this, although he's trying every trick he can think of." She frowned. "The jury pool is dismayingly small."

"Add th' Queen's Handmaidens?" Mags suggested. "They're all highborn. They should qualify, aye?"

"I'll suggest it. But what should have been simple has been overcomplicated by all the strings he's trying to pull. Virtually every bit of Court business today was hearing and dismissing petitions from his debtors."

But what Abi was thinking about was not the trial—it was how Fenris Remp's inevitable incarceration was going to free his son to do pretty much anything he wanted to do—at least, outside the walls of the Palace. She'd heard he held grudges, and he certainly had a powerful one against her. She was going to have to tread very carefully. Legally, he was old enough to completely take over his father's estate and wealth, and that meant he'd have plenty of money at his disposal. From this moment on, she was going to have to watch what she said and did even more carefully than she usually did. Just in case.

Then again, he still has no idea what kind of person he's up against.

A person—for instance—who had plenty of backing.

She waited until there was a lull in the conversation. "Is Dudley Remp likely to take over for his father, or is Remp's wife?"

Amily frowned again. "Mari Remp is a nonentity. It will probably all fall into Dudley's hands. He's old enough by Valdemaran law. Why?"

But Mags got it immediately. "Because th' young barstard 'as a powerful grudge 'gainst Abi, love. She humiliated 'im, broke 'is finger, an' got 'im tossed outa the Blues."

"And he holds grudges, and I wouldn't be at all surprised to learn he has his own fingers in a lot of dirty pies," Abi said frankly.

Mags pondered this a moment. "Whatever ye do, make sure ye got witnesses. If'n anybody starts accusin' ye of anything, demand Truth Spell; yer Mama an' I'll be willin' to put it on ye anytime, any place. But what I think 'e's like to do is get ye thrown outa the Blues, like 'e was. An' I jest had a notion for that." He chuckled. "I'll be havin' a word with yer teachers."

"How can you—?" Because she knew exactly what her father was talking about. The likeliest thing was that Dudley would set things up to make it look as if she'd cheated. And how could her father prevent that?

"If'n I tell ye, it won't be a surprise," he admonished. "Jest leave it up t'me."

And she had to be contented with that.

The trial was a sensation, though Abi suspected it was more because of the dirty secrets Fenris Remp was expected to reveal about those indebted to him than anyone's interest in a strongly disliked man on trial for organizing a petty theft ring comprised of children.

If so, it was a relief to those who had secrets to hide and a vast disappointment to those who wanted to learn those secrets that the King himself ordered it to be a trial by Coercive Truth Spell. Given Remp's history with Mags' family, King Sedric had Herald Jered set it, rather than Mags or Amily.

The courtroom was literally a Court Room; one of the common

rooms of the Palace that had had the furniture cleared from it, a podium brought in for the judge, a seat for the accused, and benches for the jury and audience. Afternoon light streamed in from the windows on the right hand side of the wood-paneled room, and though they were open, the air felt stale and stuffy.

Abi was in the courtroom, although she took care to disguise herself thoroughly with a ginger wig, abundant freckles, and a very expensive gown borrowed from Kat. She was within eyeshot of Dudley Remp, whose eyes skimmed right past her as he scanned the crowd. She wondered what he was looking for. Friends? He wasn't likely to see any. Enemies? Possibly. Or maybe just people his father had leverage over, who might betray themselves by their nervousness—Fenris Remp probably hadn't handed over the secrets of *those* names to his son, and those names would be very valuable indeed.

The judge in the case was the High Court Judge of Haven, the Honorable Bader Genberg, whose reputation was as spotless as his white judicial robes. There was no hope for preferential treatment there. Abi watched with amusement as Remp was brought into the court, objected to being subjected to the Truth Spell, had his objections dismissed on the spot, and then sat down in front of Herald Jered.

Within moments, Fenris Remp was surrounded by a bright blue glow as he scowled and sweated.

"State your name," the judge ordered.

"Fenris Iven Remp," Remp growled.

"Why were you in the tent from which you were seized at the Fair in Haven four days ago?" the judge asked crisply.

Remp told him. Told him *everything.* From how he had coerced people who owed him back rent into signing their children over to him as indentured labor, to discovering that people paid a fraction for the labor of a child of what they would have for the labor of an adult, to hitting on the notion of setting up a theft ring as soon as the Fair arrived in Haven. He described how he had thought about petty theft but realized pickpocketing was going to be much more profitable after consulting with an actual cutpurse—Shackle, the man he'd left in charge of the operation. He related how he had the man literally teach the children what to do, and when the first day of the Fair arrived, set them to work. Abi felt a little sick when she thought of those children. Now they knew how to steal, how easy it was. How many of them would go right back to stealing on their own once the trial was over? And they'd be caught, of course. When caught by the Watch, child thieves were generally sent away to a correctional school to learn a trade and pay back the people they had stolen from. But they generally weren't caught by the Watch. They were generally caught by the people they were stealing from, and . . . that seldom ended well.

By the time Remp was done, sweat poured down his face and neck from the effort of trying to resist the spell. Abi wondered if the judge was going to have him describe the methods by which he'd frightened, bullied, or beaten the children into obeying—

But the judge did not, and after a moment of looking over the jury, Abi realized why. Other than the couple of Handmaidens in the jury box, these were not people who would be moved by Remp's treatment of a few children whose parents were *clearly* no good, since they'd willingly signed over their own offspring to clear their back rent. "The apple doesn't fall far from the tree," they would tell themselves sagely. And it was entirely possible that Remp's defense would be to muddle everything by pointing out that the children were probably thieves before Remp ever got to them.

So the judge was avoiding all that. Right now he was sticking to the facts; it was just incidental that those facts were going to outrage everyone on the jury.

"Do you have anything to say in your defense that relates to what you have told us already?" the judge asked, when the flow of words slowed to a trickle, and then stopped.

Is he going to—? she wondered.

But no. The Truth Spell still compelled him. He knew very well the children hadn't been thieves before he had them taught to be. "No," he said, between gritted teeth.

"Very well then. Herald, you may dismiss the spell. Bailiffs, you may return the accused to custody. Ladies and gentlemen of the jury, you may retire to consider your verdict."

The bailiffs removed Remp, who glared at the jury out of piggy eyes that tried to bore holes in them. The jury studiously ignored him, and filed out to the deliberation room behind the courtroom. The audience whispered among themselves. Dudley continued to scan them while his mother wept into her handkerchief. He made no effort at all to comfort her.

It couldn't have been more than a quarter candlemark before the bailiff assigned to the jury returned and led the jury back in. The man they had appointed to speak for them stood, while the rest sat.

"I am to assume you have reached a verdict," the judge stated.

"We have, your Honor," stated the man, whom Abi did not

recognize but whose clothing proclaimed him to be at least as prosperous as Remp. He handed the bailiff a slip of paper, who in turn handed it to the judge. The judge read it.

"Bailiffs, you may inform the accused that he has been judged guilty on all charges. I hereby sentence him to ten years in gaol for every child in his contemptible enterprise, sentences to be served consecutively, for a total of one hundred eighty years." The judge banged his gavel on the bench. "Remand him to custody immediately. Jury, you are dismissed. Clear the courtroom."

The voice of Remp's wife, giving vent to her feelings in a wordless wail, soared over the babble. The judge cast a single look of pity in her direction, then left.

The trial was over.

Abi had expected to feel elated, or at least satisfied, but . . . instead, she was only filled with a sense of discontent. She hung back while the room cleared, trying to analyze her feelings, but couldn't come up with a reasonable explanation. Eventually, she left the now empty room, sure of only one thing.

This wasn't over yet. Not for her.

It proved pretty easy to follow her father's directive that she wasn't to do anything without witnesses; after all, she spent almost all of her hours when she was not at classes either studying with Brice, Emmit, and Rudi, or with Trey, Niko, and Kat. Or with all six, since getting together for math help had gotten to be a regular event. Regular enough that King Sedric decided to give the three actual appointments as royal tutors and *pay* them, much to their delight and amazement. If Dudley tried any schemes to accuse Abi of anything, she never heard anything about it, probably because of those precautions.

She and Kat and Perry did get down to the Fair again for a run at some of the entertainments, all three of them dressed as apprentices. They managed to squeeze in an acrobat show, a play, an animal show, and a dance troupe, all in the same afternoon. But despite Kat's urging, neither she nor Perry were particularly interested in shopping. Maybe because except for when they were actually in the tents, enjoying the shows, the two of them kept looking out of the corners of their eyes for cutpurses and those who might be acting as distractions.

When weeks passed and nothing at all happened that was any worse than difficult schoolwork problems, anyone else might have decided that Dudley had forgotten about her, or had far too much to do with running his fathers' business than to worry about the girl that had humiliated him in public.

Abi knew better.

"Honestly," Kat said one day, as Abi checked her book bag compulsively to make sure there was nothing in there that shouldn't be. "Why are you letting that dolt obsess you like this? I swear, every time we walk out you check your shadow to make sure it's not his. He's got his hands full right now, and I'm sure he's forgotten you."

"Except that he doesn't have his hands full," Abi countered. "I checked. His father set up a very careful trust a long time ago—I suppose in case he died or became incapacitated, since I'm sure the idea someone might catch him and put him in gaol never entered his mind. Dudley has absolutely nothing to do except spend the allowance the Trust gives him—except maybe try to wheedle more money out of his mother from her allowance. All the important decisions are made by a panel of Trustees.

If he wants to spend his own money on property or some other business venture, he can, but he can't touch a penny attached to his father's business beyond what's doled out to him until he turns twenty-one."

Kat whistled as they strolled back to the Royal Suite. "That can't set well with him."

"One more thing to blame me for," Abi sighed. "I know he's planning something. I can feel it. I just wish I knew what it was."

"He'll be trying to set you up as a cheat, no doubt." Kat nodded her thanks as the right-hand Guard opened the door for them.

"And how do I stop that if he's being really clever—or more like, has a clever flunky to help him?" she asked, helplessly. "I feel like I'm sitting under an ax that is hanging by a hair, waiting for it to fall!"

"Didn't your father say he'd thought of something?" Kat countered as they took their favorite seats in the solar and got out their history books.

"But he won't tell me what it is!" Abi countered in despair.

"Depend on it, it's clever," Kat soothed. "And that when that ax falls, it's not going to fall on you."

Abi just groaned.

"*Abi!* This is your father! The King's Spy! If you don't think he can outthink one fat dullard and his scummy friends, then shame on you!" Kat scolded. "This isn't a lot of Karsite agents or Sleepgiver assassins! This is a former schoolboy and whatever support he can dredge up from his father's flunkies."

Abi blinked at her, then realized she was absolutely right. If Mags couldn't be more clever than Dudley Remp and his (probably unwilling) helpers, he might as well give up the position of King's

Spy and take up riding Circuit in the Field, because he would have lost whatever edge and cleverness he had.

"I keep forgetting it's not just a random Herald," she said sheepishly. "It's Papa, and you're right. And even if he himself hadn't thought of anything, he could have consulted Lord Jorthun and Grandfather."

"That's the spirit!" Kat crowed. "Now . . . help quiz me on this section. I've got a test tomorrow."

Kat was not the only one with tests. Once the Fair was over and gone and the instructors had given their restless pupils a chance to settle back to work, it was time for a veritable barrage of tests. So far as Abi was concerned, the most important was the Combined Math test, which took an entire afternoon and covered every single one of her classes that involved any kind of math. There were fiendishly complicated problems that involved geometry, trigonometry, and algebra, in combinations she'd never seen before, besides many of the usual single problems.

It was a grueling session, and nothing less than an ordeal for many of the Blues; one boy actually broke down in the middle of it and needed to be taken out of the room. It was hard, hard work for Abi and she had a terrible headache when it was all over. She was so tired she was actually sick, and went straight home and laid down in her dark room, only coming out for supper—and then only to drink a lot of tea and eat some fruit. This was literally the hardest she had ever worked before in her life, and it was an entirely new experience. She was used to learning quickly and getting things right easily, and on the one hand, if this hadn't been something her entire progress in the Artificers was being graded on, she'd have enjoyed the challenge. But it was, and she thoroughly sympathized with the boy who hadn't been able to bear the pressure. More than once, she'd wished her Gift hadn't put her in this position and envied Perry.

The physical headache was gone by morning. But there was another headache about to occur.

It always took several days for all the exams to be looked at and graded. Four days later, Abi got called out of class in midmorning, and her stomach began to churn. Because she was certain—this was it. This was the moment Dudley struck. Somehow, some way, he had rigged things to make it seem as if she was cheating. But if she said anything now, if she insisted Dudley was trying to disgrace her—it would look as if she was guilty and was trying to head off an accusation. Besides, who would believe anything so absurd? Dudley had been expelled, he was now (nominally at least) in charge of his father's business, and he had much more pressing things to think about than one girl. No one would ever believe he was holding that kind of grudge and could be that obsessive and petty.

She went where she had been sent—to Master Ketnar's office, where she sat, hands clenched in her lap, stomach roiling, head pounding, while he looked through two sets of papers on his desk. They looked, from where she sat, like exam papers. Hers, and someone else's. He said nothing to her; she might as well not have been there. She swallowed convulsively, not daring to speak.

Finally the door opened, and another Blue came in—she knew him by sight but didn't know his name. "Ah, Geoffers," Master Ketnar said, finally looking up. "Have a seat. I have a few questions for you."

The boy took the chair, looking smug. *He knows. Of course he knows.* Master Ketnar made a great show out of looking through the papers one last time before speaking again. "Geoffers, your teachers have made an interesting observation. You and Abi seem to have identical exam results, right down to what was scratched out and how the problems were worked. Can you explain that?"

"'Course I can," the boy replied arrogantly, with a grin. "She cheated. She copied my work."

"But you were seated on opposite sides of the room!" Master Ketnar exclaimed. "How could she possibly have seen your paper to copy it?"

The boy snorted. "Simple. We all know she's got Gifts. She's probably got Farseeing, and never told anyone about it. That's how she does so well. How else could she be getting the kinds of grades she is, when she only just joined the Artificer Blues? She's been cheating all along, using Farsight to copy all our papers!"

Abi's stomach knotted up and her eyes and cheeks grew hot, and she struggled to keep down a sob. And there it was—the one accusation she had no way of disproving. How do you prove you *don't* have a Gift? Because if she was good enough, she could hide it from Heralds themselves! After all, she knew all about all kinds of Gifts, she even knew how to Shield, and she could have been hiding almost anything behind a Shield!

"Well, that's a very interesting theory," Master Ketnar said . . . and his eyes narrowed. "There's just one tiny little problem with it. You two didn't get the same exam questions."

Abi felt as if someone had punched her in the stomach. *What?*

The boy gaped at Ketnar, taken as much by surprise as Abi was. "What?" he blurted.

"I said, you didn't get the same exam questions. The answers Abi got and the work she did match the questions she got. But the answers you wrote and the work you did do not match the questions you got. But the answers do match Abi's, down to the smallest detail." Ketnar got up from behind his desk and loomed over the now cringing boy. "Do you have an explanation for this phenomenon?"

"I . . . I . . . I . . ." the boy babbled.

"Would you like to give that explanation under Truth Spell?" Ketnar continued. "It seems a pity to get a Herald to trot down here for such a petty reason as cheating, but both Abi's parents have already volunteered to do so any time I discovered someone was trying to get her in trouble. So . . . are you prepared to tell me now, or must I summon one of them?"

"Oh, gods—" the boy blurted, then buried his face in his hands and began to sob. "I—it was Dudley Remp. It was him!"

"And just how, exactly, did Dudley Remp accomplish this amazing feat?" purred Master Ketnar.

"I don't know!" Geoffers said in a panic. "He just told me that when you called me in about the exams I was supposed to say *she* cheated and copied mine, and she used Farsight to do it! That's all I know!"

"Well, you can thank your friend Dudley for the fact that you are being expelled," the Master replied ruthlessly. "I wish you good fortune explaining to your parents how this came about. You'll be escorted off the Palace and to your sponsor, who will be told what you have done and will deal with you as he sees fit. Do not set foot within the Palace walls again."

Abi felt a little sorry—a very little—when he burst into tears. But there was no hope for it. Master Ketnar summoned one of the Palace servants to escort him off the grounds, and that was that. He wasn't even allowed time to collect his books from the classroom he'd been in.

"Now you know why your father was so secretive about how we were protecting you, Abi," Ketnar said, when the boy was gone. "We didn't want the slightest chance of this to get out. Now the mystery is how your answers ended up on his exam paper."

In a blinding flash, at least one explanation occurred to Abi. "Someone got hold of a blank exam copy," she said. "Then they got Geoffer's paper and my paper and copied my answers onto the blank, and put Geoffers' name on it and slipped both back into the pile. But it would have to have been someone that didn't know math, or they'd know the answers didn't match the questions on the blank."

"They'd also have to have been in a hurry, concentrating only on the answers, or they would have noticed the questions themselves didn't match." Master Ketnar nodded. "I think my next move will be to talk to the scribes who copy out our exams for us. This should be very interesting." Finally he smiled slightly. "I'm sorry if I put you through any anxiety, Abi, but your presence here was necessary."

"It's all right, Master," she replied, although the headache that now bloomed behind her eyes was absolutely monumental, and her jaw hurt from clenching it too tightly. "I understand. In case you couldn't get him to confess, you needed to make it look as if I was the one in trouble." But now that she knew what had been going on, anger smoldered inside her. Would it have been so very hard for her father to have told her what he and Master Ketnar intended to do?

You're a good actress, Abi, but not that good. You wouldn't have been able to feign the panic when you thought Dudley had trapped you.

True. But still!

"I don't feel well, Master," she said finally. "May I be excused for the rest of the day?"

Finally, *finally*, he looked at her, and his reaction was everything she could have wished. "Good gods, child, you're as white as snow! I didn't mean to frighten you that badly, I promise you! Yes, indeed, you may be excused. I think you should lie down for a while. Do you need someone to go with you to your rooms?"

"I don't think so, Master," she said. "Thank you. I'll be going now."

But she hadn't gotten farther than the Palace proper when Kee and Tory came charging toward her out of nowhere, accompanied by Gryphon. She was so startled she stopped dead in her tracks.

"Abi, Abi, we're here to help!" Tory said, holding up a wet towel. "Put this on your neck! And lean on us!"

"Yiss!" Kee echoed. "Here!" and he grabbed her hand and put it on his shoulder. "We'll help you home!"

Touched by the attention—too touched to be irritated by the fact that the two of them had obviously been spying on her by Farsight again—she accepted the towel, and pretended to "lean on them," although she didn't put any weight on their young shoulders. The wet towel was actually a good idea, it was wonderfully cool on her neck and went a long way toward unknotting the knots in it. The littles weren't satisfied until she was lying in her own bed with the towel across her forehead. And even then, Tory asked anxiously if she wanted tea, or Mama, or a hot brick at her feet.

"I'll be fine now that I'm in bed," she promised them—and

actually, she did start to feel a bit better. They tiptoed away to go back to whatever they were up to in the center room, and she worked on relaxing those tense neck muscles and unclenching her jaw.

I'm surprised I didn't splinter my teeth. . . .

But the windows were open, Kee and Tory whispering together was rather soothing and blended nicely with the birdsong coming from the other side of the room.

The next thing she knew, the center room was full of chattering people and her father had just sat down on the edge of her bed, which was what had awakened her.

"Feelin' better, poppet?" he asked sympathetically. "I told ye I was takin' care of it, didn' I?" There was just a hint of admonition in his voice that she hadn't trusted him.

There were a lot of things she could have said at that point, most of them accusatory about not trusting *her,* but she decided to say none of them. "The headache's mostly gone," she said instead.

"Well, good." He patted her hand. "Yer Mama read me a lecture on leavin' ye outa plans what concerned ye," he added. "So . . . I'm right sorry." He let the sentence trail off, then cleared his throat self-consciously. "Master Ketnar an' me had a little palaver wit' th' scribes, an' you was right. One on 'em kept a copy of th' test, put Geoffers' name on't, an' got inter th' place where the finished exams was an' copied yer answers. Then 'e swapped the real exam fer the cheatin' one."

"What's going to happen now?" she asked.

Mags made a face. "Not much. Scribe was turned out. Geoffers was expelled. But Dudley? Not much c'n be done t'touch 'im. Tisn't a *crime* as such, an' there ain't anyone like t' take it serious.

Not serious 'nuff to bring the law on 'im."

She wanted to cry out that this wasn't fair—that almost having her life ruined *was* serious. But . . . how would her life have been "ruined," exactly? She couldn't be thrown out of her home. Being dismissed by the Artificers would not have made her strange Gift vanish, and it *was* more than useful, and if no one else, the Heralds and her father would have a lot of use for it. She could have gotten tutoring from a Master who didn't believe the cheating accusation. No one who cared about her—or who she cared about—would ever have believed she had cheated. Just people whose opinions didn't count.

Still . . .

"I *hate* this," she said instead, wrathfully. "There should be some way to make Dudley pay for what he did to me!"

"Well, we thought 'bout thet," he said. "We c'd bring 'im inter civil court. An' we c'd even make 'im go under Truth Spell agin, and make it all come out. An' then wut? Mebbe git some money from 'im, but 'ow much's cheatin' worth? 'Member, this'd be a civil judge an' jury useter goats an' 'ouses an' things wut ye c'n put a number on. An' no one'd trust 'im, a-course, but no one trusts 'im now, leastwise, not anyone with sense. An' 'e'd 'ave even more reasons t' 'old a grudge 'gainst you. This way . . . ye got a chance 'e'll find somewhat else t' go after."

She sighed, feeling utterly and completely cheated. Angry, frustrated, and sick all over again. But her father was right.

"Not even us Heralds c'n make everythin' right, poppet," he said, sadly. "All we c'n do is try an' make 'em better."

She couldn't help it. A couple of hot tears of rage and

disappointment coursed down her cheeks. But he was right. Damn it all, he was right.

"We bested 'm twice, poppet, 'member that," Mags admonished. "An' if 'e tries a third time, we'll do 'im agin. 'E thinks 'e's smart, but 'e ain't nearly as smart as 'e thinks." He offered her his hand. "Git some supper. Ye'll feel better. Tory 'n Kee 're worried 'bout ye."

She took it, and as he rose, she got off her bed. "Nobody's as smart as all of us put together," she said, finally.

Mags smiled. "Tha's the truth. Now le's eat."

8

A bi actually got to enjoy the Harvest Fair.

There was nothing, absolutely nothing, that needed the attentions of Mags, and by extension, his family at the Harvest Fair. Now, this was not unexpected; Harvest Fair tended to be concentrated on farmers and their harvests rather than entertainment. There was some entertainment, of course, and vendors, because farmers with money in their pockets could be tempted to part with some of it, particularly if they had done well. But most of the entertainment was in livestock shows, livestock contests, and expanded versions of the sort of contests (archery, feats of strength and agility) every sizable village, town, and city in Haven put on at this time of year.

So there was plenty to see for free; since entertainers really could not compete with "free," they confined their performances to evenings when there were no contests going on.

As a treat, Abi took Tory and Kee to everything they wanted to see for several days of the Fair; granted the Royal Family always made a joint appearance at the opening and closing of every Fair, but that wasn't *fun*. They'd walk through the Fair surrounded by the Royal Guard after officially declaring the Fair open, compliment a couple of vendors, see one or two of the most important contests, such as the archery or the Prize Bull, and leave.

Amily had never been able to get away to take Tory and Kee to any of the Fairs, and until this fall, Abi and Perry hadn't been free to do so either, and they certainly weren't old enough to go on their own. So this was their first full Fair, ever, and both of them were round-eyed with excitement. Living in Haven all their lives, they'd never really seen anything smaller than a horse and larger than a chicken—there were chickens and dovecotes and even rabbit hutches at the Palace, but aside from the horses, cats, and dogs, these were the only animals they knew from outside of picture-books.

The sheep—especially the show sheep, with their wool washed and brushed for the competitions—absolutely enchanted them. A couple of indulgent shepherds allowed the boys to bury their hands in the wool of their ram's backs and touch the curly horns, to their absolute delight. The goats frightened Kee a little with their strange eyes, but Tory coaxed him into petting a nanny and feeding her wisps of hay. Geese and ducks were new to them; they liked the ducks, but the aggressive behavior of the geese caused them to watch the flocks being auctioned off from a safe distance and marvel at how the goosegirls managed to boss their flocks around. Cattle were a strange mystery to them—big as a horse but nothing like a horse. And the huge pigs with their tiny, squinting eyes and grunting were of no interest whatsoever except as something to be wary of.

The actual shows for most of the animals bored them; they couldn't see what made one goose or sheep better than another, and truth to tell, neither could Abi. But the human contests and the horse and dog shows, now, that was a very different matter.

Especially since Lady Dia was showing some of her mastiffs, including the ones she'd bred out of the ones Perry had brought back from his adventure for her.

Familiar with riding horses, they marveled at the strength of the huge beasts bred to pull enormous drays and tug plows through tough turf and clay-heavy soil. Beautiful gaited horses with shining coats of every color thrilled them, and made them both declare that they wanted one—Kee wanted a palomino, and Tory a black destrier with feathered feet.

But it was the dog shows that held them spellbound.

"I never knew there were so many kinds of dogs!" Tory exclaimed, after sitting through the competitions of the lurchers, the bloodhounds, the greyhounds, the spaniels, and the hunting hounds. But Abi didn't get a chance to say anything more, because it was time for the mastiffs and to cheer Lady Dia on.

She won, handily, and joined them in the viewing stands after collecting her prize medal and sending her dog back up to her kennel with one of her servants. "Have you enjoyed the shows so far?" she asked the boys with a twinkle in her eye.

That unleashed a flood of words as they poured out their enthusiasm. With a smile and good graces, she let them babble for as long as they liked, and when they finally ran out of words, she said, "Well, next you are going to see something truly remarkable. Sheepdogs!"

"Dogs that are like sheep?" Kee wondered aloud as he settled onto the hard wooden seat of the stands, perfectly prepared to sit through anything if Lady Dia said it was something special.

"No, dear, the dogs that take care of sheep," Dia replied. "They are extremely clever, and so clever I don't think I am clever enough to train them. Look, here come the sheep now."

Sure enough five nervous sheep were herded into the arena, where they milled about uncertainly, while the first competitor and his dog eyed them from the sidelines. The dog was a shaggy little black and white thing that didn't look to Abi as if it could herd a duck, much less five sheep that were each four times its size.

But the judge blew a whistle to start, the shepherd made a motion with his arm, and the dog was off like a falcon.

For the next quarter candlemark they all watched in amazement as that dog made those sheep do everything but stand on their heads. Abi had never seen anything like it, and Tory and Kee were laughing and applauding the entire time.

The next dog wasn't quite as good as the first, the third fell a bit short as well, then the next two seemed to do as well. The contest ultimately came down to a second trial between the first dog and the tenth, in which the first dog won by successfully driving one sheep into each corner of the arena and the fifth into the center, and keeping them all in their places despite their natural instinct to come together as a flock. The other couldn't manage to keep the one in the center put.

The proud shepherd and his prancing partner collected not only their prize medal, but a handsome prize of money as well.

"Why didn't you get any money, Lady Dia?" Kee asked, since the sheepherding contest was the last dog competition of the day.

"Because I will get money every time my dog goes to make puppies with another mastiff," Dia explained, matter-of-factly. "That's what the real prize is for many of the farmers here. If they have the prize-winning bull, or gander, or ram, other people will pay them money for many years for what are called 'stud fees.' And for a farmer who has to depend on weather and doesn't know from one year to the next what his crop will be like, to have the certainty of money coming in every spring is very important."

There was no doubt that all of this was very new to both boys, and they listened with wide eyes. But they were not the only ones listening to Lady Dia; from behind them in the stands, someone cleared his throat, and said, "Well, if you're to be tellin' these lads what a farmer's life be like, I can be helpin' with that."

They all turned to see a weathered, but kind-faced, gray-haired man dressed in a smock and canvas trews; he was looking, not at Lady Dia, but at the boys. Dia didn't get a chance to answer, because both of them practically burst out with "Yes, please!"

So the rest of the afternoon, they not only heard what a farmer's life was like, but were taken around to see the beasts this particular man had brought to show and sell. They also met his wife, who had entered cheese and preserves in contests, and six of his twelve children. Three of the ones who were not at the Fair were married and taking care of their own farms, and the other three had stayed behind to tend the family farm in the absence of the rest. By the time they all went up the Hill in the wagon, Abi reckoned the boys had gotten one of the best educations on farming in a single afternoon that they were ever likely to see.

After that long a day around animals, Abi ordered both of them to make a complete wash-up, and got one for herself, before they all went to their rooms for supper. Not even traipsing around the Fair all day had repressed Kee's energy; he chattered at high speed to Kat and his nurse when Abi delivered him to the door of the Royal Suite. Abi was exceedingly grateful that Tory was less talkative.

Mags was in very good spirits when he joined them, and so was Perry. The first words he said over dinner explained it.

"So, did ye like m'agent, then?" he asked of Abi and Tory. "I've allus found 'im a good feller."

"Seth Wrenmarsh is your agent?" Abi exclaimed. "He's a very nice man!"

"Th' whole Wrenmarsh fam'ly," Mags corrected. "Though proper speakin' 'e was yer Granther's agent afore 'e was mine."

"I saw you at the dog shows, so I asked him to keep an eye on you, since he had a dog in the sheepherding contest anyway," Perry said proudly. "After all you did have Kee with you. I wanted another safe pair of eyes on our little Prince."

"Did he win?" was all Abi wanted to know. "Wrenmarsh's dog, I mean."

"Came in second," said Perry. "Wrenmarsh wasn't put out though; his dog is just a pup, and it'll do better next time."

Abi didn't honestly expect to hear anything more about the kindly farmer ever again, but the next day, she was to get a surprise, when she was called out of class by her father.

Mags didn't say anything to her at all other than, "Abi, there's a problem ye might could help with," before he led her to the King's Lesser Audience Chamber. And there, much to her astonishment, was Seth Wrenmarsh, who had evidently just finished explaining something to King Sedric.

"And here's the girl who might be able to help you, Goodman Wrenmarsh," the King said cheerfully as she and her father entered after being announced.

Wrenmarsh's brow furrowed. "I mun say, Highness, I were expectin' some'un older."

"Just tell your tale all over again, and we'll see," the King urged him.

He shrugged. "It be short enow. We be neighbors t' the Lord or Lady of Asterleigh Manor, time out'o mind, as be most'o the freeholders 'round it. Now, ye mind I said 'freeholders,' aye, young mistress?"

Abi nodded. "So you all hold your property and farms in your own right, not renting them from the Manor."

"Aye that. Manor has 'un's own Home Farm, an' that's all. Happen they had more, betimes. Every farm round about milord's manor was rented from 'em. But milady's great-granther died, an' the fortune couldna be found."

"Wait . . . what do you mean, *couldn't be found?*" Abi asked.

"Happen th' old man had it hid an' didna tell the wife afore he broket his neck. She were his second, an' young, and mayhap he didna trust her to be sensible like." Wrenmarsh shrugged. "So there was some bad years, rents was down, family sold off the land, piece by piece, 'til it come to t'day. Lady Asterleigh's a good wench and doesna want t' lose her only home, so I comes t'King, on account'o our special business, t'see if the Crown might do aught."

Abi sensed there was a great deal more to this story than Wrenmarsh was saying, but she held her peace. She had not been her father's daughter all her life not to know that some secrets were not for telling to just anyone.

"I suggested that the lady sell the property and come join the Queen's Handmaidens, but it appears there are difficulties with that," the King said, without elaborating on the "difficulties." "Wrenmarsh suggested that perhaps a Master Builder might be able to find the hiding place of the family fortune, where the efforts of the family had failed. I thought of you. Abi, is it possible that your gift might betray a void in the walls where searching has not?"

Abi had been practicing that Gift daily, and at this point, all she had to do was close her eyes to see the flow of pressure and stresses in any built object. To her inner eye it looked like slowly flowing water, with a color variation showing where the stress was strongest. But could that reveal a hidden void?

"I don't know," she admitted. "Maybe? I've never had any building to try it on."

"'Tisn't far," Wrenmarsh said persuasively. "Nobbut a few candlemarks."

"Perry can go with you," Mags suggested. "There's always the chance mice might know about such a hiding place."

Well, why not? She'd never been outside of Haven, and even if this wasn't anything like Perry's epic adventure in the Pelagiris Forest, it should be fun and different, and she certainly could not make matters worse. "I'll go make up a pack," she said. "Then I can leave when you're ready, Goodman Wrenmarsh."

"Yer a good lass," Wrenmarsh said warmly. "No matter what, the Lady'll be grateful to ye."

Wrenmarsh's business at the Fair wasn't concluded for another two days, which gave her plenty of time to get study assignments from her teachers and make up somewhat more than a pack to take with her. She, Perry, and Larral, with Rolan carrying their packs for them, walked down into the city to the half-dismantled Fair on that third morning to find Wrenmarsh, his three now empty wagons, his six children, and the sheepdog waiting for them, all ready to go. The farmer and his children, the youngest of whom was Perry's age, greeted Rolan like an old friend when they saw him and fed him two beautiful apples before everyone decided who was riding with whom and the wagons departed. Perry, Larral, and Abi all rode in the third wagon with the youngest of the six children driving.

"Do you all work with my father?" Abi asked, when they were safely away from prying ears.

"Oh, aye," the lad said cheerfully. "Not that what any'un but Pa's done anythin' special. We mostly jist keep ear t'ground and eyes lookin' fer anythin' that might be troublesome." He elbowed Perry, who was on the driver's seat beside him. "An' sometime now an' agin, it'll be this layabout we'll be talkin' to."

Perry grinned and elbowed back. "Just no more traveler's tales about goat-sucking monsters."

The boy shook his head so his blond hair flopped into his eyes. "No foolin' you, city boy," he said ruefully.

Abi just kept quiet and let the two of them banter on. It seemed that not only did Perry know Rafi Wrenmarsh very well, but that the Wrenmarshes were the very proud owners of two of the mastiffs he'd brought back from the Pelagiris Forest—the very last two he'd given away before returning to Haven. By sitting quietly on her pack in the wagon bed, she learned pretty much everything she would have asked without needing to go to the effort of breaking into their conversation.

She learned, for instance, that she and Perry would be dropped off at Asterleigh Manor on the way to the Wrenmarsh farm and that Lady Asterleigh would be expecting them, thanks to a message sent yesterday via another of the freeholders from the area. She learned that Lady Asterleigh had a very sound plan regarding the missing inheritance should it be found. The Home Farm was not large enough to be anything more than self-supporting, but by converting almost all of the arable land to herbs, she should be able to make a profit, since the farm was near enough to Haven to permit regular deliveries the year around of either fresh or dried herbs.

And still, there was a gaping hole they were all dancing around. Just why was it that Sussena, Lady Asterleigh, could not simply sell the place, move to the court, become one of the Handmaidens, and save the money from the sale of her property as a potential dowry. This was making Abi exceedingly curious. It wasn't age— she was just a little past nineteen and certainly neither too old nor too young. It was a mystery.

Perhaps she was just one of those people who was painfully shy around strangers. Lady Dia could certainly cure her of that, but she might not know that.

Asterleigh Manor wasn't one of those walled edifices, but it was bounded by what must have once been a very handsome and imposing hedge that towered well over their heads but showed by its unkempt appearance that it certainly hadn't been seen to in a good many years. The iron gates let into the hedge, hung from gateposts of stone, stood wide open, and it didn't look to Abi as if they had been closed in decades. From the gates, it was a short distance indeed to the house, which was less like the sort of manor she was accustomed to see in Haven and more like a sprawling, enormous farmhouse. It was two stories tall, with an attic, made of gray stone with a thatched roof. The main entrance, a pair of substantial wooden doors, was in the very middle of the house. The doors opened as they were half way up the short driveway, and a single male waited for them to come to him.

The cavalcade of three wagons pulled up in front of the house, and now that they were practically on top of it, the decades of neglect were a bit more obvious. There was a great deal of "whitewash" dripping down the sides from the nests in the thatch overhead, and the thatch itself was old, gray with age, and left a litter of bits on the ground around the base of the walls. Wrenmarsh senior descended from his wagon as Rafi handed Abi out, Larral leaped out of the wagon bed on his own, Perry hopped down off the bench seat, and Rafi began handing down the packs to Perry.

"Well," said the senior Wrenmarsh. "Here she be, as promised."

The man looked Abi over, dubiously. He was dressed not unlike Wrenmarsh save that his smock was much mended, as were his moleskin trews, and his boots were more patch than whole leather. He peered at Abi from beneath a pair of bushy brown eyebrows, and his thick moustache wiggled as he considered the new guests.

"I were 'spectin' some'un older," he said, echoing Wrenmarsh's words. Given how his gaze flitted between her and Perry, she suspected he had also expected someone male.

"The King himself sent her, Tobin," came a laughing, girlish voice from inside. "I should think the King knows his own business by now!"

"I be nawt so sure," Tobin muttered, but he picked up half their packs, leaving Abi and Perry to pick up the rest and follow him.

And there the mystery of Sussena Asterleigh was solved, as just inside the door they were greeted by a very pretty, dark-haired girl sitting in a peculiar chair mounted on wheels. The two in the rear were very tall, the two in the front were smaller. She wore a very plain linen gown, which showed careful darning. The antechamber was small, all of the same stone as the exterior and unfurnished. "Hello!" she said cheerfully. "Forgive me for not greeting you at the door, will you? I'm Sussena."

Wrenmarsh spoke up. "Milady, this young scamp be Peregrine, an' the young leddy be Abidela. I'll be lettin' 'em speak fer thesselves."

"I'm Perry, and my Gift is Animal Mindspeaking. I'm going to be using my Gift to see if the animals on your property have spotted the missing inheritance. This's Larral; if we find it, he'll guard it. M'sister Abi has a Gift that lets her see where all the stresses and strains are in buildings, so she'll be looking for places hidden in all the walls."

Sussena shook her head. "I fear you will find far too many of those stresses and strains to be of much use to you, Abidela. My beloved home is in very poor repair."

"Call me Abi. And that might actually help, milady," Abi countered.

Sussena looked doubtful, but said nothing. "At any rate, I hope you'll forgive the state of things. As all the bedchambers come well equipped with winds whistling through the cracks in the shutters and cold running water every time it rains, we all live in the kitchen and old dining hall. And by 'we,' I mean just the five of us: Tobin, his son Hob, his wife Hansa, their daughter Lori, and I."

Abi wasn't sure how to react to this statement, but Perry just nodded and spoke for both of them. "As long as you aren't expectin' me t'share a bed with anyone but Larral, that'll be good enough, milady."

"How we're bein' t'feed t'at gurt monster, much less two more mout's . . ." Tobin muttered, looking at Larral. Sussena blushed crimson.

"If you have wild rabbits about, Larral can feed himself," Perry said pointedly. "And we paid Master Wrenmarsh to bring the extra food you'll need for all of us even if you don't have enough rabbits. We thought this out carefully. We're here to try to solve your problem, milady, not add to it."

Now Sussena was a brilliant scarlet, and she looked absolutely mortified. She looked as if she would have liked to have apologized for Tobin, but really, he had been looking out for her interests. Abi felt a great surge of sympathy for the girl. This couldn't be easy for her. Whether or not she herself had known better times within these walls, she was certainly conscious of how low her family had sunk.

"Lets get you settled, at least," she managed, finally.

"An' I'll be takin' m'leave, milady," Wrenmarsh said. "Rafi'll be here with extra provender in a candlemark or twain. Niver ye fret, m'lady. Wutever ye c'n think of, we'll 'ave taken care of."

Before Sussena could answer—and she looked to Abi as if she would very much have liked to have refused the extra food but knew her slender means would not stretch to feeding two more souls without that help—Wrenmarsh turned and left, and the sound of the wagons moving off came through the still open door until Tobin closed it firmly. The girl flushed again but turned her chair and began rolling it toward an open archway at the rear of the entryway, using her hands to push the bigger wheels forward. Tobin carried the packs behind her, leaving Abi and Perry to bring up the rear.

The room they entered had a huge fireplace in the rear wall, one that obviously shared a hearth on the other side with the kitchen. While the other three walls were ancient, dark wood, the wall with the fireplace in it was mostly stone that matched the exterior. Obviously there were ovens built into it on the other side, and it had been made to keep a much bigger household than this one fed. Tobin dropped the packs unceremoniously down beside a pair of cots beside the hearth. "Bath's bucket i' kitchen," he said gruffly. "Outhouse be outside. None o'yer Palacey folderol 'ere."

"*Tobin!*" Sussena finally exclaimed, exasperated. "They're here to help. Stop treating them like . . . like a nest of mice!"

"Mice 'ud be more use," he muttered, and he stalked out through a passageway on the right of the hearth into the kitchen.

Sussena now flushed with utter mortification. "He's taken care of me all my life," she explained, unable to look at either of them. "So he thinks he has—never mind."

Abi dropped her packs beside the others and went to pat Susenna's hand. "Never mind, we understand," she said. "And it's not as if we're here as guests, anyway. We're here to do a job."

"Do you have any old stories that would tell you where to start looking?" Perry asked. "This is a pretty big house, and I noticed there are several outbuildings too."

Sussena sighed. "Nothing," she replied. "If there ever had been, they were forgotten years ago. The lost fortune was such a sore spot with my grandfather that he refused to speak of it at all."

Perry and Abi exchanged a look of resignation. "All right, then," Abi sighed. "Let's start with the dairy."

They passed through the kitchen, where Hansa was bent over a pot of soup, and went straight out the open door into the kitchen yard. A half-hearted attempt to clean the yard of weeds had resulted mostly in keeping them to no more than ankle height. Hens clucked and pecked contentedly as they passed across to the building that was obviously the dairy.

Like the main house, the dairy had been built of good, stout stone, with a thatched roof. Unlike the main house, the roof had been allowed to go completely to pieces, so that entire sections of the thatch were missing, exposing the rafters, which now were likely compromised. "Damned shame," Perry said, as they surveyed the interior. Abi nodded. In order to keep the dairy cool in summer the walls had been built triply thick; the floor was smooth slate, the countertops where pans of milk would sit for the cream to rise, and where butter would be worked, were built of polished granite. Even the racks for storing cheese as it ripened had been made well. Now those racks were piles of sticks, and it was obvious from the gaps where racks no longer stood that those sticks were being taken to use as kindling on a regular basis. Obviously no one had any hope that the dairy would ever serve its old function again.

"Still, look at those walls," Abi continued. "Plenty of room to hide a fortune in them."

She closed her eyes, and waited for her Gift to start working.

The last two days she had been practicing on the Palace and the buildings around it, realizing that although there were no hidden places within their walls, there were things *like* hidden places: ornamental niches, fireplaces, even serving hatches. These were all things built into walls that had similar characteristics as voids. And it turned out that if she "looked" deeper than the surface—and she could—she was able to see the stress forces flowing around those areas. Perry had helped her test this by taking her into a room blindfolded and challenging her to find such places.

But in a triple-thick wall, and one in which the beams of the structure might be compromised, this wasn't going to be easy.

First she had to recognize and discard all the distractions of other things going wrong: rotting roofbeams crying out their pain, places where the stone itself had started to crack, or, more often, spots where the mortar between the stones was not what it should have been, shifting the stresses in the entire wall or part of it. But eventually, as Perry initiated silent conversations with mice, she eliminated all those things and settled down for a good, long communion with the stone.

It was suppertime by the time they finished, and for the last quarter candlemark the smell of fresh bread and soup coming from the kitchen had been a terrible distraction. As they crossed the courtyard again, she realized she had been at her task longer than she had thought. It was nearly sunset.

She and Perry went straight to the kitchen door, where Hansa,

Tobin's wife—who clearly served as the cook—had just placed that kettle of soup and a loaf of bread on the table, while a young girl, who must be the daughter, Lori, put out wooden bowls, pottery mugs, and spoons. Like Tobin, their clothing was carefully patched, and their blouses looked to have been turned at least once. Sussena was already at the table, her chair pulled up to it, and a boy about a year older than the girl (that would be Hob) was washing his hands under the pump at the sink. There were five cots stacked up out of the way in a corner of the scrupulously clean kitchen—which was far larger than it needed to be for such a small household, even serving as it did as a communal bedroom as well as its original purpose. In its glory days, this manor must have had a staff of at least twenty people, plus the resident lord and his family.

Larral was under the table, looking perfectly satisfied, so he must have found the hunting to his liking.

Sussena looked at Abi hopefully. Abi shook her head. Sussena shrugged a little and smiled. "It's a lovely soup tonight," she said brightly. "Your dog brought us two rabbits to go into it!"

"Rabbits ain't gonna last long wi' that gurt beast abaht," Tobin grumbled.

"Shut up, ol' fool," said his wife, in the tones of someone who said that a lot. "Milor', mileddy, sets where ever ye please an' hep yersel'. We don't keep no state 'ere."

"Cain't afford no state," Tobin muttered.

Abi and Perry ignored him, as his wife was doing, although it seemed poor Susenna's cheeks were never going to be less than a mortified red. They settled down at the end of the table nearest their hostess. The soup *was* very good, and though the bread might have lacked butter, there was plenty of broth for sopping up, so Abi didn't miss the butter.

"So where did you look first?" Sussena asked, between bites.

"The dairy," Abi replied.

Tobin barked a laugh. "What sorta gurt fool'd hide a treasure inna *dairy?*"

"The kind of fool that doesn't want it to be found?" countered Abi. She was getting very tired of this contrary fellow. He might be loyal to Sussena, but that didn't excuse his constant rudeness.

"An' why wouldna it be found?" Tobin shot back.

"Because people like you think a dairy's no place to hide a treasure!" Abi replied sharply.

"Tha's cause on'y a gurt fool'd hide it there!" cried Tobin.

"Shut up yer face, old man," his wife snapped. "An' stop connerdictin' yer betters."

He turned on her and wagged his spoon at her. "An' wut makes a slip of a fool gurr-ell me better, I'd like t'know!" he demanded.

"The fact thet th' King sent 'er an' she's got more sense inner liddle finger than you has in yer entire body!" said his wife. She turned to Abi. "Don't pay 'im no mind. Cause 'e ain't got one t'speak of." And she laughed heartily at her own joke.

You could have baked bread on poor Sussena's cheeks. Tobin's children were evidently used to this; they paid no attention to either their father or their mother, but gulped down their food, took their bowls and mugs to the stone sink, and went outside, presumably to finish their evening chores.

Tobin finished his meal, grumbling under his breath the entire time, and went out to do the same. Hansa gathered up the remaining dishes and took them to the sink. "M'lady Sussena sleeps wi' us, so if she needs anything i' night, one on us is there t'help. We keeps country hours 'ere."

"I'm afraid that's true," Sussena confirmed. "We keep candles and rushlights for emergencies and go to bed with the sun."

"Then we'd better do the same," Perry offered. "Goodnight!"

Abi followed him out into the "dining hall," and looked around for a place to change. "I'll just slip into the antechamber," she said, finally, getting her nightclothes from her pack.

"Seems as good a place as any," Perry replied. And by the time she was back, he was already on one of the cots, buried under the blankets they'd brought with them. She'd thought bringing bedrolls had been a silly idea, but it turned out Perry was right to have insisted. The thin blanket already on the cot was fit only to be folded several times and used as a pillow.

9

The barn, the stable, and even the chickenhouse—all made of the same stone and all in the same dilapidated condition as the dairy—got the same treatment as the dairy had and with the same results. She included the floors in her search, although she wasn't as certain of her results there, and set Perry to tapping and scraping, using the skills he'd learned from several master thieves to try to detect if there was anything buried beneath the floors.

Somehow Sussena managed to keep her spirits up—but perhaps she'd never counted on them finding her lost inheritance in the first place. Abi wished, more than once, that she shared some sort of Mindspeech with Perry. Keeping her thoughts to herself was harder than she had imagined. She really had to wonder just what it was about this place that kept Sussena here. Obviously she'd be better off if she just sold it; granted, the acreage that came with it wasn't much, but it was near enough to Haven to make some wealthy merchant a fine summer home—once it had been rebuilt. Was it just stubbornness? Was it family loyalty? Was it fear that the money simply wouldn't last long enough? She didn't feel she could ask Sussena any of these very personal questions, but she would have loved to have been able to discuss them with Perry.

Day by day, they eliminated every possible option but the manor itself.

Finally, with the outbuildings eliminated, it was time to work on the manor; it couldn't be put off any longer.

"Happen ye'll breakit yer necks," Tobin said over eggs and bread the morning they proclaimed they were ready to search the main house. He seemed very pleased with the prospect.

"Shet up, old fool," his wife said crossly. "I been up all them rooms. You ain't." She turned to Abi. "The lad an' lass hev been clearin' rubbish, or leastwise, anythin' thet'll trip ye up. Floors be still sound. Ye'll be a'right."

Abi had come to trust Hansa more than her always pessimistic and critical husband. "We're going to start in the attic," she said. "Have they been up there?"

"Aye. Breakit yer necks," Tobin reiterated. "Nobbut up there but fambly stuff gone t'pieces."

"Nobbut up there a-tall," Hansa corrected sharply. "Every bit uv anythin' got hauled downstairs an' used or sold. Doncha remember? Curtains and bed'angin's went for clothes. So did sheets. Blankets went fer cloaks, them as we ain't usin'. Beds went t'Wrenmarsh ten years agone, cupboards an' chests t' Lotham, chairs t' Danferth, an' what weren't fit t'sell we burnt."

Abi expected that this litany in proof of her impoverished state would have brought another blush to Sussena's cheeks, but all she did was nod in confirmation. "All that useless furniture made us many a meal," she confirmed. "There should be nothing up there but thatch."

Well, as Abi and Perry discovered when they climbed the creaking staircase into the attic, that was not *quite* true. There was plenty of evidence that a pair of barn owls had raised several broods up there, and the litter on the floor proved that there were mice and sparrows making free with the single long room as well. Abi found herself sneezing quite a lot, as the dirty, disintegrating thatch disgorged dust every time they trod a little too heavily on the floorboards. Fortunately it didn't take her long to dismiss the attic floor and the chimney—the only places where anything *could* be hidden up here—and descend to the bedrooms below.

Here things were somehow sadder than the attic. There, the entire room had been stripped of everything useful. Here . . . there were still signs of what had been. Bedsteads too large to move had collapsed in on themselves before they could be taken apart and sold. Plastered walls showed stains where rain had come in— and more plaster was flaking and falling off the ceiling with every footstep they took.

Perry sat down in the middle of the room and began communing with whatever small creatures might be in the walls. Abi went to work. And when they were done with that room, they moved on to the next.

By the end of the day they had finished all the second floor rooms. That left only the first floor, and the storage rooms in the cellar beneath it, and Abi's hopes had begun to dim.

"There's still the first floor—and the cellars," Perry pointed out. "If I were going to put my bets on anything, it'd be the cellars. Don't worry," he continued, before she could even voice her concern that if there was a hiding place in anything but the walls, she would never find it. "I've got two years of training in how to find hiding places under floors. It's harder to keep those concealed than most people would like to think."

"But what if it's not *in* a hiding place, if it's just buried?" she asked, feeling her heart sink.

"Still harder to hide than people think," he said with confidence. "Besides, think about what we know. This wasn't just one old miser hiding his hoard forever. This was a place the lord of the house regularly put money into and took money out of. He couldn't just keep burying it and digging it up again. Because even if he had been stupid enough to do that, someone was going to notice before too long and there would go his hiding place. No, this was an actual, built-in spot designed for access, probably quick, easy access. Something that's been here ever since the house was built. If it's in this house, we'll find it."

"And if it's not in this house?" She had the feeling that she was more anxious about this than Sussena.

"Then maybe the answer is it was never here at all; maybe he had an account with the Goldsmith Guild instead. The King can order them to look. And if we *still* don't find anything, well, I think we should recruit Wrenmarsh to help us talk her into selling the place and using the money to buy a snug little cottage in Haven. She can still keep Tobin and Hansa, and their children can get jobs in Haven." Perry shrugged his shoulders. "It's pretty clear to me that she can't stay here much longer. I should think even in the shape it's in now, this place could provide enough money to keep her."

But Abi knew what the answer to that would be—for surely Wrenmarsh had tried to persuade her to do just that for years. And there was no guarantee that Sussena *would* net enough money to keep her in Haven, not with her needs. So what other solution could there be that would still satisfy her and satisfy the need to provide for her very loyal servants?

She didn't have any answers. Maybe there weren't any.

Two days later, it was a very dejected group that gathered together in the kitchen. Supper, eaten in an atmosphere of gloom was over. Even Tobin refrained from making carping comments. "I just don't have any answer except the bad one," Abi said, finally. "Short of tearing down the entire building—" She felt as if she was about to cry. There was a knot in her throat, and a lump in her stomach.

"And then where would we live?" Sussena said, with a little laugh, but a laugh that sounded altogether too much like a sob. "I have to thank you and you, too, Perry. You certainly did everything possible to try to find my lost inheritance. I can't imagine anyone else who would have done as much. Well, we'll just have to go on as we have, I suppose. We've managed all right so far."

But Abi could tell she was putting a brave face on it for strangers. Behind that smile, a last hope had died. A forlorn hope, to be sure, but it had been a hope. Sussena would never escape this crumbling house—unless it was by selling it before it deteriorated further. Life was going to go on lurching from one emergency to another. They were always going to be worried about the next meal, the next illness, the next piece of the house falling in. And one day it would be one emergency too many, and the careful juggling act would all fall apart.

Abi stared at the fireplace to avoid looking at Sussena, whose eyes were much too bright, suggesting she, too, was close to openly weeping. The great fireplace was the heart of the house, it was the most prominent feature of the place, with its massive chimney structure, designed to hold the heat built up in it over long winter nights. The hearth and chimney walls were massive, thicker even than the walls of the dairy. Massive enough that Abi had even considered that a hidden chamber might have been built into it in one of the bedrooms on the second floor or in the attic. But no. She'd checked all that thoroughly. It was just one solid superbly made tower of stone.

As a structure, the Artificer in her admired the work that had gone into it. On the dining room side, there was an iron spit where a whole adult pig could have been roasted in more prosperous days, and slices carved off to serve directly to the diners on festive occasions. On this side, there were two smaller spits, two cranes for kettles, a broad hearth where things could be baked on the hearthstone, and five proper ovens, two for cooking and one for keeping things warm until they were called for on the right and two for cooking on the left—

Wait a moment. Everything on the kitchen side is paired. Why is there only one warming oven?

She got up so quickly her chair fell over, and she moved to the chimney as if in a dream. Two baking ovens for meats and other baked dishes, with beautiful cast-iron doors, to the right and left of the fireplace below. Two more for bread, with wooden "stops" kept soaked in water to the right and left above them. Then, on the right, an open warming oven. And on the left . . .

She closed her eyes and reached out with her Gift. And they flew open again in startlement.

"Perry!" she cried out. "Get a chair! Help me!"

She dragged a chair over to the left side of the fireplace so she could reach the spot where a warming oven *should* have been, and she felt gingerly around the edges of the place where she sensed—yes! A void! Perry saw what she was doing and dragged a stool over to join her. His fingers, cleverer than hers, felt the hot stone carefully, then felt along the side of the chimney itself.

There was a sharp *click*.

And a crack appeared. Abi clawed at it but couldn't get a purchase on it. Perry jumped down and came back up with a fireplace poker. He inserted it carefully into the crack, and slowly, agonizingly, levered it open. Finally, it swung out on hidden hinges.

Abi tried to reach inside, but it was too hot, and she pulled back her hand with a curse.

"A candle!" Perry called. "We need a candle!"

A moment later someone thrust a lighted candle end into his hand, and the two of them peered into the darkened recess.

"There're metal strongboxes in there!" Perry exclaimed. He reached in. "Ow! They're too hot to touch!"

"Hop down, lass," commanded Hansa from behind her, and Abi obeyed. The woman had gotten the bread peel out of the corner. "Git that poker under 'un, lad. Aye, that's right—" She thrust the peel into the recess, grunted with satisfaction, then grunted again with surprise. "Kernos' Horns! Thet be heavy!" She looked over her shoulder at Tobin, whose mouth was agape in astonishment. "Stir thy stumps, old fool, an give 'un a hand!"

Belatedly he leaped to his feet, and the three of them, he, Hansa, and Perry, managed to maneuver the strongbox out of the recess and onto the table. Abi climbed back up and peered inside with the help of the candle. "There's another!" she crowed.

In the end there were three strongboxes, much too hot to touch, sitting on the kitchen table. Without being prompted, Lori fetched another pair of candles so they could all stare at them, hardly daring to breathe.

"It might only be papers," Perry pointed out.

"Too 'eavy for papers," Tobin averred.

"'Sides, papers'd hev crumbled up i' th' heat," said Hansa with authority.

They all stared some more. In the candlelight, it was obvious that all three boxes had been padlocked.

"We don't have the keys!" Sussena finally cried, a touch of hysteria in her voice.

"To the nine hells with keys," Perry said roughly and turned to Tobin. "Get me a hammer."

For once the man had nothing to say. Instead, he scrambled off into the darkness, fumbled around in the corner of the kitchen where he kept his tools, and returned with a hammer.

Perry tried holding the padlock, but it was still too hot to hold. Without being asked, Lori pulled off her apron, folded it into a pad and handed it to him.

He began tapping on one side of the lock near where the arm

went into the block. It seemed to take forever, but suddenly there was a snapping sound, and the arm came loose and pivoted out. With a cry of elation, Perry pulled the lock off the hasp, and flipped open the lid. They all bent over the box, candles held close.

It was full of small leather bags.

For a long time, no one moved. Then Perry waved everyone back. "This is yours, Sussena," he said, picking one of the bags up by the thongs. He spread the apron over her lap to protect her from the heat, then dropped the bag in her lap. "Yours is the right to find out what's in these."

With trembling hands, Sussena worked the top of the bag open, the leather cracking more than a little, until finally she could pour the hot contents onto the apron, where ten round, flat objects gleamed in the candlelight.

Gold.

—————

The first strongbox held bags of ten gold pieces each, the second bags of ten silver each, and the third and heaviest, bags of fifty copper each. Sussena held the contents of that first bag in her lap, half laughing, half crying, while Tobin sent his boy over for Wrenmarsh, who was the nearest neighbor with a horse and spare sons. Wrenmarsh himself arrived with Rafi and a crossbow. Larral stationed himself at the kitchen door, while Rafi stood guard at the front door.

"You'll be makin' a account with Goldsmith's Guild," Wrenmarsh said, sensibly, which was just as well, since all of them, including Abi, were just sitting there like a lot of dunces, wanting to play with the still warm coins. "Termorrer, you an' me, m'lady, an' Abi an'

Perry an' two on my biggest boys are takin' this t'Haven and settin'
up account wi' Goldsmith's Guild."

"Phaugh!" Tobin objected. "Wut's use-a them, I ast ye? We got
perfec'ly good place for 'un!" He waved at the open hiding place.

"Shet yer face, old fool," said Hansa. "See where trustin' t' hidey
holes got m'lady *an* all 'er kin? And it ain't no hidey hole no more,
now that eight of us know 'un! Two c'n keep a sekrit, iffen one's
daid. Goldsmith's Guild! Nothin' could be safer!"

And so that was what they did. Wrenmarsh went home, leaving
Rafi to help guard the hoard all night, and in the morning he
returned with two huge young men and a small wagon, just big
enough to carry all the people and Abi and Perry's packs. One of
the young men lifted Sussena up onto the board beside Wrenmarsh,
lifted her chair into the back of the wagon with the packs, and off
they all went.

"I thought abaht sendin' a lad on ahead," Wrenmarsh said, as
they rolled out onto the road. "But then, I thought that'd be sendin'
a signal on ahead thet we 'ad somethin' worth takin'."

"Good thinking," Perry agreed. "But we're not without our own
bag of tricks, are we, Larral?"

"Righ!" Larral agreed, sounding smug. And sure enough, they
had just about made the halfway mark back to Haven when four
Guardsmen cantered up, much to the relief of Wrenmarsh's
two sons, who stopped clutching their cudgels so hard that their
knuckles were white.

After that, the rest of the trip was anticlimactic.

"So how much was in there, anyway?" asked Kat, after Abi had finished her story.

The two of them were lounging on Abi's bed, which she was very glad to see once again. The cots had been all right at first, but the longer you lay on them, the more hard spots you seemed to find.

"More than enough to completely rebuild and refurnish the manor and the outbuildings, hire more people, plow up all the arable land, get all the herb seeds Sussena could possibly plant, and enough left over for any emergency." Abi felt very smug now that it was all over. And . . . maybe a little stupid, too. "Wrenmarsh has three Master Thatchers and their helpers on the manor and it should be finished before the snow falls. Sussena is finally going to get to sleep in a real bed in her own bedroom for the first winter in her life. In fact, she's getting one of the bedrooms that has the chimney coming up through it, and her own fireplace. I just can't believe I didn't even consider the chimney as a hiding place."

"But you did. Just not in the kitchen," Kat pointed out. "And why would the lord of the manor ever be found in the kitchen anyway?"

"That's a good point. It just proves how clever he was, I suppose." She considered that.

"Well, that's the problem with being clever," Kat replied with a laugh, lying back on Abi's bed. "Being clever gets you in trouble. Being *smart* gets you out of trouble. You do know what this means for you, though, don't you?"

"That my Gift works really well?" she hazarded.

"That you're going to be very much feared by anyone with a hidden chamber or secret passage, because you can reliably find it," Kat corrected. "On the other hand, anyone that actually has such a thing is probably going to be on his best behavior from now on so you won't go looking for it." She sucked on her lower lip. "I wonder if you can find hidden compartments in ships and wagons?" But before Abi could answer that question, Kat suddenly sat straight up again. "Oh! I just had a tremendous idea for Sussena! She hasn't committed to anything past mending the roof and refurbishing the manor yet has she?"

"I don't think so," Abi replied. "It's the wrong time of year to be doing any building, anyway. The only reason there are thatchers crawling all over the roof now is because Wrenmarsh is a very influential man among the farmers thereabouts."

"Excellent. Let me get a map from your father and then we'll go see mine." Before Abi could object to disturbing the King so close to dinner, Kat had already left her room and gone to Mags' workshop room. By the time Abi was out of her room, Kat had a rolled-up map under her arm and was heading out the door. Abi could only follow.

The guards at the Royal Suite seemed a bit nonplussed to see the Princess moving so quickly. So was Abi, for that matter. Kat generally presented herself as a little bit lazy and it wasn't often she bestirred herself. *Maybe being Chosen has had an enlivening effect on her . . .*

Abi had just reached the doors when Kat called out from inside. "Papa! Are you busy?"

Abi heard the King answering, though too far away for her to make out what he had said. But she assumed the answer was in the negative because Kat was not in the public rooms of the suite. Logically, then she must be in the King's private study.

When she finally got to the (surprisingly small) room, Kat had spread out the map on her father's desk, and they were both bending over it. "So you see!" Kat crowed. "It's just a little off of center for the—oh, there's Abi now."

"Kat seems to have worked out a plan that will save Lady Susenna a great deal of money, and be quite beneficial for the Crown as well," the King said, looking at his daughter with a bemused expression, as if this was the last thing he would have expected of her.

"Well, I just remembered something from the Logistics class I'm taking—that currently we—the Crown that is—are running a little short of both horse farms for the Guard and Guard training posts. And when I asked the teacher what the Guard looks for in a place, he said that right now they were looking for properties within a two candlemark cart distance of Haven. Lady Sussena's manor farm is three candlemarks, which is not too far, and it's got just enough land still attached to it to serve as either, at least according to this map."

"What—" Abi began, then "Oh!" she said. "So if she was willing to rent the place out to the Crown, *the Crown* would be putting in all the improvements on anything other than the manor itself, at no expense to her!"

"And she'd be getting regular rent regardless of how harvests in that area are," Kat replied, nodding vigorously. "So she gets the best of both situations, she can stay in her family home *and* get a regular income without actually having to do any additional labor."

"I am going to send a note to the Lord Marshal and the Seneschal right now and arrange for them to meet with you, Kat, before your first class tomorrow," King Sedric replied, as seriously as he would have to an adult making the recommendations. "I'm pleased that you're taking the welfare of our subjects so much to heart, and I'm

equally pleased you've thought of something that benefits the Crown
as well as milady." Then he smiled broadly. "Well done, my love!"

Kat made a little bow to her father. "Thank you!" she beamed.

This was clearly a dismissal, and Kat took her map and left the
King to whatever business she had interrupted. Abi went with her.
Kat was back to her usual leisurely pace as they returned to Mags'
suite. Kat returned the map to its labeled cubby and curled up on
a cushion on the floor of the central room, looking unspeakably
pleased with herself.

Well, she should be!

"I think I just figured out what I want to do with myself," Kat said
as Abi joined her on the floor. "I want to go all over the Kingdom
looking for problems like Lady Sussena's and fixing them."

"Don't Heralds do that anyway?" Abi asked.

"Well, they *do*, but people have to wait for their Herald to get to
them on his Circuit, and they don't always want their problems made
public," Kat pointed out. "The only reason we knew about this one
was because Wrenmarsh has a connection to your father and decided
to say something. You know what I like best about this solution?"

"That you came up with it?" Abi teased.

"No, silly. Well . . . yes . . . but—this would have worked even if
you hadn't found the missing inheritance. We could have paid her
the first year's rent in advance and done the repairs with Crown
money, and she'd have had enough money to furnish the private
rooms and some left over for winter provisions." Kat flopped over
onto her stomach. "What do you think she'll prefer, breeding horses
or training Guardsmen?"

"Breeding horses," Abi replied promptly. "I don't think she'd care for having hordes of strangers all over her property. And Tobin would be a nonstop grumble mill."

"He sounded like a grumpy old goat," Kat agreed. Then she frowned. "I wonder if the only reason he stayed was because he hoped to find the inheritance himself?"

That had occurred to Abi as well, although she hadn't voiced her suspicions. "That's not why his wife stayed," she said, slowly. "But he did seem eager to persuade Lady Sussena to leave the treasure where we found it instead of making an account with the Goldsmith's Guild. I don't know if that just means he hates change—which he does—or because he wanted a chance to steal some of it."

"Well, if that was the main reason, we'll soon be hearing from Wrenmarsh that the entire family abandoned milady," Kat said, after a moment of thought. "And if he's nothing but a cantankerous old goat, then he'll certainly stick with her, expecting some reward out of all that service for next to nothing all these years."

"That's a perfectly reasonable expectation," Abi agreed. Secretly she hoped that Tobin was just a chronic complainer who had served because of loyalty and feeling sorry for Lady Sussena. *Lady Sussena would probably be heartbroken if he and his family ran off on her.*

"Well, no point in trying to solve problems that haven't even happened yet," Kat said cheerfully. "Or that people really ought to be able to solve for themselves. I'll make sure to suggest to the Seneschal if he likes my idea that the farm should be given over to breeding horses and mules for the Guard. It's in the middle of a lot of other farms, after all, and I'm sure the other farmers would have some objections to a lot of people tramping around and fighting and making noise."

"Not to mention having fruit filched from their trees," Abi pointed out. "Guard Trainees are at a prime fruit-snatching age and probably would look on it as a clever adventure to outwit the farmers."

"Havens, you're right. Even the Trainees up here aren't immune to that," Kat groaned.

"Says the Princess who found out that the ornamental apple trees in the garden produce fruit that tastes like sour wood," Abi teased.

"Don't know why we can't have trees that have *nice* fruit instead of ornamental ones. . . ." Kat grumbled. "And that makes me hungry."

You didn't have to be a Mindspeaker to know what was going to come next. Abi jumped up and offered Kat a hand up, and they both went down to the Collegium dining hall, where it was pocket pie night.

They collected their shares—helpfully marked on the crust so you could tell which kind was which—and went outside, where several Trainees had built a bonfire of windfall just inside Companion's field. It was already quite dark, and there was just enough of a chill in the air that Abi was glad of the thicker wool of the tunic she'd put on this morning.

It was not the first time that Abi had experienced a feeling of disconnection when sitting down among the Trainees. Here the topics of most passionate discussion were the Kirball teams, who was paired up with whom, and examination results. It all seemed a little unreal, compared to Lady Sussena's very real troubles, and the excitement of hunting for actual treasure.

Then again . . . who else here has the parents I do? Who else here trained to be Kat's bodyguard from the time I was old enough to hold a knife?

Kat seemed unusually contented tonight, as she bantered with the others and munched her pocket pies. Then again, as she'd said, she'd finally figured out what she wanted to do—aside from being a Herald, that is. Trey and Niko had always known what they wanted to do, although Abi suspected that either of them would have been just as happy had their roles been reversed. But Kat hadn't really had a concrete goal in mind. "Problem solver" seemed to suit her.

"So where have you been all this time, Abi?" someone asked from across the fire.

"Oh," she said, with a little smile. *All righty; you aren't Mags' daughter without being able to come up with a plausible story that is also actually true in a matter of moments.* "An emergency building inspection."

———

A very proud Kat rode out with two Guards and Abi three days later to present her solution to Lady Sussena Asterleigh. A sudden frost had turned all the leaves on the trees to brilliant colors overnight, and both of them wore thick wool cloaks against the chill morning air, although by the time they arrived at Asterleigh Manor, they'd been able to roll them up and tie them behind their saddles.

The Manor looked very different this morning; there were men crawling all over the roof now; three Master Thatchers and their helpers made quite a crowd. The entire end had been rethatched, and there were three separate crews of men working—one stripping the old thatch, one replacing the lathes that underlay it, and one laying new thatch. They would certainly be done by the end of the month and long before the autumn rains. The new thatch, gleaming golden in the sun, made the old, gray, disintegrating thatch look even sadder than it had when she'd first seen it.

Hob was out in the front of the building, helping the thatchers by tying a rope to each bundle of new thatch so they could haul it up, when he turned and spotted them. He ran into the house and came back out with Tobin in tow.

So the whole family is still here, Abi thought with relief, *he wasn't just a treasure hunter.*

"'Ere naow—" Tobin began, but warned by Abi, Kat was prepared for him.

"I am Princess Katiana," she said, in a voice that reminded Abi strongly of her father's Command Voice. "I am here to see Lady Asterleigh."

That literally staggered Tobin, who stepped back a couple of paces. Then he began bowing awkwardly—probably the presence of two Guards as well as Kat's Companion was enough to keep him from questioning her identity, "Aye, 'Ighness," he croaked. "Right this way, Majesty."

Abi tried not to giggle.

At least Tobin led them in the front door into the dining hall, where Sussena was seated in her chair, working on what looked like a new gown of brand new fabric—a nice, thick brown wool. She smiled at Abi in recognition, but she looked bewildered at Kat, who was dressed in very fine Dress Grays. Now Abi stepped in.

"Lady Sussena, this is Princess Katiana. She comes from the King with an offer for you."

Sussena dropped the gown and it slid to the floor, where Lori retrieved it and backed out of the way, clearly not sure of what else to do.

Kat stepped forward, reaching into a belt pocket and removing a folded map that was an expanded view of all the farms around and including Asterleigh Manor, as up-to-date as she could manage on such short notice. Abi fetched a small table from beside the hearth and Kat spread the map out on it and detailed her proposition. At this point, she'd had a couple of days to elaborate on it with the help of the Guard Herdmaster, so she proceeded with confidence.

". . . we'd leave your kitchen garden, the chicken coop, and even expand the kitchen garden to allow for more produce for the new workers we'd bring on. Your old cow barn would become the broodmare barn, the dairy would become quarters for the Master of Horses, and your old stable quarters for his helpers. These fields, here, here, and here would all be allowed to go fallow, your existing meadows would remain meadows. We reckon to add about ten workers to the property: the Horse Master, the Farrier, and eight hands."

"You wouldn't be putting anyone in the manor house?" Sussena asked.

"Not unless you wanted them there. The Crown is prepared to start paying you rent and start work fixing and renovating the buildings immediately. We think we might have them done in time to bring the mares here in early summer, and the first crop of foals will be the spring after next," Kat told her. "That is, if you are prepared to accept the Crown's offer."

By this time Tobin had gotten over his awe and had crept into the room to listen. "Be a mort less work nor raisin' her-ubs," he pointed out. "An' steady income. Nobbut so much's hevin' a damn good year, but a sight better'n hevin' a wet one where ever'thin' rots i' field," he finished, with a decisive nod.

"Would we be expected to feed all these people?" she asked.

Kat nodded. "The Crown would supply the provisions, plus

produce from your kitchen garden, as the Crown would supply all provender for the horses other than grass, but your staff would be expected to cook and clean for the new workers."

Sussena looked at Tobin. "Th' auld 'oman c'n do't wit' two, three more kitchen girls an two, three more 'ousemaids."

"You'd have been adding that much staff anyway, what with all the new farm workers you'd have needed to care for the herbs," Abi pointed out, as Sussena wavered a little. "I'm sure Hansa can handle them."

"I'm sure Hansa could handle an army," Sussena said, and then she smiled. "Tobin, you are finally going to get a well-deserved promotion, then. You will be my farm manager; all these new horse people will answer to you. Hansa will be the housekeeper. We might as well hire on someone to cook so she can concentrate on managing." She turned to Kat. "I believe, your Highness, that we will accept the Crown's offer. You may send your crews to start work immediately."

Kat grinned and extracted a small pen and a tiny, stoppered jar of ink from her belt pouch. "I was hoping you would, milady. Now, if you can just sign here. . . ."

IO

Abi rested both her hands on the parapet that abruptly cut off the end of Stonebridge road and stared down into the deceptively calm waters of the river below. High summer brought the lowest water of the year, and the slowest current. Three years and four moons ago there had been a bridge here; it had disintegrated, practically beneath her and Kat, and only her Gift had given them both warning in time to save the people who had been on that bridge at the time. Since that time, all the Master Artificers had studied the river in flood and declared that there was no safe way to rebuild that bridge—unless one was to create a bridge entirely out of sword steel, which was clearly impossible. And since that time, there had been a steady clamor from the people of Haven that the bridge *must* be replaced.

In one sense it had been; there was now a suspended rope-and-plank footbridge here, which could carry riders on horses, but nothing heavier, and which was far too dangerous to cross in icy weather. But that was not a replacement. People wanted what once had stood here, a substantial object able to hold the largest of wains and the cargo such wains could carry.

Not possible. The original bridge had been borne on the back of three stone half-circle arches which in turn had rested on piers sunk into the riverbed. The piers were still there; as Abi peered down at the water, she saw them beneath it, shimmering a green white, stone beneath algae, just under the rippling surface. But every Master Artificer said that the columns built on the piers had been the weak point, the place where the bridge had failed; that the thundering waters in flood and the debris they carried would weaken every conceivable bridge support built on those piers. That nothing could withstand the battering, the temperature changes season by season, the continued etching of sand and pebbles and even boulders and tree trunks when the river was in flood. That no stone, no mortar, not even supports carved of single pillars of stone, could hold forever. The bridge would eventually fail, probably without warning, and without someone with Abi's singular and rare Gift to sound the warning, there would, when that failure came, be an intolerable loss of life.

Without the bridge here, Abi felt just fine. Better than fine, in fact. No shadow haunted this place for her. But she stood here studying the river, the banks, and the piers because she was not entirely sure all the Master Builders were right.

There had to be a way to bring a broad bridge here again. If only she could think of it. And she desperately wanted to think of a solution, because it was time for her to produce a Master Work, and this place, this lost bridge, called out to her personally.

Or maybe I shouldn't take it personally. Maybe I should pick something I'm not so emotionally invested in. . . .

Of course, that's not what I want to do. And something one of the Masters had told the class rung true to her. *"Pick a project you are passionate about. Your passion will help you find a way."*

Oh, of course technically this span could be bridged by a single arch instead of three—but that would create a bridge so tall that the ramps up to it would be impossibly steep, and the bridge itself would be ridiculously high. Anything of a reasonable height would place the footings down in the water or, at least, too close to the water, and then there would be the same problem all over again, this time with two points of failure instead of four.

Not an option.

Two points of failure would certainly bring the bridge down as fast as four, if not faster.

She studied the banks where the bridge had stood with her Gift, looking for places where the strain showed signs of weakness, and found nothing. Everything flawed had been carried away when the first bridge came down. If she could just find a way to make the span carry all its strain into those banks, it would stand, if not forever, then certainly so far into the future that it probably *could* be replaced with sword steel, because by then, people would have been able to figure out how to make beams and trusses of sword steel.

Finally, as night came on, she turned away from the river and continued in the direction she'd been heading in the first place. Midsummer Fair. *Now* she was old enough to prowl the aisles of the Fair at night on her father's behest. And in male disguise because she wasn't *stupid*, and Mags had no interest in ordinary crime. That was for the Guard and the Watch, not the King's Spy.

The Fair at night was an entirely different creature than the Fair by day. Probably three fourths of the booths were closed, canvas sides pulled down over the tables where goods would have been displayed and lashed down tight. The booths themselves, however, shone in the darkness, like giant lanterns, because no one left his booth unguarded and unprotected. The trays of goods, removed from the display tables, had been piled in the center of each booth, and there were at least two people sleeping there as well.

As for those whose booths were still open, most held two people, one to sell and one to keep a hawk-sharp eye on the goods. The Watch could only do so much, and shadows are a thief's best friend.

Each booth had at least three lanterns suspended over the goods, and even the most mundane or tawdry objects tended to sparkle and gleam enticingly in their light. As Abi drifted along with the crowd, she kept her ears tuned for scraps of conversation that had nothing to do with commerce. Her training in the day Fair had been mostly preparation for this.

Somewhere Perry was prowling as well, but more than likely, he was slipping like a shadow in the spaces behind the booths.

". . . can find better gemstone beads from Hollistown," said a man with a faint accent, dismissively.

Both the accent and the words alerted her. Hollistown produced apples and applewood, and there were no mines, of gems or anything else there. And the accent could only come from the southeastern Border of Valdemar. And that was the Border shared with Karse.

She almost rolled her eyes. When would they *ever* stop trying?

On the twelfth of never.

She slipped both hands into her pockets and lightly squeezed a sponge filled with an odorless, clear, colorless liquid her father extracted from urine. Well, it was colorless to humans. . . .

She timed her move exquisitely, so that when she stepped in between two people trying to get around the booth, one of them stumbled into her, sending her stumbling into the man who had spoken. "Bloody *hell!*" she swore, as she grabbed the edge of the booth table and the drape over it in her left hand, and steadied herself against the man with her right, leaving invisible palm-prints on both.

"I beg your pardon!" she said to the booth owner and the man she had tagged. Both of them assessed her clothing—which was commensurate with that of a young man of means—and their expressions changed. The merchant's became dismissive; the speaker's, sour, but no longer angry. "Damned crowds, don't you know! Pardon!" And she moved on.

"Puppy'll have his pocket picked before the night's half over," the merchant said to the speaker, as she moved on.

Got it. That was not her thoughts. That was her father's Mindvoice in her head, for Mags' Gift was strong enough he could make almost anyone hear him, whether or not they were Gifted. The only ones he couldn't reach were the very rare souls with natural Shields that were as strong as his Gift. *Sending Larral and Perry to shadow them.*

The liquid might be colorless to humans, but not to Larral. Perry would mark the booth from the rear in some subtle fashion that humans could see, and then follow the speaker wherever he went, while another of Mags' agents would set up a watch on the booth. If the speaker stayed on past the Fair, he'd already have been marked as a spy, and before a sennight was over, every one of Mags' operatives in Haven would know his face.

It was, all in all, a highly efficient operation. It was also unique to Mags and his family—but Abi supposed that her grandfather Herald Nikolas had had his own unique operation, and whoever came after Mags—probably Perry—would have his. The business of being the King's Spy meant you had to be flexible and adaptable, after all.

Abi worked her way around the vendors without encountering anything else that aroused her suspicions. She ignored the food tents; they were all staffed and owned by local people. If they were running a huge tavernlike operation, Mags already had one or more operatives working there as servers. If it was a simple one-food booth, Mags already knew whether they were someone that should have an eye kept on them.

Larral and Perry had been given their targets, so they'd be busy; that meant it was time for her to prowl the entertainment tents.

Specifically, the "mens' shows."

There were many licensed houses of pleasure in Haven, and the proprietors would absolutely brook no competition from a lot of outsiders with no accountability and no reputation. And those houses sent enough of the girls down to the Fair at night to ensure that no one would successfully freelance for long. But since the pleasure houses were in the business of sex rather than entertainment, they had no problem whatsoever with shows that offered titillation without satisfaction. In fact, many of the pleasure houses had agreements with the shows to allow their girls in for free. Everyone won; the performers didn't get pawed or mauled, and the girls got customers.

That might have seemed unlikely, but the girls in these shows were performing from sundown to almost dawn, continuously, and they had no time or energy for prostitution. And the proprietors made more money offering dancing than they would have done offering sex. The per-head admission fee might not be much, but the men were packed in shoulder to shoulder, so the owners more than made their money on quantity of customers.

The shows were a good place for agents to meet and pass on information, however. When a performer had just dropped her last veil, eyes and ears would be on her, and miss one man slipping a sheaf of papers to another in the crowd.

"Tha's why I want you there, Abi," her father had said, grinning. *"I know you won' be distracted."*

Well, that was not altogether true . . . there were a couple of girls who performed feats of unclothed acrobatics that had Abi both startled and envious of their flexibility. But for the most part, her father was completely correct about her ability to remain undistracted.

She caught one exchange of information and tagged both parties; the second man very nearly turned on her in anger, but she was prepared for that. "Ready for the real thing, milord?" she whispered, and slipped him a bit of pasteboard printed with the sign of a brothel where one of her father's agents was also the proprietress. And as luck would have it, she spotted one of the girls in the crowd. "Iris there, she'll make you smile," she added, and caught the girl's eye, nodding toward her target. Iris's eyes lit up, and she moved through the crowd to their side.

"I'm Iris," she cooed, taking the man's arm. "And who might you be, my handsome lad?"

Abi moved away; she couldn't help but notice that her target made no attempt to remove Iris's hand from his arm.

Nicely done, Abi, she congratulated herself.

And that was as eventful as the evening got. Now that she was supposed to be working on her Master Work, she didn't have classes to worry about, so she was able to prowl the Fair until the entertainments shut down, just before dawn. Since Mags hadn't contacted her, she decided to leave the fairgrounds and wait for sunrise in the ruins of an old temple that Mags used to train Auntie Minda's littles in rooftop running. Abi, Perry, and now Tory trained there too. Some said the building dated all the way back to the Founding; its collapse from disuse certainly predated the time of Vanyel. The ruins were picturesque in themselves, and the grounds were littered with enough debris to discourage camping by those who had traveled to Haven just for the Fair.

She knew this place by heart and could climb it in the dark. She scrambled to one of her favorite places to just sit, the top of an arch where the still intact arc of stone fed into a half-ruined wall. It looked like the sort of place where there had once been colored glass windows, but any fragments of glass had vanished decades ago, if not a hundred years or more. She tucked herself into the secure spot where arch met wall and waited for sunrise.

The curve of the stone was particularly gentle, so the perching place felt secure but not uncomfortable. The stone was still warm after baking in the sun all day. What was left of the architecture was actually quite interesting; this building used techniques that had been lost or abandoned over the years. Which only made sense since fashions in buildings, as in clothing, fell into and out of favor.

But there were some things here that you just didn't see anywhere else, not even in the very oldest parts of the Palace, which predated almost everything. Things like the subtle curve of this arch, for instance, a segment of a circle instead of—

Suddenly her mind felt as if it had caught fire.

A segment of a circle, instead of a half-circle!

Something her teachers swore could not support its own weight, let alone the weight of a building.

Or a bridge . . .

Trying not to feel too excited, she reached out with her Gift. After all, this could be a fluke. It might not be a weight-bearing structure. This might be an effect to fool the eye. This might—

The stress of weight and pressure flowed smoothly over and through the ancient stone beneath her, transferring its weight, and the weight of the stone above it, into the walls on either side, and down in a sure, strong column into the bedrock beneath. An arch of a segment, perhaps no more than a fourth, of a circle. An arch with such a subtle curve she hadn't noticed it was an arch until just this moment.

An arch which her teachers swore could not stand. They would have said it was only an ornament, that it was not, could not be, load-bearing, and yet, it was.

Yet it stood here, strong, after other parts of the building had fallen to pieces.

Why did no one notice this before?

Because they weren't looking for it. You weren't looking for it until now, and you've been all over these stones since you were eight.

She wanted to wait here until the sun rose and drink in every detail of this construction. She wanted to sit and contemplate it, run to the Fair for drawing materials, sketch and measure every thumb-length of it.

That's what she wanted to do. Instead, she very sensibly climbed down, made her way through the sleeping city and up to the Palace. She greeted the Guards at the gate and made her way up to the family suite. It was dark, and silent; Mags, Perry, and Larral were probably still down at the Fair.

So, still acting sensibly, she went to bed. The arch would still be there when she woke up, and the last thing she wanted to do was to make a mistake in measuring and sketching.

But sleep was long in coming. And when it did, her dreams were full of the gentle curves of beautiful stone arches.

"In this case," Healer Sanje said to Abi, "It is time to trust your Gift and work backward to the numbers."

"But that—" Abi began.

The Healer interrupted her with a single upraised finger. "But that is precisely what you have been trained to do. The Artificers intend for you to use your Gift first, and justify it afterward. Any Artificer can begin with the numbers, and that is why they have all insisted that an arch can only be a full half circle. You have a unique Gift that shows you additional truths; they intend you to use it to find those truths, then justify those truths in a way that other Artificers can understand. And, in fact, your doing so now will be your true Master Work, not the bridge."

Sanje had met Abi at Abi's request in the herb garden. She waited patiently while Abi mulled over what she had just been told.

"That makes sense," she said, finally. "But how do I do that? I don't want to go out there and take that arch apart. For one thing, I'm not sure I can without wrecking it before I can learn anything, and for another, it's not mine."

Sanje shrugged gracefully. "I do not know your Gift as you do, nor the discipline of the Builders, but . . . perhaps start small?"

"With a model. And test to destruction." Abi nodded and grinned wryly. "And this is *so* backward from how I have been taught to work!"

"Sometimes this is not a bad thing." Sanje rose. "Good luck Abidela. Not that I think you will need it."

———

The exact model of the Temple arch held an astonishing amount of weight. Half-circle arches directed all of the weight of the loads they were carrying straight down into the pillars that they rested on, or into the ground; but the segment carried it into the supports at either end, which stood in for the riverbanks. But the exact model of that arch still had too high a rise to be practical for the heavy wains it would have to carry. So once again, Abi worked backward, deciding the maximum rise practical and the maximum angle the wains could manage, then finding the segment that fit that parameter, then building the model and testing the load it would bear.

And then she worked backward to prove her design.

It was early autumn when she presented her proposal paper to Master Ketnar. And it was nearly a moon before he called her before the tribunal of Master Builders who would render judgment on her proposal.

To say she was nervous was an understatement. She stood before the three of them, her hands clasped behind her back to prevent them from shaking, her hair already damp with sweat.

The three Builders in their sober robes looked like a trio of judges, and she just could not read any of them. Were they skeptical, even after viewing her proofs and her explanation of how she had gotten them? Would they deny her the Work? And if they did—what was she going to do?

"This proposed Work is . . . extremely ambitious, Abidela," said Master Ketnar where he sat between the other two. "I actually cannot recall a more ambitious proposal in my entire tenure as a Master Builder. And that includes my own." He smiled, faintly, and Abi tried not to get her hopes up.

"Normally," said the Master on her right, "we would deny such a project outright, since you do not have a patron prepared to pay for it, and it is a public work that the Crown is likely to deny on the grounds that you are untried and unpracticed."

Her heart sank.

"However," the third one continued, "we have replicated and tested your models. We have triple-checked your math. We even went to view the arch that gave you the inspiration in the first place. We find no fault with your proposal. Because there has been a steady clamor from the populace of Haven to replace that bridge, because of your unique Gift, and because the King has informed us on occasions far too numerous to mention that he would very much appreciate if we managed to *rebuild that thrice-damned bridge before he punches the next petitioner in the nose,* we are approving it."

The approval broke over Abi like a wave, and for a moment she thought she might actually faint with happiness.

"However," Master Ketnar said, raising a finger. "This is a *very* ambitious work. And we foresee that there will be problems in bringing this project fully up to scale. So we are adding a caveat. We are approving it only if three current Master Builders work on it with you, Master Builders who will be familiar with your design and concept and are in complete accord with it, and at least three students who will also receive their Master Builder accolade when the bridge is complete. I think you already know and will approve of the three students—Brice, Emmit, and Rudi."

I think I may explode. "And the Masters?" she asked, trying very hard not to squeal.

"Us," Master Ketnar said, as the other two broke into huge smiles. "I don't believe any of us have been so excited about a project since the building of the Temple of Alessar."

"And I wish I had known about semicircular arches then," sighed the Master on the right.

Master Ketnar continued. "Rudi is second to none of my students in working with wood as a building material, and we believe you will need his expertise and mine in constructing your scaffolding and your full-scale pattern. Master Edders has taught everything he knows about stone, the carving of stone, and the selection of stone to Brice; they will alternate at the quarry and at the building site. And Master Renold specializes in reinforcement, as does Emmit. Master Renold foresees a possible problem in scaling up, and he already has a solution should the full-scale model reveal he is correct." He rubbed his hands together in anticipation. "So, Trainee Abidela, are you ready to go to work?"

———

Building the full-scale model out of wood took all fall and winter. It wouldn't have been possible for the work to have continued through the winter at all except that the Sisters of Betane of the Ax cleared their sanctuary as a place to do the construction. "We owe Herald Mags and the Crown itself for uncovering the fiend who was persecuting women two decades ago," the Prioress said. "And the project will be of immense value to the City in which we live." Then she smiled. "Besides, this pattern-model will be of wood, yes? An ax hews more than men. Betane will approve."

As expected, problems did arise in the building of the full-scale model. The first problem was with the spandrels, the supports on either end of the bridge. According to the math and Abi's design, the bridge had to be thin at the middle but broaden downward at each end in order to distribute the weight properly against the bank. The load-bearing arch would actually form the bottom of the span; the spandrels and roadbed would be built atop that. But careful measuring showed that the spandrels would be under water during the worst flooding, according to all of the records they consulted.

That would put potentially intolerable force against the spandrels and create a problem similar to the one that brought down the last bridge.

At this point the model was mostly on paper and a set of huge plans drawn on linen fabric for durability. Abi's Gift was not going to help her here.

She stared at the plans showing one of the spandrels, frowning, and thought, noting how the roadbed lay above the arch. *I don't want pillars between the roadbed and the arch because that would just replicate the problem the first bridge had. We need holes of some kind in the spandrels, but what will distribute the forces evenly and put them right back where I want them, into the riverbank?*

Then, after two days of staring at the plans, it occurred to her. Curves had distributed the forces evenly in the initial design. Why not go back and use arches again? Would arches within arches work?

Well, why not? If I break it down, there is still force being moved along a curve.

Carefully and deliberately, she sketched in three more semicircular arches of ascending size within the right hand spandrel, did a very quick set of calculations in her head, and called to the three Masters, who were discussing something else. "I think I have a flood solution," she said.

They hurried over to her, and once they saw her sketch, all four of them went to work.

She didn't go to bed until late that night, and not for several nights thereafter, but when the marathon was over and some small adjustments made, they were all satisfied. The arches within the spandrel would work, and work magnificently. Not only that, but they reduced the weight of the bridge by more than fifteen percent!

Plank by plank, the wooden version of the bridge took shape, fitted together like a puzzle, and every bit of it pegged and glued until it formed a single, solid structure. This was because it was going to be taken apart—cut apart, in fact, and each separate piece used as the template for a corresponding stone block or slab, creating a giant puzzle in stone that would be reassembled on the banks of the river. The main arch would eventually be made of twenty-eight "relatively" thin slabs of limestone, each long enough for two big wains and a balustrade. On top of that would come the three spandrel-arches on each side of the bridge, and on top of those would come the rest of the spandrel and the roadbed. The roadbed itself would have an incline of no more than a few degrees.

Meanwhile, Rudi and Master Ketnar created the plans for the scaffolding to support the work. Because the scaffolding would only have to last as long as the construction went on, they could use the existing piers to support it, and during a dry and clement spot of weather, work actually began laying stone on the old piers while the water was low. This work to support the wooden scaffolding got laid in long before the model itself was more than a quarter built.

Every night, Abi went to bed late, tired but happy. The only regret she had was that she saw so little of her family and Kat. Maybe one supper in seven or eight was at home. They were far enough from the Hill that generally the lot of them shared meals with the Sisters of Betane. Such meals were fairly simple and a far cry from when she and the Royals would beg food from the Palace kitchen, but truth to tell, they were all so involved in the work that half the time Abi didn't even notice what she was eating. But as Midwinter passed and Spring approached inexorably, she realized she missed doing the spycraft work for her father that was keeping Perry so busy, she missed being with her family, and she began to wonder if Mags resented that she was no longer available.

Finally she came home late one night, long after dinner, to see a light still on in the room Mags called his workshop, and on impulse she headed there instead of to her own bed.

Mags was deeply involved in constructing something—from where she stood, it looked as if he had hollowed a booklike box and was in the process of turning it into an identical replica of a book—a replica in which you could hide something. Amily stood beside him, holding an actual book—the one he was using as his model. She cleared her throat.

"Work done for the day, Abi?" her mother asked. "Come squeeze in, your father is almost done with this part of the project."

Now she saw that he was engraving lines in the edges of the box that represented the pages, to replicate the actual pages of the book her mother was holding. The wood-chisel he used was hardly bigger than a horse-hair, and sent up a long, curling thread of wood that was surprisingly pretty. After all the work on the pattern-model she had a much keener appreciation for fine woodworking than she had had before.

"Thet'll do fer now," Mags said, sitting up straight and laying the "book" and the chisel aside. "Strike me, iffen I'd known 'twas so much work t'make one on these things, I'da never started i' th' fust place." He turned in his seat to face his daughter. "Long days, m'lass. Hope they're wuth it."

"I can't even begin to tell you," she said, brightening, as she thought about the latest puzzle they had solved, the one Master Renold had anticipated—a way to strengthen the span by using iron dovetails between the blocks. "But that's not why I'm here. I—I want to apologize because—"

"Hush," Amily interrupted, raising her hand. "You are not to apologize for not being here. You are not to apologize because you haven't been out doing your father's work. Your father managed that perfectly well before you were old enough to help. And it's time for you to do your *own* work."

"She's a-right," Mags said, putting his arm around Amily's waist and holding her tightly. "Perry's been doin' all right, an' wut Perry cain't do, Auntie Minda's littles can, an' wut they cain't do, I got plenny people i'Haven t'pick up. But you—" He pointed a finger at Abi. "On'y you c'n do wut Abi c'n do. Didn' ye prove that already? *Nobody* been able t'figger out how t' rebuild that blamed bridge, but you did! We need ye t' do thet, not creep aroun' t'Fair."

For a moment she thought she might cry at those comforting words. "I was afraid you were disappointed, that I wasn't like you or Mama, that I wasn't a Herald or at least helping you like Perry—"

Mags laughed. "Pleny'a Heralds. On'y need one King's Own. Perry'll make a good King's Spy, an' Lord Jorthun wut used ta' be King's Spy was niver a Herald. There's on'y one Abi, wi' th' Gift t' see how thin's stay up or fall down. You go right on bein' thet Abi. 'Sides, it's nice t'hev some'un I c'n brag on wi'out givin' away a secret!"

There had been quite a bit more of that from both her parents before Abi went to bed, sure now that she had not disappointed anyone. The talk had been a huge relief, erasing a burden she hadn't even been aware she had been carrying—and yet it had been one that had been eating at her for a very long time, ever since she'd started her Master Work, in fact. It had been at that moment that she had understood she was no longer involved in the Artificers and Builders because she wanted to use her abilities to help her father but because this was something she desperately wanted for herself. This bridge had become like a living thing for her, something beautiful as well as useful that she felt she *had* to see created—and besides that, it was something she wanted her name on, in public, for everyone to see.

And as long as all she did was work for her father, creeping in the shadows, doing things she couldn't talk about, she would never be recognized for what she was capable of.

She thought now that she understood part of Lady Dia's passion for breeding her dogs; as long as there were dogs out of one of her famous lines, her name would be recorded for others who cared about such things. Lord Jorthun didn't share the same impulse, but he already had his name and his familial record—all highborn did. But this was the same impulse that must fuel a merchant to label his business with his name, not just the name of what he sold.

She knew that there were plenty of people who didn't feel that way, but she did—and that wasn't a bad thing.

Mags cared on her behalf but also on his own. That bridge would carry her name, but it would also carry his. . . . *it's nice t'hev some'un I c'n brag on wi'out givin' away a secret* . . . Even if no one ever knew what he'd done once the current leaders were gone, he'd still be the father of Abidela, who had rebuilt the bridge everyone had been sure could never be replaced safely. He would still be the father of Abidela, who discovered, or rediscovered, a new principle of building, one that would make stronger, safer bridges and buildings for hundreds of years to come.

Perry didn't seem to care . . . *But on the other hand, Perry's name was attached to a tale already. No wonder he doesn't show that kind of ambition— it's been satisfied. How many people get to save the entire Kingdom from a one-man horror?* There had been nothing that needed to be kept secret about Perry and Mags' confrontation with that psychopathic lunatic out in the Pelagirs; in fact, since the Council had had to be informed about what was going on, it would have been impossible to do so. So Perry was a hero; at least among a very chosen few, and his name was certainly in the Chronicles.

And now that she thought about it, Mags himself wasn't entirely anonymous. *Papa has done things that are in the Chronicles—the madman in the Pelagirs and uncovering the devious plot of the priests of Sethor the Patriarch. So he knows what it's like to be valued.*

He really, really does. And he wants me to have that on my own.

Now buoyed by gratitude as well as relief, she set her mind on the problem of how many slices the bridge would have to be cut up into until she fell into sleep.

II

"I'm sorry that I almost never see you anymore," Kat said, surveying the bridge model, which at the moment was being sliced up into careful pieces according to the marks painted on all four sides. "But I'm also not sorry, because we're getting *this*. You do know it's pretty much all people can talk about, right?"

Abi nodded with satisfaction. "We've added a fourth Master candidate, a Journeyman rather than an Artificer Trainee or a Builder," she said. "He's a stonemason, and he's designing and carving the—well, I can't call them parapets that will be on the side, because they aren't going to be that bulky. Handrails? Balustrades? Anyway, they're beautiful—gorgeous little pillars making a rail across the top. They look like stone lace. There won't be another bridge in Haven like it. But how's your Circuit among the Law Courts going?"

Kat smiled. "As you'd expect, because no one knows I'm the Princess most of the time. Lots of swearing up and down that the other fellow is a liar until I get trotted out, and then suddenly no one wants Truth Spell invoked and people are obliging and willing to settle just like magic. Of course, if it's a criminal case, no one gets the option of whether or not I'm involved."

But then Kat sighed. "What's wrong?" Abi asked.

"I envy you. Look at this beautiful thing! And you're responsible for it! If it weren't for you, Father would *still* be getting petitioners coming in at least once a week demanding that he replace it! And me, with no special Gifts, I'm in charge of intimidating boring petty quarrelers into behaving themselves in—"

"Stop right there," Abi commanded. "You're forgetting something. What you're doing now is just the Circuit work any new Herald would get, probably because the Circle doesn't really know you. You've completely forgotten how quickly you put together Lady Asterleigh's problem and a logistics hole for the Guard. Remember now?"

Kat struck her forehead with the palm of her hand. "Of course you're right. I've been so immersed in feeling sorry for myself, I forgot what I'm really good at." She brightened immediately.

"So go talk to the Lord Marshal and remind him. And whoever's in charge of Guard logistics too. Maybe they can relieve you of Court duties early, or entirely, and put you to work doing things you excel at." Abi grinned, pleased she'd been able to lighten Kat's mood. She didn't blame Kat one little bit; Mags often got called for a round of Court duty as the cover for him not being on Circuit like other Heralds, and while he took these stints in good humor, and sometimes even got decent leads from what he learned while on duty there, the assignment was probably one of his least favorite things about being a Herald.

"But then," he'd add, *"I c'ld be doin' this while sloggin' through th' mud an' snow an' livin' i' Waystations. 'Stead, I sleep in m'own bed, w' m'lovely wife, an' eat li'cherally like th' King. So I reckon I got it good."*

"And you could be doing the same thing, essentially, while slogging through thunderstorms and blizzards and living in Waystations," Abi reminded her friend, echoing what her father had said. "Instead you get to come back up to the Hill every night and sleep in your own comfortable feather bed."

"Not to mention not cooking my own food." Kat laughed. "You have put things in their proper perspective."

Having seen and marveled at the bridge in its deconstructed form, Kat went on her way, back up the Hill to a fine dinner, probably at her father and mother's side with the Court. Abi returned to discussing the iron dovetails with Master Renold. "We'll want soft, flexible iron," he told her. "So the bridge can flex a little, according to traffic and weather." He showed her the two slots he would have carved in the ends of each of the twenty eight slabs of limestone that would make up the main arch. The iron dovetails themselves would be shaped like a capital letter "V" and be carefully hammered into place while red-hot.

"Won't that crack the stone?" she asked. "The heat of the iron, I mean."

"That's one reason why Master Edders chose limestone," he told her. "Granite might crack. Marble certainly would. Limestone is not as beautiful, but it will do everything we ask of it for this bridge."

"I can't wait until we can start assembling it!" she exclaimed. He beamed at her, and it was quite clear he felt exactly the same.

Behind her, footsteps approached, and Master Ketnar cleared

his throat. She turned. He was wearing a slightly troubled look and was accompanied by her mother.

Abi cast a quick look at Amily, but there was nothing in her mother's face that suggested a family emergency, so Abi tamped down on her alarm and waited to hear what Master Ketnar had to say.

"We have an . . . interesting opportunity that requires someone of your singular abilities, Abi," said the Master. "But the unfortunate part of it is that it will take you away from seeing the actual construction of your bridge."

Wait, what? She clamped down on her dismay as well as her alarm. Best to see what it was Master Ketnar was talking about first before she got herself all wrought up for nothing.

He gestured to her mother.

"I know geography was not your strongest subject," Amily began, with a twinkle in her eye to take the edge off the non-compliment.

"I hate maps," Abi sighed. "I mean, I really loathe them."

"Well, try to cast your mind back to your geographic studies anyway. The southwestern Border of Valdemar and the northwestern Border of Rethwellan and Menmellith have quite a lot of land between them that none of those countries officially claim," her mother said. "That's not to say the land is uninhabited, because that's definitely not the case, but it's ruled over by a patchwork of self-styled nobility and independent city-states and even tribal councils. And that means they are all subject to predation from outside forces and fighting among themselves. It's official policy that the law of Valdemar stops at the Border, so we don't intervene—unless and until those people come to the Crown and ask for our protection."

Abi nodded, still not seeing what this had to do with her.

"A fortnight ago, a delegation representing over two dozen of these communities arrived at the Court to enquire about just that," Amily continued. "Valdemar's protection, and expanding Valdemar's Border to include them. And, normally, we'd grant it, and send Guard troops and Heralds and the usual functionaries and begin bringing them into the Kingdom. But this time was different. They're not suffering the kind of predation that would make this step urgent, and they want to know, well, to put it bluntly, just what *else* we can offer in return for their taxes and fealty."

"When the King asked the Council what we could put together, I suggested that the most concrete form of help we could demonstrate would be to have a group of Artificers and Builders show them how we can improve or repair their roads and bridges—and perhaps important buildings." Master Ketnar smiled. "Our own experience with your bridge certainly demonstrates just how quickly the loss of a bridge or a stretch of road escalates from 'annoying' to 'urgent.' And to be brutally frank, having you along in this group would certainly make an enormous difference in how quickly we could identify problems and either fix them ourselves with local labor, or lay out a plan for the locals to make the repairs themselves. But this thing needs to be put together quickly, while the weather is still good, and that would mean you wouldn't be here for the construction of your bridge."

Abi bit her lip. Here it was, the chance for some travel, maybe a minor adventure or two (though hopefully nothing as dramatic and life-threatening as what Perry had gone through!), the opportunity to do much more than build a single bridge, and a way for her Gift to be useful in a diplomatic application as well as the practical one. Weigh that against—not seeing her bridge go up. And—

"The Guild has met and unanimously said that you will be made a Master on the spot if you go, just on the basis of the design of your bridge," Ketnar continued. "We feel the design alone is a Master Work, and we want there to be no question of your authority among other Masters."

"And Master Edders thinks you will certainly be back in time to see the finishing touches put on your bridge," her mother said persuasively.

The balustrade, she thought forlornly. *Which will be pretty, but not the same as seeing my arch put in piece by piece.*

Still, it was the Crown. And this was not the sort of expedition that should be mounted in anything but good Spring and Summer and early Autumn weather. None of these people would be seasoned travelers; all of them were accustomed to living in comfort.

Master Ketnar gazed at her encouragingly.

Fleetingly the fear went through her that he might claim responsibility for the bridge in her absence—

—but no. For one thing, this was Master Ketnar, who had never been known for such chicanery and who, moreover, had just gotten a commission to design a great, expensive manor on the outskirts of Haven, where the newly rich were now forced to build, given there was no more land available on the Hill. This was a major commission, and the only thing more impressive would be a very large, new temple or sanctuary. And those sorts of commissions came around only once in two lifetimes—or three.

She sighed. Her mother read her assent in that sigh before Abi could say a word. "You're doing the Crown a great service, Abi," she said, happily.

She didn't say, "You won't regret this," because she knows I will almost certainly regret this many times before the trip is over, Abi thought wryly. *If there's one thing I can count on from Mama and Papa, it's stark honesty.*

"The Guild will owe you a tremendous favor," Master Ketnar said, which meant rather more than the Crown getting a "great service." The Guild Council were the ones who recommended specific Masters for specific projects if someone came to them without a Master in mind. *I can do worse than having the Guild owe me a tremendous favor,* she thought, feeling a *tiny* bit better about this whole thing.

"All right," she said. And added, giving both of them a hard look, "If I'm killed by a bear, I'll haunt you forever."

A sennight later, she wasn't so sure she had made the right decision. Fourteen meticulously carved slabs of limestone had been arranged on either side of the river for the twenty-eight slabs of the whole arch; the smaller keystone for the arch was on the side nearest the Hill. The footings for the two spandrels had been laid and built up to the roadbed. A pair of Master Blacksmiths had complete forges set up on either side of the river to make the dovetails and hurry them red-hot to the arch to hammer them in. A small mountain of lumber had been turned into the scaffolding to support the arch until the keystone was slotted into place. Almost everything was in readiness to begin the bridge itself.

And she was packing the last of her packs for this trip.

Not happy, she thought, trying to decide if she should pack in more soap or more underthings, and being reminded by the decision that where she was going, she might have to do her own laundry. In a stream. With frogs and snakes.

Ugh.

On the other hand, there were, so Master Ketnar promised, going to be support people along. What that meant, she had no idea. When the highborn went off on journeys, they had carts full of tents and furnishings, and servants who went on ahead to set it all up. They had every sort of servant they'd have at home, and all they did was ride from one set-up encampment to another and arrive at each to find their food cooked, their laundry done, their water drawn—even baths prepared, should one be desired.

Somehow I don't think that's what he meant.

On the other hand, Heralds traveled only with what they could carry, sometimes a pack-beast, except on rare occasions.

They *did* get to stay in Waystations, which were quite solidly constructed little buildings—

—which we won't. We'll have tents when there are no inns, I guess. And Kernos only knows the quality of the inns down there. We could be sleeping all of us in the one bed, or on the dirt floor of someone's hut.

And meanwhile her bridge was going to be built without her.

But it was far too late to change her mind.

Dammit.

As if she even could have changed her mind, after her mother had all but begged her to do this.

Parents always know what strings to pull. After all, they tied them there.

On the other, other hand (*is that three hands?*) she was going to be surrounded by several Master Builders and Artificers, and it was one thing to learn about techniques in a classroom. It was quite another to see them demonstrated under less than ideal circumstances. This would be incredibly educating.

But . . . tents. And dirty inn floors. And bugs. Ugh.

She tied up the last of her packs and put it outside the door of the suite for a servant to take down. Take down to what? She didn't know. No one had bothered to tell her exactly how this expedition had been organized. Was there a wagon? Several? Were they riding wagons or horses? She hadn't ever ridden anything but a gentle pony, or Rolan. What if they gave her a horse that was determined to scrape her off its back?

The suite was empty; presumably everyone was waiting at the stable where she'd been told the group was to gather so that they could say goodbye. She collected herself and put on a brave face. No use in allowing her parents to think she was having second thoughts. And third thoughts. Especially not ones as ignoble as fussing over sleeping on a dirty inn floor.

With fleas.

She lingered as long as she could, making one last pass over her belongings, trying to intuit if she would regret not having this or that with her on this trek. But eventually there was no point in delaying further. It was time to go.

The first thing she saw as she left the Palace was the whole family, and Kat, waiting at the roadway halfway between the Royal Stable and the Palace. When they spotted her, they all started moving toward her as a group; she ran toward them, and they all met in a jumbled embrace.

"Have a great adventure, and come back safe," Amily said; Mags just reinforced that with a tighter hug.

"I'll keep an eye on your bridge for you," Kat told her. "So you can keep your whole mind on your job."

"Thanks." Abi found herself with a lump in her throat. "I'll do that."

Like his father, Perry said nothing, just squeezed her tight.

"Bring me back a story," Tory said. "One Kee will like."

"I can certainly do that," she promised. "Lots of stories."

She understood instinctively why they were saying goodbye here and not at the stables. They didn't want to embarrass her in front of people who were now her peers by making it look like she was a child being sent off by her parents. The other three Masters certainly would not have a knot of family hugging and kissing and asking for stories. So this way she got her goodbye and still retained her dignity.

Eventually, there was nothing more to say. One more hug, one more kiss, and Kat headed for the Companion Stables and her daily trip down into Haven, Tory followed his mother back into the Palace, and Perry, Larral, and Mags headed for one of the lesser gates into the complex, going—somewhere. She stood quite still as they turned back a last time before moving out of sight, and waved.

Then, with both anticipation and more than a little anxiety, she made her way to the Royal Stables.

She cheered up quite a bit when she saw the three-wagon cavalcade waiting for her. Two were wagons with canvas covers that held a lot of packs and other supplies. But one was an old friend.

This was the caravan that her father and Perry had taken to the Pelagirs, posing as traders. It slept six comfortably. There would be no sleeping on dirt floors with fleas, or under leaky tents. And there were seven people waiting for her, three on the wagons and caravan, all of the riders on sturdy mules (not horses, oh blessed gods!), with a fifth mule saddled and waiting for her. The one sitting on the box of the caravan—was dressed in Herald Whites. But there was no sign of a Companion.

She ignored that for the moment, and went to greet the others.

The oldest-looking man, who seemed to be the one in charge, greeted her first. "Abidela! I am Master Vance. This good fellow is Master Padrick, and this is Master Beyrn. And may I say, we are all great admirers of your new bridge, Master Abidela."

Master Vance's hair was pure white, but he was lean and fit-looking, and Master Ketnar must have reckoned he was suited physically for this journey. Master Padrick was as short as she was, stocky, and his brown hair was liberally sprinkled with gray. Master Beyrn was the youngest of the lot, an earnest-looking chestnut-haired young man, probably in his middle twenties. Abi smiled at all of them, and got perfectly friendly responses. She addressed Master Padrick first.

"I know this caravan," she said, "and you and I need to toss a coin for which of us gets the top cupboard-bed in the front and which gets the bottom. We're the only two that will fit."

"I give you first choice," he said graciously.

"Top, then." She turned her attention to the fourth rider, a tall, stolid-looking woman with blond hair cut as short as a man. "I'm Abidela," she said, and waited for this unknown to introduce herself.

The woman smiled slightly. "I'm Jicks. I'm part guide, part bodyguard, and part cook, since I assume none of you know how to cook. The lads on the other wagons are my squad. We'll make sure nothing gets at you."

She had an odd accent that Abi couldn't quite place. "Are you from where we're going?" she hazarded.

The woman grinned. "Got it in one. Merc company, Hanson's Harriers. We came guarding the delegation and we three stayed behind when we heard what your King had planned, and as I hoped, he's not been backward in paying us for work that's a sight easier than bashing idiots' brains in. For now, I'll be taking up the last bunk in your caravan, the boys'll each sleep in the wagon they're driving. If you decide you want more privacy, the boys can take the bunks and you and I can sleep in the wagons."

Abi nodded, assuming that her father would have done his usual work and gotten a good solid grasp on the reputation of "Hanson's Harriers" at the very least. Hopefully on Jicks and her "boys" as well.

She felt a sense of profound gratitude that Jicks was also going to sleep in the caravan. Not that she was getting any sort of . . . uneasy feelings about any of the three Masters, but with Jicks in the picture, she was fairly sure none of them would even feel tempted to abuse their position and make any kind of unwanted overtures to her. Jicks looked as if she could make an ornamental knot out of all three of them.

"Oh! Well, it's quite a relief to know you're prepared to defend us, lady Jicks!" said Master Vance. Jicks gave him a skeptical look, as if to make sure he wasn't making fun of her, then nodded.

"Pleasure, Master," she replied. "'Specially at the rates we're being paid."

When everyone genuinely laughed at that, Abi was sure that they'd all get along as well as any seven people that didn't know each other.

Well, that left the Herald, sitting there patiently on the box of the caravan, reins loose in his fingers. Abi tilted her head at him.

"I'm Herald Stev," he said. "And I'm here as your link back to the Hill."

"I don't follow, Herald," said Padrick. "And where is your Companion?"

"I have an extremely strong Mindspeech Gift, but only with my Companion," the Herald elaborated. "We actually have not found a distance over which we fail to hear each other. Unfortunately, both his forelegs were broken in an accident. While they healed, it was suggested that a good use of my ability would be to go with you and send back reports to him. In his turn, he can inform Rolan."

"And Rolan can tell my mother, who can tell the Council and the King." Abi filled that in for the Masters and Jicks, who were all looking baffled. "He can report on our progress and send back orders, using Mind-magic."

"Any chance you can get us some help if we get into trouble?" Jicks wanted to know. "You know any other kind of magic?"

The Herald shrugged. "The only magic I know of is Mind-magic. And as for getting help, I won't know until we get out there. But be assured I am going to be testing that contingency before things degenerate into an emergency."

"Well, my friends, are we ready to start this journey?" Master Vance asked, cheerfully. "The road is not getting any shorter as we linger here."

The Stablemaster approached them before the rest of them had a chance to answer and cleared his throat. "Just a word afore ye go. Ye all be riding and driving the best hinnies I've ever had the pleasure of havin' in the Royal Stable, so if ye'll listen to me a bit now, it'll ease my mind."

"Hinnies?" Master Padrick asked.

"Stallion father, donkey mother instead of the other way around," Jicks told him, nodding. "They're mules, too, they just have a little bit different personality from mules with a donkey father."

"Aye, lady," the Stablemaster beamed. "I see ye know your mules. Hinnies are a little slower, a little more careful about how they move. That's why I chose 'em for you, since you'll be traveling over some chancy trails. They'll be much better over loose rock than mules. All the ones you're ridin' are gaited, so they'll go smooth for ye. And they'll eat just 'bout anything, where a mule's more picky. They're smart, smarter'n horses, and if you're in danger, trust 'em. They'll know what t'do better nor you will. If they don't want to go somewhere, don't make 'em, it means they know somethin's wrong even if you can't see it. The one thing to remember about 'em is this—they're not stubborn, they're *smart*. Be good to them, an' they'll be good an' loyal to you and take care of you."

Jicks grinned, leaned forward and scratched behind her chestnut hinny's ears. "We're already good friends. I'll see to it this herd is well looked after. Thanks for picking this lot out for us."

"All right then," the Stable Master said, satisfied. "Off you go, and fair weather and good luck to ye."

Abi mounted her bay hinny and immediately noticed how the handsome creature stood rock solid for her, not even shifting a tiny bit. Already she liked this hinny. She noticed that the bridle had a brass plate with a name engraved on it. *Belle.* "You're a sweet girl, Belle," she said softly, and was rewarded by seeing the hinny's ears flick back to catch her words.

Jicks clicked to her mount, and the hinny obediently moved into a brisk walk, heading for the main gate. Master Vance's mount immediately followed. Belle wanted to go, so Abi gave her rein and a little nudge with her heels, and off they went, with Master Padrick and Master Byrne and the wagons and caravan bringing up the rear.

Before they were even out of Haven, Abi had cause to bless the Stablemaster's choices. The hinnies moved right through the worst of the congestion in Haven without so much as a shiver or a misstep, not even when one careless little ran right under Belle's nose to cross the street, an action which would have caused a horse to shy, rear, or even bolt. And once they were out of Haven, they all took up a comfortable, ground-devouring fast walk. So far as Abi was concerned this was a very good omen for the rest of the trip.

Once they were well out of Haven, Jicks held back her hinny so that she could ride side-by-side with Master Vance. "You're the purse-holder, so here's my question to you. It'd be cheaper to buy and eat provisions than to stop at inns for meals while we're on roads that have inns. But buying and eating provisions is going to make for more monotonous meals. Which do you want to do?"

Master Vance chuckled. "I'm frugal, and I don't think any of us is too particular in the way of food. Are you?" he called back over his shoulder.

"I once ate most of a stale loaf without noticing anything wrong with it, except it seemed to last longer," said Master Padrick. "I was drawing the plans for my Master Work at the time."

"I thought cheese rinds were the best part of the cheese," laughed Byrne. "Actually, I still do."

"Food is fuel," Abi said briefly.

Jicks laughed out loud. "Well, all right then, I have my answer.

The lads and I are used to merc's rations, so it sounds as if we're all on the same page. Good. That means we'll make better time." She touched her hinny with her heels, and moved back up to the front of the procession.

It seemed that she really was serious about covering as much ground as quickly as the hinnies would let her, because Abi's stomach was actually growling when she called a halt at a bridge over a stream. "Dismount, take out the bits, let your hinnies graze a bit and drink," she said as she dismounted. "If you don't know how to slip the bits, wait for me and I'll show you."

While their mounts and the draft hinnies ate and drank, Jicks distributed hard sausage, cheese, and hard biscuit, which seemed like a perfectly good lunch to Abi. About half a candlemark later, they were back on the move, and they didn't stop until dusk, when Jicks led them into a clearing at the side of the road.

The clearing looked like a place where people stopped to camp quite often. It had been grazed clean, and there was a firepit in the middle. They arranged the wagons in a triangle around the firepit, and unharnessed all the animals. Slipping the bits on the bridles— which essentially turned them into halters—Jicks picketed the hinnies out on a long line that allowed them to graze on anything within reach. The two "lads," a couple of tall fellows alike enough to be brothers, poured out a very small measure of grain for them as well, and led them one at a time to a pond to drink, Stev got water for the camp with Abi's help, while Jicks started a fire, slung a kettle over it and began making . . . something. Abi came over to watch when the water casks were full.

It was stew of some sort, from the root vegetables and dried meat she was putting into it. Abi took careful note. Jicks cocked an eye at her.

"Want to learn how to cook?" she asked.

Abi nodded.

"Just watch, then." When she was done chopping vegetables and dried meat into the water, she gestured to Abi to follow. "See this, here?" she asked, opening a small box and taking out a tiny fabric packet. "All the herbs you need for one pot, plus salt. Already got them all done up, so no fussing when it comes time to stop. When I'm about to run out, I'll take a candlemark or so to make more."

She took the packet to the fire, shook out everything that was in it into the pot, and put the empty fabric back in the box. "That stew and traveler's biscuit will be supper. When we're done, I'll clean out the pot, put in oats and water, and bury it in the coals and ash. That'll be breakfast. I'll put in raisins tonight. Tomorrow, it'll be chopped cheese rinds. So we'll get sweet one morning, savory the next."

The lads' names, as Abi learned over supper, were Bart and Bret, and they actually were brothers. They referred to Jicks as "Chief" and deferred to her in all things. Other than that, they were both brown, tall and broad, and looked like any of the Watch Abi had ever met. Purposeful men who knew their business.

With the meal, Jicks had supplied willowbark tea. As she sat down to eat, Abi suddenly understood why.

It had been a long day, and Abi was not used to spending that much time in the saddle. Neither were the other three Masters, who had declared themselves very stiff and sore on dismounting and, after supper, groaned on getting up. Abi herself felt that she had been using a great many muscles she was not used to using, and was very grateful for all the weapons training she had done with Master Leandro. If she hadn't had that, and all the attendant exercise, she was pretty sure she'd be feeling crippled at this moment.

"I'll be making allowances for you in the morning, Masters," Jicks said politely, although Abi had the feeling she was having a hard time keeping a straight face at their expense. "I counted on this, you being city-bred and all. Don't worry, it'll get better."

"I certainly hope so," said Byrne, wretchedly, as he hobbled off to bed. The other two followed him. Abi waited by the fire for them to get settled, then climbed into the caravan, feeling her aches, and in the dim light from a single candle-lantern, climbed into the upper cupboard-bed and closed the curtains. The older men were already snoring, and she was just dropping into sleep when she felt the caravan move slightly as Jicks and the Herald climbed in. So ended her first day on the road.

———

She was not the first up, but she was the first of the Masters awake in the morning. She heard the sounds of people moving around outside. She squirmed into her clothing, trying not to make the caravan move too much, and slipped out into the cool dawn light.

The air was a little damp and full of the scent of torn foliage from where the hinnies had been eating all night. Jicks and the lads were already up as well—and practicing.

They all had the same kinds of wooden practice blades that Master Leandro used, and at the moment, the two lads were doing strike-and-block exercises as Jicks quietly counted out a cadence. Watching them, Abi felt an impulse and gave into it.

"Can I join?" she asked softly.

"I'd like that too," said Herald Stev, who had come up behind her so quietly she wouldn't have noticed if she hadn't been trained by her father.

Jicks raised an eyebrow. "There's practice blades in the—"

"Oh, I have my own," the Herald chuckled.

"Me too," Abi added. They grinned at each other, and at Jick's surprise, and went to the wagon holding their packs. Both of them got out practice blades and leather armor. Abi's rig differed from the Herald's only in that she had double knives instead of a sword. They both pulled on the leather tunics, arm guards, and shin guards and buckled wide, heavy belts over the tunics. When they were ready, they rejoined the mercenaries on the cleared area of ground they were using to practice on.

Jicks eyed Abi's knives dubiously. "You know, we have a saying about bringing a knife to a swordfight. . . "

Abi just shrugged. "Then I'll get thwacked."

"Your bruises. I'll go easy on you. Lads, put the Herald through his paces. Have at, girl." Jicks took a guard stance and waited for Abi to attack.

Which, of course, Abi was not going to do. Not until she had seen what Jicks could do. She waited, patiently for Jicks to make the first move.

Finally Jicks got tired of waiting, came in with an overhand strike, and they were off.

Jicks was good, very good. But Abi had been trained by Master Leandro and her father. Very soon, Jicks was no longer "going easy on her," and Herald Stev and Bret and Bart were no longer practicing; they were watching the two of them spar. Abi found herself grinning maniacally, she was having so much fun, even though she was sweating like a galloping horse.

Finally Abi felt something—a twig or a pebble under her foot— skid. It was at just the wrong moment, and she lost her balance, flailed a little, and started to go down. Jicks sensed her chance and came in at her fast. It was all over in a blur.

They both froze. Abi was half-sprawled on the turf. Jicks' sword was trapped in the quillons of Abi's right-hand dagger, though she *could* have freed it with a twist and hit home. The point of Abi's left-hand dagger was in Jicks' stomach.

Jicks looked down.

"Huh," she said.

Bret began clapping, slowly. A moment later, his brother followed. Stev stood there with his arms crossed over his chest, grinning as if he had expected this.

Which . . . if he's Papa's agent . . . he was.

Now, Abi was absolutely certain that Stev really was an extraordinary Mindspeaker. And that his Companion really did have two broken forelegs. And that everything he'd said about the reason for being on this expedition was true.

But at that moment she was also as certain that he was one of Mags' rare agents among the Heralds as she would have been if her father had told her as much. But, of course, Mags would have expected her to figure that out for herself.

Stev looked right at her and winked.

Jicks backed up, then held out a hand to Abi, who took it and hauled herself to her feet. "You're good, girl," the mercenary said, with a nod of appreciation. "Go run some drills with Bret. Now I want to see what this Herald is good for."

Stev made a flourish with his sword, spinning it once and coming to rest in a guard position. "When you're ready, Chief."

Jicks grinned.

12

Once they all became accustomed to riding all day, the journey proceeded at a purposeful pace. Every day was fundamentally the same. Jicks and her lads, Stev, and Abi got up first, had a practice session, then got some sort of wash-up, either a full bath or just the basics with a rag and a pail, depending on whether they had stopped by a body of water or not. Abi got used to these ad-hoc baths in uncomfortably cold water, though admittedly she didn't like them and hurried through them as fast as she could. Then everyone would eat. The other Masters would make whatever sort of bath they could manage while Jicks and the boys cleaned up the campsite and harnessed up all the animals. Stev and Abi helped with the hinnies. Then they'd be on the road, and if provisions were running low, they'd stop at the first village that had any sort of marketplace to replenish them. If there was a baker in the town selling pocket pies, Abi would always use some of her own money to get some for everyone, to vary their supper that night. She learned that every village had its own sort of traveler's biscuit, every baker claimed his was tasty, and every one of them lied.

Twice on the way Jicks allowed a full day at a village, to get laundry done and allow everyone to have a proper hot bath. Which was just as well, because otherwise Stev would have started to look like a Trainee in Grays, rather than a full Herald in Whites.

The farther south they got, the more rugged the landscape became. Gently rolling hills became steeper and taller, the road got rougher, and there were fewer farms with tilled land and more with herds of sheep and goats and, occasionally, odd, shaggy red cattle. The craggy, towering hills were covered in brush and grass; trees grew only along watercourses and down in the valleys.

And the farms got fewer and farther apart. Not only were there flocks of sheep, goats, and the odd herds of cattle roaming the hills, there were also occasional herds of red deer or single stags. Despite being farther south, the air was cooler and damper, and the prevailing scents on it were bracken and gorse. It rained as often as it was sunny, and when it did, she, Jicks, and the Masters rode in the caravan. Mostly they listened to Jicks' tall tales when they were confined to the caravan.

Abi was used to having a lot of people around her, used to Haven, and all that empty land and silence broken only by the sounds of far-off sheep, birds, and wild animals was . . . unnerving.

As the days grew longer and longer, they stopped later and later and covered more ground. By now, though, their camps were models of efficiency, and the hinnies practically put themselves and the wagons in place without needing to be guided, so they spent a lot less time getting set up. Which was a good thing, as in these hills, once the sun set it got dark very quickly.

"Where are all the people?" she asked Jicks, finally, after a full day of seeing nothing and nobody. They were all sitting around the fire, wearily waiting for the stew to finally finish cooking. Stev had taken Abi out to forage to add to their plain meal; the peppery, fresh taste of watercress added a much needed touch of flavor, and Stev seemed to know exactly what mushrooms were safe to eat and which weren't. He'd taken his bow with him as he always did, but luck hadn't been with them that night. No hares had been startled up out of the bracken to add to the pot.

Jicks chuckled. "Where you can't see them," she said. "Those cattle, sheep, and goats you've been seeing all need watching. The cattle are pastured in the valleys but away from the road. Each herd has a woman watching; they live in summer huts and guard and milk the cattle and make cheese all summer long. Then they are joined by some of their family to drive the cattle back to the family farm for the winter. The sheep and goats are in their summer pastures too, and every flock and herd in the hills has a shepherd or two that stays with them all spring and summer and into fall, when they're brought back down to the homestead to be cared for over winter. And the homesteads are hidden in the valleys away from the road to prevent casual thieves from spotting them."

Bret got up, peered in the pot, gave it a stir, and sat back down again. "Lots of cattle thieves in the hills," he said laconically.

"But Valdemar doesn't have casual looters," Abi protested. "We have the Guard to keep people safe."

"This wasn't always part of Valdemar," Jicks reminded her.

"Outside of the villages, people are wary of strangers. Some of these homesteads have been here for centuries. Some of these clans have a tradition of cattle and sheep theft from each other going back that far. Plus, there's bandits, the closer you get to the Border. The kind of bastards people hire the Harriers to get rid of, over on the other side where your Guard won't go. So you don't make your buildings obvious, you make them blend into the countryside or even hide them if you can, and hope they aren't spotted." Jicks poked at the fire with a stick. "And speaking of the Border, we'll be there in a day, two at the most."

"And then our real work can begin!" Master Vance said, rubbing his hands.

"And then we'll be staying in villages until our work is done in each one," added Byrne, forlornly. "I'd like a proper bath more than once a fortnight."

The three mercenaries exchanged amused looks, but they kept any comments to themselves. There was a pause in conversation, though, and the fire crackled and threw sparks up into the night.

"First stop is just about a day past the Border station," Jicks said. "Especially at the rate we've been traveling. Not sure if they'll have anything you can do for them, but that's the first sizable village, and we need provisions, so we'll be stopping overnight at the very least." She poked the fire again, thoughtfully, releasing the scent of resinous wood they'd gathered from beneath the trees. It was trees that they looked for now for their nightly stops, rather than water sources. There were plenty of the latter. These hills were alive with tiny springs, little threads of creeks, rills, and brooks, which did, indeed, to Abi's delight, 'babble' as books said they did. "I'm going to assume that since we brought up an entire group, they are all still speaking to one another and not feuding, and I can ask whoever is in charge if he knows what most needs mending thereabouts."

"Or replacing altogether," Padrick reminded her. "If they have the labor, we have the ability to help them completely replace anything that's tumbled down."

"I'll keep that in mind."

This time it was Bart who checked the pot and sat back down, disappointed. Abi passed him a fistful of cress. He made a face over it, but munched it stolidly anyway. Jicks put another log of their limited wood on the fire, carefully, so as not to bring the temperature of the stew down. Bret gestured to Abi to pass the cress, and he stuffed two handfuls into his mouth. The silence was broken only by the sound of two sets of jaws munching leaves as assiduously as a couple of cattle, the snapping of the fire, and a great many crickets.

"You seem troubled, Jicks," Vance said into the silence.

"Oh, just superstitious," Jicks replied, with a wry chuckle. "This trip has gone too smooth."

But Stev laughed. "That's because we're in Valdemar, milady," he replied, bowing a bit. "I promise you, things will start to fall apart as soon as we're across the Border."

Jicks contemplated that for a moment. "If that's supposed to be comforting, it's not," she retorted, but with an upward twist of her lips. "Still. I don't think the three of us are comfortable unless we're up to our asses in snapping turtles and shit."

"It ain't natural otherwise," put in Bret, asking for more cress with a gesture.

"Oh, one more thing," Jicks said, helping herself to cress. "Once we're across the Border, when we're camped out like this, we'll need to stand guard watches."

"With four of us, that won't be too onerous," Stev noted.

Jicks smiled. "I was hoping you'd volunteer."

Stev shrugged. "What else am I doing? It wouldn't be the first time I've taken a watch shift. But just what are we watching for? I thought this consortium that sent a delegation were all friends and allies now."

"Bandits probably won't trouble us; we're too much trouble. Too little gain for too much potential danger with four trained fighters they can see. But there's wild creatures. Bears."

"I *knew* I was going to get eaten by a bear!" Abi exclaimed, unable to help herself. "I just *knew* it!"

Bret and Bart snickered.

Jicks rolled her eyes but continued. "There's also lone thieves who'll try and filch something from the camp while we're sleeping. If there's a storm and we're along a watercourse, we'll need to pack up and move to higher ground, no matter how far away the storm is." "Won't that make us a better target for lightning?" Abi asked.

"Better that than get everything washed away in a flash flood. Then there's . . . things." Jicks' voice took on an ominous tone.

"Things?" asked Stev. "What things?"

"Unnatural things." Jick's seemed perfectly serious, but Master Vance frowned.

"My lady, I do hope you aren't attempting to pull some sort of hoax, so that you and your lads can have a hearty laugh at our expense," he chided. "We have neither the time nor the patience for third-year Trainee jokes."

But Jicks seemed perfectly serious. "There's magicians on the other side of the Border, real ones. Hell, we have three in the Harriers. They can conjure things up, and sometimes those things get away from them."

"And how are we to protect ourselves from these *things?*" asked Vance, still skeptical.

"Mostly by staying out of their way. The locals will know if there's anything about to worry ourselves over. That's why I asked you, Stev, if you knew any other magic. It'd help to have a Mage along." She gave Stev a *look*, as if she suspected he was somehow holding back information from her.

But Stev shook his head, as Abi had known he would. "The only magic in Valdemar is Mind-magic," he said. "But since I do have Mindspeech, I can run a periodic sweep to see if anything like a human is thinking hostile thoughts about us."

"That'll have to do."

Any more conversation, about *things* or otherwise, was cut short by the stew finally being ready.

The Border crossing was guarded by a single Guard post, but a very complete one; there was a full barracks, a stable, and a resupply warehouse, since it was from here that Guard patrols would range along the Border and northward, looking for trouble. The crossing itself was literally nothing; just a small bad-weather shack and a single man watching the road.

"I thought there would be a wall," said Beyrn, sounding disappointed, as the Guard waved them past.

"What bloody use would a wall be?" Jicks asked, laughing. "There's not enough Guards in Valdemar to keep a watch on it.

Anybody that wanted to get over it could. An army could just bring up a siege engine and knock part of it down. And there's nothing on the Valdemar side that's any better than what's on the other side, so why bother making the crossing at all?"

Beyrn looked *very* offended at this statement, but he kept whatever retort he would have liked to make behind his teeth.

Jicks was quite right about things being the same as in Valdemar, though. There was a very nice village—town, really—full of beautifully made stone houses with slate roofs on the other side of the Border, actually a much nicer village than anything they'd seen on Valdemar's side for leagues. Jicks told them it was called Ellistown. It was situated along the road in a winding valley, and it was very probably there because of traders going northward. Everyone brightened up when they saw it, and Master Vance seemed particularly pleased. "There should be plenty of projects here we can offer advice on," he said, gleefully.

A little too gleefully, actually. *Oh no*—Abi thought with alarm *Don't say it!*

"This should be very easy."

Oh, gods. Now he's done it. We're going to be cursed for sure.

The village mayor—which was what they called the fellow in charge here—came out to greet them and welcome them officially to the village before a large and appreciative crowd. There was just one problem.

They couldn't understand a bloody word he said.

It *sounded* like Valdemaran, sort of, but with a thick accent and absolutely unfamiliar words sprinkled liberally throughout. And he didn't seem to be using words that they did recognize in the same way that they were used in Valdemar. So they just nodded and smiled where it seemed appropriate, everyone appeared to be happy, they all shook hands and the mayor and the audience departed back to their own business, leaving them all alone in the village square, with their wagons and gear and no idea what to do or where to go next. Or at least, that was true of the Valdemarans. Jicks, Bret, and Bart appeared to be completely at ease with the situation.

"Jicks," Master Vance said, as they all stood there on the hard-packed dirt of the village square, "I . . . believe we have a problem."

Jicks smirked. "No, *you* have a problem. The lads and I don't. Aye unnerstanet owt. Tha unnerstanet nowt." She laughed. "Nay, tha'll be reight."

"That's exactly what I mean!" Vance said, despairingly. "I haven't the faintest idea what you just said! How are we to help these people if we can't understand each other?"

"Because, Master, I allowed for that. Just get back in your saddles and follow me." She hauled herself onto her hinny and sent her moving down a side street. Perforce, they followed. The houses were set extremely close together, and right down on the street, just as if they were all in the older parts of Haven. The only thing missing was paved streets; these were just dirt.

She led them to a house that might have been a touch more prosperous looking than the ones on either side of it. It had a plaque mounted above the door showing four mountains. She dismounted and knocked on the door, which was answered by a middle-aged woman in a brown linen blouse and skirt and a spotless apron. By concentrating very hard, Abi *thought* Jicks said,

"We have five people to buy a spell from the" . . . something. Sorcerer? But she wasn't entirely sure.

The woman bobbed her head and gestured to them to come in.

Abi, the Masters, and Stev all crowded into the tiny stone-walled room she would have called a solar if the house had been manor-sized, while Bart and Bret stayed behind to manage the hinnies and give people room to squeeze past the wagons. It was clean to a fault and sparsely furnished, which was a good thing, because if it had had so much as a chair more than it did they wouldn't all have fit in.

They waited for a few moments, and then a man appeared in the doorway.

He wasn't all that impressive to look at. Weedy, middle-aged, going bald on top, dressed in comfortable-looking robes of some soft brown fabric she couldn't identify. He and Jicks consulted quietly for a few moments, then Jicks spoke up.

"All right, if you've never had a spell worked on you, there's nothing to worry about. This one's very tame. The only thing is, for a few breaths you are going to feel as if your head is too big for your body, and your thoughts will seem a bit scrambled and not your own. Then everything will settle, and you'll know every language and dialect and accent that I do."

Wait, what? was all Abi had time to think, and before she could ask any questions, or make any objections, the man made a few flamboyant gestures in the air, spoke several strange words aloud, and light exploded in front of her eyes.

In the next breath. . .

Her head felt too big and too tight. There were things swirling around in her thoughts she couldn't identify. It was as if there were a dozen people trying to Mindspeak to her, and she couldn't understand any of them—

And just as suddenly as the effect had occurred—it was gone again.

"That'll be five Valdemaran silver pieces apiece," the sorcerer said politely. "That would be a total of twenty-five. Thank you for providing the template, Jicks, that made things much easier."

"What, you can't give me a discount for providing the template?" Jicks asked.

"That was with a discount. I have to eat, you know." The sorcerer crossed his arms over his chest and grinned.

Jicks looked at Master Vance and coughed. He came out of his daze and fumbled for his belt pouch. "Uh, yes, of course, quite." The sorcerer held out his hand, and Vance counted out twenty-five silver pieces into it.

"Nothing I like better than a customer who pays promptly." The man stowed his fee in his own belt pouch and nodded with satisfaction. "I really don't know how you people manage to learn languages over on your side of the Border."

"The hard way," Abi said dryly, though she was having a hard time getting her head wrapped around the fact that she had just "learned" several of them instantly, not to mention a number of attendant dialects. What the people here spoke, she understood now, was just a dialect, a kind of polyglot of Valdemaran and whatever they spoke farther south.

"Did—did we just—" Poor Beyrn was still trying to come to grips with what had just happened. "How can—that's not—"

"It happened, so it's obviously possible." Padrick had recovered from his shock completely. "Thank you, magician. Whatever your name is."

"It's Steen," said Jicks. "He used to be with us, the Harriers, until he decided to strike out on his own here."

"That's because I was about as useful as teats on a bull with the Harriers, Jicks," Steen chided. "Lots of practical, simple spells, but damn-all combat magic. Hellfires, a hedge-wizard would have been more use than me; he might have had some healing spells."

"Well, your heart wasn't in it," Jicks told him in a kindly tone of voice.

"If that was a 'practical, simple spell,' I wouldn't like to see combat magic," Beyrn blurted, voice shaking.

Vance reached across Abi and patted the younger Master on the shoulder, as if trying to comfort him. "And we won't. It's all right, Beyrn, this is not all that different from Mind-magic."

"You're not likely to find a powerful Mage able to do heavy combat magic out here among the likes of us, anyway" Steen told the younger Master. "First of all, they're rare, and second of all, they go to where they can command gold for their services, and lots of it." He laughed. "I don't think there's ten gold pieces in this entire village. Mostly I do mind tricks like the one I just did on you, help find lost things, and work with water. My single most powerful spell is a parlor trick that makes me popular in the summertime." He leaned back and called toward the back of the house. "Aubryana! Mint tea for my guests."

The serving woman appeared with a tray full of glasses of pale green liquid. Steen muttered a few words and made a couple of gestures, and the glasses suddenly frosted over. "Here you are, my friends," he said, handing the glasses out. "Just what you need on a hot summer day."

Abi's glass, when she took it, was so cold that it misted when she breathed on it.

"I can make lots of ice for gatherings," he said, and shrugged. "But unless an army happens to be standing knee deep in still water, it's not exactly a useful trick for combat."

"Remarkable!" marveled Vance, as he sipped the ice-cold drink.

"It brought me lots of friends, which isn't a bad thing for a magician, given that the first person people look sideways at when a cow dies is the local magician," Steen chuckled. "But I'm taking up your time, and you're taking up my sitting room. Time for you to go back and talk to Rufous about the old bridge, among other things, and me to get back to my garden."

The woman collected the glasses as they filed out obediently, though poor Beyrn was still clearly disturbed at the fact that magic existed at all. Abi wasn't—but then she'd heard her brother's and father's stories. It wasn't that magic didn't exist in Valdemar; it was that there was a protective power in Valdemar that drove Mages out or drove them insane, and at the same time made it hard even to *think* about "real" magic for very long.

There were dozens of questions she would have loved to have had the time to ask Steen, but as he had pointed out, they were here to do things, not stand around and talk. She followed the others out, and Steen closed his door behind them.

Rufous, as it turned out, was the name of the village mayor who had greeted them with a speech they hadn't understood, and he was delighted to have them come back and tell them about the bridge. In fact, he was delighted to show them.

On the outskirts of the village to the west was a road that led to a swiftly flowing river and continued on the other side. But where a bridge should have been was nothing but a few pilings driven into the bank.

"It washed out this spring, you know," Rufous the mayor said sadly. "It washes out every spring, but there's usually enough left to rebuild it. Not this time."

Abi studied the situation from every angle. "How deep is it?" she asked.

"Deeper than it looks. Well over my head in the middle," said Rufous, unconsciously standing up as tall as he could. "It's a good source of tolls for the village. When it's there, that is."

The river ran along the bottom of a flat valley, without the sort of bank that would make it possible to build a stone bridge like the one Abi was so proud of back in Valdemar. *But they probably don't have the skilled labor, or the lifting machines that would allow them to do that either. What they need is a bridge they don't have to keep replacing, or something that you could haul out of the way in flood-time . . . or both. Hmm. We could give them the plans for a different sort of stone bridge that they can build out of smaller stones, and while they're building that. . .*

"I have two ideas," she said. "First, we'll help you build either a bridge out of a series of floating platforms you can haul out of the water when floods threaten or a simple ferry you can power with a single horse, ox or mule that will be large enough for a single wagon or several passengers and beasts. That will do for now, and when that is complete, we'll leave you instructions on building a stone bridge."

"But . . ." the mayor began to object.

"Don't worry, we'll give you instructions of a sort that the same people who build your houses can follow," Padrick assured him. "You're lucky the river is narrow at that point; we can give you a high-arched bridge that the flood-waters won't touch."

"But . . ." the mayor repeated, weakly.

"Of course, this means the bridge will be quite high compared to the roadbed," Vance continued cheerfully. "But I'm sure someone in the village will have extra animals that can be hitched to any wagons temporarily to get them over the hump, as it were. You could even include that in the toll."

"Ah," the mayor said, brightening. "I see!"

"I'll get the instruments from the wagon and start surveying the site first thing in the morning," Abi volunteered. "I'm sure I can find good sites for both the floating bridge and the eventual stone bridge."

"I'll begin drafting plans for each floating platform," said Padrick. "And for the ferry."

"And you and I will work out how much material and manpower we'll need for the floating bridge and the ferry, you can determine which you want, and once you've decided, you can begin," Master Vance said cheerfully. "We'll begin in the morning. Meanwhile, is there a good place for us to set up our camp?"

"I think you ran right over the top of poor mayor Rufous, Master Vance," Jicks observed, as they sat down to an absolutely delicious supper provided by some of the local women. Abi had considered herself indifferent to food, but that had been before all these days of dried-meat stew, porridge, and not much else; by now the mere thought of a roast set her mouth watering.

And a roast was what had been delivered; a fine roasted leg of mutton, and fresh bread with butter, a spicy vegetable stew, and berry tarts.

"I've dealt with bureaucrats all of my life, my dear," Vance replied. "They're like a nervous horse. If you give them a chance to think, nine times out of ten they freeze, and the tenth time they balk. The only way to handle them is to rush them at and over the problem before they get a chance to get a good look at it."

"And in every case, the problem is manpower and money," Padrick added. "Yes please, a nice thick slice of that mutton would be—ah, perfect. Never let them have a chance to think about manpower and money until everyone they are accountable to has a chance to build expectations and clamor for what you want to build. And that would be where you two come in." He pointed his knife at Bret and Bart and went back to eating.

"Who?"

"Us?"

"Yes, you." Padrick's mouth was full, so Vance took over again, as Beyrn listened intently. "You were planning on going to the pub tonight to fill yourselves full of beer right?"

"Uh—" They both looked sheepish.

"My dear boys, that's exactly what we want you to do. And tell everyone about the magnificent ferry or floating bridge, and the even better stone bridge, we are planning for them. Tell them how wonderful the plans are—yes, I know they don't exist yet, but they don't know that. Make it all sound splendid. And in the morning, when I get done figuring how may men it will take, and how much wood, and he starts to get cold feet and wonder how it's to be paid for, the townsfolk will turn up on his door demanding these things be built *right now.* They might even volunteer to work, or offer wood, but the important thing is that they demand these projects begin immediately. And that will get our reluctant horse over the jump. A spot more of that bread and butter, please."

Beyrn was not the only one listening intently as they sat around a very nice fire, with the leg of mutton kept warm on a spit to one side, the big clay pot of vegetables just in the coals, and the bread and butter and tarts on a makeshift table made of a couple of storage chests and some planks. Abi listened with all her concentration. Seeing Vance at work today and listening to him now had made her realize that it was not just creating good structures and executing them that made a Master—it was knowing how to manage the people that would make sure the project got built in the first place.

That, it would seem, was an art in itself.

When no one could manage another bite and the last of the food had been stored safely away from vermin and insects, Bret and Bart strolled happily away to the pub—beside which they had made their camp—the Masters took themselves off to bed, and Stev propped himself on a saddle beside the fire for his nightly communion with his Companion.

Abi decided to take a stroll through the village to get herself acquainted with it. There was a full moon, and plenty of light, and she wanted to walk off a certain restlessness.

There was a low stone wall at the southernmost end of the village just past the camp that seemed meant for sitting on. And there was a spectacular view of three tall, craggy hills in the moonlight, with the moon glinting off all the little watercourses and tiny ponds that lay beneath them. Abi sat and stared; she'd never seen anything like this in all her life. Moonlight over the Palace gardens wasn't half as awe-inspiring.

She heard footsteps approaching, and identified them as Jicks without even a second thought. A moment later, Jicks lifted her legs over the wall and sat down close beside her.

"And this's why I'll never live in a city," Jicks said, after a very long period of silence. Then, without any warning, she put her arm around Abi and kissed her.

Abi was so startled she didn't react at all. Even her thoughts were a sort of blank, a blank that only resolved itself when Jicks pulled away again. And . . . she didn't know what to say. Without thinking, she lifted her hand to her lips, blinking a little. *She just kissed me. Oh, dear.*

The awkward silence between them grew. Abi didn't know how to break it, and Jicks was clearly waiting for some sort of reaction.

Finally Jicks sighed. "No spark?" she asked. "Nothing?"

Abi felt her face flushing, but more out of chagrin than anything else. "I'm sorry. . ." she said. "I . . ." *Oh, hell. But I never—*

"I couldn't help but see the lads weren't doing anything for you, even though they were spreading their tails and all but dancing for you, so I thought I—" Jicks sighed again. "I thought I might have a chance. I guess I'm just too—"

"No, it's not you," Abi managed to interrupt her. "Actually, it's not anyone. Not even my best friend Kat. Or Rudi or Emmit or Brice or—well, it's not anyone. It's never been anyone." The last was said with a kind of wonder, because—

—well, because she'd never actually thought about this before. But it was true. It wasn't anyone. All the giggling and carrying on and whispers and what people fondly thought were secret romances that had gone on around her, and there'd never been a spark of anything between her and anyone else. Oh, she loved Kat and Trey and Niko to bits. And she loved Brice, Rudi, and Nat. But . . . she loved them the same way she loved her brothers. She'd never thought about that, she'd just accepted it. And if anyone had ever been flirting with her (like Bret and Bart?) she'd been oblivious. It just wasn't that important to her. Actually . . . it wasn't important at all.

"Ah, well, then, at least it's not me." More silence, broken only by the far off whoop of an owl. "Friends, then?"

That startled her. Why shouldn't they still be—

Ah, well, one more thing she didn't understand. "Of course," she said, warmly. "We've been together enough for me to know you're one of the best friends I have."

"Good." They watched the silver moon creep higher into the sky. "You must be like my Sergeant back in the Harriers. Women, men, doesn't matter, he's always alone in his bunk and for all I can tell, he likes it that way. One Midwinter I watched him get roaring drunk, politely brush off girls that were literally hanging on his arms, and go to his bunk alone." Jicks picked up a rock off the wall and threw it out into the darkness. "Well, maybe it's all for the best. Messy things, love affairs. Worse when they get in the way of doing your job."

Abi didn't even have to think about that. Although it hadn't affected her, or anyone in her circle of acquaintances, she remembered very well how messy things had gotten among the Bardic and Healer Trainees when love affairs had gone awry. And

Brice was always getting his heart broken by girls he was attracted to when they paired up with someone else; he'd go moody and hard to work with, sometimes for more than a moon. *If that kind of mess is routine, then I'm much happier being the way I am.*

"I had no idea these hills were so beautiful," she said, finally. And she sensed Jicks relax.

"Nights like this . . . I don't even mind taking a watch."

13

As Master Vance had predicted, spreading the word that there was a short-term *and* a long-term solution to the crossing problem led the people of the town to clamor for both. As work on the series of floating platforms began, so, too did work on the eventual stone bridge begin. In the case of the latter, the local stonemasons worked under the direction of Master Vance in building up the two piers that would eventually anchor the arch of the bridge. That meant building out along the riverbank as well as up—to guide floodwaters smoothly past the piers so they wouldn't be washed out.

Abi and Master Padrick worked on the floating bridge, once Master Padrick had drawn up extremely detailed plans of how to build the scaffolding that would hold the arch in place until it was self-supporting with the addition of the keystones. That left Master Beyrn with nothing to do.

Finally, he approached the mayor himself, on one of the latter's many visits to the riverbank. "Are there any dams around here that need inspecting?" he asked, a little desperately. "Any buildings that need reinforcement?"

"Well, there's the old dam up the river that way," Mayor Rufous replied, doubtfully, after some thought. "It's stood forever, though. We don't know who built it; it was here when the village was first founded." He waved in the general direction of "upriver." "You're welcome to look at it, but I doubt you'll see anything."

But Beyrn, who by this time was fidgeting with inactivity, saddled his mule himself and left immediately. Abi didn't even give him a second thought; she and Padrick were too busy testing the first of their bridge platforms to make sure it could hold the weight of a wagon and horses without tipping as the wagon moved from one platform to the next.

That is, she didn't think anything of it until Beyrn and Bret, who had gone with him, came pounding back, having somehow persuaded their hinnies to return at a gallop. Beyrn's face was white as marble, and Abi, who was the first to see him, ran to him and grabbed his hinny's bridle. He moved his mouth, but nothing came out.

She clapped her hand over his, which seemed frozen to the reins. "Deep breath," she ordered, and he took one shuddering. "Another. Now what's wrong."

"Th-th-the d-d-d-dam," he stuttered. "It's failing!"

———

"I don't see what all the fuss is about," Mayor Rufous said crossly, looking down at the runnel of brown, muddy water at the base of the dam. "It's just a little leak. I'm sure we can patch it up with a few rocks."

But Master Vance whirled, grabbed the man by the shoulders and shook him, hard. "Listen to me, you blithering idiot!" he hissed. "It's *not* 'just a little leak! Beyrn's right! That 'little' stream means that water has worked a channel all the way under that dam, creating an unstable area that could literally collapse at any moment!" he let the mayor go, and wiped his forehead with his sleep. "Dear Gods, man, how much water is backed up behind it?"

The mayor gulped, shocked. "I . . . don't know. Acres . . ."

"We've got to lower the water level, Vance," Padrick called from up on the hill that overlooked the dam. "And we've got to do it *now.* Otherwise a wall of water this high is going to roll down on the village and when it passes there won't be a living creature left. And you all had better get up here now, just in case it decides to let go while you're standing there."

Vance shoved the mayor at the horses—they'd borrowed horses, because horses were a lot easier to coax into a gallop than the hinnies. "Go!" he shouted. "We need men with shovels and picks and we need them here *now,* if you want to save your village!"

Abi scrambled up beside Padrick, and gulped. Behind the ancient earthen dam was what had once been a wide, meandering valley, probably fed by a river that joined the one that the villagers needed bridged. It was easy to see why the dam had been built in the first place; if the village was having trouble keeping a bridge in place through flooding now, it would have been impossible with this tributary feeding it. And Padrick was right. When the dam caved in, all the water was going to rush down into the river and from there into the village. She tried to envision it; a wall of water, raging the way the Terilee in Haven raged at flood, and her imagination failed. All she could be sure of was that the result would be catastrophic. "Can we plug the hole?" she asked Padrick, feeling sick and cold.

"Not in time, maybe not at all," Padrick replied grimly. "We've got to release water in a controlled manner and drain that basin to let pressure off the dam." He looked around, as if he expected to find a shovel or a pick-ax right at hand. "Here would be the best spot."

He pointed to a point just below their feet where the dam met the hillside. Abi nodded; not only was the hill probably more stable than the dam, it appeared to be solid rock right there, where the dam was just earth and fill-rock.

Beyrn lay flat on his stomach a little higher than they were, peering down at the water at the center of the dam. "I don't see any actual flow," he called down to them. "So right now, it's just a seep."

"It won't stay that way for long," Master Padrick said, grimly, then called down to Vance. "Vance, get up here! We don't need to lose you if it decides to let go while you're standing there!"

Vance peered up at them from beneath the shade of his hand. "But think of the observational data I would get!"

"Which would die with you! Get up here!"

"Point taken," Vance replied, and began laboriously climbing the steep slope of the hill to get to them. Once he reached them, he strained his eyes in the direction of the village. "What's keeping them?" he muttered.

"The difficulty of herding people who have no idea how dangerous this situation is," Padrick replied, turning his gaze in the same direction. "You heard the mayor. 'The dam has stood forever,' so it's difficult for them to imagine it's failing."

It seemed to take forever before Padrick spotted the villagers approaching in the far distance—and even longer before they finally got there. When they finally arrived, it wasn't Rufous who was in charge.

It was Jicks. And with her was the village magician.

She didn't make any explanations about her presence, just got the men to work on the spot Padrick had chosen, and only when they were chipping away at hard-packed earth as tough as pure stone did she turn her attention to Master Vance.

"I brought Steen," she said, "In case he can do something."

"I don't know what you think I can do," the sorcerer replied, frowning. "I'm not going to be able to heal that breech—"

"Wait," Abi interrupted. "Can you freeze the water in it?"

Steen looked at her as if he had never seen her before. "Actually," he said, slowly, "I think I can!"

And without waiting for anyone to say something, he scrambled down the slope to the seep, stood a little to one side of it, and began gesturing. He took longer this time than the last two times Abi had seen him work, but eventually there came a flash of white light from his hands that made her flinch and look away. When she could see again, Steen was bent over, hands on his knees, clearly unable to speak. She slipped and slid her way down the slope herself to see what he had done.

Up close, Steen was a pasty white, beads of sweat standing on his forehead, and panting. But he wore a smile of triumph, and no wonder—the seepage of water had stopped, and all the grass around the area where the seepage was lay covered with a thick rime of frost.

"He did it!" she called upslope, and was rewarded by a "Well done!" from Master Vance.

"How long will that last?" she asked the sorcerer.

"Don't know," he confessed. "But ice stored underground can last most of the summer. Should hold long enough to get the water down." His head sagged with exhaustion for a moment, then rose again. "I'll stay here till that happens, regardless. I can probably do the trick once or twice a day if I have to."

"You're a good man, Sorcerer Steen," she told him, warmly.

He waved off her praise. "I live here too," he reminded her. "Besides, you're the one who thought of it."

"You're going to be a hero," she pointed out. "People here won't care who thought of the idea, they'll care about the man who made it happen."

Still bent over his knees, he managed a shy smile. "I'd like being a hero."

Then he looked up at the men trying to chip away the corner of the dam. "I think I can help up there, too," he said, and he shoved himself erect again. Abi was dubious, but she helped him climb the slope anyway. He studied the situation and made a couple of complex gestures, then sat down again. "Work on the water side, gentlemen," he suggested. "I've done something to pull some moisture into the earth to soften it up a bit."

Whether it was Steen's doing or just dogged determination by the townsfolk, the earthen dam began to yield to their efforts. And once they got down to the waterline, they got some real results.

They were able to tear big pieces out of the dam with their picks, and soon water began running down the face of the dam.

"Get out of the gap!" Vance ordered, and they hurried to obey him. He watched the water flowing down the improvised spillway for a while, then directed two, and only two, of the pickax men to dig a bit more at the spillway—and do so from perches they carved out above the waterline.

"I'm watching for things to get to the point where the water will do the work," he told Abi, as the water carried rocks and clods that had been chipped out of the soil down to the base of the dam. "Any moment now—there! Jump away, fellows, the lake will do the work now!"

Sure enough, there was mud in the water even after the last of the work the pickax men had done had been carried away.

As sunset neared, Vance stood watching the water flowing, deep in thought. Finally he gestured to Bret. "Would you and your brother be willing to stand watch here at night?" he asked.

"Aye, if the chief'll bring us food and our bedrolls," Bret replied. "Why?"

"I'm not expecting the dam to suddenly wash out and collapse, nor for the spillway to enlarge so fast it will create a downstream flood . . . but that's a possibility," Vance said, and he looked at Abi.

Abi shrugged. "All I can tell is the whole dam is under strain, there's a weak spot where we know the drainage is, and another where we put the spillway."

He nodded. "So, you see, if the spillway shows signs of suddenly getting bigger in an out of control fashion, or if the seepage at the bottom of the dam turns into a stream, someone needs to be here to see it and run to warn the town."

"Aye, we can do that," Bret agreed.

Steen sighed. "I should stay. If that starts to happen, I can make an ice dam and slow it down to a safe level again. Plus, I need to keep an eye on that blockage I did underneath." The wizard shook his head. "This is more work in one day than I've done in a moon."

"Well, I hope it won't be necessary, but that is a noble offer on your part," Vance replied, clearly warming up to the sorcerer.

"I'll ride back to the town and let everyone know what's going on, and I'll make sure you get some creature comforts up here," Abi offered, and she headed for the horses. She managed to get hers (reluctantly) into a canter, but his reluctance turned to eagerness once he realized he was pointed in the direction of his stable.

She found a crowd of townsfolk and Mayor Rufous gathered at the edge of town, waiting anxiously for some word from the dam. She reined the horse in and held up her hand, commanding their attention.

"We're releasing the water slowly, so the river is going to start to rise. The men will be coming back soon; we don't need them now. We need to move the work on the floating bridge back about a dozen furlongs from the current riverbank. Steen plugged the hole under the dam with ice, and is going to stay at the dam and keep it plugged until the lake has emptied."

Cheers, some a little hysterical with relief, rang out at this good news. She waited for the noise to die down, then continued. "He is staying up there to keep an eye on things; so are two of our men, who will ride to warn the town if for some reason the dam fails despite our efforts. They need provisioning and—"

Well, she didn't get a chance to say anything else, as townsfolk scattered in every direction. One man brought his mule and cart, a couple of women brought what must have been their own family's supper, and several more brought blankets and water flasks and what looked like a small tent. Without a word, the man with the cart hopped up on the seat and headed for the dam when the cart was full.

The men who'd come up from the town to chip out the spillway came trickling back; the last one arrived just as the sun dropped behind the hills. Abi waited, since she could see a clot of figures in the distance, which turned out to be the three Masters, Jicks, and the man with the cart.

"How is it looking?" Abi asked, anxiously.

"Stable," Master Vance decreed. "I wish I knew how long it would take to empty out that lake, though."

By morning, the river was appreciably higher, and the water was full of mud. Abi and Master Vance rode up to the dam to see what progress had been made.

The improvised spillway and the water level were both a lot lower. Steen looked as if he'd gotten some rest and at least two meals in. "The plug is holding, but I had to reinforce it," he reported. "And last night I had to put in a temporary ice dam, but either the water has hit some harder soil, or the pressure against the dam is lower, because things slowed down again around dawn."

"Probably both," said Vance, getting up on the hill to look at the lake. "Looks like the lake isn't as big as I feared."

"But what are the townsfolk going to do once the lake is drained?" Abi asked.

"That's going to have to be up to them," Vance replied. "We can't stay here forever. They'll have to decide if they want the dam back or are willing to do without it. If they want it, I'll have Beyrn draw up plans and explicit instructions for repairing the old dam, but they'll be on their own unless they have decided to join Valdemar."

Abi was of two minds about that; it didn't seem fair to leave this town on its own with regards to the dam on the one hand—but on the other, Vance was right, and there were more towns and villages to be seen to, and they couldn't allow this one to take up all their time.

On the whole she was glad she wasn't the one in charge of the group; this was not the sort of decision she was comfortable with making.

The floating bridge was complete by the time the lake had finally drained. The river was still a bit muddy, but Master Beyrn assured everyone that eventually it would clear. Not that it mattered; no one in the town used river water for anything; there was a well on every street. Virtually everyone from the town had gone up to marvel at what the receding waters revealed—which included the remains of another town! This one looked about half as large as Ellistown, but the buildings must have been much taller, given the fact that the ruins were three and four stories tall. No one from Ellistown quite knew what to make of it; there had never been so much as an old tale to tell them the place had ever existed. Abi hadn't seen it in person yet; she'd been too busy helping with the construction of the floating bridge and the scaffolding for what would become the stone bridge.

Master Vance and Abi would have loved to have crawled all over those ruins, as they were in a style neither of them had ever heard of—but the mud on the floor of the former lake was at least waist deep, and it wasn't going to dry up any time soon. Beyrn was just relieved that the crisis was over so far as he was concerned. He'd been happily drawing plans and explicit instructions, complete with pictures, of how to repair the existing dam or build a new one.

Back at the encampment, he showed them to Abi, who checked them over for him. "I don't think they're likely to do anything about it this year, though," she told him. "Mostly, they seem to be waiting for the mud to dry so they can treasure-hunt in those ruins."

"Honestly I hope they don't replace it," he said fervently. "And I don't care if all my plans have been drawn up for nothing. That is a *terrible* place to put an earthen dam—or rather, downstream from it was a terrible place to put a town. What were they thinking?"

"That the dam was going to last forever, obviously," she replied, shaking her head. "Sometimes I don't understand people."

Herald Stev had come over, curious as to what they were looking at, and overheard that last. "No one understands how fragile a human is like a Healer," he observed. "And no one understands how fragile an object is like an Artificer."

"That's probably true," Beyrn agreed. "Speaking of fragile, how is the magician? He put in a remarkable effort."

Stev—snickered. Abi tilted her head and looked at him sideways.

"If I didn't know your father and thus you, I'd never say this in front of you, Abi," Stev replied. "But magician Steen has been the recipient of so much gratitude from the ladies of this town that he's having trouble walking."

Beyrn looked blank. Abi burst into peals of laughter. "Oh!" she gasped. "Oh, that's good. That's good!"

Finally Beyrn got it, and turned red. Stev raised an eyebrow at him. "Don't pretend you haven't been taking advantage of the same thing, Master," he said pointedly. "You're the one that discovered the breach in the first place. And I know you haven't been spending all your time drafting dam repair plans."

Beyrn turned even redder, and clamped his mouth shut. Abi decided that teasing him would be unkind.

But she was sorely tempted.

"Is there any word back from Haven about us?" she asked Herald Stev instead.

He shrugged. "'You're doing well, carry on,' is all that's gotten back to me. I've sent three reports so far since we've been here. I didn't really expect to hear anything else."

"Have you seen the ruins yet?" she asked him. He shook his head.

"Then let's take a couple of the hinnies up the river and—can you Send what you're seeing back to your Companion?" she asked.

"Yes, but what would be the point?" he replied.

"Maybe someone will recognize what style those buildings are in. Maybe some scholar will want to document them. It's knowledge. Knowledge doesn't always have to have an immediate use." She felt a little exasperated with him. Had the man no curiosity at all?

"If you say so. At least it's a good day for a ride." He led the way to where the hinnies were picketed, as she mentally shook her head.

The river was a bit higher than it had been when they'd first arrived, but the footings for the stone bridge were well back from the new banks, and so were the mooring points for the floating bridge. Abi was quite curious to see the ruins for herself; she hadn't been back to the site since Master Vance had declared the water was safely draining.

In fact, what she wanted to see, besides the ruins, was the place where the water had worked its way under the dam.

They passed the spot where the newly released river joined the one that went past the town. She was surprised by how small it was.

"That doesn't seem like much of a reason to have put that dam there," she said, pointing at a "river" that Rolan could easily have jumped across.

"But we don't know why the dam was put there," Stev reminded her. "It might have been for flood control—when a heavy rain hits these hills, water can rise faster than you can blink. It might have been as a reservoir for dry years. Or it might—hmm—" he said, and stopped, frowning.

"What was your third reason?" she prompted him.

"It might have been to hide the remains of that town," he said slowly.

The words hung in the air between them, the silence broken only by the hoofbeats of their hinnies.

"Because—?" she ventured.

"Because an enemy not only wanted the town wiped out, he wanted it utterly forgotten, taken off the map," Stev replied grimly. "Because there was a plague, so the town was drowned along with whatever victims were still there. Because something happened there that was so terrible whoever lived there wanted it lost to memory. Or . . ."

"Or?"

"There was something *in* the town that whoever lived there didn't want to escape," he said at last. "You remember what Jicks said about *things*. Magical *things*. Maybe there was one of those in the town and the only way to confine it was to drown the entire town."

"And now . . . we've drained the water . . ." She swallowed.

"However, I am pretty certain Steen would have said something if there was some terrible magic monster still alive in those ruins," the Herald replied, with a shrug. "And I am far more inclined to believe in the evil of man than the evil of monsters anyway. I'd place my bets on an enemy that wanted all memory of the place erased."

"All the more reason for you to send images of it back to Haven," she pointed out. "And besides that, there's a reason you didn't mention."

"What's that?" he asked.

"That whoever lived there was so *evil* that good people wanted all memory of them erased."

He snorted, but smiled.

Near the dam the "new" river was shallow enough that the hinnies were willing to wade across. That put them on the side where the dam was mostly intact, and there was actually a switchback path that took you up to the top of the dam that the hinnies had no trouble climbing. Once at the top, Abi looked down, and quickly found the roundish hole near the base of the dam that was the source of the seepage.

"Doesn't look all that big," Stev said doubtfully, following her gaze.

"The fact that we can see it at all means that the dam wasn't that long from failure," she said soberly. "These things don't just leak out slowly in a controlled fashion, like opening up a bathtub drain. When they fail, they take a huge bite out of the dam, and everything rushes out in a wave."

"I'll take your word for it." They both raised their eyes to the ruins in the center of what had been the lakebed; right in the middle of the valley, with the river cutting its way through the mud right down the center of the cluster of buildings.

They were strangely unornamented, three and four story tall gray pillars with tiny windows. They didn't seem to have roofs, unless the roofs were flat. The buildings huddled together like a covey of frightened quail, as if they—or the people who had built them—were afraid of the hills around them.

"Huh," Stev said, sounding surprised.

"I wonder how they were made," Abi said aloud. "Look how flat their surfaces are! They look as if they were *cast* rather than built."

"I can't imagine living in a place like that," Stev replied, but his voice sounded as if he was preoccupied and not really talking to her. Which meant he was Sending what he saw back to his Companion.

I'm glad I nagged him into it.

She turned her attention back to the ruins, and decided she agreed with him. She couldn't imagine living in a place like that. Why such tiny windows? Surely the winters couldn't be *that* bad here—after all, no one in Ellistown had windows this small.

Then again, appearances might be deceptive. She had no point of reference in that sea of mud. Maybe the windows weren't small. Maybe the windows were normal sized, but the buildings were bigger than she thought.

It didn't look like a place that could spawn a monster. It looked more like a place that would spawn soulless bureaucrats.

She continued to stare at it, until finally Stev said, in a much more normal tone of voice, "Ready to go?"

"Definitely." She sent her hinny down the switchback trail ahead of his. "I can't imagine there being anything worth looking for in those piles."

"I'm inclined to go with a modified version of your reason for why the place was drowned," Stev replied from behind her.

"Oh? What's that?"

"Those things were too tough to knock down and spoiled the view so badly the only thing to be done with them was drown them. And their Artificers, so they could never build an abomination like that again."

Abi had to laugh.

14

"Frankly, I expected more whining," Beyrn said to Abi, as their little caravan left the town, heading eastward, paralleling the Border with Valdemar. "The only thing we finished was the floating bridge."

"Plenty of distractions, I suspect," she replied, holding back her hinny so he could ride up alongside her. "Someone pointed out that all that drying mud is probably the best soil for miles around, and now besides wanting to crawl through those ruins looking for treasure, the farmers all want to spread cartloads of the mud on their land. They're already turning everything they can into a cart."

"Huh." Beyrn blinked. "Is that going to do any good?"

"Probably quite a lot," she told him. "The land around here is poor. That's why you don't see the kinds of huge farms and fields of grain you do up near Haven. Buckwheat will grow here, and oats, and some vegetables, but it all takes manuring and a lot of tending. Whether or not people find anything in those ruins, that lake soil is pure gold. And I'm sure all the dead fish left behind will help matters."

"I thought you always lived on the Hill!" the young Master exclaimed. "How did you learn about farming?"

"Keeping my ears open," she said with a straight face. "Our fellow Trainees of all three Collegia come from all over Valdemar. All you have to do is listen and you learn a lot." Then something occurred to her. "If you don't know anything about farming, how did you know that dam was about to fail?"

Beyrn colored. "Dams are my life," he muttered, as if he thought she was going to make fun of him.

"And I'm beginning to think bridges are mine," she replied cheerfully. "Just think, if these people do decide they want Valdemar's protection, you could come back here to Ellistown and give them something better, and be the one to personally direct the construction."

She might have told him that his true love was waiting around the next bend. He just lit up with a rare smile. "That's true, isn't it?" he said. But before he could say anything more, Jicks joined them.

"What's our next stop?" Abi asked. "And how far is it?"

"About two days, and a village a lot smaller than Ellistown and a bit harder to get to," Jicks replied. "That's all the information I have." She paused, then gave Abi a sidelong glance. "Now . . . I'm curious, and given your connections, I suspect you might have an answer for me. Just *why* is Valdemar going to all this trouble for a lot of villages that are barely self-supporting? Why do you even want them?"

Beyrn looked indignant, and as if he was about to burst out with something confrontational, but Abi caught his eye and shook her head. "It's . . . complicated," she said. "The most obvious thing, and the thing anyone on the King's Council will tell you, is that by expanding our borders, we prevent someone else, some unfriendly power, from moving in. So it doesn't actually matter that these little towns and villages have nothing to give the kingdom. What matters is that we prevent someone hostile from taking over here— or prevent this area from turning against Valdemar by itself."

Jicks nodded. "All right. I can see that. But you said it's complicated."

"There are reasons someone not from Valdemar probably wouldn't understand." She shrugged. "Let's just say that Valdemarans don't like to see people who need help and protection not getting any. But we can't just ride in and force people to accept that help."

Jicks barked a laugh. "So you want me to believe you're all doing this out of the kindness of your collective hearts, and you're so sensitive you won't come knocking on peoples' doors until they invite you to? Pull the other one."

Beyrn got red in the face, but one look at Abi and he bit down whatever he was about to say.

Abi just shrugged. "I told you that you'd have to be one of us to understand it."

Jicks chuckled and sent her hinny up to the front of the line to lead the way. Beyrn shook his head angrily. "That . . . rude . . . *cow!*" he spluttered. "Ignorant, pig-headed, blind . . ." he went on in the same vein for quite some time before he ran out of words. Interestingly, none of them were obscene. *Wherever he's from, he's had a very gentle upbringing.*

"No one true way, Beyrn," she reminded him. "If that's what her experience has left her with, well, that's sad. But don't let her make you lose your temper over it."

He huffed a little, but gradually his anger ebbed. "Here I was thinking she was so well-traveled and had seen so much of the world, and I admired her for it! She's nothing but an insular *sell-sword!*"

"And that's precisely why she's so cynical," Abi pointed out. "She's a mercenary from the South. Most of her experience is with the worst of humanity, not the best. She doesn't know how to recognize altruism when she sees it and probably thinks it's just a granny's tale that only children would believe in." She looked ahead at Jicks' erect back. "That doesn't stop her from being kind when she thinks she can afford to be, or honorable, or good company. She's still the same woman whose stories you laughed at a fortnight ago."

"I suppose," Beyrn admitted, reluctantly, after a very long pause. "Do you suppose Bret and Bart think the same way she does?"

"I think Bret and Bart are as dumb as a pair of posts and don't think much past tomorrow's breakfast," Abi replied, in a lowered voice so the two "lads" would have no chance of hearing her. Beyrn smothered a laugh behind his fist, which he hastily shoved in his mouth. "But they're strong, good fighters, and loyal, and have very good tempers, and on this trip that's all that matters. So, tell me about dams."

Beyrn was only too eager to oblige, and it was very clear once he started that dams really were his passion. Well, actually, any construction meant to hold back water. He was extremely knowledgeable about everything from a simple berm meant to divert water to a complex stone dam. She learned quite a lot in that day of riding.

Meanwhile the road they were taking was quite challenging, and Abi was extremely glad that they had hinnies both to ride and to pull their vehicles, because she was fairly certain horses would have been a problem. And near the end of the second day of travel, Jicks stopped them all and pointed up.

"That's where we're going," she said, matter-of-factly. And after a bit of squinting, Abi realized that what she had taken for the exposed, bare stone cliff at the top of one of the hills was actually a village. She gaped.

"Why on earth are they up there?" she asked.

Jicks shrugged. "You have to admit, it'd be hard for anyone to get at them there," she pointed out.

"But . . . where do they get water?"

"The top's a big cistern cut right out of the rock. Plenty of rain hereabouts." Jicks shook her head. "Not how I'd care to live, but nobody's going to get to them without losing more men than it'd be worth to raid a dirt-poor little village."

The journey up that hill, which was a mere trail barely wide enough for their wagons, took the rest of the afternoon. And once they got to their goal, the entire village, all dozen families worth, had come out of their houses to greet them.

Once they arrived, Abi saw that the "houses" were mere facades; the actual buildings were dug out of the rock of the hill itself. And the rock was granite. It made her mind spin to think how long it must have taken to chip out decent-sized dwellings up here.

She'd been afraid that there would be no place for their wagons, but it turned out that there was room for them. Barely. Abi prayed she would not need to get up in the night. She'd probably misstep and fall to the road beneath the village if she needed to use the wood-shielded, stone bench over the cliff that was the village "outhouse."

The needs of this village proved to be very simple; they wanted some sort of system to bring water down out of the cistern so people didn't have to carry it down twice a day. Master Padrick worked out a simple system for them using a minimum of metal parts involving a bucket-chain worked from below and clay pipes; two days later—most of which time was spent teaching them how to trouble-shoot any problems—and they were on their way.

It was at the third town that things turned . . . odd.

This was a walled town, with guarded entrances and exits that were closed at night. And instead of being greeted with smiles when Master Vance announced who they were and why they had come to the gate guard, they were met with scowls.

"Wait here," the grizzled, heavily armored guard told them. "I'll send a runner to the mayor. We'll see if he wants to see you."

"The mayor sent to the King of Valdemar expressly—" Master Vance began indignantly.

"That's as may be," the guard cut him off. "I don't take the word of a lot of scruffy strangers." And the man retreated into the guardhouse, making further speech impossible.

"What on earth . . ." Master Vance said, with exasperation.

Jicks shrugged. "Maybe this lot only went along with the delegation because the others urged it on them. Look at these walls! They probably think they don't need protection from your Guard and army." She snorted. "They've never seen a siege engine either, I'll be bound, or they wouldn't be so smug."

Abi examined the walls, which were stone, and pretty impressive to her mind. At least two stories tall, they had enough room at the top for guards to walk up there, protected by a parapet. There were four guard towers too, two of them visible from where Abi stood.

They stood there, cooling their heels, for the better part of three candlemarks, before someone finally turned up from inside the town. This person, a middle-aged, scrawny man with black hair and beard, wearing what looked like livery, ignored them to go straight to the guard and talk to him in a low voice for quite some time. Finally the guard gestured to them abruptly. "You can go in," he said, with a brusque tone that bordered on rude. "But you follow this fellow, and you do what you're told, and you don't wander off pretending to be lost. Understand?"

"Quite," Master Vance replied, making it clear with his tone that he was offended. He didn't even speak to their guide, he just gestured to the fellow to lead.

They went in through a tunnel under the wall; as Abi expected, there were iron portcullises at either end, and stout wooden gates as well. The tunnel gave out into a street nearly identical to similar walled towns in the South of Valdemar: narrow, with houses and shops whose doors were right down on the street itself, wide enough for a single wagon with space for a pedestrian to squeeze by on either side.

I don't know why that guard warned us not to wander off, she mused. *We'd be pretty obvious if we tried.*

The fact was, that rude greeting made absolutely no sense. And when confronted with something that made absolutely no sense,

Abi's first instinct was to become very cautious and keep her eyes and ears open.

What she saw did not make her feel any better. The few townsfolk they encountered glared at them, frowned, or actually turned their backs on them. It was almost as if they had somehow done these people some great wrong—at least, that was the impression she got.

It can't have been the lake we drained. That was too far away to have affected them. Are they angry because we installed bridges they might have to pay tolls to use? That makes no sense; they can't have found out about that yet. And that water system Vance worked out—that can't be it, either. Something is very wrong here.

Unlike the last two places, this town featured buildings made of brick as well as stone, although stone predominated. Like Ellistown, the buildings were tall and narrow and literally built so closely together that you couldn't have gotten a sheet of paper between them.

There were also a lot of lingering odors; pleasant ones, but mostly slightly unpleasant ones, including a lingering odor of urine and dung. It wasn't hard to see where that came from, either. The houses might be stone, but the streets were unpaved; urine from animals just soaked into the hard-packed earth, and dung that wasn't immediately swept up by an enterprising urchin got trampled into it. Plus it was obvious that they weren't as careful about cleaning their latrines as people in Valdemar were.

It made Abi wish for that village perched atop its hill again, where a constant wind ensured that you smelled nothing worse than gorse.

Finally they came out into a square, with a pump and stone trough in the middle. They stood directly across from a very imposing, three-story tall building of gray stone with actual glass windows that took up all of the back side of the square.

Their guide led them to that building and finally spoke. "You're to come in with me," he said, abruptly. "I'm to take you to the mayor."

Master Vance turned his back to the man to speak to the rest of them, but Jicks spoke up first. "Me and the lads will stay here. Stev—"

"I don't like the feeling about any of this," Stev replied. "I don't think you should all go in there. If nothing else, people might do our wagons and beasts a mischief. My advice is for Masters Vance, Padrick, and Abi to go in, and the rest of us to stay out here."

Jicks nodded, and looked meaningfully at Abi. Abi didn't need to have Mindspeech to know what she was thinking. *Are you armed?*

Abi almost smiled, given that she was never *un*armed. She nodded slightly.

"I agree," Jicks said. "Be careful."

Their guide had been waiting impatiently, actually tapping his toe to demonstrate how impatient he was, as they spoke. When they turned toward him, he heaved an exaggerated sigh, and strode briskly toward the building, leaving it to them to keep up. Another demonstration of rudeness—if Masters Vance and Padrick had not been very fit and vigorous, they'd have been left behind completely.

Inside, the building was not at all unlike the Asterleigh manor, just much larger; outer walls were stone, inner walls were wood, and the floor of the first floor was stone. A foyer with banners hanging from the ceiling led to a large reception chamber that went all the way to the roof, with stairs going up to the right and left, a door in the rear of the room, and doors beneath each staircase. The minion led them up the right hand stair to the top floor, and from there through a series of three rooms, each fitted out with desks and clerks who looked up at their entrance and stared at them silently. Their destination was the fourth room.

And there they found the mayor, sitting behind his imposing desk, wearing a scowl.

The minion bowed his way out, closing the door behind himself. The mayor looked them over, top to bottom. He was an old man, bald, with a fringe of gray hair, dressed in a brown and red striped velvet tunic, the collar of a white linen shirt showing at his neck.

"Well," he said, in a very unfriendly voice. "You certainly have nerve, showing up here again, after what your other lot did."

Master Vance opened his mouth, but Abi put one hand on his arm. "I beg your pardon," she said politely. "But we have no idea what you're talking about. We set out from Haven two moons ago. It took us one moon to get to the Border, we spent the better part of a fortnight and a half to deal with problems at Ellistown, then two days travel, then three days at Cliffedge, then two more days here. We were the only party that set out from Haven, and we left less than three days after your delegation left."

The mayor looked as if he had plenty to say—right until Abi hit him with the barrage of dates, and the fact that they were the only party to have left Haven coming here. He stared at her as if he were not quite sure what to believe.

"If you don't believe me," she said, still in the same reasonable tone of voice, "You can talk to the Herald who is with us. He'll tell you the same thing. Heralds cannot lie, as I am sure you know."

Not *quite* true, because her father, for one, had done his fair share of lying over the years, but these people had only heard rumors of Heralds, and she could probably convince them of almost anything.

A play of emotions ran over the mayor's face. Doubt, skepticism, chagrin, anger, bewilderment. It was when bewilderment finally settled in that he spoke again. "Then who were the *other* people here who ruined our wall?"

"I'm sure I have no idea," Master Vance replied. "But whatever they ruined we can help you fix."

"And why should I—" the mayor began, then shook his head. "Never mind. You can't possibly make it worse. *Benjon!*" he bellowed, making them all jump.

The flunky, the one wearing the brown tunic that definitely *was* livery, entered the room. "Mayor?" he said, looking as if he expected the mayor to order the three of them thrown into gaol.

"Take this party to the ruined wall," the mayor ordered. "And give them what they want. If they're not lying, and they fix the wall, we have a problem."

The wall was a wreck. Stones tumbled everywhere from a V-shaped gap that went all the way down to the ground. Abi and the other three Masters stared at it. Jicks tilted her head to the side. "Looks like a siege engine hit it, except there's no sign of battering on the downed stones," she observed, and moved closer to the breech to examine the fallen stones more closely.

Master Vance turned to Benjon. "What happened here?" he asked.

Benjon sniffed. It was very clear that he didn't trust them at all, no matter what his master had said. Abi suspected that he expected them to know exactly what had gone wrong.

But he answered anyway.

"The wall developed a crack we were unable to stop," he said.

"Your Valdemarans—"

"They weren't ours and weren't from Valdemar," Padrick interrupted him, eyes flashing.

Benjon sniffed dismissively. "The *strangers* then—said they could fix the wall overnight. They painted something on it, and left, telling us that the wall would be healed in the morning. In the middle of the night, there was a clamor, and this is what we found."

Padrick, Beyrn, and Vance stared at each other. "I don't—" Master Vance began.

"I do," said Jicks. She came back to the group. "You're an idiot," she said to Benjob bluntly. "I'll bet your own stoneworkers told you there was no way to repair a crack like that by *painting* something on the stone. I know exactly what happened. What got painted all over the mortar was plain old water. And what brought the wall down was simple magic. Someone snuck back here in the middle of the night and rapidly froze and thawed the water in the mortar with magic until the mortar crumbled and the wall fell apart. And these Valdemarans *don't have magic.*"

Benjon gaped at her. "But . . . but . . . but . . ."

"It's a trick our Mage-engineers in Hanson's Harriers like to use in a siege if they can, though usually they can't get close enough to a wall to work the trick. And usually, they don't get off enough freezing and thawing cycles fast enough to do more than weaken the wall for the engines. But I've seen it done and more than once." She gave Benjon a gimlet eye. "Bet you didn't ask these tricksters for their credentials from the King, did you? Bet you just took their word for it, didn't you?"

Benjon got stony-faced. "I'm not privy to that information."

"Of course you aren't." Jicks snorted. "So eager to get repairs made for nothing, you couldn't hand the keys to the castle over fast enough. Well, now Masters, what do you want?"

"We need all the loose stones piled on either side of the break," Master Padrick said. "And any stones that are still in the wall, but loose, knocked out and added to them. First we'll need to address why the wall cracked in the first place before we can allow you to repair it." He looked down his nose at Benjon. "Give the orders, please, then run on ahead of us. We're going back to the mayor to properly present our credentials, including the petition *he* signed that brought us here in the first place."

By now, a crowd had gathered, and although it wasn't particularly friendly, it seemed that Jicks's commonsense words had fallen on ears willing to hear them. There was a lot of murmuring, and it looked to Abi as if they were going to get the benefit of the doubt, at least for now.

Benjon got rather red in the face, but he'd had his orders from the mayor, so there wasn't much he could do. He bustled off, his spine radiating how indignant he was.

Abi and the other three Masters prowled around the ruined wall, but she saw Padrick was right. There really wasn't much they could do until they uncovered the site of the original problem.

"And this is something you will encounter constantly as a Master," Padrick sighed to Beyrn and Abi. "People who are taken in by charlatans who promise to do something free or very cheaply. Then they come wailing to you when disaster strikes."

"I think there's more to it than that," Stev said, glancing over his shoulder at the crowd that had gathered and still had not dispersed.

"The people who did this didn't ask for money. So why did they do it?"

"That's not our problem," Vance said dismissively. "We're not able to read thoughts—well, all right, *you* can, Herald, but the rest of us can't. Our problem is to repair the reputation of Valdemar, fix the original problem, and get these people rebuilding their bloody wall."

But Abi didn't agree with him that it wasn't their problem, and from the look she got from Stev, neither did he.

Credentials presented and sheepishly accepted, crew assigned to move the stones, they accepted quarters in the massive building that was both the Town Hall and the Guild Hall for every guild in the town. Abi found herself paired with Jicks, sharing a smallish room that at least had two separate beds. And it was going to be nice to be in a bed that she didn't have to curl herself up in to fit.

They both fetched their belongings from the wagon, which had been wheeled into a carriage house attached to the Town Hall, and Abi followed Jicks up the stairs to the upper floor above the Great Hall itself, where the guest chambers were. These were not anything like "plush" accommodations; the rooms were simple and plain, furnished only with two beds and a tiny table between them, and a chamber pot under each bed. The rooms opened up into each other in a long string just under the rooftree, and the ceiling sloped sharply down on either side—but at least there were gable windows to let in light. They'd probably be freezing cold in the winter.

But it wasn't winter, the rooms were clean, and they weren't in the caravan. And this stop would allow them to get the linens from the caravan laundered. And baths! The town had not one, but three bathhouses, and Abi intended to make use of one of them.

Jicks slung her bag down onto the right-hand bed. She looked at Abi with an expression that told Abi she was feeling very awkward about being together in a room they shared, after trying to kiss her. Abi herself wasn't at all sure what to say. *So probably it's best to leave it unsaid.* "I must admit it'll be nice to sleep in a bed that doesn't move every time someone gets up to visit the bushes in the middle of the night," she said instead, opening the windows to let the breeze come through. Jicks managed a smile. Abi took that as a good sign.

Their meals were to come from the inn across the square from the Town Hall, but the parsimonious mayor had decided that the meals were to be sent over from the inn and subject to his orders, not eaten off the menu. So when they all gathered at a very small table set up in the enormous Great Hall, they were greeted with what was probably the cheapest fare the inn had to offer. Pease porridge flavored with bacon, bread and butter, raisins, and thin ale served from a pail.

Bret and Bart dug in without a word. Abi and Jicks exchanged a look and a slight headshake, and Master Vance looked as if he was going to explode.

"No point in getting upset, Master," Herald Stev cautioned him. "This man is going to pinch every penny he has until it screams for mercy."

"Well, he's just guaranteed that we are *only* going to find the root of his problem, *tell* him how to fix it, and move on," Vance huffed. "Really! I've no doubt he's sitting down to roast pork and baked apples this very moment!"

"This is better than my cooking, Master Vance," Jicks pointed out diplomatically, then followed the example of Bret and Bart and dug in herself.

Just as they all were finishing their meal with a handful of raisins, Stev coughed meaningfully, and nodded when Abi looked up. She slowed down her eating, so that eventually everyone had left the table except her and the Herald. By that time the sun had set, with blue dusk visible outside the Great Hall windows. "Let's take a walk," Stev said, and she followed him across the shadow-shrouded Great Hall and out into the stableyard, which was deserted at this late hour.

"I don't like this," Stev said, without preamble. "It's all very well for Master Vance to say that the *why* of this is not our problem, but someone was specifically impersonating our group, and to me, that's a problem."

She nodded. "I was thinking the very same thing. Someone has something to gain by discrediting Valdemar. I don't think it's the mayor."

"I don't either. He'd have to be the best actor in the world to have convincingly put on the performance he did today. Either he should be on the stage, or he was honestly angry, then shocked, then full of chagrin. All my instincts say the latter."

She leaned against the stable wall. "How good is your Mindspeech? Good enough to read surface thoughts?"

"If I'm close enough to the source." She was very pleased that he didn't quibble at what some Heralds would have considered an invasion of privacy—then again, her father wouldn't have bothered to recruit him if he had those kinds of qualms.

"Well then, you know what you should do," she replied. "And taverns are probably the best place to do it. I am absolutely no help to the other three when it comes to this wall problem, so tomorrow I am going to drift around the area where that breech is and listen to the women gossip. I may not learn anything of value, but I can at least get a clearer picture of what the imposters looked and acted like, how many of them there were . . . well, just as many details as I can."

"Good plan," Stev replied, nodding agreement. "All right, the other reason I asked you out here was that I want you to watch out for trouble while I talk to my Companion. These imposters may only be one-time opportunists, or they may be more than that. Either way, your father needs to know."

And that pretty much cemented the assumption that he was her father's agent into certainty.

"Easy done," she replied, and kept careful watch as he slid down the wall of the building to sit with his back to it and apparently nod off.

About half a candlemark later, he "woke up" again, stretched, and got to his feet. "I'm for bed. Looking forward to one that doesn't move six times a night."

She smiled in the darkness. "I think I said the same thing to Jicks before dinner."

———

In the morning, she put on the single skirt she had brought with her, a shirt, and a modest bodice, and after a cheap breakfast of bread and butter and the same thin ale as last night, went out to meet the ladies of Gescony.

She joined the thin crowd of onlookers who were watching a crew of local men move the stones away from the wall and arrange them in neat rows out of the way. It was already warm, although the morning was young, and about half the men were shirtless, so many young ladies were in the crowd, using any excuse they could think of to loiter. Using her talent of being unobtrusive, she joined a knot of women about her age who were off to one side, gossiping. Mostly she learned about which of these men the young ladies admired most, but she did glean the location of the washing well nearest the breech in the wall.

Having learned that, she went back to the wagon, gathered up her own laundry and soap, borrowed a basket, and sought it out.

Now, her clothing was definitely different from the local women, and there was nothing that she could do about that—their blouses had square necks finished with embroidery, while hers had a drawstring neck, they had loose, bell-shaped sleeves, she had tighter ones, their bodices were embroidered black canvas, hers was brown leather, their skirts were black, worn with white aprons, hers was brown, with no apron. But she was fairly sure that if she appeared to keep herself to herself, and seemed to be concentrating on scrubbing, after a while they'd speak freely in front of her. Very likely they'd assume she didn't understand them.

And after a candlemark or so, they did, indeed, start to gossip, as she had hoped.

For three candlemarks of hard scrubbing, wrinkled hands, and a wet blouse, she had learned the following. There had been four of the strangers, and they had not been accompanied by anyone like a servant. They had ridden into and out of town on ordinary horses. None of them had claimed to be, or dressed as, a Herald.

And one of them had stood back while the others had saturated the mortar of the wall with their "curative" liquid. Not doing anything. Just apparently watching.

Had this one been the Mage? Had he been ensuring that the water penetrated deeply into the mortar, using that trick Steen had used at the dam?

It seemed very likely.

The strangers had all spoken the local tongue like natives—so the Mage had probably been able to do for them what Steen had done for the real party from Valdemar.

She carried her basket of heavy, wet clothing back to the Town Hall, got some rope from the wagon, and when Jicks returned to their bedroom from whatever she had been doing, she was greeted by a zig-zag of rope festooned with drying clothing. She regarded the transformed room from the doorway for a moment, hands on hips.

"Sorry," Abi said from the far side of the room, where she was just draping the last pair of stockings over the line. "I didn't expect you back so soon."

"Gathering information at the washing well?" Jicks asked.

Abi once again felt a moment of commonality with the mercenary. "You think there's more to the story too, don't you?"

"It's enemy action, as far as I'm concerned," Jicks replied, but very quietly so her voice didn't carry beyond the room. "There aren't that many people who knew we were going to be doing this, and most of 'em are in Valdemar. There was no reason to specifically pose as us, if all this group wanted was to weaken the wall for an attack or an invasion later. But if the main goal was to discredit Valdemar . . . this may be the first time we've caught them at it, but I'll bet it isn't going to be the last."

"What possible motive could there be, though?" Abi asked. Not that she didn't have her own share of speculations, but she wanted to hear what Jicks had to say.

"Could be someone local to this town that doesn't want to be gobbled up by Valdemar," Jicks replied, ducking under the clothesline to get to Abi. "But my gut says it's bigger than that. My gut says it's someone who doesn't want this whole strip of territory to join up. And that still could be someone local; someone who wants to consolidate this area for himself, or someone who's anxious that all these little towns and villages remain disunited and easy pickings. But my gut doesn't think that's right either."

"So what does your gut tell you?" Abi asked.

"That I haven't guessed the right answer," Jicks said, her jaw set. "But there is one thing my gut knows for certain. We haven't seen the last of them."

15

"Well, there's our problem," said Master Padrick, prodding a soggy patch of ground with his toe. Now that the blocks of stone had been cleared away and the ground had been revealed, all four of them were making faces.

The ground dipped here. It was already at the bottom of the hill. And the ground was . . . wet. Wet ground was shifty ground; it only took one part of the wall being a trifle heavier than the other to have caused that initial crack that had brought the fake Valdemarans here in the first place.

Master Vance nodded with agreement. "Look how green the grass is, too." He turned around and looked at the backs of the buildings that stood behind the wall. Abi noticed that there was a row of outhouses behind those buildings, and that they too were uphill from the wall. "There is not a hope of getting those people to clean out their latrines on a monthly basis," he said with resignation. "And they'll never believe this isn't a spring that just somehow decided to break through at this spot. Or just something temporary."

"Or that wet ground can cause problems in the first place," Abi pointed out.

"So?" asked Padrick.

"So, we pour concrete footings for this spot and build the wall on that. No more shifting ground."

"I haven't seen any concrete in this entire city," Padrick replied, worried. "There isn't even a word for it! They have nothing but mortared walls."

"Then we'll teach them how to make it." Master Vance, then scowled. "This is going to take much more time and work than I wanted to allow."

"Charity, Master Vance," drawled Stev, *not* in his Whites, strolling up beside Abi. "'Tis a great virtue. So I'm told."

Master Vance growled something under his breath and turned to his crew of predominantly shirtless, burly, thick-thewed, and mostly thick-headed workers. "Have any of you any notion of how to create . . ." He swore. "Damnitall, he's right, there isn't even a word for it in your tongue . . . it's like mortar, but you make entire slabs out of it. It hardens into something like stone. Anyone?"

The men looked at each other and shrugged. The more intelligent looked as if they thought Master Vance was crazy.

"Seven hells," he muttered. "We're going to have to make it from scratch and teach them how." He turned back to his crew. "You and you!" he barked, pointing. "Get me a cartload of sand. You and you, get me a cartload of gravel no bigger than this." He held up a rock chip. "You and you, get me a cartload of lime. You get me a cartload of that white clay your potters use. You get me several cartloads of wood, and you get me a cartload of fire-bricks, because we're going to have to build a bloody damned kiln."

They all gawked at him.

"Don't just stand there staring like a bunch of owls! Hop to it!" Jicks shouted.

Well, they recognized the Command Voice when they heard it. They hopped.

Master Vance sighed as they disappeared. "Sennights of pease porridge," he moaned.

"I can always make stew," Jicks offered.

———

Abi had always taken cement for granted in Valdemar. The components were generally available, separately, if not premixed. In fact, the actual formula for it hadn't been taught in her Artificer classes. After all, why would an Artificer need to know how to make it, since every mason already did? Now she got a quick lesson in how it was made, and she marveled at Master Vance's depth of knowledge. He even knew how to build a kiln!

But most of her time, as the components of cement were created, was spent in trying to learn about the four men who had impersonated Valdemarans, by loitering all over the city—just as Stev was. He'd immediately gotten a suit of the local clothing, and so had she—boy's gear, and women's. They each went where the other could not, at least not without being conspicuous.

What she mostly learned was that the imposters had not been housed in the Town Hall but had paid for rooms in an inn near the wall, staying only two nights. Naturally, she posed as a chambermaid to get a look at those two rooms, but the imposters had left absolutely nothing behind. Their stay had been very brief. They had arrived in the evening and hired the rooms, presented themselves to the mayor in the morning, inspected the cracked wall that afternoon, applied their "treatment" the next day, stayed overnight, and left sometime before dawn. By the time the town was awake, the damage was done. Riders had been sent out to look for them of course, but they had completely vanished.

She and Stev pooled what little information they had, while the Masters burned the clay to get the final components they needed.

They sat across from each other, conferring at the table they used for eating meals, in the echoingly empty Great Hall. Light poured in from second floor windows on both sides, touching the banners of all the city Guilds hanging from the rafters. "I haven't learned much more," he admitted. "Whoever these men were, they spent as little time as possible talking to the locals. Most of their interactions consisted of ordering meals. They were even highly secretive about their 'wall-healing potion,' but that's most probably because they didn't want anyone to know it was just water."

Abi drummed her fingers on the table. "Did my father tell you about any would-be warlords down here, or anyone looking to increase his holdings or consolidate these people under his rule?" She paused. "Or hers. Women have as much ambition as men, after all."

"No. In fact, everything his people down here told him indicated the locals were united on one thing: they were all so jealous of one another that they didn't want anyone from along this stretch of territory to rule over the rest of them." He smirked a little. "I think that's why they hit on this scheme of coming under the umbrella of Valdemar."

So there was no answer there. *I need to know the why of this. Knowing the why should tell me who is responsible. But who would have a magician or Mage at his disposal? That's nearly as important. And how difficult would this be? Steen told us that we'd only see really powerful Mages in places where there was a lot of money to pay them, and I certainly haven't seen any signs of wealth so far.*

"I wish Steen were available," she fretted. "He'd know how easy or difficult it is to break a wall apart with that freezing trick."

"There are three magicians in town, and I think we should ask one or all of them," Stev replied. "Look, there's no point in skulking about anymore. People know now that we're the real Valdemarans. They know we're actually *doing* work to fix the wall, not pretending to. Let's just approach these magicians openly and ask their opinions."

She stared at him, wide-eyed. "You mean . . . just *ask?*"

He laughed. "I know, right? We never do anything openly. Well, as my Companion would say, there is a first time for everything."

"Well, I know of one of the magicians, she's got a shop—I suppose you'd call it a shop, even though she doesn't actually sell anything—not far from the washing well I used. I can go talk to her," Abi offered.

"And I'll have a word with the one right here, near the Town Hall." Stev stood up. "At least we can give the appearance of being useful."

————

Abi knocked on the door of the "shop," and when no one answered the door, cautiously tried the latch. It wasn't locked, and she pushed the door open. A bell set over the door jangled as she did so.

It looked like an ordinary shop inside: narrow, a door and a window in the street-side wall, lath and plaster walls on the inside, with counters and shelves on the left and back, and a door into the back half of the place behind the rear counter. And now that she was inside, she saw it wasn't *quite* true that there was nothing for sale. There were a few weapons—several daggers, two swords. The daggers were displayed on the counter, the swords on the back wall.

The door at the back opened, and a woman with the shoulders of a brick-carrier or a blacksmith entered from the rear. Her red hair was as short as Jicks', the sleeves of her shirt were rolled up over her biceps, she wore a leather apron over her shirt, and her arms were muscular enough to match her shoulders.

I thought this was a Mage, not a smith. . . . "I'm sorry," Abi apologized. "I was looking for Mage Evelie—"

"You came to the right place, dearie," the woman replied, sounding like someone's grandmama, amused, but kindly. "You're one of those Valdemarans, aye?"

"Well, yes, but . . ." she glanced again at the weapons on the counter.

"I'm a Mage-smith. I hammer spells into metal," the woman explained with a laugh. "Now, I'm not one of your legendary types. I don't make unbreakable swords, or daggers that never miss, or gods-forbid bleeding talking swords, and why you'd want one of *those* I can't imagine. I just make weapons that are a good bit tougher than your ordinary sword or knife, with edges that never need sharpening, weapons that never rust. Once in a while I make one you can use as a torch, in a pinch."

Abi had to remind herself that she wasn't here to talk about magic swords, much less buy one, even though a dagger that could be used as a torch sounded awfully useful. "Well, I was wondering if you might be willing to help me. Would you be able to tell if the false Valdemarans used magic to bring down the city wall?"

The woman stroked her chin. "Maybe, if there's anything left to find. They might have wiped out their work . . . though I should be able to pick up some traces. Did you want me to go have a look at it? There'll be a fee whether or not I find anything."

"If you could do that, it would help us a lot," Abi admitted.

The woman nodded. "I dunno why that dolt of a mayor didn't ask one of us to come have a look in the first place," she said, lifting up a section of the counter that swung up on hinges and coming out into the shop. Now that she was out from behind the counter, Abi saw she was wearing breeches not unlike Abi's, only with leather patches on the thighs and the front of the lower legs, and stout working boots. "No, wait, I do know. Skinflint didn't want to pay us." She barked a laugh, and led the way out of the shop, pausing only to lock it behind her.

There was a lot of activity at the wall site. There was a kiln going full blast, Master Padrick had marked out the rectangle where the footings would go in string tied around pegs pounded into the ground, and there were two men digging it out to the depth of about a hand. The ground was saturated, but there wasn't a puddle forming in the excavated area, so the cement footings should set regardless of the condition of the ground.

The Mage ignored them all, stalking up to the place where the wall had been, closing her eyes and scowling with concentration.

She stood there a lot longer than Abi would have expected. But finally, she nodded, turned, and stalked back to Abi.

"Three spells, no doubt of that. What three spells, I couldn't tell you; not my specialty. But since everybody knows you Valdemarans don't use magic, if they were your people, I'll eat a set of horseshoes without salt." She said it loud enough that everyone around the breach in the wall could hear her. Then she held out her hand. "One silver."

Abi put two into the waiting palm.

She grinned. "Pleasure doing business with you," she said, giving Abi a little two-fingered salute, and stalked off again, the workers quickly getting out of her way.

Master Vance gazed after her in astonishment. "What was the force of nature that just came onto my worksite?" he asked incredulously.

"Mage-smith Evelie," Abi replied. "She makes magical weapons. She was also able to confirm that there were three spells used on the wall, as we guessed. I'm betting one was to pull water into the wall, one was to freeze the wall, and one was to heat it."

Master Padrick joined them, nodding. "It just occurred to me that you wouldn't need to freeze and thaw the wall several times to make the mortar crumble. Once would do it if you could get it cold and hot enough, suddenly."

"Well, I'm glad she trumpeted the fact that it couldn't have been our people to everyone in earshot," Vance said. "She's local, and probably trusted. This should spread."

Abi nodded. That was why she'd paid the woman the second silver piece.

When Stev turned up, he was relieved to hear that Abi had been successful in her quest. "Because I certainly wasn't," he said ruefully. "The old man was deaf as a post, and I'm not entirely certain he had all his wits. He kept trying to shove me out the door, yelling 'I don't make love potions, young man! You'll have to win her yourself!' at the top of his lungs. I couldn't get it through his head that I was there on other business."

"We've got our confirmation that one of the four fake Valdemarans was a Mage," she replied. "Can you think of anything else we can do? The fact that the quarry has fled and wasn't native to this city limits our options."

"Let's go to the third Mage, just in case he can tell us more," Stev decided, after a moment of thought. "Unfortunately, he's all the way on the northern side of town. It's a long walk."

Abi leveled a *look* at him. "I'm not a Herald. I don't have a Companion. I walked the entire Fair about thirty times every day it was open," she said scornfully. "You're the softie used to riding everywhere."

"Ouch." He stepped back a pace. "Point to you. Let's go."

The northern side of town had not been one of the places where Abi had needed to go until now. And the closer they got to the area marked on Stev's rough map, the more oddly at home she felt.

Because this was the mirror image of the part of Haven where her father had his pawn shop. She was absolutely sure that if the other three Masters had known where Stev was taking her, they'd have had hysterics.

Jicks, on the other hand, was likely to say, "Why didn't you take me along? I miss all the fun."

Stev's white uniform would have drawn a lot of attention, so it was just as well that he wasn't wearing it. As it was, he was getting second and third looks, given that his clothing hadn't been worn to rags, then patched up to wear again. For that matter, so was she, and she had the distinct feeling that this would not have been a good place to wear a skirt.

She adjusted her tunic so both knives showed, at the same time that Steve put a hand on his sword hilt.

The bystanders quickly became uninterested. And those who might have been following them somehow found a reason to peel off in other directions.

"Not the part of town for an evening stroll," Abi observed, trying not to inhale through her nose, because this part of town was a lot more odorous than its counterpart in Haven.

"Or any other time, actually. But at least in daylight we can get them to back off with a show of strength."

The stench here wasn't a sewage smell because, not so oddly, that component wasn't any stronger than it was in the rest of the city. No, it was another sort of smell, compounded of unwashed bodies, sickness, rot, mildew, with the stench of a tannery somewhere nearby, urine baked into the street, and a harsh, acrid stench she couldn't identify. As she'd told that Bardic Trainee back at the Collegium, urine and dung were valuable, and she'd bet her last copper that while the latrines in this part of town were probably filthy, they were also emptied religiously. And the rare bit of dung from donkeys or cart horses probably had three or four urchins competing to sweep it up before it hit the ground.

Conditions improved a bit as they got nearer to the city wall, but it was still quite clear that this was the poorest part of the city—just that the nearer you got to the walls and the guards on top of them, the more "poor but honest" it became. It was also the lowest part of the city, which probably meant that in a heavy rainstorm, every nasty thing in the streets and gutters washed down here. And if there was enough rain that part of the city flooded, it would be here. And the muddy streets here would be the last to dry.

Their goal was another shop, this one with the sign of a black bird over it. They found it in the last street before the wall.

Stev opened the door without knocking.

There was no bell to jangle at their entrance, but there was a skinny lad standing behind a counter filled with little bags made of a scrap of cloth tied with a bit of thread, carefully sorted by fabric color. "We're looking for Korlak," Stev said, loudly.

The boy stared at them, or rather, their weapons, and stood frozen as a frightened rabbit.

"I said, we're looking for Korlak," Stev repeated.

"He's not here," said a voice that was probably supposed to be a child's piping soprano, but was clearly an adult's strained falsetto. *"He's gone to visit his sister. He probably won't be back, ever."*

"We can pay," said Stev.

"Well, why didn't you say that in the first place?" said the Mage Korlak, opening the door the whole way and gently pushing the boy to one side.

Korlak looked a little like a shabbier, more desperate version of Steen.

He could have been younger, but Abi placed him between twenty and thirty, though what was left of his hair was a grimy white. His robe had either once been black and faded to patchy gray, or pale and accumulated so much grime that wouldn't wash out that it had achieved the same effect. It had definitely been turned several times and mended carefully.

A tentative sniff told her that he and the boy at least were accustomed to bathing, though there was a medicinal, bitter smell about him that had nothing to do with a lack of cleanliness.

And there was a crow on his shoulder. It was definitely a live bird. It looked at her and cawed derisively.

"Don't be rude, they have money," Korlak scolded. He turned back to them and looked them up and down. "Ten coppers for your initial consultation," he said.

Stev started to fumble out coppers. Abi slapped three silver on the counter. Korlak's eyes bulged.

"Ah, ah," she cautioned, as he reached for them. "First you tell us if you can do what we want. And what we want is for you to look at the place where the fake Valdemarans brought down the city wall and tell us more about the magic that did it than just the fact that three spells were used. If you can do that, you can have those. If you lie to me, we'll know, and you'll get nothing."

He pulled back his hand, and he and the crow eyed her with about the same expression, or lack of it. "The wall was wrecked by magic?"

"Not initially," Stev corrected. "The initial crack was caused by soil instability under it. The fake Valdemarans used magic to break the entire wall down."

"You should probably go ask Albemarle," Korlak sighed. "As you've probably guessed, I'm not the best Mage in the city."

"Albemarle kept yelling at me about love potions," Stev said flatly. "And the smith is who told Abi that there were three spells in the first place. We need more information and we need it now."

"If you're willing to wait, Albemarle usually comes out of those fits in two or three days and has about a day of being lucid—"

"No," Stev and Abi said together, interrupting him. They looked at each other. "We're under some time pressure," Abi said. "The Artificers want to get out of this city as soon as we've got a footing set for the wall repair. Let's just say they aren't happy about conditions here."

"I see you're getting the benefit of our mayor's notion of hospitality," Korlak said dryly. "All right. We'll do what we can. But no guarantees. Magic is sometimes unpredictable, and mine in particular is unreliable." He glanced at the counter, and the little bags lined up in neat rows. "I can offer you each a potion by way of compensation if I don't come up with anything."

"Do they work?" asked Stev.

"The bellyache tea does," the boy behind the counter spoke at last.

"Two bellyache teas, then," Stev said, and Abi took her hand away from the three coins. Korlak snatched them up, put them somewhere inside his baggy robes, and came out from behind the counter. The boy gave Stev two faded green bags, and Korlak followed them out into the street, crow and all.

"If you don't mind, can we take the long way around, by way of the wall?" Korlak asked nervously, once the door shut behind him, casting a glance at the less-than-welcoming streets they would have to cross.

Stev sighed. Abi cast him a mocking glance. "I'd prefer that myself," she said. "I don't mind walking more."

They didn't actually have to go the whole way around. It wasn't even a quarter of the way when the state of the houses and shops told both Abi and Stev that they were in "respectable" neighborhoods, and it was safe to cut across the city from there. When they reached the breach in the wall, it was late afternoon, and the site for the footings had been dug out, and framed in with scrap timber. It looked to Abi as though the damp ground wasn't going to cause a problem with the concrete curing as long as Master Vance got the right mix.

"Ah, there you are," said Vance, when he spotted them. "The last batch of clay is in the kiln. It should be burned off by morning. We'll be able to mix and pour the cement then, and if all goes well and it sets and cures properly, we can be out of this place the next day, and they can rebuild the wall as quickly as they please."

"And if it doesn't?" Stev asked.

"It will!" Vance snapped. Clearly his temper had been tried by day after day of monotonous, poverty-level food. Not that Abi blamed him. Especially not after the generous way in which they'd been treated back at Ellistown. The food wasn't going to kill them, but it wasn't what they were all used to. In fact . . . unless she was very much mistaken, he'd lost weight.

"We *might* not get a good cure because we are not using components that have come from people who do nothing but make cement," Master Padrick said, soothingly. "It won't take long to find the proper mix if that happens. And we made plenty of all the ingredients for several batches. And as a bonus, the couple of more intelligent fellows we have here are learning how to make cement. So we've brought something new to the city."

"Not that they'll be grateful," Master Vance growled.

Abi did not fail to notice that Korlak was carefully keeping Stev and her between himself and Master Vance. "Can we just get on with this, please?" the Mage whispered, timidly.

"We have another Mage to look over the wall, Master," she said.

"Fine, fine, whatever." Vance waved a dismissive hand at all three of them. "Go investigate your mystery. I'll see you back at the Town Hall. Jicks said she's going to have a word with the people at the inn that's supplying us. Maybe that will bring an improvement in the food."

He and the other two Masters stalked off in the direction of their host building. Korlak drifted over to the wall, looking down for a moment at the excavation with bemusement.

"What, exactly, are you going to do here?" he asked.

"The ground's wet here, and it's unstable. That's why the wall cracked in the first place. We're making a stable platform for the stones of the wall out of something called"—she used the Valdemaran word—"*cement*. It will fill this form and harden as tough as a stone."

He eyed the extent of the form, which extended into dry ground on either side. "Would a single stone slab have worked as well?"

"Do you people have stone slabs that size lying around here?" she countered. "Do you have the means to transport blocks of that size and place them without cracking them?"

"Well, yes, I mean, we have the means and the men to cut and transport something of that nature, but the mayor won't pay the stonemasons for a job that complicated," Korlak admitted. "Even with all the men he threw at you, this isn't costing him a fraction of the price of a job that size. This lot is all unskilled labor, and they cost coppers, not silver."

"I'm glad the Masters aren't here to hear that," Stev put in. "The way their tempers are right now, if they knew all of this could have been done by getting a big enough slab of stone in, there'd have been an explosion." Abi nodded.

"Why don't you have a look at the wall," Abi suggested to the Mage.

Korlak picked his way around stones and got to the wall itself. He put both hands on the section still standing, closed his eyes, and his head sagged. The crow on his shoulder froze, not moving a feather.

They stood like that for some time, long enough for the lengthening shadows to make considerable progress and for all the men except the ones manning the kiln overnight to go off home. Abi and Stev sat down on two of the stones. The sounds of the city reached them faintly; the murmur of voices (now and then one raised, shouting something incoherent), the noise of hoofbeats and rolling cart wheels, the steps of the guard on their section of the wall, approaching, then receding.

"Sweet Mother of Kernos!" Korlak shrieked.

Stev actually fell off his stone. Abi leaped to her feet, daggers out.

Korlak had somehow leaped a good cartlength backward away from the wall. He stood there, frozen, eyes wide, pupils dilated with shock. The crow on his shoulder flapped its wings and made alarm calls.

Abi ran to him, sheathing her daggers, as Stev picked himself up. She seized Korlak's elbow to steady him, with one eye on the crow in case it took the notion to attack. "Magician! What happened? What did you see?" she asked urgently.

Korlak began shaking, as if he were standing in the middle of a blizzard.

Then his eyes rolled up into his head, and he dropped to the ground.

Or started to. Stev caught him before he got too far.

The crow startled up into the air as he started to fall and landed on Abi's shoulder, making pathetic, whimpering sounds. "Let's get him to the nearest tavern and get something into him," Abi suggested.

"Good idea. I can carry him, he probably weighs less than you do," Stev replied. "Lead the way."

Unconscious people carried out of the Green Dog Pub were not an unusual sight, but an unconscious person carried in was something else again. They managed to attract a small group of well-meaning drinkers, some of whom were drunk enough that they weren't all that far from resembling Korlak and none of whom had any useful suggestions.

Except one.

The cook came bustling out of the kitchen, made Stev put the Mage on the floor, pulled his legs up and draped them over a bench, then patted his cheeks until he moaned and opened his eyes. "Get him up slow," she said, brusquely. "I'll be back."

She bustled out and bustled back in again with a wooden cup. "Drink," she ordered the Mage, raising him into a sitting position and shoving the cup under his nose. Obediently, he drank.

"Brandy?" asked Stev.

She snorted. "Hot honey-water. Like's not he ain't et since breakfast, if then." Satisfied that the Mage was not going to die in her pub, she bustled back out again, looking remarkably like a busy hen.

Abi and Steve took his mug, then helped him up into a sitting position on the bench.

The crow hopped back onto his master's shoulder and rubbed his beak against Korlak's cheek, crooning.

Korlak huddled in his seat, leaning on both elbows on the table, mug clasped in white-knuckled hands, sipping and shivering. One of the serving girls turned up at the table and slapped down a plate of stew with a fat chunk of bread and butter on the side in front of him. Abi paid for it without a second thought and began coaxing him to let go of the mug, pick up the spoon, and eat.

The crow hopped down to the table and began helping himself, looking up at Korlak and helping himself to more, as if he were trying to show the Mage what to do. Finally the sight of his pet eating seemed to rouse him from his terrified stupor, and he did as Abi asked, slowly spooning stew into his mouth. Then he put down the half-empty mug of honey-water and tore off small bits of buttered bread to give to the crow, who looked anxiously into his face before devouring the tidbit.

Stev sat down across from him, Abi next to him. That seemed to steady him more, too.

"Better?" Abi asked.

He took in a huge breath and let it out in a sigh. "Yes . . . and no." He shivered again. "Do you suppose you could tell me why a party of fake Valdemarans would have someone along who conjures demons?"

———

". . . so we escorted him back to his shop, and I paid him a gold piece for his troubles," Abi concluded. She cast a glance around the table. The other three Masters were sitting there with their spoons in the plates, staring at her, open-mouthed. Jicks' jaw was set hard. Only Bret and Bart continued to eat, jaws moving in unison like a pair of munching horses.

"*Demons?*" Master Vance sputtered incredulously.

She nodded. "That's what he said. One spell to pull the water into the mortar. One spell to invoke a demon with powers of heat and fire, one spell to invoke a demon with powers of cold and ice.

He says he doesn't know how they managed to control these things, or how they managed to keep them working on the wall without being seen, but he also says he couldn't tell if the demons were also invisible, which is possible."

"Demons?" sputtered Master Vance.

"I've heard of Mages that can call them up," Jicks said, her jaw still set. "Never saw them myself, but plenty of people I know and trust have. But there's one set of people I've heard of that can reliably call 'em up and make 'em dance that's got a connection to you people, and if tales are true, a very powerful hate on for you."

"Us?" Master Padrick bleated, bewildered and alarmed.

"Not you, specifically, Master," Jicks amended. "You, Valdemarans." She looked to Stev, who nodded grimly, and they spoke as one. "Karsite Priests of Vkandis."

16

Karse, it seemed, wasn't much more than a name to the three Masters, and "Vkandis" wasn't even in their vocabulary. So they weren't much help. They knew Karse was an enemy country, but that was about it.

Then again, they were no hindrance either, as Stev, Jicks, and Abi tried to put what they knew together with what was happening down here. As Masters, they knew to listen when they were ignorant, because you cannot learn when your mouth is open.

"I've never heard of Karsites coming this close to Valdemar outside of their own borders," Jicks mused. "Then again, they haven't made a major move in . . . years, if not decades."

Stev and Abi both grimaced. "Well, you wouldn't," Abi replied. "And it hasn't happened in my lifetime, but there've been Karsite agents inside Haven in relatively recent memory," Abi replied. "Not the Mage-priests, though. They can't handle crossing the Border."

"Heard about that," Jicks said laconically. "Makes you wonder what'll happen to the Mages here if you people extend the Border the way you're planning."

Abi grimaced, because that suddenly interrupted her line of reasoning. She hadn't thought of that, and she knew it was something she should have. What would happen to Steen, Albemarle, Korlak, and Evelie? It didn't seem at all fair that they'd find themselves driven out of their own homes and businesses because the Kingdom of Valdemar itself, and not the people of Valdemar, didn't want them there.

"It's something we hadn't considered, because we just don't have Mages," Stev admitted. "I'll include that in my report tonight." He didn't add that it was difficult even to think of magic inside Valdemar, so it was going to be a bit difficult to get this properly seen to by the Council.

And I'll nag Kat about it, Abi decided. Kat wanted to solve problems for Valdemar? Here was a very perplexing one for her to solve. And Kat had been exposed to the concept of magic a lot, because of associating with Mags' family, so she wouldn't forget.

"So I can think of plenty of reasons why Karse would want to discredit Valdemar," Jicks continued. "And this is a good, cheap way to do it. Not only will it leave the people in this strip of land angry and disinclined to join your Kingdom, it'll make your allies think twice about your promises. Karse doesn't even need to move in here themselves. All they need to do is poison the well."

"But how did they find out we were here in the first place?" Stev wanted to know. "And find out fast enough to get agents here as soon as we did?"

"It wasn't a secret," Abi pointed out. "We rode out openly, and plenty of people saw us go."

"But it wasn't well known either." Stev drummed his fingers on the table. "There's something we're missing. I just can't put my finger on it."

"Karsite agents in Haven again?" Abi suggested. "All you need is one really *good* one and a network to relay information quickly." *And father will be turning the air blue with curses to think that he missed catching someone.*

"Possible," Stev admitted grudgingly. "I'd like to think we're better at winkling them out than that."

"I'd like to think so too, but let's not let our vanity rule what we consider as likely." Abi tried to think of something useful, but nothing sprang immediately to mind. "They're going to keep doing these things," she said. "Making things worse, wrecking things. That's why they're here in the first place. We need to catch them and stop them before they do something that gets someone killed."

"Better idea," Jicks interrupted. "We need to send your Masters home before *they* get killed. This time it was just a wall, an inconvenience, and people were just annoyed at us. The next time, like you said, someone could get killed, and your Masters are going to find themselves dancing on the end of a rope before we can convince anyone that we're innocent. Mobs are impossible to reason with."

Abi bit her lip. Stev nodded. "You're right. And let's not forget the fact that when we catch up with these imposters, one of them is a Mage who controls demons. The Masters can't protect themselves, and I don't want to see them turned into hostages."

"But what about fixing what these Karsites are breaking?" Abi retorted. "We need the others! If we don't do that, we don't fix Valdemar's reputation!"

"You're a Master," Jicks pointed out, and waited while she tried to think of a response to that.

I am, but . . .

She didn't have the depth and breadth of experience the other three did. She hadn't known how to make concrete, for instance!

So you would have gotten them to cut and fit a stone slab for the new footings. There's always more than one answer. Isn't Valdemar built on that very premise?

But there were so many things she didn't know!

So you improvise, using what you do know. You're not Mags' daughter if you can't improvise. . . .

"I . . . can try," she said.

"Good." Jicks nodded her head. "So let's figure out how we can convince your three Masters to go home, and head out on the track of these Karsites." She looked ready to start right that very minute. It occurred to Abi that thus far Jicks' life had been very tame. And while she might have enjoyed that for about a moon, clearly she was itching to bash something in the head again.

"Wait—this isn't what you signed up for," Stev said, holding up a hand. "What do you mean by 'we'?"

Jicks just grinned. "What I said. You, me and Abi. When we track these bastards down and put a hole in the priest, there's going to be a very big reward for me. A nice reward from your King, I'm sure, because your King is pretty generous, and an even nicer one from Menmellith, because they have a standing bounty on these Mage-priests. Between the two, I'll have enough to buy that pub I want to retire to."

"Huh," was all Stev said.

She's never going to retire—oh wait. A pub. Where she can have a nice bar fight every evening if she wants, just to remind her of old times.

"All right, then," Abi agreed. "So, we send the Masters back with your boys?"

"And the caravan and one of the wagons." Jicks nodded. "With only three of us we won't need all the supplies, and the three of us can fit in the wagon to sleep."

Abi thought regretfully of that nice, comfortable bunk in the caravan, but had to agree. They didn't need any of those things . . . *And, oh, gods, I cannot believe I am about to say this but . . .* "We don't actually need the wagon either," she said, cringing a little. "And we'd be faster without it. You remember what the Stablemaster said: the hinnies can eat just about anything. We could take all the riding hinnies, use two of them for pack animals, and . . ."

"Personal opinion, bad idea," Jicks countered. "One, that leaves someone with no experience driving a wagon. Two, I want the supplies. In fact, I want most of the supplies—Master Vance has money enough to buy meals at inns all the way back home. Three, thunderstorms around here can be deadly; I want something we can shelter in."

"I agree on all counts," Stev said. "Remember, we may be encountering hostile locals, and I'd rather know we have food we can trust, and not eat a plate of mushrooms that has me curling up and rolling around like a hoop."

Abi gulped a little. She knew just enough about poisons to know he was absolutely right.

"Right!" Stev continued. "Step one: Get the footings done, because we'll never get them out of here until the Masters are happy with what they're leaving behind. Step two: get them on their way."

"That'll be a lot faster than getting down here," Abi pointed out. "They're used to riding all day now."

"Step three: figure out which way those bastards went. Step four: make sure we're all outfitted as closely as possible to the locals. We're going to say we're from Ellistown from now on. Then—"

"No plan survives contact with the enemy," Jicks interrupted. "That's good enough for now."

"I'll go talk to Haven and tell them what's happened and what we've decided," Stev said. "They'll argue with me, I expect, but they're there and I'm here, and we've all already decided to go through with this, right?"

Abi and Jicks both nodded, but Abi could only think of what her father and mother would . . .

. . . or maybe not. She was older than Perry had been when *he* got caught up in a dangerous situation. She wasn't alone—she was with a very experienced Herald, and an equally experienced fighter, and as much of a mercenary as Jicks was, Abi also had seen plenty of evidence that she was just as honorable. So . . . they'd worry, but they wouldn't immediately demand that she come home.

"You can go home too, you know," Jicks said suddenly, looking at Abi. "I could bring one of the boys. You know how to drive and you're good with the hinnies. You're awfully young to go diving into danger like this."

For a moment, she was tempted. If she went home now, she'd be back in time for most of the bridge building. But after a moment of thought, she shook her head. They not only needed people to take out the Karsites, they needed someone to repair damage and Valdemar's reputation with it. "How old were you when you first signed up with a Company?" she countered.

Jicks grinned. "Fifteen. Point taken. And it seems you know what you're getting into. I sure as hell had no idea when I first signed on."

"I'll vouch for that," said Stev.

"All right then, you go commune with your horse. I'll dig the boys out of the pub and tell them what's going on. In the morning we tackle the Masters."

"No, after they pour the footings," Abi corrected. "And then only if it goes well. Otherwise I am afraid we'll have a Master-Vance-shaped tempest on our hands."

The mixing of the cement went well, with all four of the Masters examining the cement critically at every stage to see if it differed in any obvious ways from cement they'd poured in the past. The pouring went well. The form filled up nicely, the cement began to firm up almost as soon as it was poured, and by lunchtime, Master Vance decreed that they could all go to lunch, leaving two of the locals to keep guard over the curing concrete.

"I don't want to see so much as a bird footprint in my cement," Master Vance growled before they all paraded back to the Town Hall. "If I do, there will be Consequences." The two men nodded, and sat down, one at either end of the poured concrete, to keep a careful eye on it while they ate their own lunches.

Jicks' little talk with the innkeeper had only produced the result that they got extra bread and butter, and there was now more vegetables and shreds of meat than broth in their soup. Evidently the mayor's parsimony weighed heavier in the scales than Jicks's "persuasion." But none of the Masters had time to comment on this minor change because Stev got right to the point of what was going on and what was going to happen as a result as soon as they all sat down.

"There are four Karsite agents, one of them a Mage-priest who can invoke their demons, posing as the Valdemaran delegation," he said bluntly. "We know this now. We know that while they haven't hurt or killed anyone yet, given that they don't care if they do, it's only a matter of time before they will. And when that happens, the moment we set foot in that town, there will be a mob looking for our blood. By the time the mob is appeased, one or more of us is going to be hurt or dead, It's too dangerous for you to be here now." Stev paused. "And another thing. As soon as they find out you're fixing what they destroyed, they'll come for you themselves. You need to go back home."

They all looked up at him, blank-faced as they digested this. Abi half expected objections, but they didn't make any; evidently they took what Stev said seriously. They looked at each other, then at Abi and Stev, then back to each other. Master Vance spoke first. "I don't like to leave a job half done," he said reluctantly.

"You'll like it even less leaving it in a coffin," Jicks said dryly.

Master Vance blanched. But Padrick and Beyrn nodded, as if this was what they had expected to hear. "Can we go straight north to the Border from here?" Beyrn asked anxiously.

Jicks shook her head. "Too much rough ground for the wagons. Retracing your steps is the only way. You'll have the caravan and one wagon and you can't take those across country or on the little tracks you'd need to take. But you'll go back faster because you won't be stopping to solve problems."

"And we're used to riding all day, so that will speed things up as well," Vance mused, and then realized what she'd said. "Wait. *One* wagon? Are we leaving one here?"

"No, we're taking it, Abi, Jicks, and I," said Stev. "We need to hunt these men down and eliminate them before they destroy Valdemar's reputation."

"Abi? I absolutely *forbid*—" Vance began.

"You don't get a choice, Master," Abi interrupted. "You three and Bret and Bart are going home the fastest way possible. Jicks and Stev and I are tracking down these Karsites. I'll be coming up with solutions to fix any problems they've caused, but we're going incognito until we make sure no one's been hurt, and only then offer to fix things. Three people and a wagon probably won't attract attention, but eight people and three vehicles will. And when we catch up with the imposters, we're going to stop them. That's what's going to happen."

"But—but—but—you're nothing but a slip of a girl!" Vance protested. "Oh, I don't doubt you can solve any problem the three of us could, but what about when you finally confront these villains?"

"Haven't you seen the girl practicing against me in the mornings?" Jicks asked quietly. "I'm not holding back, you know. Abi's not some sheltered little scholar who doesn't know which end of a sword to hold. She's *good*. I'd have her at my back in any fight."

Master Vance stared at the mercenary for a long time.

"Isn't this the business of the Guard?" he said, finally.

Stev actually smacked himself in the face with his palm. "Please tell me you're not that naive," he begged. "Send the Valdemaran Guard *past* our Border to hunt down Karsites? Not only would we never get another ally to trust us again, we'd never get any of these people to agree to—"

They had been so intent on their conversation that not even Abi had noticed that a half dozen people had entered the Great Hall until the mayor cleared his throat ostentatiously. And they all jumped, turned in their seats, and stared.

The Mage-smith elbowed the mayor, who also jumped. "Uhm . . . it has come to our attention . . . that . . . uhm . . . the vandals who broke our wall were agents of Karse," the mayor said nervously. "There's a standard bounty on agents of Karse posted by the Crown of Menmellith, which we honor here, especially the ones that can summon demons. I've been asked to give you authorization and deputization to find them and deal with them. If you will. You don't have to. But—"

"Oh, for Vutan's sake," said Evelie, the Mage-smith, shoving the mayor aside. "I swear, I am going to run against you next year, you useless waste of air, and you can go back to swindling children out of their pocket money." She snatched some rolled-up documents from the mayor's limp hand. "This gives you all the authority you need to do whatever you want to do with the Karsites when you find them," she said, thrusting the documents at Jicks. Jicks took them. "If you want the reward, bring back something to prove you put them in the ground. Please don't make it anything that rots." She took a bundle of leather away from a boy who looked as if he was working on the same set of muscles she had, and handed it to Abi. "Saw you favored knives. These aren't my work, they're my teacher's. She said they were 'special,' 'good against evil,' and her Master Works. Better Mage and a smith than me, but not real articulate. I'm only *lending* them to you, understand," she added. "I expect you to bring them right back to my shop when you're done. Same for you," she added, taking a longer bundle from the same boy and giving it to Stev. "You get to *borrow* the sword of the set."

Abi peeked inside the oiled leather. The knives, from what she could see, were exceptionally fine. Better than anything she currently had with her.

"Anyway," Evelie continued, turning to the Masters. "We'd appreciate it if you three gentlemen can see to the wall being rebuilt, and we'll load up your wagon and send you on your way back home. That's it." She spread her hands wide.

"Well, this does take care of possible international incidents," Stev admitted wryly.

"But I have to say, if I were you, I wouldn't advise your King to go bringing an army down here," warned a third man, one extremely well dressed. "At least, not until I can reconvene the same delegation as before and we can agree to such a step. And we would be far more likely to hire our own mercenaries than invite your Guard, at least until we can agree we are joining Valdemar proper."

"Ah," said Stev. *"There* it is." He looked at the three Masters as if to say *I told you so.*

Then he stood up, and shook the hands of everyone who had come trooping in here. "I think we all agree on all points," he said. "With one exception."

"What would that be?" asked Evelie, sounding suspicious.

"That you do something about the food you've been serving

us," Stev said. "Please. 'Master' isn't just a pretty title. All four of our Masters are the equivalent of any of your Guild Masters, and you've been serving them peasant swill. Rude, don't you think?"

Evelie glanced down at the poor fare on the table and lifted her lip in a sneer of contempt. "Oh, I very much agree with you, Herald," she said, bestowing a glance on the mayor that made him shrink visibly. "I'll see to this myself."

To Abi's relief the cement was curing nicely when they returned to the site. "Seven days," Master Vance breathed. "Seven days, and we can start rebuilding the wall. These may be the longest seven days of my life. I swear, I will be looking over my shoulder every night for Karsite demons."

"Well, that's easily fixed," Jicks said cheerfully. "Go round up every priest you can find in this city and have them bless your sleeping quarters. They're demons, right? Should be *some* god out there that can keep 'em away."

Master Vance cheered up immediately. "By Jadus, you're right! And while I'm at it, I'll talk to that formidable smith. Maybe she has some blessed iron we can hammer into the beams to keep things at bay."

He, Beyrn, and Padrick went to find a city map showing where all the temples were. Jicks heaved a sigh of relief. "Let's get to the wagons and get supplies sorted out," she told Abi. "The sooner we're out of here, the better the chance we have of catching up to the imposters before they realize they're being tracked. And *track* is what I'd like to do. I'd like to get caught up enough to them that we can actually track them and then take them on ground of our choosing."

"Seems solid," Abi agreed, and they retired to the dusty carriage house to sort through the contents of both wagons, deciding what they needed and what they could leave for the others.

"There's no point in leaving any food that requires cooking, It's not that the boys can't cook, it's that they don't care what they eat. So they're as likely to serve burned or raw food as anything decent." Jicks just shook her head. "I don't know how they do it. I swear they're half goat."

"I think it's funny that Vance, Beyrn, and Padrick all said they didn't care what they ate, and I think they didn't, until they got here," Abi replied, shifting a bag of oats from the wagon they were leaving to the one they were taking.

"There's a difference between monotonous but decent, plain food and shitty food," Jicks replied bluntly. "The little talk I had with the innkeeper? I learned a few things. That mayor ordered us to get the stuff that not even the lowest of the inn staff was eating. Our rations were literally leftovers no one else would eat, made into soup, and I'm surprised none of us got sick."

"That's just wrong," Abi frowned. "Just because someone else tricked him, that's no reason to take it out on us."

Jicks shrugged. "Some people are like that. And I wouldn't be at all surprised to discover the City Council gave him a certain amount of money to feed and house us once we proved ourselves, and he decided to skim as much of it as he could. That's why he fed us far away from anyone else, so no one else knew what he was doing."

Once they had all the supplies moved, it was suppertime, and they joined the others in the Great Hall. And waited. And waited.

Finally just as Master Vance, stomach growling, was about to explode with anger, a boy appeared in the door. "Will ye not come over to the inn, Masters?" he said, in a tremulous soprano. "Yer dinner been waiting there this half candlemark."

Master Vance's demeanor completely changed. The anger washed from his face, and his entire body relaxed. They all got to their feet and followed the boy out the door, crossing the square to the inn on the other side.

When they got to the inn, oh! The change! They were ushered to a good table on the hearth. Slices of leg of lamb right off the roast at the fire were cut for them, and placed on a bed of roasted root vegetables to absorb the juices. There was good, strong beer, not the ale that they now knew had been collected from unfinished mugs and thinned down with water, and some kind of nut tart to finish. "Ye'll be eating here from now on," said the innkeeper, when they tendered their compliments and satisfaction. "And it's ashamed I am of the swill Hizzoner had me send to ye."

Abi was pleased to see that the three men were so satiated that they had temporarily forgotten about Karsites and demons, and went up to bed in a jolly frame of mind, talking about how they intended to rebuild that wall.

———

With Stev on the box of the wagon, Jicks and Abi mounted up on their hinnies. The sun wasn't even up yet, and Abi glanced up at the attic of the Town Hall, dark against a lightening sky. "They'll be all right, won't they?" she asked anxiously.

Jicks laughed. "As all right as we are, probably better." She nodded at the wagon, which had had diagrams and symbols written all over the wooden bed and the canvas top in indelible ink, and countless little charms sewn onto the front and rear canvas flaps. Even the hinnies had charms fastened to their bridles and saddles. "Once the Karsites find out about us, and they will, eventually, we'll be the rod that attracts lightning. The Karsites won't even look for the others."

I'm not quite sure how comforting that is.

They were waiting for just enough light to fill the streets that the hinnies wouldn't stumble over anything. Just as real dawn began, and Jicks picked up her reins to urge her mount to move out, someone ran—well, if you could describe a flapping chaos of oversized robe hurrying in the gate as "running"—toward them.

"Wait!" cried the Mage Korlak, breathlessly, as he stumbled to a halt at Jicks's side. His crow flapped down out of the sky to land on his shoulder. "You'll need a Mage. Take me with you!"

"I thought your magic was unreliable," Jicks said, raising her eyebrow.

He blushed. "Better unreliable than nothing," he retorted.

"And I thought you were terrified of demons," she pointed out.

"Anybody with any sense is terrified of demons." He stared at her stubbornly.

She leaned down over her saddle-bow. "All right. I'll bite. *Why* do you want to come with us? The real reason."

He flushed a deep and brilliant crimson. "I . . . can't tell you."

Jicks sighed. "And yet, you will. One night over the campfire, you'll get some wine in you, and you'll proceed to tell us a long, sad, and hopelessly entangled story about how your master was attacked by Karsite demons, and you didn't stay to help him, he died, and the demons turned your hair white overnight. Not necessarily in that order. And we'll sympathize with you, because only a monster wouldn't, and then when we do encounter the

Karsites, you'll do something stupidly brave to make up for your failure and get killed."

He had gone from red to white, and his mouth fell open. "I— but I—"

"You aren't more than thirty. Twenty-five, I'm guessing," Jicks continued ruthlessly. "I'm a good judge of a lot of things, Korlak, and age is one of them. Telling who the people are who are desperate to redeem themselves is another. Now, how much of that did I get wrong?"

"Only that I didn't run," Korlak muttered, looking at his shoes. "I fainted."

"Well, good, I'm glad we got that over with," Jicks replied. "Now . . . just how do you think you'll be useful to us?"

"It's not so much me," Korlak replied, looking up again. "It's this." And he held up a small, leather-bound book. "It's his book of spells."

Jicks sat back in her saddle and nodded slowly. "That's more like it. I'll tell you now, from what I know of Mages, that a lot of your unreliability is due to semistarvation. Eat, and you'll be fine. Study that book for anything specific against demons. All right then. Climb aboard the wagon, Mage Korlak. And keep that bird from crapping on the bedrolls."

Instead of taking the route she had planned out of the city, Jicks went through the marketplace; there was one weaver setting up her stall, and Jicks had Abi buy blankets enough for a fourth bedroll. Other than that, Korlak actually had made as adequate a set of preparations as his poverty allowed; he had two changes of robes and more smallclothes bundled up on his back, plus eating utensils and his wand and knife. "I'm from the Red River School," he explained to a bemused Stev as they sat on the wagon-box. "We use sigils and runes for casting spells, not components."

"How's your healing?" asked Jicks.

"It's not bad, when I'm not hungry. . . ." His voice trailed off.

"Good. There's travel biscuit in a satchel under the seat. Eat it until you're not hungry," she ordered.

He rummaged and put the satchel on the seat between himself and Stev, removed a packet, and started eating. "This—this's *good!*" he exclaimed. "Why does everyone always complain about this stuff?"

Jicks exchanged a look with Abi, one that said *Like I thought. Not hungry. Starving.*

He went through two entire packets of the biscuit before he sighed and put the satchel back under the seat. "I feel like I need a nap now," he said, with chagrin.

By this point they were out of the city and on route to the next scheduled stop.

"So go make yourself comfortable back there and have a nap," said Stev. "I very much doubt we're going to have any trouble that we can't see for leagues."

He gestured at the road before them, which wound along the side of a river valley between craggy hills. From her reading, Abi had a good idea what ideal country for an ambush should look like. This wasn't it.

Korlak didn't have to be asked twice; he climbed into the back of the wagon, and nothing more was heard from him.

"How did you guess what had happened to him?" Abi asked Jicks.

Jicks shrugged.

"I didn't guess," she said. "When you're in charge of a fair number of new recruits, which I often am, you come to figure out what reactions go with what stories. Nobody goes into a mercenary company, or into a mission like ours, without motivation. Yours— yours is to set things right for the people the Karsites are hurting. Stev's is to make sure Valdemar's name is cleared. Right?"

Stev nodded.

"Mine's twofold. Money is the primary one, but secondarily, I've heard a lot about these Karsite bastards, and I would be quite pleased if I could remove some of them from the face of the world." She smiled grimly. "I suspect, *I've* heard rumors of what *you* know, Stev. That they're child-murdering monsters."

"I've got proof of that," Stev said quietly. "Every child who shows signs of Mind-magic is sacrificed to their god. Every child who shows signs of your sort of magic is conscripted into the priesthood, and failures are sacrificed to their god. All that is quite apart from the fact that they enforce their rule with demons, which kill indiscriminately."

"Good to have my intel confirmed," she replied. "That just moves my motives around. Money's nice, but nobody kills a child on my watch."

The look that passed over her face at that moment literally set Abi aback. She'd never seen that look on anyone's face before. It was absolutely murderous.

What in the nine hells is her *story?* she thought.

But even as she thought that, she knew she would probably never learn the answer. Jicks would never let a relative stranger have that kind of hold over her. Not even Abi.

Korlak and his bird emerged from the wagon when they stopped for lunch and to water the hinnies. He rubbed his head with a hand encased in his voluminous sleeve as he walked toward them. "How long did I sleep?" he asked.

"Just till noon," said Stev, and offered him trail biscuit. "Hungry again?"

"Actually—I am! Thank you!" he replied, and shared the biscuit with his crow, holding it up for the bird to stab a bite out of it, then taking a bite of his own.

"Where did you get that crow?" Abi asked, fascinated. "Will he let me pet him?"

"He just showed up at my shop door one day," Korlak told her. "He just decided to adopt me. He's a lot bigger than any crow I've ever seen before. He's almost raven-sized. I didn't think I'd be able to feed him, but he seems to keep himself, and sometimes me and Zac, fed."

"Zac?" asked Stev.

"My cousin. The boy in the shop. Albemarle was sane the other day and I asked him if he'd take Zac as an apprentice because I'd already decided to go with you if you let me. He said yes, so Zac went to him." Korlak sighed. "I don't know how much or how little he'll learn, but his grandmam had the same troubles as Albermarle, and Zac took care of her until she died. He knows what he's getting into—but he also knows he'll get plenty of food and a good bed with the old man, which is more than he was getting with me, and that was more than enough to make up his mind. I should have sent Zac to him a year ago, but his mother probably would have had a cat."

Jicks looked thoughtfully at her half-eaten biscuit. "That's as good a bargain as most people would ask for," she said, mildly.

Meanwhile, Abi stared with fascination at the crow, who stared with equal fascination back at her. He bobbed at her. Tentatively she held up her wrist. He jumped to it.

To her surprise, his feet were warm. He looked meaningfully at her biscuit, and she offered it to him. He took a corner in his beak, broke it off, tilted his head back and swallowed it. The feathers at his throat rose as the bite went down.

"He likes it when you scratch his head with one finger," Korlak said around a bit of biscuit.

She offered her finger. The crow didn't bite it. Instead, he pushed his head into it, and looked at her again.

She started scratching. He closed his eyes and leaned into the scratch, looking blissful. Absently, Abi put her biscuit down and handed Korlak another one just as he finished his last bite of the one he had been eating.

Jicks laughed. "I think you've been adopted by a stray," she said, with only a tinge of mockery.

But for the life of her, Abi couldn't tell if Jicks meant the crow or the Mage.

17

They made good time, and found a great camping spot next to the river, with plenty of bracken and rough grass for the hinnies to eat and low trees within walking distance for firewood scavenging. Abi reflected, as she helped set up the campsite, that she literally could not have imagined a more peaceful setting, back in Haven. *I wonder if Perry prefers places like this, or the city?* Since coming back from his adventure, he'd shown little sign of wanting to hare off to the wilderness, but she had no idea if that was his own preference or feeling that he needed to stay to help their father. She had the feeling that if her future included more places like this, and less time in cities . . . she would not be at all unhappy.

The three of them arranged the supplies inside the wagon for the most possible comfort (oat bags on top) when they would go to bed later, and even Korlak managed to relax as Jicks made stew. They admired the sunset, ate, and listened to a particularly melodious nightbird singing in the bushes. The sky blazed with reds and oranges and even deep purple, and the hills cast wonderful, long shadows as the sun set behind them. The stars came out in the east and slowly propagated westward. The fire that Jicks was about to bank sent up a few sparks while the wood crackled and popped. She was about to suggest bed and offer to set up the oatmeal to cook overnight.

And then the bird abruptly stopped singing.

At exactly that moment, Abi suddenly felt as though someone was watching her. Stev's head came up, and he stared at her. Under the cover of his voluminous sleeves, the Mage began frantically sketching tiny sigils in the air between his legs, and Korlak's crow went as rigid as a stuffed bird.

Even the hinnies stirred uneasily. Only Jicks seemed unaffected, but her eyes narrowed as she paid close attention to the rest of them.

"We're being scryed," Korlak mouthed. Abi nodded slightly.

She didn't need to tell them to act normally except for poor Korlak, who just hid his hands in his sleeves and slumped over, staring at the fire. She and Jicks and Stev began what would have sounded like an ordinary conversation to an outsider.

"I want to try for a couple hares tomorrow," Abi told them. "We're making such good time I think it's worth my going off the road for some fresh meat to put in the pot."

"From the look of the countryside and the tracks on the road, your odds should be all right," Jicks told her. "I don't see signs of a lot of travelers coming this way."

Stev chimed in with his favorite recipe for hare and another for grouse. Jicks scoffed at the idea that he had ever hunted grouse; he replied with indignation. Abi teased him. And all the while, she felt those unseen eyes on them.

Then, as abruptly as it had begun, the feeling ended. Korlak's fingers wove, and his posture relaxed. "They aren't watching us anymore," he said aloud.

But Jicks didn't relax at all, and neither did Stev. "We let the fire die down, and smother the coals in ashes," she said tersely. "We crawl into the wagon. When I give the signal, we crawl out the back, each take a hinny and make for the trees."

"But—why?" Korlak asked, bewildered.

Abi answered before Jicks could. "That scrying probably means the Karsites were looking for us. If they've decided they've found us, they'll attack tonight. We can afford to lose the wagon. We can't afford to lose the hinnies. All that magical and priestly protection on the wagon might hold, or it might not, so we don't want to be inside when the demons attack. But the hinnies don't have much of that protection, and the demons will almost certainly attack them if they are within reach."

As Korlak's eyes widened, Stev picked up the narrative. "Every briefing I have ever had on Karsite demons said that they are sent to specific *places* to attack, rather than sent to attack specific people. They're not that bright and can't tell humans from anything else, much less tell humans apart. So they're sent to a place, allowed to run rampant for a time, then recalled. Anything in that spot that isn't protected will be minced." He grimaced. "When the Karsite priests send demons, they don't particularly care who gets in the way. They always say 'The God will know his own.'"

Jicks nodded. "So we're going to get out of this spot. And when the demons come, we'll be—hopefully—out of their sensing range."

The fire was out. The only light came from a half moon, but the line of trees in the distance seemed clear enough to Abi. She slipped out first when Jicks nudged her and got her hinny, Belle, from the picket line. Jicks followed. Stev and Korlak, Korlak's crow riveted to his shoulder, each took one of the wagon hinnies. Following Jicks, who seemed to have eyes like a cat, they made their way through the darkness to that distant line of trees.

She stumbled a lot, and it was Belle who kept her upright, waiting patiently, steady as a rock, for her to get her balance again. Eventually instead of trying to lead the hinny, she draped her arm over Belle's back and let Belle lead her. She got the sense that Belle was "feeling" her way with her feet, finding roots and stones and holes before Abi could. And the entire time they crept their way through the gorse and bracken, she kept expecting to have that sense of eyes on her again.

Somehow, although it seemed as if they had been moving through the night forever, when they got to the shelter of the trees, Jicks looked up at the stars, and whispered, "Not quite midnight." She urged her hinny to lie down, and lay down beside her. Abi copied her. Korlak had some trouble until his crow cawed, very softly, twice; then the hinny folded up her legs and went down nicely.

Stev had already gotten his hinny down.

Abi lay down next to her hinny and looked back in the direction of their wagon. *Now* she saw why Jicks had taken this position. Besides making themselves less of a target, hidden in the shadows under the low trees, from this angle the wagon stood out clearly, a stark black patch against the night sky.

"If they come, they'll come at midnight," Stev said quietly.

"If they don't, no harm done," Jicks replied.

And so they waited, in the insect-buzzing night, with another of those birds nearby singing its heart out.

Until it stopped.

And an unearthly howl came from the direction of the wagon.

Abi's blood froze in her veins, and she was so terrified she couldn't have moved if she'd wanted to. Belle went into a paroxysm of shivering but didn't attempt to move.

The howl was joined by a second, a deeper note, and the night air, no longer peaceful, filled with such horrible cries that Abi clapped her hands over her ears trying to shut them out, in vain. She literally could not move once she'd covered her ears, and she didn't want to look, and yet her eyes were pulled to that black patch where the wagon stood.

She only caught a vague glimpse of something, something moving too quickly for anything but a sense that there was something there, around the wagon.

If the trip across the gorse to the forest had seemed to take all night, waiting in the trees seemed to take forever. The tiny bit of Abi that was still able to think was certain that if the screaming and howling went on for a single moment more, she'd go mad with fear.

And yet it did, and she didn't.

This was terror that turned her insides to water, that almost stopped her breath, and yet inexplicably allowed her to take shallow gasps that didn't seem nearly enough. Now she thoroughly understood what poor Korlak must have endured, and she could not possibly have felt more sympathetic toward him.

That was when she felt warmth penetrating her tunic and breeches at each hip.

Somehow, fighting the terror that *assured* her that if she moved at all, she'd be spotted and torn to small bits, she brought her right hand down to that patch of warmth. Her hand closed around the hilt of one of the two daggers that the Mage-smith had given her.

And the second her hand touched it, the fear ebbed.

It didn't vanish, but it no longer left her paralyzed and unable to think. She pulled the dagger from its sheath—and, gods be thanked, it *did not glow*, since that would be a dead giveaway to anyone watching where they were—and pressed it to her chest. The warmth spread from the dagger into her frozen body, and with every passing moment, she was able to think more clearly.

Moving as slowly and imperceptibly as her father had taught her, she clasped the dagger against her with her left hand and edged over to Jicks.

Jicks was rigid to the touch; all her experience had not saved her from that same paralysis of fear. Abi unsheathed her left-hand dagger, felt for Jicks's hand, and pressed the unsheathed dagger into it.

Almost instantly, she felt Jicks relax. Several long moments later, as the howls and screams continued to fill the valley, Jicks patted her shoulder, and she edged over to Stev.

In his case, she shoved the flat of her dagger against his hand, sharing the warmth, and when the hand and arm relaxed, guided it down to his sword—which was also, as she had hoped, radiating warmth.

Good against evil . . . it might not be a lot of help, but it's something, and I'll gladly take the gift.

Now she moved past Stev to poor Korlak, fearing the Mage had passed out cold. But she found him still alert; rigid, but listening to his crow, who was muttering into his ear. She grabbed his hand and pressed it to the hand holding her dagger, and she heard him let out a faint sigh that was half sob as he too felt some of the fear ebbing away.

The time they spent besieged by terror were the longest candlemarks in her entire life. It wasn't just that those howls invoked fear. It was what was *under* the fear.

You are alone. You will always be alone. You will die alone and no one will care.

You are nothing, and no one. Insignificant. You matter less than a grain of sand.

And everyone knows this. When they think of you at all, which is almost never, they laugh at you and your pretensions.

The world would be a better place with you gone from it.

Die. Give up. Now.

She got the sense that even if someone escaped the terror and the claws of those beasts, this relentless message would burn itself into their souls and send them into a despair from which the only escape would be death.

Korlak squeezed the hand holding the dagger, and she reached out and caught Stev's free hand in hers, and she hoped he stretched out his to Jicks. Because that, and not the warmth and magic of the daggers, was what drove that message out of her heart and showed it to be a base lie. Here they were, a human bulwark against despair. They mattered to each other.

Then, all at once, the howls stopped. So did the terror. And after an interminable silence, a lone, brave bird began to sing.

Exhausted, Abi let go of Stev's hand, and Korlak's, and she put her head down on her arms and, somehow, slept.

She woke instantly when Jicks moved, raised her head, and saw that the first fingers of dawn had broken over the hills. Jicks was getting stiffly to her feet, dagger still held loosely in her hand as if she did not dare let go of it. Abi got slowly to her knees; Stev and Korlak were doing the same. She peered in the direction that Jicks was staring. The wagon still seemed to be there, though whether or not it had been ransacked was impossible to say from this distance.

"Are they scrying us?" Jicks asked quietly, never taking her eyes off the wagon as her hinny lurched to her feet.

"No." Korlak seemed quite sure, and Abi was inclined to trust his judgment. She got Belle up at the same time as the other two hinnies, and with Jicks leading the way, they limped, stiff and sore, to the encampment.

As they got to the halfway point, she thought the wagon looked a bit odd. As they reached the three-quarter mark, she realized why. The canvas and wood had been splashed with red.

But it wasn't until they got right to the encampment itself that she understood that red was blood.

It looked as if the demons had scoured the area in a clearly defined circle and slaughtered every single animal within that circle. Blood was everywhere, and bits of fur and skin. Poor hares. And—was that a hoof?

"As I said," Stev said, with unnerving calm, "Demons aren't too smart."

"Bloody hell," Jicks muttered, looking at the trampled and torn up campsite, the blood, the sheer carnage, she shook her head, then hung it. "This is . . ."

"The Karsite way. So I'm told, anyway." Stev held his hinny's bridle loosely and looked from Jicks to Korlak and back again. "Now what? We didn't move as you'd planned while we were still under the cover of the darkness. If we move now, all they have to do is scry this spot to know we escaped. Wagons don't move by themselves."

"Maybe we can use that to our advantage," Abi said into the silence. "They probably *will* scry this spot soon."

"Not soon; calling up demons and controlling them takes a lot out of you." This was the first thing Korlak had said since they'd left the camp in the night. "But you're right, Abi, they will scry this spot to see what the demons did."

"I think they'll want to make sure," Abi continued, trying to think what she would do, if she were in their shoes, as Mags had taught her. "How good is scrying, Korlak? I mean, what can you actually see?"

"If these priests can control demons, they can see very clearly." Poor Korlak chewed his lip, and the crow nodded as if it understood.

"So we need to clean up the bits so all they see is blood," Abi decided. "If we do that, I think they'll scry first, then come in person to look for body parts." *I cannot believe I just said that. . . .* "Can we set up an ambush?"

Jicks's head came up. "That's the best idea I've heard in two days," she replied, eyes alight. "Stev, can they invoke demons in the daylight?"

"I—" He paused. "I've never heard of them doing that."

"Well, that's good, if it's true. Do you have any idea how these priests dress?"

He looked at her as if he wondered about her sanity, but answered. "Normally, long robes, either red or black. But they're passing as us, remember? They'll be dressed normally, probably in clothing they bought somewhere around here."

"Or stole from someone they murdered," Abi muttered.

"Bloody hell. So they can come across country without getting tangled up, which means instead of coming up the road, they could come from any direction—"

That was when Abi noticed something as she finally went to sheath her dagger. While it wasn't glowing—the point was blood-red.

That's . . . odd. Experimentally, she moved it around. The further away from south-southeast she pointed it, the less of the point was red.

"They could—but they won't," she said, as sure of that as she was of her own name. "Look."

She held up her dagger. Jicks blinked, then lifted the second, temporarily forgotten dagger and repeated the experiment.

And grinned.

"Now we can set up an ambush."

But to Abi's bewilderment, the first thing she did was go to the wagon. "Abi, make us something to eat, please," she said, handing out supplies. "Korlak, start cleaning up the bits. Your crow—"

"—is already eating them," Korlak said. "I think we can leave him to it, there are not that many bits left. I think the demons must have eaten most of them."

"Good, then come here, please." As Abi portioned out traveler's biscuits and dried meat, Korlak went to the back of the wagon and came away burdened with the grain sacks Jicks had thriftily stowed away as they used them for the entire trip. He staggered over to where Abi was eating and resolutely ignoring the crow, who, having stuffed himself, was now carrying more bits off to hide in the grass, bracken, and gorse.

"Oh! Grass suits!" exclaimed Stev, who evidently recognized immediately what she was about to do.

"If those bastards stay passed out long enough, we can have ourselves four sets by noon," Jicks said, with a grim smile. "You show Korlak what to collect. Bring a big pile--I want these things done right." She sat down with a traveler's biscuit between her teeth and began unpicking the seams of the bags. *Well, I can do that,* Abi thought, and joined her.

When they had twelve bags unpicked, Jicks started sewing them together. "Three bags per suit should be enough," Jicks said. "Make it like a burlap blanket."

Meanwhile, Korlak and Stev went out into the area around them and began selectively harvesting long grass, branches of brush that were not gorse, and bracken fronds, making three separate piles. By the time Abi and Jicks got done sewing together four burlap "blankets," they had three tall piles.

"All right, now watch, you two," said Jicks. "Pay attention to how Stev and I attach the stuff to the burlap. That grass is going to serve as our yarn. I don't have time to unravel this burlap, and even if I did, it's the wrong color to blend in around here." Abi watched carefully as she poked holes in the burlap with her knife, threaded hanks of grass through, and used the grass to knot the bracken and branches to the burlap, laying it all in one direction. Korlak proved surprisingly adept at this task, and with all four of them concentrating on it, they had four blankets of foliage they could use to hide under some time after noon. Abi's fingers were sore and a bit cut by the sharp edges of the grass, but she was pretty pleased with her result.

"All right, you can see what we're going to do, I'm sure," Jicks said. "Now we're going to move some supplies, the hinnies, and our hides back to where we were in the forest. Korlak, can you tell from where we were if they start scrying the area again?"

Korlak seemed to have grown in confidence since yesterday. He nodded.

Without any further ado, they loaded up the hinnies with the camouflage mats and the supplies and got into the shelter of the trees as fast as they could. Jicks was taking no chances that the priests might wake up from their stupors and start looking for evidence that they really were dead.

The hinnies were just as happy with the brush and sparser grass under the trees as they had been with the better pasture out in the open. The four humans settled themselves in a rough camp. They'd brought their bedrolls along this time, and they took some time gathering more bracken and spreading their blankets over it.

Meanwhile, the afternoon grew warm, insects buzzing everywhere. With a full belly and water, Korlak and his crow on the watch, she sat down on her bedroll and felt she might be able to relax.

And the next thing she knew, Jicks was nudging her awake with more traveler's biscuits and a water bottle, and the sun was setting. "Any sign?" she asked.

"Nothing," said Korlak, cross-legged on his bedroll, squinting at his master's spellbook. "Kaw is out there on the wagon until sunset. If he feels someone scrying, he'll come to us."

"Kaw?" Jicks said incredulously. "You named your crow *Kaw?*"

"It's his name," said Korlak indignantly. "I didn't name him, he named himself."

Jicks gave him an incredulous look but didn't comment further. Clearly, though, she thought he was making it up.

"Can they scry in the dark?" she asked instead.

"They won't see anything more than they'd see if they stood out there in the dark themselves," he said with confidence. "They probably won't bother, so I told Kaw to come back to us at sunset."

"That means we'll actually get a good night's sleep," Jicks sighed.

"Unless they send the demons back instead," he reminded her.

At sunset, Kaw came winging back in a leisurely way that suggested no alarm on his part. Jicks moved the hinnies so they could resume browsing and made sure they couldn't wrest themselves free if overcome by fear. After some thought, Abi settled into her bedroll. After all, if the night remained quiet, she might as well get as much sleep as she could, and if the demons came back, she might as well be relatively comfortable while terrified. Jicks still had her second dagger, Stev had his sword, and hopefully Korlak had figured out some sort of protective magic he could use on himself.

As soon as the sun set, she closed her eyes.

She woke up in the middle of the night; by the stars, it was about midnight, which was when the last attack had taken place. She couldn't help herself: She tensed up, waiting for a repeat of the previous night.

But nothing happened, and eventually she dozed off again.

They were all awake in the predawn. No one said anything, but Abi could tell from the furtive, restless movements under the blankets that no one could sleep anymore.

As soon as it was light enough, Korlak sent Kaw out again.

Finally, she spoke. "It'll be today if they actually decide to check for themselves. So what do we do if they don't?"

"Original plan," Stev suggested. "With the added benefit that they might be more careless, thinking they've gotten rid of us."

"But do you think they'll still follow their own original plan?" Abi countered.

"They've got nothing to lose and everything to gain." Jicks seemed quite sure of this. "They'll thoroughly destroy Valdemar's reputation down here, and they'll have gotten rid of four of her best Masters. They might as well. They're following the same course they'd be taking to head home anyway."

"It takes less time to wreck something than it does to build it." That was Korlak, sitting up in his bedroll. "I'm going to get up and keep studying the spellbook. I'll send Kaw back out to the wagon."

"Dare I suggest something unorthodox?" Abi asked, "If they, and we, follow their original plan, that we make every attempt to avoid a confrontation? And, yes; I'm suggesting we don't confront them, just go along fixing their messes."

Jicks regarded her as if she thought Abi had gone mad. "That makes no sense."

"There are four of us and at least four of them, since there are supposed to be four Master Artificers coming to the selected places to help," Abi retorted. "And we know they can summon at least two demons. That makes us outnumbered and out-maneuvered. If we attack the demons, how do we protect ourselves from the priests? And if we attack the priests, how do we protect ourselves from the demons?"

"Korlak can cast a shield to ward us from firebolts," said Jicks confidently.

"Korlak is busy researching things against demons, not shields," came the retort from where the Mage sat with his nose apparently in the book. "Korlak can research shields or demons, not both."

"It's not a terrible idea," said Stev unexpectedly. "We know the route. We know the last place with problems. We could follow them to make sure they aren't going to continue their antics and then let them go when they seem to be well on their way home."

"But—that's like letting enemy scouts come and go as they please!" Jicks sputtered.

"They're not in Valdemar," said Stev. "They're in a strip of land that *might* decide to join Valdemar. Not my problem."

"And what if they *do* decide to join Valdermar?" Jicks crowed in triumph.

"Then whatever drives Mages out of Valdemar will keep them and their demons out," Stev said serenely. "Still not my problem."

Jicks seethed for a moment, then shook her head. "I must be getting soft," she said. "I'm not getting paid to make it my problem either. All right. If they decide to believe their scrying and wander off to make trouble again, we'll do that. It means I won't have to risk my skin fighting them."

But she looked peeved, and Abi had a good guess why. Abi had pointed out there were at least four priests, and Jicks had mentally leaped from "two bounties" to "four bounties." Abi was pretty sure Jicks figured none of the others would have the inclination to collect blood money, which meant she also wouldn't have to share those bounties. And now she could see all that money slipping away.

Then again, Abi had just reminded her she wasn't going to have to put herself in danger, either. *Hard to spend money when you're dead.*

Jicks made a show of getting up to check on the hinnies and making sure they had water. Korlak's crow sat, a tiny, black dot on a larger beige blob that was the wagon.

And then it wasn't. It was speeding off, at right angles to the direction it would have taken to them.

Korlak frowned. "I wonder if he saw something, or if he's felt someone scrying. . . ."

Well, that answered my question about Animal Mindspeech, Abi thought.

But as they continued to watch the wagon, the crow came flying in under the branches, to land on Korlak's hunched shoulder.

"That mean's they're scrying," Korlak proclaimed. He closed his eyes, frowning in concentration. "Yes, they definitely are."

Abi was not inclined to doubt him, though Stev looked skeptical.

He was probably thinking that Korlak had seemingly been the worst Mage in the city, and now he suddenly was claiming to be able to do, or learn to do quickly, all manner of magics. That either Korlak was lying, or he was another Karsite agent.

He doesn't have my experience. Abi had been taught how to see and analyze the smallest details of people and their behavior. Korlak wasn't lying, and he wasn't an agent. For the first time in a very long time, Korlak had gotten regular meals, as much as he wanted to eat, and suddenly his mind, numbed by starvation, had sprung to life again.

Stev was good, but he wasn't a son of Mags.

"Go back out and come back to us when you don't feel the scrying anymore, please," Korlak said to his crow, who bobbed his head, and flew off in quite another direction than the wagon. And, eventually, a crow appeared, coming from the opposite direction in which it had disappeared, to land on the wagon in a slightly different spot.

It wasn't there long. Whatever examination the Karsites were making, it had to be a cursory one. The crow roused, as if from a stupor, shook its feathers, and flew directly back to them.

"Now," Jicks said with satisfaction, "we set up our ambush."

She directed them to put the hinnies on a much lighter line, something that, if they got too hungry or thirsty, they could snap by all pulling in the same direction—which they would. Then they carried their burlap disguises out into the bracken past the wagon, putting the wagon between themselves and where the Karsites would be coming from, according to the daggers.

"Now comes the hard part," Jicks said, her voice muffled by the camouflage. "Trying not to die of boredom or bug bites before they show up."

Abi had tucked the edges of her cloth in under existing plants, which was probably an unnecessary detail, but it gave her something to do. Following Jicks's orders, she cut two eye flaps out of the side facing where the Karsites would come from. And after that . . . it was just waiting.

18

It was surprisingly warm under all that grass and bracken. On Jicks's instructions, they had all cut eyeholes in the front of their hides, and she had a fine view of the wagon and the field beyond. Now it was a matter of waiting.

She was glad she'd had a good night's sleep, or she'd have nodded out under all this.

Should I have negotiated with Jicks to abandon the ambush? she wondered. *If they come here and don't find anything, wouldn't it be better to just let them go?*

Then she realized she was not only second-guessing herself but that this was totally wishful thinking. These priests would, of course, have some way of telling whether or not humans had died here. It would be ridiculous of them not to; Stev had made the point that this kind of indifferent slaughter was what they did. And given what a mess the demons had made with a few wild creatures, the priests would want to verify what they'd torn to tiny pieces.

Plus, there is no way I could have stopped Jicks once she had heads with bounties on them in her sight. Jicks might have said at the outset of this trip that she was happy, it was easy money for not killing anyone, but the longer they had gone without a fight, the more restless she had become. She had welcomed the chance to hunt down these Karsites. *She's probably so used to being in fights that if she goes without one for too long, it's like a regular drinker being without a drink.*

Combine that restlessness with the bounties available . . .

Then something occurred to Abi. *Huh. I think she knows herself better than I thought. She said she wanted to buy a very particular pub. I bet it's one that gets rough customers. So she'd be breaking up fights and throwing people out regularly, which would solve her need to periodically break skulls.*

A crawling sensation distracted her from her thoughts. Was that a bug? Was something moving around her leg? She worked her hand around to the spot and tried to squash whatever was between her leg and breeches. Hard to tell if she was successful, but at least the sensation stopped. *It's a good thing I have a lot of practice at waiting. This isn't that different from shadowing someone Papa wants watched.*

Then movement at the edge of her vision made her lose interest in bugs or anything else. There was something bobbing up and down on the horizon, moving above and below the bracken. Someone was coming.

Heads. Those were definitely human heads.

Two someones. Now two figures against the horizon. Then three. Then four.

At least the odds are—

Five and six.

Oh . . . hell.

She tensed, ready to throw the hide aside and attack. The ambushers would become the ambushed. Even though the odds were not in her favor, if the three of them with bows could take out three of the priests on the first volley, they'd bring things back in line. Her breathing shortened and her heart raced. *Wait for the signal. Wait for it. Wait for it . . .*

An owl hooted. She threw herself erect, sent the hide flying off her shoulders with a gesture, bow in hand, sighted, and shot. And hit.

And her heart sank. *Oh, hell!*

She, Stev, and Jicks had all picked the same target. One of the strangers went down, well feathered with arrows. She picked another, but something like a bubble had suddenly shimmered into existence around him, and the arrow she loosed literally bounced off.

Not good!

Her next internal curse was one Amily would *not* have approved of, as she switched to another target, only to find all of them surrounded by those same shimmering bubbles. Fear—of the energizing, not paralyzing sort—galvanized her entire body.

She dropped her now-useless bow, but everything was happening much too quickly to properly react, as four of the five men shouted something in unison, the air opened up in front of them, and out stepped four—things.

She almost vomited when she saw them, they invoked such complete revulsion in her.

They were the color of rancid butter. They were vaguely human in form, but that was where the resemblance stopped. They were naked, sexless, and their hairless heads were mostly mouth. The mouths were full of needlelike teeth. They were muscled in some obscene parody of a carnival weightlifter or wrestler; their arms were longer than a human's, their legs shorter, and hands and feet ended in claws as long as Stev's middle finger. And almost as soon as they appeared, they launched themselves into an attack.

Oh, gods. We're all going to die.

Abi drew sword and dagger, hoping against hope that at least one of them would be of some use, and knowing the thing had reach on her. Unless she was extraordinarily lucky, it could lacerate or grab her before she could reach it even with the sword. Her body tensed to throw her out of the way in a desperate dodge, but the thing was faster than she'd thought and it was going to—

—bounce off the shimmering bubble skin that suddenly appeared between her and it.

The thing clawed and bit at the barrier, to no avail. Everything it tried slid off. It even backed up and rammed its shoulder into the protection that had saved her, but it just bounced off again.

That didn't seem to make any difference to it. It continued to raven at her, a mere double-armlength away. As Stev had said, the things clearly weren't too bright. It had a target, and it had fixated on that target.

I guess Korlak found something that works against demons and *is a shield. We might survive this!* If this shield stayed up, she could just ignore the demon and go straight for one of the Mages—

But then, the thing opened its mouth, howled right at her, and the terror began. But this time, she had the dagger in her hand, and instead of rendering her helpless, the terror remained within bearable levels. Barely, but she could think and move, which was better than nothing!

Ignoring the demon clawing to get at her, she fixated on the Mage nearest her. He had been smirking until he saw she was looking at him. He frowned.

And then he made a throwing motion, and she had to dodge as a small ball of fire hurtled toward her.

It hit the place where she had been standing and set the bracken smoldering. She barely had enough time to roll away to her feet when the second fireball hit where she had landed. Around her the air filled with fireballs, aimed at her and presumably the others, and she prayed that the spell that protected her was not something that Korlak had to concentrate on. And she prayed he'd had the sense to stay in his hide as he'd been told to do when she, Jicks, and Stev had leaped to their feet in what Jicks had been so certain was going to be the perfect ambush.

The dagger in her left hand burned whenever a fireball hit the shield. The demon followed her every step of the way, alternately tearing at her shield and howling at her. Smoke filled the air, an acrid smoke that made her eyes water and fight to keep her coughing under control. *How soon before we have to dodge a wildfire?* If these Mages were smart, they would realize all they'd have to do would be to start one behind their foes, and all four of them would be trapped between the fire and the Mages. And the fire would win the fight for the Karsites.

Do something! she screamed at herself. *Anything!*

And in desperation, when she saw the next fireball coming at her, she swatted at it with the dagger, as if it were a ball in one of those games her friends hated to play with her.

Finally a burst of luck! It connected, squarely, on the flat of the blade near the hilt, and it went scorching back toward the Mage that had cast it.

She got a glimpse of his startled face before the fireball cut through his shield as if it weren't there and exploded in his face. She got a sickening glimpse of burning skin and bubbling flesh, and he dropped, screaming for a little while, as he continued to burn.

With a popping sound, the demon attacking her vanished.

Before another of the Mages realized she was free, she made a run for the next nearest. He saw her coming for him and switched his barrage of fireballs to her, but she made a dive for the turf and got under them. She hit the ground, rolled, and stabbed him in the groin with her dagger.

It went right through the shield.

He collapsed with a shriek, blood fountaining out of the wound, a lot of it splattering all over her.

His shield vanished.

She gagged, rolled to her feet, continued on past him, and only paused to look back when his shrieks took on an entirely new level of pain.

One of the two demons that had been attacking Stev had turned away from him, thrown itself at the downed Mage, and—

—"eviscerated" was too mild a word for what the demon was doing to the Karsite. Blood and bits of flesh and organ flew everywhere, and within moments, the Mage stopped screaming, and that demon, too, vanished with a *pop*.

She gagged again, but there was no time to be sick. Things could turn against them again as quickly as they had turned in their favor.

She pivoted to look for the third Mage that was left; he had just realized that his companions were down—but not necessarily what had happened to them. He flung a fireball at her and quickly realized his mistake when she batted it back at him with her dagger.

It skimmed past his head, neatly piercing the shield, landing behind him and setting a smoldering fire in the bracken. His eyes widened, he shouted another word—

—but never finished it, as Jicks's dagger lodged in his throat. More blood spurted everywhere, but at least this time she wasn't in range of it.

She dashed past Abi to snatch the dagger out of the body. This time there was no *pop*, and one of the demons was still following Jicks, ignoring Abi.

Jicks executed a move worthy of Master Leandro. She grabbed the dagger, turned the grab into a somersault, turned, and lunged at the demon with all her strength.

The demon bounced off her shield and into the wagon, which now had only rags of burning canvas on the supports. With a glance at Abi, Jicks turned and ran. Abi intuited what that glance had meant. While Jicks ran for the second Mage left, Abi pinned the demon between her shield and the wagon.

It ignored her and tried desperately to free itself to run after Jicks. When that didn't work, it finally turned to her and howled at her. The terror drove her to her knees, but she clutched her dagger to her, and kept it pinned, until it, too, evaporated with a *pop*.

She turned just in time to see Stev literally chop the remaining demon in two as it hesitated between two targets. Its hesitation cost it. Jicks threw her dagger again (while inside Abi shrieked *never throw away your weapon).* This time it struck the Mage in his shoulder; he went down with a scream, and his shield vanished.

It's over. Oh, gods, it's over. And we lived.

Jicks went back to the last Mage she'd killed and began rummaging in his shirt.

Then she cursed and tore the clothing off the corpse's body, clearly searching for something. Then, as Abi fought down nausea and sank to her knees in the bracken, she cursed even louder and began kicking the dead body.

"These bastard's aren't even *Karsite!*" she screamed, kicking it again and again.

Stev paused, his swordpoint at the Mage's throat. "Is that so?"

"What the *hell,* Stev?" she screeched at him.

"That's what I'm about to find out," Stev said, far too calmly.

Abi looked down at the ground a moment to control her stomach, wiped blood off her face, and by the time she looked back up, the blue glow of the Truth Spell surrounded the prone Mage. And the faint glimmer of shielding was gone from around her and the other two. *Thank you, Korlak.*

"Are you Karsite?" Stev asked the captured Mage.

"No!" the Mage spat, "Holy hells, man, get your knife out of me! I surrender! You Valdemarans have to take a surrender!"

Stev pondered a moment. "I think we'll leave the knife where it is for now. Why are you here?"

Abi couldn't control her stomach anymore; she vomited. But that didn't keep her from hearing the man's answer.

"To keep you crazy people from annexing this area. *Get it out! Help me!*" The Mage's hand kept reaching for the knife as if to pull it out himself, but then he seemed to lose the courage to do so. Which was probably all for the best, as the wound would certainly start bleeding badly if he did get the knife out. But Abi could scarcely believe how indifferent everyone else seemed to be to his pain.

Abi, you idiot, he tried to murder us all! He could have killed other people if he'd rigged a bridge to fall!

"I like the knife where it is. It looks good on you," Jicks said, and sat down in the bracken as Korlak and his crow approached.

"Sorry I didn't do more," Korlak said apologetically. "I was putting the fires out. I mean, literally putting them out." He looked pale, and a little sick, but no worse than Abi felt. He glanced at the enemy Mage, and his lips curled up, just a little.

"Just as well you did, or they'd have had us pinned down for the fire to take," Jicks told him, thumping his shoulder. He staggered. "Good thinking."

He shrugged. "There wasn't much more I could do, anyway. Nothing else I tried seemed to work."

"Help me!" the enemy Mage shrieked.

"That's an odd demand from someone who was trying to kill us a few moments ago. Why were you doing this?" Stev continued, doggedly.

"We were hired! *Help me! You're a Herald! You're supposed to help people!"*

"I'm supposed to help Valdemarans," Stev corrected. "And you're not a Valdemaran. Who hired you?"

"Some rich bastard." The man struggled against the Truth Spell, trying not to reveal the name, speaking what was literally the truth, but obviously not the whole truth.

Stev, however, was a veteran at this sort of interrogation, working methodically through questions designed to get the most information in the least amount of time. "And what was the rich bastard's name?" he persisted.

The Mage's eyes bulged and his face reddened as he did his utmost to foil the spell. But Stev's Mind-magic was too strong, and finally he burst out with, "I only heard it once! I'm probably wrong!"

"What was the name?" Stev leaned over the man. "You know, I'm going to find it out one way or another. You might as well make this easier on both of us."

Does my father do this? Silly question. Her father dealt with the worst of the worst. Of course he did. Meanwhile, the man was weeping in agony, hand hovering over the dagger he didn't dare remove, or he'd probably bleed to death. "The name," Stev repeated.

"Kemp! Lemp! Hemp! That's all I remember!" the Mage cried.

"Was it 'Remp'?" Stev asked, cold as ice in Midwinter. "Dudley Remp?"

That startled Abi out of her nausea. *Dudley Remp? What on earth was he up to, here?* What could he possibly gain from meddling with the politics of a few small cities on the Menmellith Border?

"Yes!" the man shrieked.

"And why did he want Valdemar discredited here?" Stev asked.

The smell of blood and even worse things made her dizzy, but this was an answer she needed to hear.

"He wants his own kingdom where he can do what he wants. Please, please, help me," the Mage blubbered, pawing at Stev's foot.

Stev glanced over at her, finally. She swallowed down the sour taste of bile in her mouth, winced at the taste of blood on her mouth, and looked the Herald straight in the eye. "You know Remp better than I do," he said. "Does that sound logical?"

She thought it over, but not for too long. "Completely," she replied. "He's always thought he should be allowed to do whatever he wants because he's rich. I can see him sending these Mages in to discredit Valdemar, hiring a mercenary company, and coming in to offer himself as the new king."

Stev's lip curled in contempt. "As in, 'this is a lovely city you have, it would be terrible if anything happened to it while your defenses are down. But of course, I have the men to prevent that'?"

She nodded.

Stev turned his attention back to the Mage. "Is Remp still on this side of the Border?"

"Yes," the Mage moaned. "He's waiting for us in Carnsbridge, near the Karsite Border."

"Well, now," Stev continued, looking down at the enemy Mage. "That's all I needed to know. The question now becomes, what are we to do with you?"

Jicks took that as a cue to come up beside Stev and rest the point of her sword against the Mage's chest. The man froze. Even the tears on his cheeks seemed to stop moving as he stared into Jicks's impassive face.

The blue light of the Truth Spell flickered and died as Stev stepped back. Jicks looked down on the man, expressionless. "That's a good question, Stev. I was looking forward to collecting six Karsite bounties. This bastard and his little friends have deprived me of a whole lot of money, and I am not happy about it."

She put a little pressure on the sword. Stev looked off to the horizon.

"You're a Herald!" the Mage screeched. "You're supposed to uphold the law! *Do something!*"

"Valdemar law," Stev reminded him. "This isn't Valdemar. And you're a problem for me. I can't let you go and alert Remp to the fact that we know his plans. And you did try to kill us. I can't take the chance you won't try again. I can't take you with us—you are way too much trouble; we'd have to keep you tied and gagged all the time, and tending to you is far more work than I care to go to. And besides, every time Jicks saw you, you'd remind her of how much money you cost her. It would be a waste of time to keep arguing with her about not killing you."

"There's no law out here," Jicks reminded the Mage. "Or if there is, we decide what it is." A drop of blood welled up from where the swordpoint rested on his chest. "I really am mightily irritated with you."

"You want to take responsibility for this piece of trash, Jicks?" Stev asked. "I mean, if I take him across the Border to account for himself, very bad things are going to happen to him because of what it's like for a Mage trying to get into Valdemar. I'm not sure he'd stay sane more than a couple of days."

Abi was . . . appalled. She glanced over at Korlak, who just seemed fascinated.

"Oh, gods, no, no, no," the Mage whimpered. "That's torture!"

So's this, Abi could not help but think.

"So it is," Stev agreed. "And torture is illegal in Valdemar. So taking you across the Border isn't an option. Jicks? Got any ideas?"

"You cost me a big fat pile of money," Jicks reminded the Mage again. "Captain Whitepants there seems to think I should decide what happens to you. I'm inclined to take my irritation out on you a piece at a time." She gazed off into the same distance as Stev. "However . . ."

"However? However *what?*" the Mage gasped, desperately.

She licked her lips, oblivious to the blood that spattered her face. "You might be worth more alive than dead. You're obviously for hire. How about if I hire you for my Company at the handsome rate of not being dead?"

His blubbering assent did not particularly impress Jicks, who glanced over at Korlak. "You know any way to make an oath binding on this piece of trash?"

Korlak smiled, slowly. "As a matter of fact, I do," he told her. "Let's get that shoulder taken care of first, though. Abi needs her dagger, and we don't want this idiot to bleed to death. Yet."

Korlak rummaged in the damaged wagon, then knelt next to the Mage with a wad of rags he'd gotten, packing them around the dagger. As the Mage moaned with pain, he put pressure on the wound, then Jicks leaned down and pulled the dagger out with a quick yank.

The Mage screamed and passed out cold.

That just allowed Korlak to work in peace. By the time the Mage woke up again, his wound had been cauterized, packed with herbal powder that would keep infection out, stitched up and bandaged, though he was still lying where he had fallen. The rest of them had had a chance to get cleaned up as well, going down to the brook one at a time with changes of clothing from the wagon. Abi just left her gore-soaked clothing in the pile of trash they'd burn before they left this campsite. She didn't want to see what she'd been wearing ever again.

"You see this?" Korlak said, holding up a wad of the bloody rags left over from treating the wound.

The Mage nodded.

"You are going to take a vow to obey every single command that Jicks gives you, and you're going to do it on your own blood on these rags," Korlak told him. "And then I am going to bind that vow to a very specific consequence if you ever disobey. Your wound will open, no Healer will be able to mend it, and you'll bleed to death in about as long as it takes you to make up your mind that disobedience was a mistake."

The Mage, already pale, turned white. Before he could protest, Korlak squatted down, grabbed his hand and shoved it over the wad of rags. "Swear!" he ordered.

"I swear to obey every command Jicks gives me!" the Mage gulped, probably wishing he could think of some prevaricating way to rephrase that.

Korlak pulled the hand away and dropped the rags on the ground beside them; then he made a few gestures, clapped his hands over the rags, and they burst into multicolored flame. The Mage blanched again.

"Now," Jicks said, "whatever your name was before, it's now Del."

"Why Del?" Stev asked.

"Because it's short, and I don't know anyone named Del." She turned back to "Del." "You are never even going to attempt to run away," she told him. "You're going to be serving my Company from now on. When I or the Commander says to do something, you're going to figure how to get it done. No excuses. Am I clear on all counts?"

"Yes, sir," the Mage replied, beginning to look as if every bit of strength and energy had been wrung out of him.

"And you are never, ever, ever to conjure up one of those *gods damned* demons again!" Jicks snarled.

He started back away from her vehemence and whimpered a little in pain as he jarred his wound.

She dropped some clothing on him. "Brook's that way," she told him, pointing, "Get to your feet, get down there, get clean and changed, and come back before sunset."

The Mage stumbled to his feet, clutching the bundle of clothing to his chest, and staggered through the bracken to the nearby brook.

Stev had meanwhile brought back the hinnies, who had been watered and were now enjoying better fare than they'd had in the forest. "You actually bound him to Jicks?" Abi said, as soon as the Mage was out of earshot.

"Total bluff," Korlak said with a shrug, as his crow cawed derisively. "He thinks I can because I made shields that worked against the demons. He doesn't know I tried three spells before that and six after. The only one that worked besides the shields was the one that put out the fires. Pure luck. I kept more of his blood on the rags, though, and I'm giving them to Jicks. If he ever does try to run, she can get another Mage to use the blood to track him down or maybe force him to come back."

"I think I'll go make sure he doesn't try to test your 'spell'," Stev said, and he followed after the Mage.

Abi looked around to make sure that Stev was out of earshot before she spoke next. "Listen, Korlak, when we get back to your city, I want you to talk to that Mage-smith. And Albemarle, if he's sane. If they do invite Valdemar to extend its borders here, you need to know that the day the new borders are set, the same thing that keeps Mages and magic out of Valdemar will move down here. You'll have to leave if you want to stay sane."

Korlak eyed her curiously. "Why are you telling me this? Aren't you supposed to be persuading people they want this?"

"Because it's not fair to you and people like you," she replied frankly. "And I'm not sure they'll tell you this before it's too late." She turned to Jicks. "And you need to talk to Steen, too. Make sure he knows this and what it will mean for him."

Jicks raised an eyebrow at her. "Isn't this going counter to what your King wants?" she asked.

"Maybe Stev doesn't care about non-Valdemarans, but I do," she replied, feeling just a tiny bit better about what had just gone on. "It's not fair to the Mages and the people who depend on them to hide what's going to happen if they accept Valdemar's offer."

Later that night, when they had all—even Del—gotten a dinner of Jicks' stew and some pine-needle tea, Abi made a bed on the other side of the wagon where the carnage *wasn't*, while Stev was communing with his Companion, relating everything that had happened today.

Today? It felt as if it had all taken a week. She was exhausted and wanted nothing except to sleep, but the presence of Del meant someone was going to have to watch all night, and she volunteered to take first watch.

Del curled up on a bed of bracken in a borrowed blanket. The rest, except Stev, fell asleep immediately. She kept herself awake by splashing water on her face, wondering if she could ever wash away the smell of blood.

Finally, when her watch was just about over, Stev roused himself and stretched.

"What took so long?" she asked.

She heard the dry amusement in his voice as he replied and knew it would be matched by a slightly cynical smile. "As you can imagine, what I had to say aroused the same sort of reaction you'd get from taking a stick to an ant's nest. Court Dinner got cut short. An emergency Council meeting was called. There's going to be an actual trial of Dudley Remp tomorrow, with or without his presence. They're not letting any grass grow under their feet on this one. I . . . might have neglected to mention that the last Mage is still alive."

"Why?" Abi asked.

She saw his silhouette shrug. "Taking him North would be torture, and torture is illegal in Valdemar. Jicks is just as wronged as I am, and she's satisfied with the punishment. Not my Mage, not my country."

She couldn't help herself. She had to ask, because his words were so cynical and so dismissive. "Why do you keep saying that?"

"Besides the fact that it's true?" Silence hung between them for a very long time. "Because Valdemar has limited resources, Abi. Tales about Herald Vanyel aside, what would happen to the people *inside* Valdemar—people who rely on our aid and protection—if everyone on the other side of a Border came crying to a Herald for help?"

She bit back a retort that this didn't matter. Because she was wrong. It did matter.

"I see you've taken my point. Remember what we Heralds do, besides all the day-to-day business of making sure the Kingdom runs smoothly. We literally save peoples'—*our* peoples'—lives. If we go interfering in matters that don't concern us, *our* people could suffer and die. And I know it's not fair, but you're Mags' daughter. You know there's no such thing in life as 'fair.' But there's no reason for us to trade 'unfair' for 'worse.' Sometimes doing your job means knowing when not to do it." He chuckled dryly. "And technically, every time I would do something on the wrong side of the Border, I'd be violating agreements between the two Kingdoms in question. Vanyel was a legendary Herald, but he was sometimes terrible at the job."

She hated hearing this. But part of her knew he was absolutely right. She went to bed with her head a complete mess, and only utter exhaustion allowed her to get to sleep.

The last thought before she did fall into a kind of stupor was, *I don't want to do anything from now on but keep my ears open and fix bridges.*

The Mage traveled in the wagon with Korlak keeping an eye on him, and they pushed their speed as much as they could. They also progressively lightened the load by giving the hinnies more grain, which meant they needed less time to browse.

When they reached Korlak's town, they got a new cover for the wagon, Abi left her daggers and Stev's sword back with the Mage-smith Evelie, and she had a word with Evelie herself about what becoming part of Valdemar would mean to Mages.

They also got rooms in the inn this time. Good ones. And in the morning when they left, Abi saw that Stev had a certain cat-in-the-cream look about him. She cornered him in the stable.

"You've heard from Valdemar," she stated.

He smiled grimly. "Every length of property and every copper belonging to Dudley Remp's been confiscated, he's been exiled, and the

Border's been closed to him. He's stuck here, with only the money he has on him. If he comes back across the Border, he's got nothing to draw on, and no one will help him. If he's caught, he'll be booted back across the Karsite Border, and bad luck to him." He went back to hitching up the hinnies, and she went back to saddling. It was a good solution. After all, Remp hadn't managed to kill anyone. And it was a solution that left a better taste in her mouth than the disposition of "Del."

They caught up with the Masters and Bret and Bart back in Elliston. And that was where Jicks and "Del" parted with them.

"You have all the funds that were meant to hold a bigger party than you'll have now," Jicks pointed out. "Abi knows how to drive and cook now, you can sell the second wagon and tie the hinny to the tail of the first."

"I'd rather give you the wagon," decreed Master Vance. "You can get a mule or a horse here, and it'll make transporting your tame Mage a lot easier. You might as well take the supplies we won't need, too. Think of it as a bonus for your work."

Jicks smiled, clearly pleased. "A pleasure doing business with you, Master. I'll make sure to let everyone know how Valdemarans are."

The last was said with a knowing look at Abi. *She's remembered to tell Steen about what's going to happen if the Border moves. Good.*

The people of Elliston gave them all one final feast, with a whole roast lamb all to themselves, and in the morning, they parted on the road, one party going north, and one south.

Abi was relieved to see them vanish into the distance. She'd learned a lot on this trip, but too much of it had been things she wished she could forget.

Still. *I'll be back in time to see my bridge built.*

EPILOGUE

Two huge wooden cranes the size of siege engines carefully lowered the last slab of the roadbed into place. The cranes stood on the two sides of completed roadbed on either side of the limestone expanse. The main arch and the subarches had been completed long before Abi had gotten home, but she was in good time to see the last stage, the roadbed itself, set into place. It, too, was an arch, a fragment of a circle rising over the river in so gentle a curve that the eye scarcely noticed what it was.

A crowd of people surrounded her, although she stood a little apart from them, in the company of all of the Artificers and workmen who had labored to bring this limestone dream to reality—in fact, crowds waited breathlessly on both sides of the bridge, here for the sole purpose of seeing it completed.

Beneath the stone, the wooden supporting structure was still in place, but once the initial keystone of the arch had been set, and the iron dovetails were in place, the bridge had been supporting itself.

Eight workmen guided the slab until it was directly over the gap. Then the crane crews cranked on their apparatus until the stone hovered within a breath of the surface.

Then the workmen slipped a dozen wedges of highly flammable pitch-pine into the gap between the slab and the roadbed. The crews cranked again, and the slab lowered to *almost* fill the gap. The workmen removed the two rope cradles. Supported by the two dozen wooden wedges, the surface of the slab stood about a thumb's-breadth above the roadbed surface.

Now the workmen lit the wedges in quick succession, starting at the outside and working in. The wedges flared up like tiny torches, burning fiercely and quickly, going from wood to ash.

With a grating noise, the slab settled into place, the roadbed now forming one surface.

The crowds cheered wildly, and the group around Abi cheered with them, slapping each other on the backs, some hugging, all of them ecstatic.

Abi stared, transfixed, hardly able to breathe. There it was, her dream, her sweet curve of stone come alive, hovering above the water like the gentle curve of a dove's wing.

Oh, it wasn't "finished" yet. It still needed the parapets and pilasters on either side for safety. But those were cut and waiting to be placed, and it wouldn't take long to get them where they belonged. But that would take a sennight at most with all the workmen on hand, so it would be done before the autumn rains.

She looked at it with her inner eyes, and the soft, muted sweep of stress carried evenly and sweetly from the crown of the bridge, down the subarches, into the arch-span, and into the riverbed walls, like the soft sweep of wind over a hill. And like the bridge in her dreams, it sang. It didn't cry out in pain. It didn't groan under a burden off-kilter and askew. It was a melody in stone.

Suddenly she realized the workers and her fellow Masters and Trainees were pushing her toward the stone. Not shouting, but urging her, "Go on, Abi! It's yours! Go show them who made it!"

When she set her left foot on the limestone roadbed, she thought she was going to cry. A few more paces, and she thought she was going to burst. The crowd went utterly silent, watching her walk, slowly along the creamy stone arch—until she came to the middle, and stopped.

Without even thinking about it, she raised her arms, slowly, and spread them, offering this, the child of her vision, to her city.

The crowd roared.

———

"That was amazing," said Kat. "I don't think I've seen people cheer for Mother and Father the way they cheered for you."

Still feeling so full of nameless emotions she thought she might explode, Abi and Kat had gone up to the top balcony of The Compass Rose, an inn much frequented by Artificers and their Trainees. The lot of her fellows carried Abi off here; Kat had arrived later. Once the serious drinking started, Abi and Kat had managed to get away from them and go up to the balcony to see if it was possible to see the bridge from here.

It was, and it looked even better by moonlight.

"I feel drunk," Abi said, staring at her bridge. "I haven't had anything but cider, and I still feel drunk."

Kat laughed. "I don't blame you," she said, fondly. "And to be honest, this couldn't have come at a better time. People are going to be concentrating on this, and not on Father's bad news."

Some of Abi's elation drained away. "Bad news? What bad news?"

"That expedition you all went on—it was all for nothing," Kat explained, leaning her arms on the balustrade and looking out over the river. "Father just got their answer today. A very politely worded refusal. They are very sorry to have put us to all that trouble, and grateful for the work you and the other Masters did, but they have determined they have more to lose than to gain by joining Valdemar, and are going to be sending a delegation to the Court of Menmellith."

It took Abi a moment to process this—and then those particular words, "more to lose than to gain," echoed in her mind. The Mages! Of course! All those people in the area who depended on their Mages, weak and strong, and so very useful in everyday life—the Mages had talked to them and to each other and had convinced them. "More to lose than to gain."

And rather than feel like a defeat, this just felt like one more victory, at least to Abi, although she was sure Master Vance, Master Padrick, and Master Beyrn would feel differently.

"Well, I bet in their eyes, they do," she said. "After all, there is no one true way."

Kat laughed. "I'll be sure to remind Father of that if I find him still grumbling when we get back. Goodness, even your bridge is a reminder of that. If we'd stuck to 'one, true way' it wouldn't be standing there now."

Abi could only smile harder.

ABOUT THE AUTHOR

Mercedes Lackey is a full-time writer and has published numerous novels and works of short fiction, including the bestselling *Heralds of Valdemar* series. She is also a professional lyricist and licensed wild bird rehabilitator. She lives in Oklahoma with her husband and collaborator, artist Larry Dixon, and their flock of parrots.

www.**mercedeslackey**.com

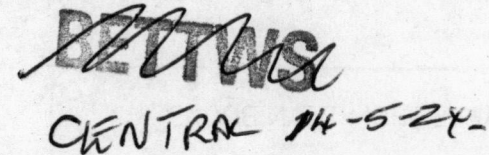
For more fantastic fiction, author events, exclusive excerpts,
competitions, limited editions and more

VISIT OUR WEBSITE
titanbooks.com

LIKE US ON FACEBOOK
facebook.com/titanbooks

FOLLOW US ON TWITTER
@TitanBooks

EMAIL US
readerfeedback@titanemail.com